KIM HUDSON NEVER LACKED PLAYMATES

From the moment little Kim Hudson first entered an all-powerful Hollywood mogul's office and was asked by the great man to sit on his lap and play a very unusual game, Kim knew she was not like other children. She learned even more exotic lessons from her fellow students in the school run by a giant film studio for its celebrated child stars, and her sensual education moved to a new level when a famous blonde sex goddess took her in hand.

But that was just the beginning for Kim Hudson, whose beauty was both her blessing and her curse, and whose body betrayed her again and again and again. . . .

ARLENE DE MARCO is the youngest of the five DeMarco sisters, whose singing team made show-business history. With her bestselling first novel, *Triangle,* Miss DeMarco made a triumphant entry into another field of entertainment. Herself a child performer, and the intimate friend of many greats in the entertainment world, Arlene DeMarco again displays her bold, spellbinding storytelling skill and her very inside knowledge in this sensational blockbuster novel.

SIGNET Books You'll Want to Read

Make-Believe Children

by
Arlene DeMarco

A SIGNET BOOK
NEW AMERICAN LIBRARY
TIMES MIRROR

SIGNET, SIGNET CLASSICS, MENTOR, PLUME AND MERIDIAN BOOKS
are published by The New American Library, Inc.,
1301 Avenue of the Americas, New York, New York 10019

FIRST PRINTING, FEBRUARY, 1975

1 2 3 4 5 6 7 8 9

PRINTED IN THE UNITED STATES OF AMERICA

To Mama with love

And to my two darling daughters, Rosana
and Melisa, who are my stabilizers through
everything

My loving thanks to Eugene Boe
who helped me get it all together

Make-Believe Children

Chapter 1

CALLING ALL STARS!

PAST AND PRESENT!

It's Reunion-Time, Scholars!

You're invited to a party.

Where?

Where else?

Back on the old reservation!

When? May 15

When again: 6 P.M.—Oblivion

That's the way the invitation read. I, Gina Spinelli, was being invited to a reunion-type party. A bash for all of us kids who had ever done time at the Studio . . . and who had picked up, catch-as-catch-can, our three R's in the Studio schoolroom. The reunion—incredibly—was going to be held at the Studio. Or what's left of it.

If you read the entertainment columns or the fan magazines, you know what's left of the Studio. You know it's a shadow, a ghost, Spooksville. You know they've parceled off everything except one sound stage and the old back lot 3. You also know they were so strapped for cash they had an auction awhile back. They hawked everything from the four-poster bed where Lance Bascome made it with Dolly Carlotta in *Came a Lover* down to Marcia Mercer's bra (big) and Tommy Rigger's posing strap (small). You probably also know that right now they're making the very last movie that will ever be made at the Studio. And when it's done, the wrecking balls will strike all the sets. And that will be that. God, that will really wind up the era that was!

Being in such sorry straits, the Studio obviously wasn't springing for the party. The invitation came from Laurie Ann Hopkins, who definitely can spring for it. Laurie Ann is married to a doctor who's known as "the gynecologist to the stars." You can bet his services don't come cheap. Laurie Ann's been out of the business even longer than I have. But if you've got a long memory or look at a lot of late, late movies on the tube, the name might ring a bell. From the time she was six years old to when she was eleven or so, she cutesy-pooed her way through about eighty-nine clinkers where she was always being kidnapped or fought over for custody in a divorce action. Kim once said, "Can you imagine anybody fighting over such a dopey twit?" But that wasn't fair. We actually both liked Laurie Ann. She was always sweet and nice. Besides, she wasn't much competition. She couldn't sing or dance or clown or act or do much of anything. Except look helpless. But she couldn't leave pictures, as the saying goes, because she was a star.

Kim. My dear old buddy of a million up-and-down years. Miss Kimberley Hudson. That must be how I got invited. That was how the invitation caught up with me out here on the draggy edges of Hackensack, New Jersey. Kim gave Laurie Ann my address. It had to be Kim. Which must mean Kim herself was intending to show. The fabulous superstar Kimberley Hudson. Was the No. 1 box-office draw four years in a row going to show up for a reunion of ex-child stars who were mostly has-beens before they were done being kids?

I cooled my curiosity until the rates changed. Then I put through a call to the Coast. I reminded myself that it was three hours earlier in Beverly Hills and that Kim rarely batted an eyelash until two or three o'clock in the afternoon when she wasn't working.

"Indiana, how nice to hear you again. It's me."

"Oh, hello, Miss Spinelli. It's nice to hear *you* again. It's been such a long time."

It had, of course. I hadn't seen Kim in over a year and it must have been six months since I talked to her on the phone. No matter how time passed, you could always count on Indiana being there. The important thing was that Kim could count on it. Next to my friendship—and Lonnie Braintree's—Indiana's devotion was surely the most lasting and stabilizing thing in Kim's life. Indiana had been with her as

2

maid, mother-substitute, and confidante for more than twenty years. The things she had seen and put up with!

"Indiana, can Her Majesty come to the phone?"

"Oh, I'm afraid she can't do that, Miss Spinelli. She's in Switzerland."

"I guess I haven't been keeping up with the columns. Are she and Mr. Glasgow at their chalet?"

"No, no. She's just there to make herself all beautiful. I mean, even *more* beautiful. She's in some clinic where she said they perform miracles."

Oh-oh. That meant something. For openers, it meant Kim was planning to drop a fast twenty pounds, get a face lift, maybe even a rejuvenation shot. The works. The meaning behind the meaning, I'd bet anything, was that something new was cooking in Kim's life. Like a new guy. Was the thing with David petering out? Could it be Kim that Earl Wilson was referring to in one of his "Secret Stuff" items? Item: "A famous film beauty, still married, is feeling very romantic about a much younger television personality."

". . . and Mr. Glasgow is in Yugoslavia. He's making another one of those horror pictures there."

"Indiana, did she say anything about a party at the Studio? Whether she was going or not?"

"She certainly did. I heard her calling some lady to tell her she'd be there. The party's the same day she's supposed to be coming back. The fifteenth, isn't it? I'm sure she's coming back that day especially to be there."

"In that case," I said, making a snap decision, "I'm coming out. I've been invited too. If she calls, tell her I'm flying out on the fifteenth. If the welcome mat's still out, I'll stay with you overnight."

"For you, Miss Spinelli, the welcome mat is always out. You must stay longer than that."

"No, I mustn't. I'm working hard on a new book and I'd feel guilty leaving the kids any longer."

Kim and I go back almost to the beginning. We met at the Studio when I was ten and she was twelve. I was the youngest of the four singing Spinelli Sisters. We were under contract to the Studio and doing a turn in some so-so musicals. Kim had just landed the part of Wendy in *Wendy and the Golden Retriever*. She filled me in on her earlier years and they were really grim. I know things about her nobody else does. In fact, I don't think anything like the truth has ever been written about her.

A couple of months ago she sent me a copy of the "bio"

3

her latest press agent had hacked out. Across the top she wrote, "Isn't this a crock?" Here's an excerpt of it:

Often acclaimed the most beautiful woman in the world, and quite certainly the ranking queen of international filmdom, Kimberley Hudson first saw the light of day in an ancestral manor house in Sussex, England. She was born Kimberley Margaret Sarah Berkeley, the Baroness of Kyneshire.

Miss Hudson was the daughter of an adventurous maverick earl who emigrated to North America to look after cattle and oil interests in Alberta. She was only two when she came to this continent. For the next eight or nine years she lived comfortably, if uneventfully, on a 47,000-acre ranch northwest of Calgary.

Nothing could have been further from the minds of the young girl or her parents than a career in films. How it happened is, in its own way, as much a part of the Hollywood legend as the discovery of the young Lana Turner, who began her ascent to stardom from a stool at the soda fountain in Schwab's Drug Store—thanks to a bird-watching movie columnist who liked the way a sweater was wearing Miss Lana.

Miss Hudson and her parents were wintering at the fashionable Desert Inn in Palm Springs. One night in the dining room they became aware of a man at the next table who was staring almost hypnotically in their direction. When he had finished his dinner, he came over and introduced himself. His name was Frank Graham and he was a talent scout for the Studio.

Struck by the uncommon beauty of the child, Graham told Kim's parents that she belonged in films. To prove he was willing to put his money where his mouth was, so to speak, he said he had a specific film in mind. The picture was to be called *Wendy and the Golden Retriever*. Kim would make a perfect Wendy, the girl they had spent months searching for.

It took enormous powers of persuasion on the part of the talent scout to overcome the objections of Kim's parents. Like most members of their class, the Berkeleys (the Studio changed Kim's surname to tone down the too-aristocratic sound of Berkeley) loved the theater and "cinema," as they called it, but they took a fairly condescending attitude toward people who worked in those professions. As for their own daughter becoming an actress . . .

4

Fortunately for all of us, Mr. Graham prevailed. The rest, as they say, is motion picture history.

Unlike so many of the child stars of yesteryear, who faded after their youthful endeavors, Miss Hudson soars higher with each passing year. Today she stands at the pinnacle of her artistry and international acclaim . . .

Ha! With the possible exception of the last paragraph, the "bio" is about 180 degrees from the truth, which is par for the course.

If I live to be a thousand (right now I'll settle for thirty-seven!) I will never, never forget the first time I saw her. She was coming out of the Boss's office. I nearly stopped breathing. She was the most breathtaking thing I had ever seen in my whole young life.

I was sitting in the reception room with Mama and my sisters. Three or four other mothers with seven or eight little girls were also there. The Boss wanted to talk to Mama and us girls about the new picture the four "amazing" singing Spinelli Sisters would be going into. A little diamond called *Tots of Tuscany*. But Mama and us girls and all the other Mamas and their daughters were there hoping the big plum was going to drop into their laps. Just then every girl at the Studio was dying to land that part of parts . . . Wendy.

The door opened and the bombshell fell.

There was a girl I had never seen before. I had never seen any girl nearly so beautiful. To nobody in particular she said, "I'm going to play Wendy."

I said "girl," but you couldn't really tell if she was a girl. Or a woman. She was short enough to be my age. But she had boobs. And she had the face of a woman. That face! It was like a piece of jewelry. Her eyes were the pure, rich green of jade. Her lips curved in a bright, thinnish ruby bow. Her hair was a color I had never seen before. Nor have I seen it since, though God knows millions of women have tried to get their hairdressers to imitate it. It was about half-way between fresh rust and burnished copper. Anybody else with anything like hair that color would have had a million freckles. She didn't have one. Her skin was like white velvet, flawless as new-fallen snow. She wore that gorgeous mane of hair long, like a woman, not in braids or spit curls or pinned up like the rest of us kids.

For a minute she just stood there by the door. Slowly—and pointedly—she pulled down her sweater. Then she smoothed her pleated plaid skirt. After another long minute she walked toward the woman who could have been her mother, though she was pretty rough-looking. I couldn't make out the look the girl gave her. It was a penetrating one, which could have meant anything: victory, defiance, even loathing.

Finally the girl started to walk out. The woman got up and followed her. Just as they got to the door, the girl turned around suddenly and stared at me. *Me!* Why me? It gave me the heebie-jeebies.

Three days later I saw her again in the commissary. I was slurping up a Shirley Temple Malted Cream Surprise just before ballet class, and she was sitting by herself at another one of those long, gloomy wooden tables that looked like they were snitched from a monastery.

She hypnotized me. I kept staring at her until our eyes met. She picked up her glass and came toward me, walking so cool and poised and womanlike as if she were at least eighteen years old.

"Hi," she said. "I know who you are. I'm Kimberley Hudson."

"Hello, Kimberley. That's such a pretty name."

"I guess so. I'm not used to it yet. I only got it two days ago."

"Mama wouldn't let them change our names."

"My mother would let them change anything," she said bitterly, "if it would get me into the movies. She'd even let them change me into a boy."

"I don't think anybody could ever change you into a boy."

"Well, they're going to let me be a girl. My new name is Kimberley Hudson and I'm supposed to have rich parents who never wanted me to go into the movies. Nobody's ever supposed to know who I really am or where I come from."

"I wish you'd tell me. I'd never tell anybody else."

"I have to talk to somebody," she said. "I saw you in the Boss's office the other day. I thought you looked like somebody I could talk to."

I knew what she meant. You might be only ten years old, but if you've been in show business since you were three, you sort of know the score. You know you're not like any other ten-year-old. When I was six I could put on my makeup like an old pro, just to take one example. By the time you get to be ten, the things you've seen and heard! And done. Things no ordinary ten-year-old even dreamed about. Still, I was thrilled out of my skin that this fantastic-looking girl, who had to be a lot older than me, wanted to be friends.

Her real name was Dora Olsen, Kim told me, and she and her mother didn't have a pot to pee in. (That isn't quite the way she put it then, but that's the gist of it.) They had lived

6

in two sleazy little rooms over a hardware store in an Arizona border town called Barton. She didn't remember her father at all. He was a loser and a drifter, her mother said. He had drifted by just long enough to make Dora before drifting across the border into Mexico to look for gold. They never had so much as a penny postcard from him.

Dora's mother slung hash in a chili parlor. Often she brought home one of the customers. He could be a "traveling man" who didn't have a place to sleep because the hotel was full up. Or he might be some "poor soldier" who had missed the last bus back to Fort Huachuca. But Dora could tell from the sounds in the next room the visitor was getting something more than just a bed for the night.

"Honey, you're pretty enough to be in pictures," Kim remembered her mother telling her from the time she could remember anything. "And that's where I mean to see you."

There was more, lots more, Kim told me about her depressing childhood, so that, pretty soon, my own didn't seem so bad by comparison. But the important thing is that her mother, in her own screwy way, did make good on her prediction.

The way it happened was pretty simple. And awful.

The Bison Hunters was being made outside Tombstone. The cast and the crew were mostly holed up in and around Barton. Many nights the director of the movie would stumble into the chili joint where Mrs. Olsen worked. His name was Terry Winters, and he was a real lush, but a fairly young and good-looking lush.

Terry Winters would soak up the juices until closing time. He never seemed to have a place to sleep, so guess whose bed he ended up in? In the morning, semi-sober, he would watch Kim making her breakfast and getting ready to go to school. He raved about her budding beauty. He swore she'd grow up to break a million hearts. By God, if he wasn't going to tell the "old man" back at the Studio about her!

Mrs. Olsen worked until midnight. Kim was usually so sound asleep she never heard her come in—unless she was bringing someone with her.

One chilly night just before Christmas Kim heard the key in the latch. She had just gone to bed. It wasn't ten o'clock yet. The floor lamp over her cot was on so she could read. She thought her mother must be coming home early because she wasn't feeling well.

But it wasn't her mother. It was Terry Winters.

"Hiya, cutie. Hope I didn't wake you up."

"No, you didn't. I can't read in my sleep."

"That's good." He came over to the cot. "Wow, have I had

7

a day! We started shooting this morning at six. I was so bushed, I was falling asleep at dinner over my enchiladas. So your good mother told me to take off. Told me to come back here and put my weary bones to bed."

"If you're that tired," said Kim, "that's where you belong."

"You're batting a hundred percent there, sweetie."

Kim's cot was in the dining room-kitchen. Her mother slept in the connecting bedroom. Terry went into the bedroom. Without closing the door, he began shucking off his clothes. He kept up a flow of cheery chatter. For once he seemed to be reasonably sober.

He came back into the dining room-kitchen in his shorts and undershirt. He shivered and clapped his hands and jumped up and down in his bare feet.

"Baby, this may be Arizona. But let me tell you one thing. It's cold enough out there to freeze the proverbial witch's titty-boos. I want to tell you I'm frozen to the bone."

Terry did some more jumping and blew on his hands. "Listen, my sleeping beauty, Christmas is coming. In the spirit of the season, could you be persuaded to give one poor frozen bum the only present that would mean a damn thing right now?"

"What's that?" asked Kim.

"Five minutes. Five minutes out of your life. Five minutes so I could crawl in beside you and get my tootsies warm."

"I knew what was going to happen," Kim confessed to me. "And I let it. He was cute, kind of. And I was sort of curious." She gave me a long, leveling look. "Are you ... well, do you see?"

I nodded. I only half-knew, but I didn't really want to know exactly what she was talking about. Mostly I didn't want to lose my new friend by being shocked at anything she told me.

"It wasn't much. It didn't hurt. And it didn't make me moan and groan like my mother. But he didn't keep his word—about the five minutes. He went to sleep. So did I after a while." She paused. "I don't think I had been asleep five minutes before I heard my mother screaming."

"I bet she was ready to kill Terry," I said.

"That's how she pretended. She called him lots of names. A filthy, low-down swine. And worse. She said she had a good mind to call the cops. She asked Terry if he knew he could go to the electric chair for attacking a twelve-year-old girl."

"*Pretended?*" I said. "Do you call that pretending?"

The beautiful green eyes narrowed into a hard glare that

8

bore right into me and made me feel like a very stupid little girl.

"She gave him the key to our apartment, didn't she? She knew what would happen. She didn't call the police, did she? She didn't even kick him out. She didn't even make him sleep on the floor. I was still wide awake when I could hear them in bed together, arguing and whispering and then giggling.

"When I woke up the next morning both of them were already up and everything was hunkey-dorey between them. My mother was bustling around making a big breakfast and they were laughing and kidding together.

" 'Good morning, little morning glory,' Terry said to me like there was honey in his mouth and nothing had ever happened. 'Your mother says you have her permission to stay out of school today if you'd like to do me a favor.'

"I asked him what the favor was.

" 'I can use you in a scene I'm shooting today,' said Terry. 'It won't be hard. I'll show you just what to do. You won't have to memorize any lines or say anything. But it's a very important scene. You'll get paid just like any other actor. How about it?' "

Kim was delighted to do the "favor," but the scene turned out to be kind of dumb. She was supposed to be a white girl who had been kidnapped by some Apaches. She was being held captive in a hogan, gagged and tied up. Her rescue came from a white hunter who charged into the hogan when none of the Indians were around. He put her on his horse and rode off with her. And that was all.

"You were just great," Terry told her.

Mrs. Olsen, who had been on the set, told her the same thing.

The next day, when Kim got home from school, her mother had some big news for her. "Guess what, honey? We're going to Hollywood! Isn't that something? They're going to give you some tests at the Studio and you're going to meet the big mogul who runs the whole works. Just look here."

She showed Kim the note Terry had written the Boss on the back of one of his business cards: "Have a look at this girl. I think you'll be impressed. She could be the perfect Wendy."

Mrs. Olsen smothered Kim with kisses. "I just know you're going to make it, baby. I just know you're going to be a big, big wonderful star. You got it a hundred times all over Shirley Temple or Judy Garland or anybody you want to name. You don't have to sing or dance because you're so beautiful. People will just want to look at you. They have classes there.

9

They'll teach you how to act. You'll pick it up in no time. You're smart."

Kim and her mother took the Greyhound to Los Angeles and checked into a flea-bag hotel off Pershing Square. The next day they were at the Studio.

Kim sucked deep on her straw and gave me a funny smile. "How do you like the Boss?"

That was easy to answer. "He's pukey."

"Have you ever been in there alone with him? In his office?"

"No."

"You're lucky."

"Mama takes us. I hate it when we go there. So do my sisters. He's always stroking our hair and patting us on the cheeks."

Kim smiled. "Can I tell you something?"

"Sure."

"It has to be a secret. You must promise not to tell anybody ever. Promise?"

Right then I'd have promised her the moon. Ava Gardner had just come into the commissary and everybody was gawking and going buzz-buzz-buzz. Ava was over at M-G-M but her new boy friend was a pipsqueak young actor working at the Studio. Some writer in a fan magazine had just called Ava the most beautiful woman in the world. But I didn't think she could hold a candle to the girl sitting across from me.

"My mother didn't want to go in to see the Boss with me. She said, 'I'll just be in the way. He doesn't want to talk to me. You're the one who's going to be the great big star. I'll just wait outside.'

"I told her I was afraid I wouldn't know what to say to him.

"'Oh, yes, you will, baby. They say he's very easy to talk to. You're such a smart girl anyway. And remember, I want you to be extra nice to him. Be just as nice and friendly as you can. You know how much this means to us. This is our big chance. They say the Boss is very keen about young girls. Maybe because he doesn't have daughters of his own. So you be just like a loving daughter to him, even if you have to put on a little bit.' "

Kim was awestruck by the size of the office. She thought it must be half as big as Barton and she doubted that the Boss's desk would fit into either one of their rooms back home.

"Come, come, come, little girl!" the Boss called to her.

His voice was gruff and she felt scared walking across the deep rug to his desk. He was still writing something and

10

waved his hand, meaning that she should sit down in the chair beside him. He didn't look at her until he finished his writing. Then he whistled almost as loud as a police whistle.

"Jesus, Mother of God!" he yelled. "You're gorjus! You're the most gorjus thing I ever laid eyes on."

Kim thanked him and he asked her how she got to be so gorgeous. She told him she guessed we all look just the way we're made.

"I don't believe it," he said. "I've just got to pinch you to make sure you're real."

He reached over and pinched her on the leg.

"He asked me a lot of junk about how old I am and about my mother and father," said Kim, "and where I'm staying now and how I liked school and what grade I'm in and if I liked the movies and who my favorite movie stars are. Pretty soon he was doing what he does to you and your sisters. He had his fat hand on my hair brushing it and then he was patting my cheeks."

Now I thought Kim and I were really friends. The same thing had happened to each of us. We were like two women of the world baring our souls to each other. Ten and twelve years old!

"You know, little girl," the Boss told her, "I don't have any daughters of my own. It's the big sadness in my life. Seeing you makes me know how much I'm missing."

Kim thanked him again, and he brushed and patted her some more.

"Come over here, little girl," he said to her. "You'll make an old man very happy if you'll just sit in his lap a minute or two and let him think he's a real papa."

Kim remembered what her mother told her about being real nice to the Boss and how important this was. She didn't need to be told. All she needed was to remember Barton and the miserable hole that had been their home. She went and sat on the Boss's lap even though she felt "dopey" doing it. She was much too big and old for that stuff.

"The Boss hugged me tight and whispered a lot of gooey things in my ear," said Kim. "His hands started to brush up and down my side and the outside of my legs. It was so silly. I just sat there. I thought about my mother sitting outside and almost started to giggle. If she could see me now! I stopped trying to think of anything to say. I just sat there.

"I guess I shouldn't have been surprised at what he did next. But I was. I nearly screamed from the surprise. His hand was under my sweater. He patted my tummy a couple of times. Then I could feel the hand crawling up. It kept crawling. Until he was poking his fingers under my bra! First

11

one side. Then the other. He almost went out of his mind when he touched them. 'Holy Jesus, little girl, they're beautiful!'

"You know, Gina, how boys and men get when they're excited."

I didn't know. But I nodded my head again. I didn't want to have her looking for some other friend who did know about such things.

"He kept whispering in my ear. All kinds of crazy things. I really couldn't tell what he was saying. He was so out of breath and sort of gasping. I could feel something getting hard under me. That's the way they get when they get excited. His hand, his right hand—Gina, you've got to swear in blood you'll never tell one word of this to anybody."

"I swear."

"His right hand started to crawl up inside my leg. I thought maybe I would scream or bite him or kick him. But I just sat there. It felt like I was sitting on a rock. That fat old hand just kept crawling. Up and up and up. Way up under my dress. Up until it was on my panties. Gina, you've got to believe me. I'm not making any of this up. He put the tip of his tongue in my ear. He was panting like crazy. He said a lot of funny-sounding things I couldn't understand. It could have been Greek or Russian for all I knew. He wouldn't stop. He had his fingers under my panties. Yes! The Boss! He was touching me. *There!*"

Kim leaned across the table toward me. Our heads were almost knocking together. She put her hands around her mouth and whispered: "He started rubbing me. *There.* 'Oh, my God, oh, my God!' he yelled.

"The next thing, Gina, he lifted me. *Lifted* me. And set me on his left leg. I heard a zip. Gina, there's his *thing* sticking out. *Honestly!* Ick! It was so ishy. All fat and red and stiff. Ick! He put his hand on it and started shaking it up and down. The other hand was still rubbing me. *There.* Then—"

I was so shocked at the dreadful things Kim was telling me I could hardly believe she had gone into a fit of laughing.

"What's so funny?" I asked.

"Gina, he was going crazy. I thought he was going to have a heart attack or something. I almost had a heart attack myself. His leg gave such a jerk it threw me way up in the air, and he let out a wild yelp. Gina, you should have seen it! There was this icky white stuff coming out of his thing. He was a mess. He got some Kleenex out of his desk drawer to wipe up the mess. Ick, ick, ick!"

It was the worst thing I had ever heard. I felt sick for Kim. I hated the Boss so much I would have kicked him and

12

spit in his face if he had been walking by. Nothing like this had ever happened to me or my sisters. Mama and Papa were always so strict with us. One or the other always had their eye on us. We weren't even supposed to think about boys. God help any boy—or man—who might try anything with us! Even with my oldest sister, who was almost eighteen.

Bad as I felt for Kim, all I could think of to say was, "That's terrible."

Kim laughed like a hard, cynical woman. "It wasn't so terrible. It was sort of funny. It wasn't like with Terry. The Boss is such . . . an ick! I just sat there. I didn't do anything. I never touched him."

"What did he say . . . afterwards?"

Kim laughed again. "He said, 'Now you be a nice girl and don't give us any trouble. You listen to your mother. Always listen to your mother. She knows what's best. You must work very, very hard. You work hard and I promise you, little girl, you are going to be a very, very good Wendy.' "

We all hated the Boss's guts. But Kim hated the man with a blazing fire. We all called him names our mothers never taught us. Everybody except Kim. She called him the Beast. I always thought of the two of them as Beauty and the Beast.

When she grew up, Kim got a charge out of shocking people with the tale of her first meeting with the Beast. When she grew up, she could employ one of the liveliest imaginations and raciest tongues to jazz up any tale she was telling. She always managed to improve on the literal truth.

It wasn't true Kim had to screw the Boss to get the part of Wendy. But that's the way she liked to tell it. Telling her version of their first meeting, she said she was just going out the door of his office when she called back to the Boss, as an afterthought, "By the way, do I have to fuck the golden retriever too?"

In the Gospel According to St. Kimberley, the Beast replied, "Over my dead cock, Princess."

One person who won't be at the reunion is the Boss. He has long since gone to his reward. The night he died, Kim took a party boisterously "on the town" to celebrate his passing.

Chapter 2

When you're pregnant, as any mother can testify, your mind hatches out some real weirdo fears. You can spend nine months in Panicsville if you start ticking off all the things that could go wrong with that little life growing inside of you. What if it's born blind? or deaf? Or minus legs or arms? What if it comes out a Mongoloid? What if it's a harelip or its face is covered with a gruesome birthmark? What if it grows up to be a wino? A junkie? A thief? A whore? A rapist? A murderer? Whatifwhatifwhatifwhatif—?

This mother can honestly tell you all these fears took a back seat to a real lulu of one I had the whole time I was carrying both Timothy and Julie. Do you know what spooked me for the eighteen months give a day or three I've been pregnant in my life? You won't believe this. Or maybe you will. With each of them the prayer I prayed over and over again was, "Please, God, I don't care what You give me. Boy or girl, twins, triplets. I'll take what I get and be grateful. I don't care what they look like or anything. Make them any way You want. But please, God, whatever You do, don't make them *talented*. I mean *showbiz* talented. I mean talented to where they'd be itching to make something of their talent. Or I'd be tempted to push it or feel it was my duty to push it. Please, God, whatever You do . . ."

What I'm saying is, I wouldn't want any child of mine—or anybody else's child, for that matter—to follow in the script of me and my sisters and most of the kids we grew up with. I wouldn't wish that screwy childhood on the Enemy, for heaven's sakes.

"More things are wrought by prayer," they say, "than this world dreams of." I can't tell you who said it first. Shakespeare? Somebody in the Bible?

Anyway, it works. Sometimes. These two times, both with Timmy and with Julie, it worked for me.

It nearly kills me to see how amazingly *normal* my kids are. Where do they get it from? Not from me, I can tell you. God knows, not from their father. Both their parents by rights ought to be branded with a big N across their chests— N standing for Neurotic.

Do you know what else kills me? How *smart* my kids are. It's all I can do to keep them from learning how *dumb* I am.

14

Book-wise, I mean. The things they already know at seven and eight years old! I really have to jump to keep a step ahead of them with their homework. I'm sure glad they go to a school where they don't teach the New Math. I could burn the midnight oil until Doomsday and I'd never get the hang of the New Math.

The other day I asked Julie and Timmy what they wanted to be when they grew up. Maybe some other mother wouldn't dig their answers too much. But I got a big kick out of them. I was plenty relieved, too. At their ages, of course, you can't hold them to anything. At least they didn't tell me what I didn't want to hear. Like, "Mommy, I wanna be like you. I wanna sing and make records and do club dates and be in the movies."

When I asked her, Julie turned those big, gorgeous, solemn brown eyes on me. "I think I'd like to be an airplane pilot for Pan Am," she said thoughtfully. I asked her why and she said, "Because then I could go all over the world and I wouldn't have to pay." Not a stewardess, mind you. A pilot, no less. Get that, Gloria and Betty and Germaine? Seven years old and she's already liberated!

Julie's brother Timothy is the original put-on artist of all time. "When I grow up," he told me in great seriousness, "I want to be a drop-out. Or maybe, maybe"—eyeing me mischievously—"a dope fiend." "Those are choices to make any mother proud," I said. Maybe I shouldn't let him see so much television or read the *Daily News*.

Their mother is about the biggest PTA-nik in Greater Hackensack. She never misses a meeting. She's so glad to be aboard. She's so grateful to be passing for the normal mother of normal kids and involved in the normal concerns of mothers who are trying to do the best by their kids. The schooling my kids are getting is such a far cry from my own dipsy-doodle "education."

It almost makes me laugh to see all the fussing that goes on nowadays about school matters. Whether to bus or not to bus. Whether or not to say prayers or the Pledge of Allegiance in classrooms. The whole bit about decentralization. Should they take the vending machines with all the junk foods out of schools? Should the hot lunches have a minimum of 20 or 30 grams of protein? Should there be time in the school day for Yoga or karate or finger painting or computer programming?

I want to laugh remembering my own crummy, hit-or-miss education. Which was the same crummy, hit-or-miss education all the other kids at the Studio got. I'm here to tell you a ghetto kid today gets a better education than any of

15

the most famous child stars ever got. A kid in Harlem or Bed-Stuy or Watts or wherever gets more book learning than Elizabeth Taylor or Judy Garland or Mickey Rooney or Shirley Temple ever got. And I'm not saying kids in the ghettos should count their blessings.

Maybe I shouldn't be mentioning names. Elizabeth Taylor or Judy Garland and Mickey Rooney were at M-G-M and Shirley Temple was at Fox. But I can't believe things were much different at M-G-M or Fox than they were at the Studio. The other day I read an interview with Richard Burton and he said Elizabeth reads all the time "trying to catch up on everything she missed." "Everything she missed" has to mean all the schooling she missed when she was making *National Velvet* and the Lassie films all the way up to *Father of the Bride* when most kids her age were going to school. Real schools, I mean.

Frankly, the Studio didn't give a damn if we grew up to be the biggest know-nothings in the world. Just as long as we were smart enough to do our tricks on camera was all they cared about. Any of us could get into the damnedest scrapes or scandals—I could tell you about some dillies!—and the Studio would jump in like Big Daddy to shut the whole thing up. Whatever it took, batteries of lawyers or press agents or fancy blackmail fees, they'd pay the price and no *kvetching*.

In a thousand ways we were pampered and petted and catered to and spoiled rotten. The bigger we were as a property, the more murder we could get away with. But I don't think we could have demanded a decent education and got away with it. If any of us—or our parents—had yelled for at least as good schooling as the kids in the Mexican section of Los Angeles were getting, we'd have found everybody out to lunch. Getting a decent education would have used up too much valuable time. The Studio had better uses for our time.

I don't know how it is now but in those days the California law said we had to be in school at least two hours a day. I never saw anybody clocking us. Those two hours were at the convenience of the Studio. You took them when they didn't need you for anything else. You went to school when there wasn't anything more important to do. When you weren't rehearsing or shooting or taking dancing or singing lessons or being fitted for costumes or posing for publicity shots or being interviewed by columnists or writers for fan mags. Then they'd suddenly remember school as a welcome excuse to get you out from under foot.

"Gina, it's time for your lessons."

"Kimberley, arithmetic class is just starting. You better hurry so you'll learn how to count up all your money."

"Tinker Wells, get over to school. Miss Bitters says you've still got a lot to learn."

Tinker Wells was there the first day Kim came to class. It was the day after I met Kim in the commissary. I had made a date with her in the commissary to take her to school her first time at the Studio. Tinker Wells must have been fifteen going on twelve, a little sawed-off half-pint with freckles and cowlick all done up in Argyle from socks to bow tie. Behind that impish All-American boy grin he was always grinning there was a lot of garbage that wasn't so All-American boyish.

If I remember right, there were a few other Famous Young Faces in class that day. Sally Strickland. Lonnie Braintree. Peggy Palmer. Hal Harper. Bunky McAllister. (You remember Bunky, the fat and funny fuck-up in all those two-reel *Just Us* comedies.) I'm also pretty sure "Cuddles" Malloy was there. Maybe you've forgotten the name. He was about one and three-quarters years old when he did the baby gig in a movie with an old dipso comedian who hated all kids in general and "Cuddles" in particular. Anybody who's ever read anything about old R. T. Handy remembers how he's supposed to have spiked "Cuddles" grapefruit juice with Four Roses during a break on the set of *It's a Wise Child* and how "Cuddles" was in no shape to resume filming. Opinions differed as to R. T. Handy's motives. Either he was being just his usual sadistic self or he was lashing back at a born scene-stealer and trying to prove that anybody under two years old was not professional enough to be in pictures. Handy's explanation was it was never too early to introduce someone to "God's nectar."

"Cuddles" was seven now and already a has-been. He had been hot as a baby but nobody wanted him as a little boy. His contract still had a year to go. His mother brought him to the Studio school every day, no doubt hoping if they kept seeing him around they'd find something for him to do.

I didn't mean to get started on "Cuddles," who isn't part of this story at all. The point is, there we all were crowded into one stinking makeshift crack in the wall calling itself a school. All ages from seven-year-old "Cuddles" to Hal Harper, who must have been seventeen. There we were in one teeny room being "taught" by one teacher who was about as qualified to be teaching school as a twenty-buck-a-night hooker. Which was what everybody said she had been before her brief fling in the flicks.

Miss Bitters was a joke. We all joked about her. Joke No.

1 was we called her Miss Titters. She had a pair of knockers that must've measured forty-six. The Studio claimed she was an accredited teacher in the Los Angeles school system. That was the biggest joke of all. During the years I did time in school, first in New York and then at the Studio, I probably racked up what you might call an elementary school education—if you were being generous. But I'll bet it's a lot more than Miss Bitters ever racked up.

Miss Bitters, when I first laid eyes on her, was a straight-from-the-bottle strawberry blonde. You could say she was crowding forty-two. That's again if you were being generous. Almost matching the color of her hair was the nail polish she put on the runs in her stockings. You could look at that puffy, dropping face and see it must have been pretty eye-grabbing in its day. Somewhere along the line she must have said to herself, "What the hell, let it all hang out." Maybe she had been trim and tight once but now she was real tummyish and fat-assy.

The story was that years ago Miss Bitters had been the special nooky of some medium-high *schmuck* in the Studio. He got her a second-from-the-left spot in the chorus line of a B-minus musical and a two-line walk-on in some long-forgotten F-plus comedy. She couldn't even cut that much, the story went, so somebody got the bright idea she could run the Studio's version of the one-room schoolhouse. Abe Lincoln trudging off seven miles every day to his one-room country schoolhouse had to be better off.

Our "school" was a narrow, rectangle-shaped enclosure between a couple of big sound stages. It had maybe fifteen battered-up old desks that must have been dug up from some junk shop or left over from some one-room schoolhouse in the wilderness. Maybe even Abe Lincoln's. The walls were done in lovely decorator burlap. They had two really stunning decorations. Up front, behind teacher's desk, we gazed at a full-length spread of our Saviour Jesus Christ, flowing beard, flowing nightgown and all. To our left, we had the awe-inspiring art of an unfurled, gigantic map of the United States of America to look at. Jesus in front of us and the stars and stripes forever to our left. Get it? Two dazzling visuals that stood for God and Country. If we got that much straight, we didn't need to know anything else.

Don't forget, this was the time when half the country went to bed expecting to find Commies hiding under the bed. Even biggie *schmucks* at the Studio thought that way. Or pretended to. At least they were smart enough to know they could make a buck out of riding everybody's hang-up. And they could make points by teaching us small fry Real Values. Like God and Country. And not much more.

Another thing. Our little school had no windows. For oxygen the door had to be kept open. That open door sure did wonders for our concentration. Can you blame us if we didn't know whether Thomas Jefferson came before Ulysses S. Grant, or what six times nine equaled? Or if when the teacher said Pierre she was talking about the capital of some state or good old horny Lucky Pierre? Who could concentrate when you couldn't hear yourself think? All you could hear was that damn splashing. And the orchestra sounding off. *And* Miss Queen Bee bitching away.

"That damn water's cold enough to stiff an Eskimo. Get it heated!"

"Has anyone cleaned that pool since the Civil War? Look at all the crud floating on top. I'm not diving into any cesspool."

"When that dame brings her kid, tell her to scram. She gives me the heeby-jeebies . . ."

I just saw the Queen Bee the other night on one of the lesser TV talk shows. She was with that Latin lover she's been bumming around the world with for the last fifteen years. People will be talking about the lover part long after they've forgotten all the lousy pictures he hammed his way through. I never thought the Queen Bee was the least bit sexy, but apparently Armando Monte Alban does. You can still giggle thinking of the expression on her face the first time he got her in the bedroom of her big Laurel Canyon shack. The way they tell it, Armando goes out to the kitchen just when things are getting hottest and comes back with a plate of something, and dumps it right down *there*! A butterscotch sundae five hundred degrees colder than her snatch.

On the Dirk Haynes Show the other night, the Queen Bee looked awful. She must be fifty-two or fifty-three now and she looked every second of it. . . . But I'm rambling. I said that outside the open door to our schoolroom were two big sound stages. One of them was the huge Olympic-and-thensome swimming pool of the Queen Bee. Plus everything that went with it. The diving boards, the rafts, the bells, the underwater lights. The works. The other sound stage was where two orchestras, each one with about a hundred musicians, accompanied the Queen Bee's water ballets.

The Queen Bee, you must have guessed, was our one and only Miss Astrid Hollins. The Divine Miss H. Short for Hell-on-Wheels. But in those days she was It. The Studio laid $2,-000,000 and more on any musical they could stick her fins in. These days a couple of M's doesn't sound like much. Sure, none of the majors want to go for any more, considering the blue funks of the movie business today. But back then two mil meant there was a star who was top drawer. A star with a track record that spelled P-R-O-F-I-T to the Studio in neon lights.

Astrid Hollins was that kind of star. She couldn't act her way out of a Christmas crostic, but in the water she was another kettle of fish. She was a sensation. Whatever they spent on her movies, they made it back in spades.

Now Astrid was making something called *The Beautiful Dolphin Meets a Minnow*. You get one guess who the beautiful dolphin was. The "minnow" was a five-year-old wonder child named Bubber.

Bubber made it into the movies faster than even a "godfather" could have arranged it. It was just one of those flukey things that could happen probably nowhere else than in Tinseltown, U.S.A. Ron Tuttle, one of the Studio's stable of writers, was loafing one weekend on the beach at La Jolla and there was little Bubber doing her stuff in the mighty Pacific. He got a big charge out of watching her. He kept thinking about her long after her parents had dragged her out of the water and taken her home for her afternoon nap. Jesus, he thought, wouldn't it be a gas to team up Bubber with Astrid! Before he left La Jolla, he had hatched out the basic story line for *The Beautiful Dolphin Meets a Minnow*.

Astrid must have been out of what mind she had to agree to such a deal. I don't care how big a star you are, if there's a kid in the picture you're in trouble. When *Paper Moon* came out, I remember Ryan O'Neal saying not so kiddingly he'd never make another picture with his own daughter, she was just too heavy to play against. The kid can steal any scene gagged and blindfolded. I don't think it took Astrid too long to catch on. I doubt whether she had in mind doing any sequels with Bubber. Nor do I think she stayed awake nights wondering how she could help Bubber's career in movies along.

The Spinelli Sisters did a turn in one of Astrid's later pictures and you could tell she had learned her lesson. By that time her popularity was slipping and musicals looked like they had about had it. But she could still throw her weight around. The script called for us to appear only in one scene. The scene was set in a nightclub, where we were supposed to "open" for a famed comic.

"Okay," said Astrid, "they get two songs. No lines or cutesy-poo business. They sing their two songs and haul ass."

With Bubber, Astrid knew she was in trouble from about Scene No. 2. You could tell it from the high C note of her bitching. "Look, I don't care what the script says, she's nowhere but nowhere when I'm doing that underwater kaffeeklatsch with the other dolphins . . ." Or she'd be trying to psych Bubber out of thinking Bubber could do anything. Dripping honey and spun-sugar candy with every syllable. "Bubber, darling, that's not quite it" (knocking Bubber's double somersault off the diving board and plunge to the bottom of the "sea" to find some rare underwater treasure to present to the beautiful dolphin). "I think you'll have to practice some more." Or she might say, "Bubber, darling, if that's too hard for you to do, we can just cut it out."

That was the scene outside the open door to our school the first day I brought Kim to school. There are thousands of days since then that I've completely blanked out on. But if I live to be a million, I'll remember that day. I was so excited. And I was bursting with pride.

The first day I ever went to any school, which was P.S. 147 back in Brooklyn, I remember I brought the teacher an apple. Corny but true. It's the sort of thing a poor, humble Italian mother would put her daughter up to doing. But this was something different. I was bringing Kim. Somehow this magnificent jewel had come into my possession. That day anyway, I owned it. It was mine to show off to the teacher, the kids, the whole world.

"Miss Bitters," I said, pulling Kim along by the hand, "this is Kimberley Hudson."

I thought Miss Bitters's eyes were going to jump out of their sockets. "Why, hello, Kimberley!"

"She's new here," I explained, "and she's going to be Wendy. In that movie with the dog."

"Are you, Kimberley? Why, that's marvelous. Welcome, Kimberley. I'm so glad you're going to be one of us."

"Thank you," said Kimberley.

"Good luck. I just know you're going to be very good."

Kim thanked her again, with a kind of serious smile.

I loved Miss Bitters that day. I loved her for being bowled over by Kim and showing it. I loved her for being so warm to my new friend. That day I would have sworn on a stack of Bibles she was a great teacher and I'd have scratched the eyes out of any kid I caught making fun of her. I swore to myself that I would try harder to pay attention and be a good pupil.

I can still see Kim as she looked that day. She was wearing a simple sleeveless dress the color of whipped egg yolks. I don't think any of the kids really saw her until Miss Bitters was through greeting her and Kim and I turned around to

21

look for empty seats. When they saw her straight-on, there was a hush like there had never been in that room.

These kids, you must remember, weren't ordinary kids. They all had something extra going for them. They were cute or funny or darling or they could do this or do that. They were all special in some way. They had to be to get where they were. Being special in their own way, they all had the smarts. They could be mean, jealous, ballsy little in-fighters. Like their parents trained them to be. They all had a sharp nose for the competition. They took one sniff of Kim and turned greener than her eyes.

I'm telling you every kid in that room gawked and gawked, open-mouthed. It was Tinker Wells who finally broke the spell. Naturally. Who else? Tinker put two fingers up to his mouth and let out a wild whistle that started Astrid swearing and screaming on top of the diving board.

"Who the fuck did that? Who the fuck's the clown who thinks he's a cop . . . ?"

Everybody howled. We all hated Astrid, who would never give anybody the time of day unless it was some hunk of ass she was either humping or wanted to hump. Most of us hated Tinker's guts too. But he could be funny. He always had a terrific sense of timing. And he didn't give a good screw for anybody.

If it was two o'clock, it had to be geography. If it was any o'clock, you knew what it had to be. An hour for everything and everything in its own proper hour. No matter who was there or how many were there. If it was ten o'clock, you got American history. If it was four o'clock, you "learned" arithmetic. How I'll always know it was two o'clock is that it was geography time.

". . . where Brazil is? Biffy?"

"Beats me."

"Lonnie?"

You could ask Lonnie a lot of toughies today and he'd know the answers. But he was only eight years old then and he had just come from England and I don't think he'd ever been in any kind of school before. Even then he was anxious to please. Because he didn't know the answer, he started to cry.

"Oh, now, Lonnie, it's not that important," said Miss Bitters. "We don't scold anybody here for not knowing an answer. Laurie Ann, can you tell us?"

"I think it's just below Mexico," said Laurie Ann.

Miss Bitters consulted the map in her geography book. "No, that's not quite right, Laurie Ann. I don't think I can

22

give you credit for that. Tinker, can you tell us where Brazil is?"

"Have you looked under your dress?"

Tinker's comeback and his puckish grin set the whole class to giggling. I watched Kim. She was biting her lips to keep from joining in the laughter. Tinker was watching her closely. Guessing that he had got to her, he beamed.

"I see you don't know, Tinker," said Miss Bitters.

"Do you? If you do, why are you asking us?"

More titters at the expense of Miss Bitters.

Tinker turned sideways in his seat and put a stare on Kim. You could tell she felt it by the way she kept her eyes fixed on the spiral notebook she had brought. Never did she return his gaze for one flickering second.

We never did find out just where Brazil was. Miss Bitters was off on a new kick. "Who knows which are the three largest cities in the world? Sally?"

Not a word from Sally. Sally was sitting a little behind me off to the left. Her geography book was open and she was poring over it. But it wasn't geography she was studying. It was the lyrics of a new song she'd be rehearsing for *The Season of Spring* right after she'd "done" her two hours.

"Sally?"

"Oh, I'm sorry, Miss Bitters. What did you ask me?"

"The names of the three largest cities in the world."

Sally giggled. "Let me see. I think first is Los Angeles—"

"Wrong!" yelled Tinker.

"Now, Tinker, please," said Miss Bitters.

"Please what? She's wrong."

"I know. But that's not the nice way to say it."

Tinker snorted loudly. Then he whipped out a note pad from his back pocket. He tore a sheet out and scribbled something on it. He folded the sheet and wrote a name on the outside. He passed it to Bunky McAllister with a sharp jab in Bunky's ribs. Bunky read the name on the note and passed it on to the person on his right. Kim.

The note stopped there. Tinker had written Kim a note. I felt sick to my stomach. I could have killed Tinker. I had never been so furious with anybody in my whole life. Just then I couldn't have told anybody why I was so mad. It was my first time out with jealousy.

Kim read the note and blushed. She avoided looking at Tinker. But as she pushed the note into the middle of her notebook, she glanced at me.

I pretended I hadn't seen anything. I was deep into my geography book. Between pages 112 and 113 I had my typewritten copy of the scene we were going to shoot the next day on *Tots of Tuscany*.

"Bubber, you're not staying down long enough. You're coming up too soon. Try it again, honey."

Astrid. Bull. It never came out but Bubber would out-underwater Astrid by a whole minute. Bubber could gulp enough oxygen to keep submerged for almost two and a half minutes. The most anybody ever stop-watched Astrid was 1:24.

Out came Tinker's pad again and he was scribbling away. Another poke in Bunky McAllister's ribs and the note was on its way to Kim. Every drop of blood in Kim's body must have rushed to her face. Her color was redder than a geranium. Very quietly she squashed the note and put it in her little white handbag.

I was in total misery until the class was over and we were ambling down the back lot together. Kim wasn't talking.

"You made a big hit," I said shyly.

"I did?"

"At least with Miss Bitters. And somebody else."

"Who?"

"You know who."

"No, I don't."

"Tinker Wells."

"Him," said Kim, frowning. "He's nuts."

That meant she liked him. I had never felt that way about a boy yet. But I knew the signs. When my oldest sister Anna started getting interested in boys, she'd always hide her feelings for anybody she liked in particular by telling us he was "real dumb" or a "jerk."

How could I blame Kim if she went for Tinker? Now she was in the very studio with the boy she had been seeing in the movies since she started going to movies. What's more, she was even in the same room with him. What's even more, he was sending notes to her! It must have seemed like a dream to her. How could I blame Kim for falling for this famous boy? Especially after he made a play for her?

I thought these reasonable thoughts but they didn't do much to calm the state of my mind. I had had Kim's friendship for just a minute and now I was about to be pushed into second place.

"Is that really Boyd Hunter?" Kim exclaimed.

"Oh, sure," I said matter-of-factly.

Boyd Hunter was just about the hottest thing in films. He was six foot two of rugged American manhood. He was one of the for-real, virile heroes in the business. The Studio had borrowed him from Paramount for a Western. For three

24

days they had been shooting a street scene. Boyd was the sheriff (surprise!) and he was fixin' to gun it out with a band of cattle thieves.

Kim went ape. The great Boyd Hunter in front of her very eyes! In the flesh. Making a picture which the whole world would soon be rushing to see. But she was seeing it first. She was seeing it being made.

I guess that's what was going through Kim's mind because it was what was going through mine. Only I was careful not to show that I was impressed. It was important that I let on that to me big stars were a dime a dozen. I'd seen them come, I'd seen them go. Stars were all part of the business, and when you had been in the business as long as I had you learned not to blow your cool. They weren't any different from you or me. Except they were more clay than you or me.

I hoped Kim would see how cool I was. But Kim had eyes only for Boyd. She didn't say a word through fourteen "takes" of Boyd slowly walking up the street to meet the bad guys. She was hypnotized. I don't know why but she was smiling. I hadn't seen her smile much before.

I couldn't budge her until the director called "Cut!" and the scene was over and Boyd was slouching back to his dressing room.

"He's wonderful," she sighed.

"Boyd?"

"Of course."

I was relieved she didn't say Tinker. Boyd Hunter could have been the man on the moon as far as mine or Kim's chances of having anything to do with him. He was too big, too far off, too grown-up. Tinker was a different matter.

I got up my nerve to go on a fishing expedition. "I saw Tinker passing you notes today."

"Yes."

Nothing more. Just "yes."

"He must like you. That's the first time I ever saw him do that. I've never seen him write anybody else a note."

"They're not missing anything."

I took a big gulp. "What did he say?"

"Nothing much."

"Don't you remember?"

"Sure I remember. It was just silly."

"Can't you tell me?"

Kim flipped through her notebook until she found the folded piece of paper. "Read it yourself."

Tinker, as the saying goes, was a poet and didn't know it:

"Sister, you're cute.
                    Honey, you is a real beaut."
"That's almost as good as Shakespeare," I sneered.
"Shakespeare?"
My God, she hadn't even heard of Shakespeare! Education-wise, things couldn't be too good in Barton either.
"You got another note," I said.
"Yes."
"Was Tinker making up a rhyme in that one too?"
"Yes."
Silence.
"Do you remember it?"
"Not exactly."
"Is that one a secret?"
"Sort of, I guess."
The sting of a bee couldn't have hurt more. "Friends aren't supposed to have secrets."
"I don't see anything wrong with secrets."
"If I got a note from someone," I said, "and you wanted to know what was in it, I'd show it to you."
"Then maybe that's where we're different, Gina."
I couldn't let her off with that. If it cost me the friendship, I had to know what was in that other note. "Please, Kim. I know a lot of things about Tinker that aren't too good. I don't want to talk about them unless I have to. But if I'm going to be your friend, I think I should know what Tinker wrote you."
"I don't think you have to know that."
"Why?"
"Because you're too young."
She couldn't have said anything meaner. I was crushed.
If you're Italian, your emotions are always riding pretty close to the surface. On top of that, you also know how to stage a scene. I got my waterworks working. Tears came flushing down my cheeks by the bucket.
Kim put out a sound that was somewhere between a heavy sigh and a groan. "Quit bawling, Gina. You can read it. It's just . . . stupid."
She opened her little white purse and handed me the crumpled paper.
Tinker's crumpled poem read:
        "Roses are red,
            Violets are blue.
                Would I ever like
                    To screw you. Woo-woo!"

26

Chapter 3

Once, when it seemed like the only time I saw much of Kim any more, I said to her, "You just love me for my home and family."

I was sort of joking. I was taken aback when Kim said quite seriously, "You know, you may be right about that."

She was not so much in love with my home and family, I think, as with the idea of home and family. Family was something she had never had. No brothers or sisters. A runaway father who didn't leave so much as a snapshot of himself behind. A catch-as-catch-can mother so dingbatty she could just barely keep a roof over their heads.

I can't tell you how I felt the first night I brought Kim home to dinner. It was an even bigger thing than when I brought her to school the first time. This was my family. Being the youngest, I had to try harder. The whole world might think I was cute as hell but to my family I was nothing too special. Bringing Kim home to dinner I was so proud I nearly popped my jumper.

"Mama," I had said, "there's this new girl and we're friends. She says her mother doesn't like to cook. Would it be all right if I brought her home tomorrow and she could eat with us?"

"Sure, Gina. You just bring her and we'll feed her up."

Dear, dear Mama! I wouldn't have had to ask. If it was something nice you were setting up, even a kindness to a total stranger, you were wasting your breath to go into it with Mama. The answer was an automatic yes.

We lived those days in a six-room stucco bungalow on La Binalba Avenue. In those days La Binalba Avenue was just about in the heart of Los Angeles. I guess it still is. That is, if you believe Los Angeles has a heart.

By the standards of De Lucia Street, Brooklyn, U.S.A., we were living in semiluxury. Three bedrooms, a living room, a dining room, a kitchen (with a window yet!), a patio, a front lawn, and a couple of cypress trees to boot! On De Lucia Street we had a sort of sunken first-floor flat (three steps down from street level) where on a clear day you might see the Williamsburg Bridge. Through half a pane in the kitchen window darkly.

In California, we were just the folks next door. The truth

is, with six mouths to feed and six bodies to clothe and the endless expense of Papa's "doctoring," we didn't have the bread to "go Hollywood." The truth is, we wouldn't have had the bread to live it up even if we hadn't been a big family and had all Papa's medical bills to cope with. The truth is, we didn't have that fat a contract at the Studio. There wasn't all that much bread coming in. A blah bungalow on La Binalba Avenue was about our speed.

Papa drove a beat-up old Chevvy that was about seven years over the hill. Papa was our chauffeur. If it hadn't been eleven miles from La Binalba Avenue to the Studio in Golden City, I think my sisters and I would have walked. We practically died of embarrassment every time Papa deposited us at the Studio gate or picked us up there at the end of the day. It seemed like everybody else came and went in a Rolls or a Caddie or a Mercedes-Benz. But there we were coming and going in a junk-yard Chevvy.

Papa was so strange that night. There were just the three of us and we all sat in the front seat. My sisters had stayed home because I was the only one of us in the *Tots* scene they were shooting that day. Papa hardly said a word. Usually if there was somebody "in the business" present, he had plenty to say. He liked to flaunt his knowledge of showbiz and give the impression he had been around the entertainment industry all his life. I thought he'd be pumping Kim about what kind of contract she got and the shooting schedule for *Wendy* and what not. Not that he'd expect any green, twelve-year-old kid to know the answers. But just to get the idea across he was Mr. Big Shot.

He didn't say a thing to her the whole ride home. At stoplights he'd turn and look at her. I couldn't tell if the looks meant he liked her or didn't like her. It made me nervous. I was afraid he might be thinking Kim didn't look like the kind of girl his youngest daughter should be going around with. I was afraid he was thinking she didn't look sweet and innocent enough to be somebody I should have for a friend. If Papa said he didn't want me hanging around her, that would be it. What Papa said went. We were an Italian household, after all, and Papa ruled the roost.

"Oh my, oh my!" Mama exclaimed, wiping her hands on a dish towel, as she came out of the kitchen to greet Kim. "If you're not something to see!"

Even then, Kim towered over Mama, who was barely five feet tall. To give Mama her complete measurements, you could say she was about five by five. Mama just gazed up at Kim, sighing, "Oh my, oh my."

"What's the matter, Mama?" I said.

"She's so pretty," said Mama. "She's prettier than a picture. You could go blind looking at her."

Mama's twitchy hands kept working the dish towel. She was trying to figure out what to do with them. Mama was never much of a hand-shaker. She either blew hot or cold. With strangers, she was usually polite and quite reserved. Meeting them, she kind of bowed her head but kept her arms stiffly by her side. "I'm pleased to meet you," she would say, or, "I am glad to see you again." In her own peasant way, Mama had class.

Mama was always shy, always uncomfortable around strangers. She lived and breathed mostly for her family. After her family came the Church. Our Lady of Victory back in Brooklyn and Church of the Immaculate Conception in Los Angeles. When Mama was greeting her family or her Church friends, she knew what to do with her hands. She stretched them out in a big, crushing hug. Now all you hear about is muggers. But Mama was the No. 1 *hugger* in the world.

Mama jerked her right hand about two inches in the direction of Kim and took it back. Then both her hands reached out to circle Kim in a huge bear hug that had Kim melting into Mama's big front porch.

Kim did not return the embrace. But she didn't do anything to break it up either. I don't think she knew what was happening to her.

"I can't believe my eyes," said Mama, giving Kim a real tight squeeze before letting her go.

My sisters were all lined up like a reception committee to see what Gina had dragged in. There was Rosa, who was closest to me in age, just thirteen months older. Then came Angelina, who was fourteen. My oldest sister Anna was almost seventeen. Anna was looking daggers into Mama.

Mama never had much schooling. Maybe four or five years. But she was sharp. She picked up cues. She got the message in Anna's look. In the next beat she was saying, "Papa, would you look at what we got here? Atlantic City. We got the Miss America contest right here under our own roof. Five raving beauties under our own roof!"

It was a quick-recovery act on Mama's part that had me and Rosa and Angelina beaming. Anna still glowered.

Papa was staring at Kim.

You always hear the expression, "Saved by the bell!" In our house, wherever we lived, we could be saved by the *smell*.

I mean if things got sticky there was always something in the kitchen that needed attention.

29

The fumes coming out of the kitchen were usually overpowering. Garlic. Oregano. Rosemary. Sweet basil. Olive oil. There was always a marinara sauce that had been simmering on a back burner for at least three days. Or you'd smell freshly grated Romano or Parmigiano cheese for the pasta that was boiling away furiously.

That first night Kim came home for dinner Mama had cooked chicken our favorite way. It looked like it was going to become chicken Kim's favorite way too. You should have seen her at that table. It was her first Italian dinner. She ate up a cyclone. It's lucky Mama always cooked more than enough ("just in case somebody's a little extra hungry") or there wouldn't have been enough to go around.

"It's so good, Mrs. Spinelli!" she exclaimed, handing over her plate for a refill of the chicken. "What do you call it?"

"It's called chicken cacciatore," said Mama.

"Chicken cacciatore," Kim repeated after her. "What has it got in it?"

"Let me see. It's got tomato sauce and mushrooms and black olives and onions and green peppers. A little olive oil."

"How do you make it?"

"Now don't you go asking me that." She laughed as she piled more fusilli on Kim's plate. "I never know how I do anything. I always say it's made with love."

Kim stopped eating long enough to gaze at Mama.

Besides the chicken cacciatore and fusilli Mama fed us fried slices of eggplant and her delicious pumanal salad, which consisted of plum tomatoes and red onions chopped fine and mixed together and dressed with olive oil and vinegar.

Another first for Kim that night was wine. She had never tasted it before. Being Italian, we always had it on hand. Mama didn't care for it, but Papa usually had it with dinner. He always poured us a little bit in a glass and filled up the glass with water, in the European fashion. It was just plain old jug wine and none of us girls much liked the taste of it. But along with everything else, Kim downed her diluted wine and even pushed her glass toward Papa for a refill.

We never did talk much at mealtime. But that night there didn't seem to be any talk at all. Kim was too busy eating and everybody else was too busy watching her. I was too nervous to be hungry.

I was worried about the impression she was making. As far as I could see, Kim had made a hit only with Mama. It wasn't hard to make a hit with Mama. She always led with her heart. You'd have to be Simon Legree or Genghis Khan or Adolph Hitler for Mama to be turned off by you. And if you liked to eat and you liked her cooking—well! You could take the dress off her back, the very food out of her mouth.

Kim didn't really get with the scene until Mama was clearing the table for dessert. That was when she first came up for air. Those fantastic jade eyes started moving around the table, taking everybody in. Behind the fantastic jade eyes plenty was going on. You could only guess what. Click, click, click, you could see her mental camera snapping away.

I never asked her what she was thinking when her eyes went all around the table, putting each one of us in the spotlight of those green lamps. I just knew she was taking in a lot. Kim's one of those people who I think just instinctively know the score. I mean about sizing up situations and people. It didn't keep her from getting into the goddamnedest messes and getting mixed up with all the wrong people. But that was something else. We all have the ability to tell ourselves what we want to believe, rather than what we know we are seeing.

Although Kim always hated school and was kind of allergic to book learning, she was keen. She had a sharp eye for a lot of things. Of all the ones who became real movie queens or so-called love goddesses she's the only one I'd say had any brains. And one other. Ava Gardner. I never met Ava, but from all I heard she goes a little deeper than the others. It says something for her, I think, that she could count among her personal friends two such famous writers as Ernest Hemingway and Robert Graves.

Kim picked it right up that Anna was having none of her. That much she told me later. And Anna's attitude never changed either. But I don't know what she could have been thinking about my two middle sisters, who only talked to each other if they talked at all. If you were being nice, you could say they were shy in the presence of a stranger. Kim, being Kim, probably saw they were jealous. Their younger sister had a friend but neither of them as yet had ever had a friend. Life had always been too frantic and pushing ahead. Up to now all we had for companionship was each other. Now an outsider had entered our nest.

Papa was something else. Not only had he not been heard all through dinner. He just nibbled at his food. I couldn't believe he found her so awful she took his appetite away. I thought he was a jerk for not saying something to make her feel welcome and asking her about herself. Luckily, she had been so busy eating she probably didn't see him staring at her. It was Papa himself who had always told us it was bad manners to stare at anybody.

"Here we are, here we are," Mama chirped, bringing in a big ricotta cheesecake she had baked that afternoon. On top of the cake, to make it look pretty; she had put citron fruits and little candies of many different colors. "I just hope you're going to like this, Kim."

Mama must have been kidding. Kim put away her piece of cheesecake in about three seconds flat. "It's delicious!"

Another piece of cheesecake quickly appeared on Kim's plate. Mama was smart to have baked the cake in her twelve-inch spring form pan instead of the nine-inch pan she often used.

"There's going to be enough left, Kim," said Mama, "so you can take a piece home for yourself and one for your mother. I bet she's never had real homemade Italian cheesecake."

I don't think Kim moved up in the popularity contest with my sisters when they heard she'd be walking off with the rest of the cheesecake. We all had overdeveloped sweet tooths and Mama's cheesecake was our favorite dessert.

Mama must have been reading some minds around the table. Like she had to justify her offering to Kim, she said, "Look at her. Skin and bones. We got to put a little fat on her."

"If she gets fat," I said, "she'll get in trouble at the Studio."

"A few pounds won't hurt," said Mama. "A few pounds and she'll be even more beautiful."

"Look at Sally Strickland," I pointed out. "The Boss gave strict orders to the commissary they weren't to serve her anything but soup and those little salads the stars eat to stay skinny. He said he didn't want to catch anybody giving her sweets. He makes her come to his office every day to get diet pills and he makes her take them while he's watching. She says the pills make her jump up and down and forget about wanting to eat anything. She says they even keep her from going to sleep at night."

"That poor girl," said Mama. "Such a crazy way to treat a young growing girl! Kim, you come here all you want. You come and we'll feed you up real good. There's always a place at this table any time you want to come."

Then Kim did something that surprised us all. She jumped up from her chair and ran to the end of the table where Mama was sitting. She threw her arms around Mama's neck and she started to say something. But she didn't get it out. She burst into tears.

It was some cry. Kim laid her face on top of Mama's head and she just let it flow. She held Mama tight around the neck and rocked her back and forth gently. The tears washed through Mama's hair and trickled down her cheek. They kept coming so fast I thought Mama might float away under our very eyes.

Nobody said anything. What could we say? We all just gaped in dumb astonishment. We didn't know what started it or what it meant. Only Mama seemed to know.

Mama stroked and patted Kim's face. "There, there, honey," she said. "That's all right."

It took a long time for Kim's tear well to run dry. When it finally did, she straightened up and got out the little hankie that was tucked into the breast pocket on her dress. With the hankie she carefully dried Mama's cheek. Then she bent over and kissed Mama on the cheek.

In the years since then Kim has wept buckets. Niagaras. *Oceans*. She's one of the water gushers of all time.

I've watched the rains come over one little stupid column item in a jerkwater paper only seven people at the most would read. I've seen them dropping to good effect in snags with writers, press agents, directors, producers, designers, and reporters. Mostly she cries for the same reason anybody else does. Rage. Frustration. Defeat. Betrayal. Self-pity. Loneliness. Depression. Fear. Helplessness.

You don't have to be a genius to guess what was making her cry during her first dinner at the Spinellis. She was crying from *happiness*. Probably for the first time in her life.

Probably for the last time in her life. At least I never saw her crying for that reason again.

"How about me? Don't I get a kiss too?"

Another country heard from. Finally. Papa.

We all nearly fell out of our chairs. I would have been far less surprised if he had said, "I don't want you in this house again." He hadn't opened his mouth all evening to give us any clue she was the least bit welcome. He had just stared at her.

I'd hate to count up the number of men Kim has kissed in her day. It could well add up to a cast of thousands, as they say. Some of them have been real dogs.

When Papa asked her, kissing men was new to Kim. With Papa, of course, it was different. It wasn't a man-woman kiss. Even so, it must have been a drag. Papa wasn't very kissable then. Once upon a time, according to Mama, Papa had been very handsome. But that must have been at least twenty-five years ago. It wasn't just that he was old-looking and shriveled up. He looked so unhealthy. He was a human wreck. There were big dark circles under his eyes because of his heart condition and brown spots all over the back of his hands. He had the wrinkles of a man eighty years old. His teeth were rotting and his breath would have had lions and tigers backing off. He had the smell of death.

Kim gamely slipped her arms around Papa's neck and kissed his unshaven cheek. Papa closed his eyes. He didn't say it but he could have been thinking, "You've made an old man very happy."

I began to get Kim into real focus only when I glommed on to one important thing about her. Though I loved her and was awed by her from the first moment, I didn't understand her at all until it dawned on me that she was one of those people who are born hungry. I'm not talking just about food. But that's part of it. All her life she'd had to fight a ravenous appetite. If she ever gave in to it completely, she'd be bigger than Totie Fields. But it's more. Kim was born hungry for *everything*. She has the kind of tapeworm that doesn't stop with the stomach. It keeps gnawing away at all of her. Body, heart, and soul. She's never wanted just something of value. She's always wanted *everything* of value.

She never asks herself, "Is it me? Is this for me?" Or, "How much is good for me? When's enough enough?" She wants it all. You could always see the wanting in her eyes and that she meant to have it all. Anything that anybody had ever thought worth having. Food. Drink. Sex. Money. Fame. Power. Possessions. Love. Idolatry.

Part of Kim's tragedy is that she's managed to get more of the quote good things in life unquote than would be good for anybody.

When I had done quite a lot more growing up, it dawned on me what was eating Papa that strange evening Kim first met my family. I guess the mystery of his weird behavior must've been stewing around in my subconscious since then. Give your subconscious a problem to work on, the psychiatrists say, and sooner or later it'll come up with the solution.

I think I was about sixteen, and one night I was either washing my hair or doing my nails when it suddenly came to me about Papa.

Papa would have loved to screw Kim.

It was that simple.

It was also sad. Papa was dying and now I think he would have died happy that very night if first he could have got it up one more time and satisfied that longing with Kim. In his day Papa had been a real ladies' man. It was something Mama, like most Italian wives, learned to live with. You just pretend not to see what you don't want to see but you know

34

damn well is going on. When Papa had his looks and his manhood, he had never been without steady outside female companionship. But that was all history.

All that strange staring at Kim was not because of lust. He stared out of the memory of lust. The shape he was in then there was no longing left in him for anything. All he had left was the memory of longing.

Chapter 4

In later years people seeing us together would ask, "How did you meet? How do you know each other?" By that time my star—such as it was—had dimmed and Kim's was blinding bright. I'm sure what they honestly wanted to ask was, "What do Superstar and Has-been have in common?" When they asked, "How do you know each other?" Kim had her well-rehearsed answer ready. It usually got the desired effect. Kim loved to shock, remember?

"It so happens," she would say deadpan, "we're in love with the same woman."

Well! Eyes popped; jaws dropped; breathing stopped.

By then Kim's love life had been heavy, to say the least, and heavily publicized. But the world had been led to assume she confined her bed partners to members of the opposite sex. The bed partners might outnumber the extras in a Cecil B. De Mille spectacular but at least they were supposed to be the "right" sex.

Don't forget this was still before we were letting everything hang out. We weren't "into" Women's Lib or the sexual revolution or a lot of other things that are in the air now. Most definitely we weren't having our consciousness raised by groups like the Gay Activists Alliance or the Daughters of Billitis.

So generally Kim got the reaction she wanted. People were shocked. My God, they must have thought, she can get any and every man she wants, but she has to have women too. Was she a dyke? And of course it wasn't exactly every day that two women were close friends because they were "in love" with the same woman.

"I see," the person would say nervously, wishing he had never asked. Or, "Is that so?" And drop the subject like a hot potato.

Kim would let it go at that. As far as she was concerned,

35

they could think what they damn well pleased. I didn't have nearly so much at stake, since I was no longer in the public eye. Who cared what I did or who I did it with? And who would bother to spread any dirt about me? Still, I always felt compelled to set the record straight. Maybe basically I'm a square, a prude. Anyway, I could never resist explaining that the woman we were both "in love" with was Serafina Isabella Martino Spinelli. My mother and Kim's adopted mother.

Until I had my own children, Mama was the only person I ever completely loved in my whole life.

Who knows how many people Kim has truly loved in her lifetime? I do know her love for Mama was the most *lasting* love of her life. It lasted from the first day I brought her home to the day Mama died.

The day Mama died, Kim walked off a set in Munich, leaving the filming high and dry so she could catch the first Lufthansa back to New York for the funeral. The funeral parlor and the church and the gravesite were banked with more flowers than you'd find in the Brooklyn Botanical Gardens, and Kim had picked up all the funeral expenses as well as donating a handsome contribution to the Waldemar Medical Research Foundation for its cancer research programs in the name of Serafina Spinelli. Such were the sentiments of a grieving and loving adopted daughter. The tears Kim shed came from sincere heartbreak.

All relationships are complicated. I don't think I'll ever understand what Kim's true relationship to her own mother has been. To Kim's credit she's never disowned her mother. She's never tried to reform her. She's never told her to shape up or get lost. I must say if I had had a mother like Kim's I'd have wanted to keep her under wraps. Since Kim drew her first paycheck at the age of twelve, her mother has never wanted for anything. But what Kim has done for her mother I can't help feeling was done out of a sense of duty. Or from habit. Or some dumb kind of loyalty. Or even pity. I don't think it's ever been out of the love that springs from the center of the heart.

"Mama," when you stop to say it, is such a warm word. Kim never called her own mother Mama. She called her Mom or Mother when I first knew her. Later she called her Lois, like they were old friends the same age or girls who worked together.

But it was only the second time Kim came to our house for dinner when she began calling my mother "Mama." The way she did it was so cute. Her plate, as before, was empty before anybody else's. Mama said, "Here, Kim, let me give

36

you some more rigatoni and sausage and some more zucchini."

"Thank you very much." A second or so later she added shyly, "Mama." Not Mrs. Spinelli. But Mama! Just like she was Anna or Rosa or Angelina or me. After that Kim never called her anything but Mama. She became like one of Mama's own.

As long as she lived, Mama saw only the good in Kim. No matter what kind of scrapes Kim got into or what kind of stories were going around, Mama's faith couldn't be shaken. In Mama's eyes Kim could do no wrong. If the gossip got too sticky, Mama would point out that a lot of people were jealous of Kim's success and were surely telling lies about her. She'd say Kim was "too easy and trusting" and let herself be taken advantage of by "bad company."

"I've never had anything like this," Kim said to me after that second evening with us.

I didn't know what she meant.

"Having a family," she explained. "Sitting down to eat with other people. I used to make my own breakfast because Mom would still be sleeping when I got up to go to school. At night she'd always be working so I'd have dinner by myself. She'd leave something like meat loaf or a casserole I was supposed to heat up and eat. But most of the time I'd eat it cold. Or I wouldn't eat it at all. I'd just have a peanut butter sandwich. I never sat down even. I always ate standing up."

The standing-up, lonely, cold dinners were over now that she had found Signora Spinelli. Saint Serafina, the patron saint of the hungry and the unloved, had come to Kim's rescue.

In my eyes Mama was a Madonna. She's been dead for years now. But there's never a day goes by I don't think about her. I still see her in my dreams. I have conveniently blocked on what that disgusting disease did to her looks. She was down to less than eighty-five pounds and she looked eighty-five years old when she died. I only remember her beauty. I see the lovely cheekbones, the unlined olive skin, the bright, dancing black eyes, and the shining black hair pulled back tightly into an enormous coil. Thirty, forty pounds lighter, Mama could have doubled for Dolores Del Rio.

I have no bad conscience, thank God, about Mama. When we had it, we did everything we could for her. Before the act split up, we managed to buy her a house back in Brooklyn near where we used to live.

Mama would have been happier if we had never left Brooklyn in the first place. She was proud of our success, of

37

course. But in her heart of hearts she would rather that we would have stayed four little nobodies, growing up like all the other kids in the neighborhood. It was the mounting pressures of our careers and our success that so often took us away from her. Without all of us to be feeding and fussing over, Mama wasn't even half alive. When we made the big time and went to the Coast, Mama was in her element. Not because we were in the big time and on the Coast. Because she had all her family together again.

I used to wonder what Mama might have become if she hadn't spent her life catering to us. She had such possibilities. If she'd had the good luck to have a little education and not got stuck with an overbearing husband and a bunch of grabby, demanding kids, who knows what she might have been? But I don't think that way any more.

Mama had the life she wanted, the only kind of life that would have meant anything at all to her. In her own simple way Mama had stumbled on a tremendous truth. She knew something not many other people ever seem to learn. Mama was wise. She knew that happiness in this world only comes to those who can love without any strings attached. The really rich and lucky ones are those happy few who put out love and never ask what kind of return they're going to get on their investment.

Kim could never forget Mama or get her out of her system. As Kim spread her wings, we didn't see too much of her. She was always in flight, pursuing God knows what. The fattest role ever created for an actress. A jewel that would make the Hope Diamond look like a poor man's engagement ring. The most delicious man on earth. Whatever she was pursuing, the long shadow of Mama always followed her. So when Mama became very ill and we were told what it was, I wrote Kim. She was on location in Spain—in Algeciras—starring in a potboiler with a bullfighting background. She was playing a lady bullfighter. I guess you'd call her a matadoress. Jesus!

Three days after I wrote her—actually three middle-of-the-nights later—I got a hysterical transatlantic phone call.

No hellos or how-are-you's. "Who says that's what it is?"

"Dr. Stackpole. He's supposed to be——"

"Never heard of him. That's just one quack's opinion. Listen. I want you to take Mama to Memorial. There's a Dr. Feldenheimer there I once sat next to at a charity thing and I thought he knew his onions. Try him first. Use my name. If he gives you the same thing, take Mama out to the Scripps Clinic. Massachusetts General in Boston. The Mayo Clinic. Everywhere. Don't stop until you've gone through every specialist in the whole goddamn country. Keep using my name. I'm paying for everything and I don't give a sweet fuck what it costs . . ."

No shopping around from clinic to hospital to specialist to specialist was going to change anything. There was no wishing our way out of the diagnosis. The monster hacking away at Mama wasn't going to quit until it had devoured her completely.

Kim stepped up the shooting schedule in Algeciras and came in ahead of time. She chartered a chopper to Madrid and caught the first TWA to New York. By then Mama was in Mt. Sinai and the end was near. I stationed myself by the reception desk on Mama's floor to intercept Kim when she got off the elevator. I wanted to prepare her for what she was going to see.

Kim never won an Oscar. It's just one of many things that make her bitter about Hollywood. She was up for the Best Actress Award three times. Each time the award seemed to go to somebody who should have won it the year before and who was being rewarded late. Par for the course. But if the Academy Awards are a popularity contest—and they are, I think—Kim just wasn't the type the movie establishment who do the voting want to give any prizes to. She didn't play the game. She didn't advertise the Industry the way it wanted to be advertised. Someone else who never got an Oscar, maybe for the same reasons, is Lana Turner. A good case could be made for Lana winning for *The Postman Always Rings Twice*. I also happen to think Ava Gardner should have won it for *Mogambo*.

But if there was any justice in this world (ha!) Kim would have won an Oscar for her performance in Mama's room at Mt. Sinai. Even though this was real life and not part of a movie. She must have nearly swooned at the sight of Mama. Could this ghastly, withered little figure on the bed be the same big earthy woman who used to almost crush her in her warm, bone-cracking embraces?

Kim didn't let herself miss a beat. "Mama," she said, sailing to the bedside, "I'm ashamed of you. You're just about the last person I ever expected to see lying around a hospital. You know as well as I do there isn't a darn thing wrong with you. Do you know there's a terrible word for doing what you're doing? The word is malingering. Malingering means somebody lying around pretending to be sick when they really aren't. And, Mama, that's just not like you . . . Now here's what we're going to do. I've got to go right back to Europe. Germany. To Munich. I've got to make a movie there. But I'm going to make it fast. While I'm doing that, you're going to sign yourself out of this depressing hospital. Then here's what we're going to do. I'm going to zip right back here and collect you. Then you and I are going to have ourselves a real vacation. Just us two. We've never really been alone together. I can't remember, Mama, you've ever had a vacation in your whole life. I can't remember the last time I had one either. So we're going to get on an ocean liner and sail to Italy, first class too. You're going to have your own private outside stateroom. The boat will probably land in Naples and we're going to see Italy from one end of the country to the other. First we'll go off for a weekend on Capri . . ."

In the corridor, outside the closed door to Mama's room, Kim said, "Gina, I want her out of that semiprivate. I want her in a room all to herself. I want that room stuffed from floor to ceiling with fresh flowers every day. I want air conditioning put in immediately. I want a color television set in there. The biggest and best you can get. I want three shifts of private nurses there around the clock. Don't tell me what any of this is going to cost. I don't give a fuck. Just get it and send the bills. I want that hokey priest over in Brooklyn to get his fat ass over here every day and sit with her. Tell him I'll endow a chapel in Mama's name. I want—" Kim ran out of steam and broke down completely. "Oh, no, Mama. Why you, Mama? Why you? The best!"

Then she let out a banshee wail that brought nurses and attendants running from every corner of the floor.

For fifty-seven years Serafina Spinelli glowed with love in a world where love seems to spark for only a second . . . now and then.

But it was Papa who made everything happen. It was Papa who put it all together, as they say now, and got us where we got to. For that we have him to thank. I can't speak for my sisters, but seeing how everything turned out for me, I don't feel very thankful.

Papa was never one of my favorite men. It's easy to put him down for all the things he did wrong. It was Papa who pushed us out of our baby carriages into an "act" . . . who pushed us out of the taverns of Albany, where we did our cutsey-pie bit and passed the hat, into the sleazy wide world of scummy nightclubs, botton-of-the-bill vaudeville, and the back corridors of Tin Pan Alley. Always Papa pushed and pushed, manipulating and cajoling and preening us until we were winning amateur contests and breaking into recording studios and radio. Papa never stopped pushing until he had maneuvered us cross-country for a chance at the brass ring of Hollywood.

Chapter 5

Wendy and the Golden Retriever, in case you've never seen it on the tube, is about this English girl who loves her dog Tobias more than anything else in the world. She runs away from home with Tobias when her parents won't let him sleep in her bedroom any more. Maybe her parents knew something the audience didn't know about Wendy's relationship with the golden retriever!

Wendy being English, the first thing they had to do was give Kim an English accent. The Studio was making so many English movies at the time starring characters who had never been nearer England than Kansas City they had this speech specialist who really was English. She had a full-time job coaching actors and actresses to sound like the real goods from Limey-land. Kim spent an hour with Beryl Hampshire every day practicing and practicing how to say things like, "But, fathah, why cahn't Tobias sleep in my room?" "Mummy, I think you're being veddy, veddy cru-el."

Though she was no scholar, Kim was keen and picked up things quick. She's what they call in the trade a fast study. She got that English accent to a "T" toot sweet and she learned it so well she never lost it completely. Sometimes, like when she's trying to impress somebody or she's doing an appearance on a television talk show, it comes back and people think this must be the true, English-born Kimberley Hudson.

At the same time, the Studio flacks were putting out all this crap about the beautiful English girl the Studio had discovered and going on about how she was approximately royalty. They gave her a long "fact" sheet to memorize so she'd be ready for the press when they got to her. She'd know her real name and where in England she came from and all about her mother and father and who they were descended from and the names of her favorite books and what her first impressions of America had been and how she liked Hollywood.

Now I'm getting ahead of the story a bit. After *Wendy*, they stuck Kim in a clutzy costume picture set in Henry VIII's England. Then they put her in a Bobby Baxter movie where she was cast as an English girl visiting cousins two doors up the street from Dr. Baxter's house. Then the well ran dry. They didn't seem to have another suitable English role for Kim.

By this time it was apparent Kim was a comer. The Studio and movie columnists were getting letters asking what Kim was going to be in next. The problem was how to keep Kim working until somebody came up with a script that called for an adolescent English girl. They couldn't very well try to pass her off as David Copperfield or Oliver Twist or David Balfour, though Hollywood has tried things almost as crazy. What to do? Simple. "Americanize" Kim. Cast her in American roles and let the flacks take over.

She's one of the brightest and most adaptable girls ever to grace Hollywood. She's been on this continent for only a year and it would take a Dr. Henry Higgins, with his keen ear for dialects and accents, to detect she wasn't native-born. . . .

Credit the movie industry with her passionate fancy for Americans and all things American. She confesses that since her first glimpse of Judy Garland in *The Wizard of Oz* she's been imitating her as Dorothy singing Harold Arlen's "Over the Rainbow" and that she almost wished she had been born one of Uncle Sam's very own citizens. . . .

Typical mo'om pitcher bullshit. But don't get me wrong. I love Hollywood. I even think it's a nice place to live—if you're a taco. Wasn't it Fred Allen who said living in Hollywood was like sinking in a warm mound of farina?

Beryl Hampshire, as I said, was teaching Kim an English accent. Others teachers were teaching her how to act and how to walk and how to sing and how to dance. Even how to fence. I don't know what the singing and dancing and fencing had to do with it. She didn't have to do any of that stuff in *Wendy*.

Cool Kim took everything in stride. It was Kim's mother who was Alice in Wonderland.

Kim's mother. The first time I saw her I turned blue. *This* was Kim's mother? This bony, blotchy-faced woman with the stringy hair and buck teeth? Honest to God, the first time I saw her she was wearing a house dress and toilet paper curlers in her hair. You looked at her and you looked at Kim and you had to think Kim was the Immaculate Conception or else her father must have been the most beautiful man in the world. More beautiful than a Greek god. Kim told me she had never seen even a picture of her father. She could only guess what he looked like. Her mother wasn't much help in describing him.

What can I say about Kim's mother? To me she was just a blah. She couldn't have been more to anybody else, including Kim. I never liked or disliked her. The only real feeling I had for her was pity. I felt sorry for her from the beginning and I've never stopped feeling sorry for her.

If they had let her, Kim's mother would have been the movie mother of all time. In the nicest way. Not a mean, driving, witchy movie mother, but the mother who dug the whole movie scene the most. She had been movie-crazy all her life. Movies had given her the only real dreams she ever had. All the drinking and screwing around, I always thought, was done just from boredom ... done as a way of passing the time of day and night.

Through a classified ad in the Los Angeles *Examiner* Kim's mother found a three-room apartment in the Coronado Flats on Santa Monica Boulevard renting for $42 a month. She bought an old flivver and she drove Kim back and forth to the Studio every day. It was about eight miles each way. During the day she planned to stay right beside Kim, kibbitzing on whatever Kim was doing.

This routine lasted for two days. They were certainly the two happiest days in the life of Kim's mother. She ate it all up. She was on cloud #37. Inside those mighty iron gates of the Studio I'm sure she could happily have spent the rest of her life.

Came the third and the gates of the Studio closed on her.

"I'm sorry, ma'am," said the guard. "I can't let you in."

"Why can't you?" Kim's mother asked.

"Instructions."

"Whose instructions?" asked Kim.

"I don't know, miss. That's the orders came down. Maybe they want the sets cleared of everybody who doesn't belong."

The sets were far from "cleared of everybody who doesn't belong." There was the usual mishmash of tourists and visiting newspaper people and hangers-on and "go-fors" *schlepping* around. It is true the Studio frowned on having mothers hanging around, coaching from the sidelines. But it was no hard-and-fast rule. In at least one case a father had been given the bum's rush. Ours. Papa was told to scram and stay scrammed when he tried to give the director some helpful hints on how to direct the first picture the Spinelli Sisters worked in.

Kim's mother had the same humiliating experience the day after she was turned back at the gate. And the day after that. "You can't come in, ma'am. Sorry. Instructions." Kim's mother sat parked in her rattle-buggy, sunk to the bottom of the world. She had had one fast peek at the inside. Now she was already on the outside looking in. She might never get back inside again.

If Kim hadn't made it as an actress, she could have become an ace detective or newspaper reporter. When she wanted to get to the bottom of something, she kept going until she got there. It bugged her that her mother was barred from the inner sanctum. Every time she looked around she could see the whole place was crawling with civilians.

"Do you know why my mother can't come in?" Kim asked Beryl Hampshire, her speech coach.

Beryl didn't know.

Kim put the question to all her other teachers and trainers, even Miss Bitters. Nobody had a clue. She asked Bigger Buchanan, the assistant director on *Wendy*, who was spending time with her every day blocking out the action of the script and interpreting for her the character of *Wendy*. Bigger Buchanan couldn't answer her question. Kim asked him to ask Sol Bryerhoff, the producer of the film. The word came back that Bryerhoff knew nothing either. The best Bryerhoff could suggest was to take it up "with the front office." That meant the Boss.

I don't think in ten million years it would have occurred to my sisters or me or most of the other kids at the Studio to ask for a meeting with the Boss. We didn't call him, he called us. We were all so happy *not* to have to see him. But Kim had no qualms about making her way through those wall-to-wall secretaries (some of the secretaries even had secretaries) in the front office until she found the one in charge of appointments.

The Boss, probably tipped off to what was on Kim's mind, wouldn't see her for almost a week. It finally trickled down through Bigger Buchanan that the Boss would condescend to give her an audience one Friday afternoon right after lunch.

That meeting was what they today would call a confrontation. It put the stamp on their whole future relationship. It started the poisonous chemistry between them. To begin with, he kept her cooling her heels for an hour and a half in the reception room. Even people barging in without appointments were pushed ahead of her.

"I hear you're shaping up pretty good," said the Boss, poring over papers on his desk and not even looking up as she was admitted to his office.

"I think so," said Kim.

"Do you have a problem, Kimberley? Can I help you with something?"

"My mother isn't allowed inside the Studio."

The Boss signed something and threw down his pen. "That's right."

"Why?"

"It's for the best. Mothers are wonderful people. I should know. My own mother—may God look over her through eternity!—happened to be the finest woman who ever drew the breath of life. She's been dead sixteen years now and I doubt a day goes by I don't think of her and wish she was here to give me guidance." The glasses came off and he dabbed a handkerchief to his owlish eyes. "But mothers have their special place. It's not being around where people are doing the dirty work of the world. Their place is keeping the home fires burning. Mothers are something wonderful to come home to when the day's work is done and she'll have a nice hot dinner waiting for you and she'll smooth away all the cares of the day. That's a mother's true role. She has no place on the ugly outside where business goes on. Why drag her away from where she should be and put her some place where it isn't natural for her to be? To tell you the truth too, Kimberley, mothers can get in the way when they go somewhere where they really shouldn't be. They don't mean to get——"

"Other mothers are allowed in."

"A few, maybe. If they keep insisting, it's sometimes easier to give in than have a big battle going on."

"Well, my mother is insisting."

As Kim recalled it later, the Boss seemed to be looking at her from the other end of the earth. When she thought about it, she marveled at that meeting. How could he sit there hardly letting on he had ever laid eyes on her before? How could he seem to have forgotten their first meeting ... when she sat on his lap while he jerked off?

"In this case I'm afraid I can't give in."

"Why is my mother different?"

"She is, that's all."

"How is she?"

"I don't want your mother hanging around here. Now leave it at that."

"She doesn't bother anybody."

"She bothers me."

"Why?"

The Boss made a hissing sound and slammed his fist against the desk. "Goddamnit, little girl, you shouldn't be wasting my time with crap like this. I make the laws here and everybody follows them. Since you put it to me, I'll give it back to you plain. We're taking a big chance on you. You

45

can't do one damn thing any of these other kids around here can do. But we're putting you in a picture. We've got an investment in you. We're trying to put you over as coming from some classy background. That'll be murder to put across. We can't have that woman around here letting the cat out of the bag."

"She wouldn't say anything."

"She wouldn't have to. She doesn't have to open her mouth. Anybody taking one gander at her is enough to blow the whole gag sky-high. Let's just face it. She's one rough-looking bird. I don't want her around. That's my last word on the subject. Nix, nix, nix. Now you get right back to doing what you're supposed to be doing and you and I are going to get along very well."

Fat chance they were going to get along at all, let alone "very well." From that day until the day he died, Kim hated him with all the adrenaline she could pump. It wasn't that he had attacked an object of love and undying loyalty. But what he said about her mother she took personally. He might as well have been saying, "Look, you come from trash and you're just a piece of trash yourself. But if we keep hammering and polishing away at you and we tell enough lies, maybe we can hawk you off as a diamond—instead of the commonest pebble on the beach we all know you are in reality."

The Boss felt her hatred and hated her right back. The feeling was mutual—and for keeps.

Making movies is a pretend business. If you've been pretending long enough, your notions about truth and reality get pretty blurry. Don't expect any big movie star to be just like Joe Blow next door. I don't care how down-to-earth he might come on. Don't be taken in by how much he dresses like a slob or goes on about how he hates the whole phony business or how his real interests are in things that are happening in the real world. Don't be taken in when you see him going out to undo the wrongs on an Indian reservation or to demonstrate for peace or cleaner air. You can be sure he'll get there in a chartered plane. He'll get out of that plane in a Dion Paoli jumpsuit and be reeking with Brut. He'll also have sent his press agent as an advance man who makes sure the television cameras are set up to record the celebrated arrival.

No matter what Star says or does or how slobby he looks, he's never going to be like Joe Blow next door. How could he be like the guy next door who drives a truck or works on an assembly line or sells neckties for a living? The guys next door get their noses rubbed in raw reality every day of their lives. But Star earns his livelihood from pretending, insulated from the firsthand experiences everybody else is experiencing.

46

The superstars always sound so bullshitty when they try to make out they're just folks. Of them all I think Kim has the most talent for coming off as Real People. At certain times. When something cuts close to her nerve endings, when she's in touch with her deepest feelings, she reacts for real. Her basic honesty takes over and you don't catch a whiff of sham or phony-baloney.

The day the Boss died, Kim told the world, was the happiest day of her life. The way she said it anybody would have believed her.

You may recall the flowery headlines and fake expressions of sorrow his death touched off:

MOVIE CAPITAL STUNNED BY LOSS OF LEADING STAR-MAKER
FILM TYCOON MOURNED THROUGHOUT THE WORLD

Commenting on the deceased, Phony Star said, "I'm in a state of shock. It's like losing my father. I owe my whole career to him."

Said Phony Director: "His passing is an incalculable loss—to the industry, to the millions here and abroad who love motion pictures, and to me personally. The industry will not see his likes again."

Kim refused to make any printable comment.

On hearing the news, she got on the phone and started calling friends, friendly acquaintances, and, finally, a few dependable freeloaders.

"Heigh-ho, the Beast is dead," she sang jubilantly, "the Beast is dead. This calls for a whoop-de-do. I'm springing . . ."

Without mentioning any names, Louella Parsons wrote in her column, "One of our biggest stars saw fit to celebrate the occasion of her employer's death with a 'spirited' party that got so out of hand the management of a distinguished hotel had to ask her and the other merrymakers in her entourage to leave. Her behavior was in shockingly bad taste. It also showed her to be a very ungrateful girl. She owes the deceased everything. He made her what she is today. This star would do well to remember that far bigger stars than she have fallen. It could happen to her unless she changes some of her ways . . ."

It could be that Kim had made an enemy out of Louella long before this, before she knew what she was doing. This was after the "Hollywood Hotel" days, so on top of reading Louella everybody knew what she sounded like. Lots of people were doing takeoffs on her, but Kim's was really a pip. To while away the boredom between scenes on the set, Kim regaled everybody with her imitations of that singsongy, gushy voice. It probably also got back to Louella that Kim was joking about Louella's ample proportions and had nicknamed her "Moosella." So you can hardly blame Louella for not missing a chance to take snide swipes at Kim in her column. Or Kim for being "uncooperative" in return as a news source for Louella.

Kim cried for her past sins against Louella the day she found out Louella was Jewish, notwithstanding her ardent Catholicism. I don't know where Kim found it out because it was a fact Louella herself had long forgotten. Kim by then had developed a chronically bleeding heart as far as all minorities were concerned. The Jews, the Chicanos, the blacks, the American Indians, the Orientals, the Puerto Ricans—her heart bled for them all. She cried to think how she had stupidly, for a few cheap laughs, contributed to the suffering of a member of one of these persecuted peoples.

By then it was too late to build any bridges to Louella. Nor would Louella have thanked Kim for the reasons behind Kim's change of heart.

Kim's love and mercy always stopped short of the Boss, a Jew. Jew or no Jew, he was always a son of a bitch of the first rank.

"I don't mind admitting I've had some morning-afters along the way," said Kim, describing her spree to toast the Boss's death, "but never anything like this. I had a hangover that would have hospitalized a hippopotamus. I was in bed for two and a half days. But believe me, it was worth it. It was worth every head-splitting, puking second of it just knowing that bastard's dead and gone to hell."

Chapter 6

We movie children never played like ordinary children. We wouldn't have known how!

We missed so much. But we had one thing other kids didn't have. We had magic at our fingertips. Everywhere we turned we stepped into wondrous new worlds. The air we breathed had the bewitching perfume of make-believe.

The Studio must have had thirty sound stages, each one a world unto itself. Each one had its own people, set in a time and a place, creating its own illusions. If you came back the next week or the next day or even the next hour you might find everything changed. Carpenters and prop men might have erected and furnished a whole new set of worlds where other people were playing out *their* lives.

It was truly fantastic. Outside, each street was a street of miracles and a walk down any of them was like a journey around the globe. Every few steps brought a sharp change of setting. On one side, a coffee plantation in Brazil. Across the street, a sky chalet in Austria. Piccadilly Circus in London. An antebellum mansion with Doric columns. The Piazza San Marco in Venice. A hacienda in Argentina. A dunesy, white-sanded desert that could be the Sahara or the Gobi. Main Street, Dodge City, U.S.A. A great hulking ship named H.M.S. *Aldershot*. The Lama's shack in the Himalayas. "Doc" Holiday's Tombstone, Arizona. An Indian village that could have been Wounded Knee. The North Woods of the Mounties. A sidewalk café on the Left Bank. The Matterhorn. A game lodge in the Scottish highlands. The jungles of Yucatan. A faded, red-brick Victorian railway station complete with waiting platform and train tracks. The Marseilles waterfront. An island in the South Seas so romantic it would start anyone humming "The Moon of Manakoora." The Plaza Hotel on Fifth Avenue with a real fountain gushing real water. An elm-shaded street on the Main Line. A Dutch village. The Administration Building of East Jockstrap State Teachers' College in Ballsy, Idaho . . .

All the back lots were lined with false fronts. Windows and doors opened onto nothing. But it didn't matter to us. So what if the buildings were mere facades made of papier-mâché? We saw them as solid and complete, our imaginations filling in the missing dimensions.

The streets on the back lots teemed with every variety of the human species the makeup artists and wardrobe staff could conjure up. There were Sioux Indians, schooner captains, Barbary Coast hookers, officers in the Lafayette Escadrille. Chain gangs, and cotton pickers, Berbers, nuns, football players, marines, Portuguese fishermen and Polynesian maidens. Basque shepherds, Chinese coolies, Japanese soldiers, stunt airmen and telephone linemen. Eskimos and hoboes and lynching mobs and cowboys and lumberjacks and gold prospectors and firemen. Factory hands, nurses, pushcart peddlers, coal miners and African tribesmen. Nazis and suffragettes and samurais and whirling dervishes—

From what I gather, all the fun has long since gone out of the movie-making business. But in those days there was fun. Things usually managed to get done on schedule. But there was always time for jokes and kidding and horsing around.

There always seemed to be lots of good, warm vibes in the air.

A child who played son or daughter to a star in some movie would often say "Hi, Mom" or "Hi, Dad" in greeting that star years after the picture was made. Some of the kids were so starved for affection that they had to cling to these fantasy relationships. The star being greeted as "Mom" or "Dad" may not have found it all that cute after a kid got to be eighteen or nineteen years old.

Sally Strickland was the biggest "Hi, Mom"-er of them all. There must have been six well-known actresses she kept calling "Mom," even when she was a grown woman and far more famous than they had ever been. It tells you a lot about Sally and the troubles that finally got the better of her.

One of Sally's screen "Moms" appeared years later in another film with Sally. By then Sally was deep into her problems. To the cast and crew she was one giant pain in the ass. She had tantrums and she had the sulks and she was always late, late, late for work. She threw her weight around as a big star by exercising her prerogative as a big star to keep the set closed to all outsiders. Not many of the big stars who had been way up there a lot longer than Sally pulled rank in that way.

Sally's old screen "Mom" was a very fine actress named Nancy Gorham. Nancy Gorham's still alive. Like myself, she has found a second career in writing. She's had a couple of good-sellers about her career in the movies. She could have a couple of best-sellers if she ever blew the lid on a lot of sensational stuff she's an authority on, including her own love life. She came to Hollywood in the age of the silents when she was about thirteen years old. The stories she could tell!

One of the stories she does tell is about making this second film with Sally. She couldn't believe this was the adorable child she had worked with a few years earlier. Sally now was sixteen or seventeen and she was top box office. She was America's sweetheart more than Mary Pickford or anybody else had ever been. Anybody who hinted she was less than the sweetest, purest, most lovable doll-baby in movies would have taken his lumps from Mr. and Mrs. America.

One morning during the filming of *The Clocks of Heavenridge* Sally set what was a record even for herself. Shooting was to start at nine A.M. sharp. At eleven thirty Sally was still a no-show.

Her dander up, Nancy Gorham took the liberty of storming into Sally's dressing room. She found Sally nervously plucking her eyebrows. "Oh, hi, Mom," she said.

"Don't 'Hi, Mom' me," said Nancy. "Do you realize you've

been keeping about a hundred and fifty people waiting for two and a half hours? A hundred and fifty people waiting two and a half hours on one person! Do you realize that?"

Sally giggled. "Yes, I know."

"Sally, I don't understand you. What's happened to the little trouper I worked with six or seven years ago? That girl was a real 'pro.' She did her homework and she was always where she was supposed to be when she was supposed to be there. She was considerate of everybody and eager to make things as pleasant as possible for everybody around her. She was a credit to her profession. Who'd ever have dreamt she'd get all swelled up with her own importance? Who'd ever have dreamt she'd think she was so special she could make up her own rules and keep a hundred and fifty people waiting? If you're bidding for attention with tactics like these, I can tell you you're getting it. But it's not a very flattering kind of attention you're getting. You may be able to get away with it now. But take it from one of the old warhorses in the industry, there comes a time—"

"Don't, Mom! I can't stand it." Clapping her hands over her ears, Sally burst into tears. "I know, I know. You're right, you're right. But don't, Mom. *Please*. I'm so tired. I'm so jittery. I can't sleep. I'm so tired in the morning and I get so scared thinking I have to go out and face everybody . . ."

"In theory and on principle I was right," Nancy wrote somewhere not so long ago. "She needed a firm hand and somebody should have given it to her. She wanted to be saved from her own excesses. But if it were happening today, I can't imagine myself being so preachy and buttinsky. So one hundred and fifty people waited and there were delays. The one hundred and fifty were all on salary and picking up their weekly paychecks. Whatever the delays, a Sally Strickland picture always delivered to the Studio. So the Studio made a little less money than if Sally had been able to operate at optimum efficiency. I had my priorities all wrong. I should have been more perceptive. I should have 'seen' into Sally and been more aware of the pressures that were weighing down on her head like a crash helmet. I should have known that there was a good reason for anything Sally did—or was unable to do. I should have known, all things considered, that the inconvenience of one hundred and fifty people was inconsequential to the private hell one poor, tragic, young girl was suffering. . . ."

Understandably it did not occur to Miss Gorham to record these impressions until some time after Sally Strickland's untimely death.

Sally Strickland was like a needle in the haystack. Literally. But we found her, Kim and I.

It was a Big Deal day. The next morning the cameras were going to roll on *Wendy*. All the coaching and rehearsals and fittings were over and now it was lights-camera-action time for Kim. I was as happy as I could be for her, taking into account how sad I was for myself. Her getting started now seemed like the end of something for me. Now she would be busier. Now there would be so many demands on her time and attention there might not be any room at all left for me.

I told Mama it was a kind of celebration day and we didn't want to eat lunch in the commissary. So Mama put up a picnic hamper for us.

Kim and I cased the back lot. Where would be the perfect spot for our picnic lunch? Where would it be the most fun to spread Mama's feast and start gorging ourselves?

That haystack!

Neither of us had ever seen a real, live haystack before. We only knew there were such things from the movies. But there it was right in front of us, honest-to-God hay piled up about fifteen feet high and looking so feathery-soft and smelling so fragrant. The hay was there for the *Good-bye to Terre Haute* picture Sally was making. The hay and the barn on the set looked dead to the world. Everybody must be off on a lunch break.

As we dug a perch for ourselves in the haystack, we heard a rustling sound a few feet away. Out popped the head of Sally Strickland. The rest of her stayed buried in the hay. She looked scared as hell.

Recognizing us, she giggled with relief. "Oh, it's you."

She moved out of the hay a little more. When her hands came up they were holding the remains of a family-size Hershey bar with almonds. She polished off the candy bar with two big bites and hid the wrapper deep down in the hay. "They'd kill me if they found me doing this," she said when she could talk. "I'm not supposed to eat sweets. But I get such a terrible craving for them. The stuff they want me to eat I don't have any appetite for. You won't tell anybody, will you?"

Poor Sally! Of course we wouldn't tell. But even then I wondered was it candy she was craving—or the sweetness of love?

Kim gobbled down her whole picnic lunch in about five minutes flat, as if the food would be taken away from her or turn to stone if she didn't put it away in a hurry. But there was something on her mind. I wasn't half through my own lunch when I could see her fidgeting.

"Come on, Gina, let's get going."

I knew she had an appointment with Maureen for some final fittings. I also knew the appointment was for one thirty and it was only ten minutes to one.

"It's early yet," I said. "What's the rush?"

"I'd like to look at Sound Stage Sixteen to see if anything's happening."

"Is something supposed to be happening?"

These were the days when the Studio was still grinding them out at the rate of one a week, fifty-two weeks a year. Almost anything could be happening at any time on any of the sound stages or back lots.

"They were supposed to start *Gorgeous* there this morning."

I hadn't seen Kim for maybe five days. But how could I have forgotten? All she talked about the last time I saw her was how exciting it would be when *Gorgeous* got started. Wouldn't it be something, she wondered, if we could visit the set and watch Sarah Blandings in action with Mark Spencer. Just to see the Giant!

The Giant was the sexiest male star in movies. He wasn't the handsomest guy around by a far cry. His nose was too big and his ears were too small. But his name at the top of the cast meant money in the bank even if the picture was a dog. Every actress panted to play opposite him. Half the women of the world panted at the thought of having him—just once. He even had his effect on men. When he stripped down in *The Sweetest Night* for a bedroom scene and it was shown he was wearing jockey shorts, it sent boxer shorts into a depression they never got over.

Sarah Blandings! At twenty-seven or twenty-eight she was already, like they say, a legend in her own time. Any movie buff remembers the story of how she was "discovered" in a malt shop on LaCienega. The malt shop was an after-school hangout for the kids from Hollywood High. Came that red-letter day when Sarah was sitting on a stool and sipping her malted and over in a booth there just happened to be a dirty old gossip columnist who just happened to be an ass man. Well! He took one squint at the ass in the tight-fitting skirt on the stool and he nearly dropped his dentures into his strawberry milkshake.

"I never hoped to see a can like that," the dirty old columnist enthused, "if I outdistanced Methuselah."

The D.O.C.'s eyes were sizing up the delicious divide in the blonde's tight skirt when she swiveled around on her stool to

53

face her girl friend. Christ! All that ass and blond hair—and a profile to boot!

The rest, like they also say, "is cinematic history."

In *Gorgeous* the Studio was teaming, for the first time, its two hottest stars.

Mark Spencer was just back from a honeymoon in Bermuda. Once he had been married to no less than Janet Maynard, who was no less than just about the classiest comedienne who ever came out of Hollywood. It must have been a real love match. Janet died young—of leukemia. Mark mourned her for years. Only in the last year or so did he start looking at women again. The woman he married was a very social type, the heiress to a chewing gum fortune.

Sarah Blandings at twenty-seven or twenty-eight was between marriages when *Gorgeous* came along. A young entertainment feature writer from the Minneapolis *Tribune* put the question to her: "Is it three or four times you've been married, Miss Blandings?"

"Oh, who counts marriages?" Sarah answered airily.

Sound Stage 16: deserted.

Everybody out to lunch here too. Way in the back a couple of men, probably lighting or sound men, were playing cards.

"Nothing's happening," said Kim, downcast.

"There's Miss Blandings's portable dressing room," I pointed out. It was up front and off a little to the left side of the set.

"Are you sure?"

"Sure I'm sure. She has her own bungalow too. But this is the portable she uses on the set. She's the only one I know of who has that full-length mirror outside the door. She always likes to take a last-minute glance in the mirror to make sure every hair's in place and she looks just right before she goes into a scene."

"It must be nice," said Kim, "having your own dressing room."

The words were hardly out of her mouth when there was a sound in Miss Blandings's dressing room. The sound of breathing. *Heavy* breathing. Gasping.

"I don't think we should be here," I said.

"Why not?" Kim asked calmly.

I didn't know why not. I just had an eerie feeling we shouldn't be there.

Inside Sarah Blandings's dressing room a man let out a terrible groan. Then came a silence that was just as terrible.

"Is he dead?" I whispered, horrified.

"Shhh!"

"That's it?" a woman's voice—Sarah Blandings's—asked. "You mean, that's it?"

No answer.

"Are you telling me that's the ball game? You mean that's all there is?"

Still no answer.

Sarah Blandings shrieked. "And they call you the Giant? Giant? Giant, my ass! You're supposed to be the great lover? Well, I've got a cablegram for you. I've had fourteen-year-old kids who could out-fuck you by miles. You got your rocks——"

"Shut up, baby."

Anybody would recognize that voice. It was Mark Spencer.

"Wait till I spread the word about the great lover," Sarah hooted. "Where's it you're from, Spencer? Montana? Okay, from now on, you'll be known as the Minute Man from Montana. He's on and he's off in a jiffy, ladies. Don't blink or you might miss the whole thing. That's why we call him——"

Sarah was stopped by something that sounded like a gigantic crack across the face. "I told you to shut up, bitch."

"You bastard! You get dressed and you get the fuck out of here. I've had better times with cucumbers."

We could hear Mark Spencer swearing and cursing as he moved around. Kim stood there in a hypnotic spell. But I was scared. In a minute he'd be coming out the door of that dressing room and he'd catch us eavesdropping. I tugged at Kim's arm. "Come on," I whispered. "Don't let him find us."

Kim clearly hated to leave. But I was in a panic to get out of there. Until I heard the "get dressed" bit I had no idea of what was going on. Now I had a general idea but it still didn't seem to make sense.

"What was that all about?" I asked Kim.

Kim looked at me as if I was the No. 1 idiot in the world. "They were doing it."

"I guessed that," I said. "But why was she so mad?"

"Because he got done too soon."

I didn't know what that meant but I didn't push it.

Kim smiled mysteriously. "It could have been *her* fault."

I let that one pass too.

"How do you get a dressing room?" Kim asked.

"You really have to be a star," I said.

"Then I'll have to be a star," said Kim. "It must be nice to have your own dressing room."

Chapter 7

Kim had a twenty-four-week no-risk contract with the Studio. That meant the Studio was hedging its bets. She had twenty-four weeks to convince them they should make her a member of the family.

Some poet poeticized about "that first, fine, careless rapture." He may have been talking about first love. He could have been talking about the beginning of anything important. The artist at the moment of conception. The intuitive hunch of a scientist that sparks a breakthrough to the unknown. Friendship in its earliest budding. The fertilization of an egg.

There is a moment, early on, that may never come back again. Call it the thrill of discovery. Once something has been discovered, it can't surprise us ever so much again, no matter how satisfying it might turn out to be. From that moment on, some of the wonder and the excitement has to diminish.

That's how it was with Kim when she made *Wendy*. It was all so new and strange and fascinating to her, the business of making movies. It could never be that new and strange and fascinating again. All the coaching and rehearsing couldn't begin to prepare her for what it would really be like once the cameras actually started rolling. Later she would do her share of bitching about early calls and lousy scripts and those lights that were like murdering suns and the endless boredom of doing the same thing over and over again and all the waiting around for things to get set up and the directors who couldn't direct and the producers who couldn't produce and the lines that wouldn't "play."

But in that "first, fine, careless rapture," everything was to be taken in and devoured and marveled at. It was almost stranger than a dream.

On the sound stage they built the interior of the Georgian country home of Wendy and her parents. In an early scene Wendy is trying to teach Tobias to kneel down and pray in her upstairs bedroom. Kim flipped over the way the walls of the bedroom could be pushed out to let in the whole camera crew.

Out on the back lot they dumped a lot of earth and shaped it into a kind of rolling land and struck some sagebrushy grasses on it. This was supposed to show up on film as the lonely Yorkshire moor. Here Wendy and Tobias romped and frisked and played tag. Here in a later scene you saw them in the middle of the night when they were running away from home.

The role of Tobias went to a golden retriever who was a professional "actor" named Colleen. Tobias was a male being played by a female. Typical Hollywood casting.

Tobias/Colleen and Wendy/Kim took to each other like lint to blue serge. Like a lot of other actresses, Kim has always had this special affinity for animals. And for children. With the notable exception of her own child.

Wendy had a shooting schedule of eighty days. Incredibly it came in just seven days behind schedule. I say "incredibly" in view of the interruptions and mishaps. Where Kim is involved, I long ago decided, the course of true love or moviemaking never would run smoothly.

Once in my presence she was being asked by someone for her permanent address. I spoke up for her, "Crisis Hall."

She couldn't buck Nature. Not when Nature wore its biggest smile the day she was born. Not when Nature was going to endow her so lavishly.

Kim arrived in Hollywood with beginning boobs. Under the ripening sun of California or whatever, the beginning boobs that were like the darling buds of May matured fast. But Wendy had to be a girl, not a young woman. Every morning Miss O'Connor from Wardrobe bound Kim's breasts with gauze, wrapping the gauze around and around and up to the armpits.

Instead of blouses that might reveal suppressed mounds, Kim wore loosely cut Brooks Brothers men's shirts, which somebody said would be just the sort of thing a country girl would wear.

Wendy was done in Technicolor. The Studio loved to turn the color on those British epics so the lawns and parks would show their dazzling green and White Cliffs of Dover would be Pepsodent white against periwinkle-blue English skies.

Hy Seligman, the director, did not like the way Colleen photographed. "She's too dark," he said.

"She's a pedigreed golden retriever and that's what she looks like," said Rex Burpee, her trainer. "I never had anyone tell me she wasn't the right color."

"On film she shows up more like an Irish setter. We have to lighten her up."

"How?"

"A peroxide bath every morning."

"She's not going to like that," said Rex. "She wouldn't like

57

it if it was just a soap-and-water bath. You know how dogs like baths."

"Yeah, well, we all have to do a lot of things every day we don't like to do. Just tell her she has to do it in the interest of art. Tell her there are a hell of a lot of other dogs who'd give their biting teeth to get the break she's getting."

"Oh, Colleen," sighed Kim, hugging the dog tight and putting her head against the dog's head, "you don't need any old dye job. You're just beautiful the way you are. If you were any more beautiful, I couldn't stand it."

But every morning, just as the director said, Colleen was given a peroxide bath. And how she hated it!

Props furnished "Sonny" Merlin a big, muscular bull-dyke, with an old-fashioned zinc bathtub placed just off the set. "Sonny" hosed water into the tub until it was within an inch of overflowing and dropped her cosmetic chemicals into it. She took a no-nonsense grip on the yelping dog and plunged her into the tub. Her rough, efficient hands saw that every hair on the dog's body was soaked and the solution carefully worked into it.

Sprung from the tub, Colleen went wild. She ran in crazy circles, barking her head off and bumping into people and props. Winded, she lay down on her back with legs kicking in the air. She rubbed her back scratchingly against the floor and moaned.

Kim wept.

On film Colleen came through as fluffy golden as the wheatfields of Kansas in an August sun.

The Studio imported two bonafide actors from the Mother Country to play the roles of Wendy's father and mother. They got top billing and Kim got the "And Introducing" bit.

Margalo Whittemore and Sir Henry Stafford were stiff and superior enough to intimidate anybody. It wasn't hard for Kim to be convincing on screen as a child who was having a strained relationship with her parents.

"My, but you're a pretty child," Margalo Whittemore said to Kim when they first met. "Where did you get your training?"

"Training?"

"Quite. Your stage training."

"Nowhere." Even then, as a beginner, Kim didn't like being bested. She couldn't resist wanting to lower that arched eyebrow of Margalo Whittemore. "I never had any stage training." She paused and then added brightly, "But I'm *toilet*-trained."

Wendy and Tobias run away from home late at night, after everybody has gone to bed and the house is in darkness. Shooting of the scene began at nine o'clock one night on the back lot. While they were setting up the lights, something happened that almost never happens in Southern California at that time of year. It started to rain.

Did the rain hold up production? It did not. "Manna from heaven!" exclaimed Hy Seligman. "Rain, rain, keep pouring down! That's just what it would be doing almost any time in England."

In the movie the scene lasts about thirty seconds. Wendy and Tobias are crossing the moor. A couple of times she stops to take a backward glance at the house they're running away from.

They were shooting that scene until one o'clock in the morning. Coming from a deserty Arizona, Kim got such a kick out of the rain she didn't balk at getting soaked. Between takes, she and the dog went inside a trailer to wait and dry off.

"Colleen's got bumps all over her," she told Rex Burpee.

"Yes, I know," said the trainer, frowning.

"What makes those bumps? Is she sick?"

"No, she's not sick. I think it's a reaction to the baths. The stuff they put in the water."

At the end of the night's shooting, Kim said to Hy Seligman, "You shouldn't make Colleen take those baths. She's breaking out in bumps all over."

"You don't know it's the baths. It could be something she's been eating."

"No. Mr. Burpee said it was the baths."

"Mr. Burpee isn't a veterinarian."

"If it might be the baths, can't you stop them?"

"Kimberley," said Hy Seligman, "you're just starting out and you've got so much to learn. Right now you'll have your hands full just remembering your lines. Let me handle all the other worries."

Three days after the night shooting in the rain, production on *Wendy* came to a halt. Kim couldn't speak a word. Kim's speechlessness led to her introduction to Dr. David Wetherbee, who finally decided she had a case of laryngitis. He decided that only after a lot of examining.

Dr. Wetherbee had an office in the Producers and Writers Building. He came to the Studio three days a week. Anyone who had occasion to see him could just drop in without an appointment.

Dr. Wetherbee was married to a widely syndicated gossip

columnist who had enough clout to subtly blackmail her husband's way into the Studio. Nobody doubted that Dr. Wetherbee was an honest-Injun doctor with an M.D., but the rumors about his background and his "professional" activities buzzed around like flies on a cow pie.

Some people said he had been a clap doctor back in New York, where his special clientele were the jazz musicians who played in the 52nd Street joints. Others said he had done a lively business in baby-snuffing, and abortions being frowned on in those days, he fled West when the heat was on. They said he used to be the house doctor at Miss Lorraine's, the Numero Uno brothel in Hollywood. There he checked out the hygiene of Miss Lorraine's girls and doctored any girl in need of treatment. In due time Miss Lorraine's went the way of all fleshpots. But as the expression that applies to everything about the old Hollywood goes, "It was fun while it lasted."

By the time Dr. Wetherbee came to the Studio he was a harmless, dirty old man. He must have been well into his seventies when he examined Kim for the first time. About all he was up to then was looking. He liked to look at the girls and go touchy. If a young girl came to see him with no more than a nosebleed, she was asked first to take her clothes off. Then the good doctor went over her from stem to stern. The part of the examination that gave him his jollies was probing the girl's vagina. "Everything all right in there?" he'd ask. "Not having any trouble there, are you?"

It was said Dr. Wetherbee had many other talents besides routine medical care for Studio employees—and drooling over young girls. It was said he provided a variety of services beyond the scope of any completely kosher doctor.

If Kim had popped in to ask the correct time, Dr. Wetherbee would have had her strip before he told her. Her first visit to him, as she joked about it later, completely discombobulated him.

"What seems to be the matter, dear?" he asked, bug-eyed at the stunning new blossom in his doorway.

"I can't talk," Kim whispered, pointing to her throat.

"Let's give you a good going over. We don't know where the trouble is. Now you go behind that screen and undress. Just leave your clothes there and come back when you're ready."

Kim stood before him nude except for the gauze binding her breasts. "Can I leave this on?" she asked. "So I don't have to go down and have them wrap me all up again?"

"Don't worry about that. I'll take care of it. Here let me help you take that damn stuff off."

The doctor's hands trembled like Parkinson's disease as he

60

undid Kim. When the ripening young melons jumped out of the gauze, he cursed. "Holy Jesus! The damn fools that run this place. What do they want to hide anything like these for?"

Dr. Wetherbee's fingertips explored every inch of Kim's breasts, as if searching for some hidden malignant growth. He took his hands away reluctantly. Still there was another goodie awaiting him. Kim watched his Adam's apple move up and down like an express elevator as he inserted two fingers gently. She saw spittle coming out of the corners of his mouth.

"Oh, no," said Dr. Wetherbee, making a discovery. He looked up at Kim and wagged the forefinger of his other hand at her mischievously. "Either you've been doing a lot of horseback riding or you've been a naughty girl. Which is it?"

"I've been a naughty girl," said Kim.

They shot around Kim for four days until she got back her voice.

Then something disastrous happened that interrupted shooting for three weeks.

It happened so fast it was all over before the paralyzed bystanders knew exactly what was happening.

The Bitch of Bergen-Belsen, as Colleen's trainer called the dyke who bathed his dog, had Colleen in the tub for a bleach job before the day's filming began. Colleen seemed to be putting up more resistance than usual. She bridled and yelped, but the Bitch had a good sturdy grip on her and kept douching away.

Once out of the tub, Colleen would usually stand still for a toweling. This time she took off like a bat out of hell, just as she had after the first bath. She ran around in circles faster than a racehorse, screaming her head off. She knocked over props and crashed into people and kept going. Rex Burpee yelled at her to come to him. She didn't hear him. The crew all had their hands out trying to catch her. But Colleen was beyond reaching.

Colleen's amazing marathon stopped as abruptly as it began. She froze not two feet from where Rex Burpee was standing and rolled over on her back. She let out the most agonizing moan. Her legs shot out stiff and then collapsed. She was dead.

Colleen raced her heart until it failed. But the real cause of her death was her allergic reaction to the bleaching solution the Bitch of Bergen-Belsen had dumped over-generously into the bath that day.

Kim screamed and wept hysterically. She lay on the floor

61

kicking her feet. She couldn't have carried on nearly to that degree if it had been her own mother. She loved that dog passionately. The death of Colleen introduced her to grief.

Dr. Wetherbee gave Kim an injection of something that was supposed to calm her down. Finally her feet stopped beating against the floor and her wild weeping gave way to sobs. A soft-hearted electrician who had taken a special liking to Kim came over to her.

"Come on, Kim," he said gently, "you can't just lie there. We can't let Colleen just lie there either. We have to give her a nice funeral and bury her. Come on, now, you owe this to Colleen."

The electrician found a shovel and put it into Kim's hands. With Burpee's permission he lifted the dead dog in his arms and led Kim out to the back lot. On the Yorkshire moor he dug and dug, down deeper than the superimposed turf, into the dry California earth. Then he laid the dog in the grave.

"We'll pray," he said, getting her to kneel beside him. "Dear Lord," prayed the electrician, "thank You for giving us Colleen. She was wonderful and we all loved her very much. We don't know why You saw fit to take her from us now but we do know there is rhyme and reason to everything You do. Please take special care of Colleen until Kim and all her other friends are reunited with her."

They dyed a French poodle pink to match the hair of Jayne Mansfield in a picture she was making. And the poodle died.

In a circus picture they shot too many tranquilizers into the ass of a lion and the lion died.

Nowadays, thank God from all us animal lovers, the Humane Society has representatives on the set where any animal is performing to prevent such cruelties.

But there are those who ask about animals' inhumanity to man. How about the chimp who bit Ray Walston?

Rex Burpee threatened a lawsuit against the Studio. The response to that threat was quick in coming from the front office.

"You tell that son of a bitch," the Boss was quoted as saying, "if he starts anything, he'll never get any goddamn animal of his in another picture. At this studio or any other studio. You tell him to get another dog the color we want and save us all that monkey-business of baths and bleaches. And tell him to make it PDQ."

It took three weeks to get Tobias II rehearsed and ready to face the cameras. For ten days, production shut down completely and there was *kvetching* about the delay and the mounting costs. *Wendy* was judged as a minor B picture that wasn't expected to pull in more than the kiddie trade and a few dog freaks.

Kim's breasts were giving her considerable pain. It seemed to be more than the gauze binding. Her nipples became hard and red and it was agony to have anything touch or brush them. The day after shooting with Tobias II resumed, she paid Dr. Wetherbee a second visit.

She pointed to where the trouble was. Dr. Wetherbee, in character, wanted to see all of her.

"You don't expect much from the stupid Chinese," said the doctor, undoing the gauze, "binding up women's feet. But I never heard of anything as nutty and criminal as this."

Between Kim's two visits she had done a lot of developing. Dr. Wetherbee whistled when he saw the change. "My, my, my!" he exclaimed. "You *are* a growing girl."

He told her to lie down on a sheeted table. "Now I'm not going to hurt you. I can see your nipples are hard and inflamed. But I don't think it's that damn binding, much as I'd like to blame it on that. It could be mastitis. More likely it's a virus that's settled in your breasts. Personally," he added with a leery laugh, "I couldn't think of a better place to settle."

It was never finally diagnosed as either mastitis or a virus. But heating pads and gentle massaging of the breasts were the indicated cure. Dr. Wetherbee applied the treatment with gusto.

"They say only her hairdresser knows," the old doctor cackled. "But that's not true. Her doctor knows for sure. And I can tell you're a natural."

To show what he meant he gave her reddish mound of pubic hair an affectionate pat.

Chapter 8

They sneaked *Wendy* in San Bernardino. Nobody from the cast went. The studio was represented by only two bottom echelon PR guys, who asked the preview audience to fill out the usual cards in the lobby after the screening. The audience was enthusiastic about the picture beyond anyone's wildest dreams. Their comments were:

"A winner!"

"A warm picture the whole family will love."

"With a kid and a dog, how can you miss?"

"Who's the dog? He's a knock-out. Who's the girl? She's an even bigger knock-out."

And so on.

A couple of days later, the news trickled down to Kim from the front office that she would be asked to join the Studio "family." She celebrated her thirteenth birthday by signing a seven-year contract that would give her a starting pay of $350 a week.

Kim and her mother never dreamed there was that much money even at the end of the rainbow.

Before she had too many more birthdays Kim had grown blasé and cynical about her good fortune. "If that bastard offered me three hundred and fifty a week," she observed, "you can imagine how much more he thought I was worth. Or how much more someone else might have been willing to pay."

With her new prosperity, Kim moved out of the chintzy Coronado Flats to a five-room apartment off Hollywood Boulevard in a newish apartment house that had a swimming pool. The move involved some adjusting on her mother's part, Kim said later, because her mother had to discover a whole new set of bars to hang out in. "But I think it was very good for her," she added, "because she met a better class of drunks."

Bound breasts again, Kim went immediately into a dreary costume epic set in the time of the Spanish Armada. She played the daughter of the captain of a frigate and had only three scenes. In one of them she's in Plymouth Harbor bidding her father a weepy farewell as he sails off to fight the Spanish. It proved Kim could cry convincingly on camera, but that's about all. The picture was a bomb. However one reviewer did write, "The only thing about this one you won't want to forget is the extraordinary beauty of young Kimberley Hudson. Give this girl a couple of years and she should develop into a full-blown siren of the screen."

When *Fair Stood the Winds for Spain* went into release, *Wendy* was still drawing raves and scooping up all over the country, and the front office was anxious to keep Kim's face before the public. Somebody came up with the bright idea she should be written into the next Billy Baxter picture. The cookie cutters who had ground out all the other Billy Baxter classics obediently came up with another gem they called *Billy Baxter Woos a Foreigner*.

Anybody could anticipate—or write—that plot. Millicent Evans and her younger brother have come from London to visit relatives who live a couple of doors down the street from the Baxters. The time is World War II and the kids are really refugees sweating out the war in America. Natch, Billy discovers Millicent. Natch, ho's smitten. For six months he hardly looks at Janie McFarland, the wholesome, goody-two-shoes girl-next-door we all know he's going to end up marrying someday. Then the war ends and it's sail-away time for Millicent and her brother. Billy's at the station seeing them off on the first leg of the journey that will take them back to their home in England. He pledges his undying love to her and swears that as soon as he's saved up enough money from his paper route and working in the Main Street Pharmacy on Saturdays he's going to come over and see her. But you know this is just a pipedream.

After the train pulls out, Billy's walking slowly, sadly, thoughtfully back toward his home. A voice suddenly jerks him out of his gloom. "Hiya, Billy," somebody calls. It's Janie McFarland breezing by on her bicycle, bright, cheerful, rah-rah, no hard feelings over Billy's neglect of her. Billy waves and watches her appreciatively as she zooms down the street. You know, the wave of the future. Billy and Janie are meant for each other. Nothing against Millicent Evans, who was a beauty and a darling. But somehow America is America and England is England, and the home-grown product will always win out over any foreign competition.

Kim was nearly fourteen when *Billy Baxter Woos a Foreigner* went into production. It was decided she could let everything hang out. Tinker Wells gave a war whoop when he saw the "new" Kimberley Hudson.

"If those things were ice cream cones," he said, "I'd be licking away to beat the band."

Kim blushed but couldn't think of anything to say.

"My old offer still holds," he said, beaming evilly.

"What offer?"

He stood on tiptoe to whisper in her ear, "To give you a good screw."

"That's not funny," said Kim.

"Who's trying to be funny? I mean it."

"You shouldn't be talking to me like that."

"A line out of a clinker movie if I ever heard one," jeered Tinker. "If you should change your mind—"

"I won't. You can be sure of that."

It was Samuel "Doc" Hull who helped Kim learn how to "take" Tinker, though he never tried to persuade her that she should learn how to like him.

"Tinker's brash and brazen and maybe no better than he should be," Doc explained to Kim. "But if you just stand up to somebody like that and call their bluff you never have much trouble with them. Personally I've always gotten along with Tinker. For some crazy reason he seems to like me and look up to me."

Kim didn't find that hard to believe. That's the way she herself felt about Doc almost from the moment she met him. Like the rest of the cast she never called him Mr. Hull or Sam or anything except Doc. His off-screen character came over much like the kindly but firm, wise, honest character of Dr. Baxter he projected on the screen.

Doc taught her about key lights and how to "stay in profile" in scenes with Tinker so Tinker couldn't maneuver her back to the camera. He also taught her all kinds of other little tricks for making the most of her scenes. Kim was grateful for the help and flattered by his attention.

Doc seemed to be held in special reverence and affection by everyone. Cast, crew, director, and flunkies. This was the ninth *Billy Baxter* movie in the making and the atmosphere was relaxed and informal. In each picture there were always two or three newcomers to the cast. Otherwise the whole cadre were used to one another from working together—more or less happily—over a period of four or five years.

Gentle and courteous as Doc always was, he had a way of holding himself apart. There was something a little stand-offish about him, a quality of reserve and privacy that everybody instinctively respected. In part, it may have been the respect for age and a head crowned with snowy hairs. Whatever, between scenes on the set no one approached the chair of Mr. Hull without some nod of encouragement from Mr. Hull.

Kim had many such nods of encouragement. Through the seven weeks of shooting and the promotional tour that was timed for the release of the film she came to know a great deal about the old man and to adore him thoroughly. By to-day's standards he wouldn't be considered old. At the time he was maybe sixty-seven or sixty-eight. But Kim thought of him as old, either because of his white hairs or his sweet, almost grandfatherly manner.

"Gina, I'd put my hand in fire for him," she swore to me one day in the commissary. "He's so marvelous to me and he sits there talking to me by the hour just like I was one of his family or somebody his own age."

Doc told her about his childhood in Mainland China. He was the son of missionaries who had been stationed in Hangchow. If he had one dying wish, he told her, it would be to see Hangchow again, which would always be the most beautiful city in the world.

Doc told her of being sent to the States to school, first to prep school at Hotchkiss in Connecticut and later to Yale. He told her of the lost but happy years when he floundered, bumming around the country and keeping himself going with all kinds of odd jobs. He told her how, when he was stranded in Denver one summer, he accidentally fell into acting with a summer stock job in the Elitch Gardens after the juvenile lead suddenly came down with a case of hepatitis.

Doc even told Kim about the ecstasies and fulfillment of a marriage that had lasted thirty-nine years . . . until the death of his beloved from a brain tumor four years before. The happiness of that marriage had been testified to by just about everybody who had any interest in proving that Hollywood was too a place where long-lasting marriages did occur.

"We never had children," Doc said. "No particular reason. We never talked about it much one way or the other. Neither of us wanted them or didn't want them. It wasn't the fault of either of us. *Physically.* It was just one of those things that didn't happen."

But the script hadn't gone according to plan, Doc said. Who'd have dreamed that his wife, ten years younger than he was and who had always been in the pink of health, would be the first to go? Without her, there didn't seem to be much point to anything. Still one had to keep going. It was something at least to have a craft and to be able to go on practicing it. Now he realized it would have been nice to have children, to have some emotional base to fall back upon.

"Every time I look at you," said Doc, reaching over to pat Kim affectionately on the hand, "I realize how much I missed not having had children."

"You make me wish I had had a father," said Kim.

"Thank you, my child. That touches me more than I can tell you. Yes, to have been your father would have been quite an experience. I wonder if I could be going into my dotage. Lately I seem to have the father thing on my mind all the time."

Chapter 9

The Studio sent the cast of the Billy Baxter film on a four-city promotion tour when the film went into distribution. San Francisco, Denver, Omaha, and Minneapolis. The tour gave Kim her first real taste of what it was like to be a movie star. Up to now everything had been secondhand, reading reviews and items about herself in columns and interviews she had done and gushing letters from fans. But this was new, this was real, this was meeting the world in the flesh. The pleasures and privileges of traveling for the Studio overwhelmed her.

I still have the cards she sent me from that tour.

From San Francisco: "Station jammed when our train came in. People yelling 'There's Wendy!' and reaching out to touch me. Have big suite in this hotel (the Fairmont), the best in town. Beautiful city. Limousines to take us everywhere. Everybody wants to interview us. Invited to about a thousand things every day. Phone never stops ringing. Wonderful!"

"At Utah Hotel, best in town," she wrote from Salt Lake City. "Beautiful city but not as exciting as S.F. Doc and I rode out in limo to Alta Lodge today, where Doc said he learned how to ski 'a million years ago.' Somebody coming to interview me from the *Deseret* in five minutes. They're lining up around the block for every showing of the movie."

"Crowds here are the wildest yet," her card from Omaha stated. "They think movie people are *gods!* Staying in Blackhawk, best hotel in town. Doc took me for a great steak dinner in a restaurant near the livestock yards. Remind me to tell you about Cal Sommers. Ugh!"

"A beautiful city!" she wrote about Minneapolis. "Lakes everywhere. Staying in the Radisson, the best in town. Some people who own a flour mill have invited us to dinner. Doc is going to rent a car and show me Minneapolis, where he made a movie a long time ago. He's the most wonderful man I've ever known."

Besides Doc and Kim and Tinker, the cast members who went on tour were Sarah Caulfield, the spunky but family-loving Mrs. Baxter; Melanie Rogers, Mrs. Baxter's old-maid sister who lived with them; Rhodie Baxter, Tim's rebellious older sister; and Jessica Stanard, who played the ever-faithful girl-next-door, Janie McFarland. No parents are allowed on the tour. But because there were three minors in the cast, the Studio sent along a chaperone who was supposed to keep watch over them. The chaperone was a slightly graying, schoolmarmish woman of about forty-five named Joy Ann Harmony. When she wasn't chaperoning minors on tour, Joy Ann Harmony was a legal secretary at the Studio.

On her way to the observation car on the train going from Salt Lake to Omaha, Kim went by Tinker Wells's compartment. The door was closed but she could hear whispers and giggling and heavy breathing. No one else was in sight so she stopped to eavesdrop. She heard Tinker bossing the show: "Give me some joy, Joy! Suck, baby . . ."

Kim was not surprised. She thought it would be fun to get the Boss's goat by telling him there should be a chaperone to chaperon the chaperone.

She wondered why it hadn't occurred to her earlier to call him Stinker. Even if he hadn't been named Tinker, she would have thought stinker was one of the best words to describe him. Everything that happened on the tour showed him up to be a stinker of the first order. She took to calling him Stinker, emphasizing the "S."

Tinker had a lot of nifties. Grinning like a Cheshire cat, he'd yell "Catch!" to a bellhop and toss a coin into the air. The bellhop, who might be four times Tinker's age, would raise his hands to catch the thrown dime. Everybody ordered meals in their suites from Room Service. But only Tinker ordered things like Beluga caviar and pheasant under glass. And vintage wines to wash them down. He shouldn't have been served alcoholic beverages but who'd have had the guts to say no to Tinker Wells? When Room Service rolled in the cart, Tinker had a cute trick. He'd roll up a five-dollar bill and throw it on the floor. When the waiter stooped to pick up his tip, Tinker would give him a finger and laugh like a hyena. Who was the waiter going to complain to? Besides, a five-buck tip was nothing to sneeze at.

In each city the cast appeared on stage between showings of the picture. As the star of the series, Tinker introduced the other members of the "Baxter family."

"You just come out and grin," Tucker instructed Kim backstage in San Francisco, "and get the fuck off."

"And now, folks, the perfectly gorgeous, heartbreakingly beautiful girl I lose my heart to in the picture you're about to see . . . let's have a big hand for Miss Kimberley Hudson!"

Kim came on stage, grinned, bowed, and started back to the wings. She was terrified. She couldn't see anybody in the darkened theater but she knew they could all see her. Walking toward the wings, she heard the cries:

"Kim!"

"Wendy!"

"Come back!"

"Say something!"

Kim came back, speechless. Helplessly she turned to Tinker for coaching.

"Tell them 'Thank you, thank you, from the bottom of my heart for your warm welcome. It's so wonderful to be here in San Francisco. I wish I could meet each and every one of you out there in the audience.' "

Tinker's arm was around her as he spoon-fed her this little speech. As she got to the last words, his hand slipped down Kim's back. With his forefinger he gave her a poke up her rectum that sent her flying into the air. The audience roared, assuming no doubt he had just given her a playful pinch on the behind.

"You ever try that again," Kim fumed backstage, "and I'll punch you in the face."

Tinker grinned. "Wanna fuck?"

During the trip Kim also had her troubles with Cal Sommers. Cal was the unit publicity man on the picture and he was the one responsible for handing out press kits and setting up interviews with newspaper reporters and the radio and television talk shows. He was young, about thirty, but far from handsome. Kim was turned off by his heaviness and his sallow skin and oily, wavy black hair. But Kim turned Cal on. Big.

It started with his inviting her to have a nightcap in the lounge car on the overnight train journey from Los Angeles to San Francisco.

"I don't drink," said Kim.

"Hell, you can have a ginger ale, can't you?"

Cal sat uncomfortably close to her, his arm draped on the banquette behind her. Occasionally he would tap her shoulder to make a point. "Kim," he said, "I hope we're going to have a chance to get really acquainted on this tour. I hardly know you and there's so much a guy like me can do to help someone like yourself. I need a lot more dope on you, Kim. Be a good girl and save me some time tomorrow at the hotel."

In the Fairmont Hotel the next day he came to her suite with a yellow legal pad. "I want to do an up-to-date release on you," he said, "so I'll need your help. Then I can hand this out to the press and you won't have to keep answering the same questions over and over again."

Cal quizzed her on a lot of things. Her favorite colors and foods. The kind of clothes she liked to wear. Her hobbies. How she liked making the movie. Funny things that happened on the set, etc.

"Kim," said Cal, "the first thing anybody asks about a girl as beautiful and—stacked—as you are, 'What are her measurements?' I know that'll be the first thing they throw at me. So what are your measurements, Kim?"

"I don't know," said Kim honestly.

"Amazing! A girl with your equipment and you don't know the statistics. God, that's rich!"

"And true."

"Now you do know what size bra you wear. I'd say——"

"Oh, Cal, I never see stuff like that about any of the actresses I read about in movie magazines."

"Maybe not. But those guys'll take one squint at you and that's what they'll be asking."

In Salt Lake, Cal came knocking at her door fairly early in the morning, hours before any of the activities of the day were scheduled to begin. He came with a tape measure.

"Kim, I got to get this measurement thing settled once and for all," he announced.

She let him measure her. First the tape went around her hips and her waist, with Cal dutifully noting the measurements on his yellow pad. Then the tape wound slowly around her breasts. In the winding Cal managed to touch each nipple and give it a small, circular rub. Cal bent down to note the measurement and then feigned forgetfulness. The tape measure wound lovingly around Kim's boobs again, his fingertips giving her nipples another massage.

"Jesus Christ, they're beautiful," Cal drooled. "Jesus Christ, do I ever hate bras. God, Kim, how I'd like to feast my eyes on these things just as God made them."

"They weren't anything at all," said Kim, "just as God made them. Two little pimples on a tiny baby's body."

Kim thought Doc would be amused by her latest meeting with Cal. To the contrary, he was incensed. She could hardly believe that this mild, gentle man could get so worked up over something she saw as a funny bit of no importance at all.

"You don't have to put up with that crap." Doc raged. "If he tries any more of it, you tell me. First I'll crack his skull in. Then I'll do my best to see to it that he's out on his ass at the Studio."

"Oh, Doc," said Kim, throwing her arms around him and kissing him, "it's nothing. He's icky but he's okay. He's maybe a little stuck on me but I can handle him. He means well."

Doc was just giving Kim a good-night kiss at her door, after their steak dinner together in Omaha, when she heard her phone ringing. It was Cal.

"Minneapolis shapes up as socko," Cal exclaimed, bounding into Kim's suite. "You and Doc and Tinker and the rest are going to do a lobby appearance tomorrow evening before the picture has its first showing there. Signing autographs and saying 'Howdy.' That sort of thing. Then I got you for a three-minute interview on the WCCO-TV news roundup at eleven. The next morning you're back there for the Cecily Adams Show, which a million people in the Twin Cities area

71

look at every morning. Then you're free all day long until seven o'clock. That's when we all pile into the limos and haul ass out to the Bancrofts in Wayzata. They're real rich bitches who live in a French château that's supposed to have been brought back stone by stone from somewhere in the South of France at the cost of about two million dollars. The old lady's movie-struck and I've heard she'd like to sink some of their flour billions into producing movies."

"It sounds wonderful," said Kim.

"Kim, you don't know the excitement you're causing. I get more questions about you than I get about the whole rest of the cast put together. Thank God, I thought to get those measurements. That's the first thing every guy wants to know. I mean the reporters and columnists and so forth."

"Is that all they want to know about me?"

"No, no. They want to know everything. They want to know one thing I never thought to ask you."

"What's that?"

"They want to know about your hair. Well, not exactly about your hair. They see this color that isn't quite like any other color they've ever seen before. You know, it's something between rust and chestnut and raspberry. Is it for real, they ask, or is it some unique kind of dye? Something hatched out just for her?"

"You can tell them it's for real," said Kim.

"I believe you," said Cal. "But I tell them that and they ask me how I know for sure."

"You can tell them to ask Dr. Wetherbee."

"Yeah, well, they're not going to go to that trouble," said Cal, "but they'd take it from me."

"Okay, let them take it from you."

"How could they take it from me unless I swore I really knew for sure?"

Kim knew what he was getting at but she was in a teasing mood. "I don't tell lies. If I tell you something is true, can't you swear you know it's true?"

"Kim, I love you for being so naïve. It shows what a pure girl you are. Just the kind any man dreams of marrying. Kim, if you were a man, you'd probably have hair in a lot of places. You'd have your head hair and you might have a moustache or a beard or sideburns and hair under your arms and on your chest and legs and above your penis and on your testicles. I hope I'm not shocking you, Kim. And all the hair has sort of the same color. If you're a blond on top of your head, you won't be quite that blondish other places. But the other hair will be light enough so everyone will believe that blond hair on your head is the real thing. Now if you're a woman, the only place you're supposed to have hair is on your head and . . . down below. Around your vagina. Now if I were trying to be crude I'd have said something like 'around your pussy' or 'around your cunt.' "

"Thanks for being such a gentleman, Cal."

"Kim, let me see with my very own eyes. Anybody ever asks me I'll be able to answer truthfully. I won't tell them how I know but I'll be able to swear that's your natural color of hair. I can tell them you don't put anything on it and you don't have a hairdresser brewing up solutions to give it a special color. Kim, just let me. You take off your things, Kim, and I promise not to touch you."

Not knowing exactly why she was doing it, Kim found herself peeling off her clothes. She wasn't going to let Cal lay her. She thought of him as a friend who had been going out of his way to do her favors and help her. She liked him without being the least bit attracted to him. Still she couldn't help getting a little excited knowing how steamed up he was getting over her.

"Holy Jesus!" Cal cried when Kim took off her bra and stood before him bare tit. "They're beauts. They're works of art. You know, they're better than Jane Russell's. Maybe not so big. But in better proportion. Holy Jesus, Kim, I wish I was an artist instead of a writer. It would take ten thousand words and I'd never find the right ones to describe them. But a good artist could capture them on canvas and they'd belong to the world . . ."

He babbled on, still standing yards away from her, as she stepped out of her skirt and pulled down her panties. When she stood before him in the altogether, he rushed over to a big table lamp with a three-way bulb and turned up the wattage to 300.

"I believe you, I believe you!" Cal shouted, staring down at Kim's triangular pubic forest. "Goddamnit, it matches. It doesn't match but it's the color it should be to go with your hair. Kim, do me a favor, honey. Just turn around slowly. Oh, goddamnit, wowie, wowie, wowie! You got it everywhere in spades, Kim. You got it up front and you got it out back. And you got a face like a goddess . . ."

Kim stood straight and still and listened to Cal become almost incoherent raving over her charms.

". . . should be loved and worshipped . . ."

Kim watched almost stupefied as Cal fell to his knees and walked on them toward her, his hands clasped behind him. "See, no hands. Like I said, I'm not going to touch you. But let me just do this. Let me kiss it . . ."

Kim said nothing. Cal took this as a green light to go

ahead. Hands still clasped behind him, he bent forward until his nose was nuzzling her pubic hair. He moistened his lips. His tongue darted out like a snake's and thrust itself inside her. Deeper and deeper it probed, sweeping around in circular motions and then going flick, flick, flick, light as a feather. Kim liked what he was doing but she tried not to let him see that she was enjoying it.

"Holy shit!" he exclaimed, coming up for air. "That's darling pussy . . . a real treasure cave in there . . ."

His tongue went deeper and deeper, like it was looking for the center of the earth. Ridiculously he kept his hands clasped behind him, as if to prove to Kim he was a man of his word.

"Does that feel good?" he asked the next time he surfaced.

"Yes," said Kim. "Keep doing it. It's the first time anybody ever did that to me."

Cal unclasped his hands. He unbuckled his belt and undid his zipper. His pants fell down to his knees and a huge elephant tusk popped out through the gap in his boxer shorts.

"Look here, Kim," panted Cal, stroking his penis. "This little guy's going crazy."

"Not such a little guy," said Kim.

"God, how jealous he is of my tongue! How he'd like to get where my tongue's been. He'd make you feel even better than my tongue did. Please let him come in, Kim."

"No."

"Is it because he's so big?"

"No, that's not it."

"Protection? Are you worried about protection? I got protection right here." He started to reach for a wallet in his back pocket.

"No, Cal, please."

"Why not?"

She couldn't tell him she thought he was sort of ugly and she didn't like him enough to want him screwing her. "My mother always told me I should be a good girl," she lied.

"Boy, if she only knew how good you are! Maybe not in the sense she meant it."

"Today I'll be half-bad and let you keep on doing what you were doing."

"Okay," said Cal, and he went back to licking her and flicking his tongue in and out, all the while stroking his penis with one hand. Until Kim's fireworks exploded. Cal nearly went wild, and he stroked his penis with increasing fury. And it erupted like a volcano.

Finally, his calmed penis dangling outside his shorts, Cal looked up at Kim. He was almost crying. "Maybe your mother's right about wanting you to stay a good girl," he said. "I know I was able to make you feel good and satisfy you. But it's not the way it should have been. We should have been in bed. I kept my word about not touching you but it's the hardest thing in the world I ever had to do. I knew if I just touched you once I'd never let go. My hands, my body, everything would have been all over you and never quit."

"Thank you for being so good," said Kim, and added, "in both ways."

"Jesus, have I ever got the hots for you. I could go for you in such a fantastic way. What a loving you could get from me! I don't mean in just the sex way, though I've got the sex drive of ten men combined. Lookit, even talking about it, that little guy down there's already standing up again and rarin' to go. But I mean loving in-the-round, completely. Loving you could even inspire me in my work. Most of the time I look upon it as just a routine hack job. Loving you, I think of the things I could do to further your career and shape your image in the public's eye. A good press agent can be developmental for his client, you know. It would give my life some sense of mission to help mold the big star I know you'll become. God, how I'd love to take care of you in every way. I got such a lot of loving to give to somebody. I'd give you twenty climaxes a day if you wanted them. There's nothing I wouldn't do to please you. . . ."

On the train the next morning Kim said nothing to Doc about her meeting with Cal.

"We'll soon be in one of my favorite cities in the world," Doc told her. "I spent a whole summer there just before the war making a picture called *Aquatennial*. I fell in love with the place and its healthy and handsome and hospitable people. Do you know what I've planned for us tomorrow afternoon, Kim?"

"What?" she asked eagerly, warmed by the sound of "us."

"We have the whole afternoon off and you and I are going to ditch everybody. We're going to thumb our noses at the rented limousines and I'm going to rent an ordinary car so you and I can get a look at Minneapolis."

In the Radisson Hotel, an hour or so before they were to make their lobby appearance in the Orpheum Theater, Doc came to Kim's suite bearing gifts. He handed her three boxes.

"For me?" she cried.

"Who else? Open them."

In the biggest box was a green chiffon dress. In another box was a pair of matching shoes with ankle straps. In the smallest box was a pair of rhinestone pins.

"They're beautiful!"

Except for the trifling gifts her mother had given her at Christmas and for her birthday each year, the experience of receiving gifts was so new and sweet to her she thought she was going to cry. She kissed Doc on both cheeks.

"Go try on your dress and shoes," said Doc.

To Kim's delight and amazement, both the dress and the shoes fit perfectly. "How did you know my size?" she wondered.

"A little birdie told me," said Doc. He was pleased that she was so pleased. "Notice anything special about the color?"

"It's green," said Kim.

"Go look in the mirror and see if you notice something special about the shade of green."

"They're the same color as my eyes," she said, blushing.

"Now come here," said Doc, "and I'll show you what we're going to do with these pins."

He pushed her hair back on both sides and stuck a rhinestone pin on either side to hold the hair in place. "Now go take a look at yourself in the mirror. I don't know if you see what I'm seeing. But I'm looking at something as gorgeous as you'd ever want to see. I'm looking at someone I keep thinking of as a little girl but who's really a grown-up gorgeous young woman. Now, come on, that's what you're going to wear tonight and you're going to kill 'em. . . ."

In the lobby of the Orpheum Theater Kim attracted even more attention than Tinker Wells. There were whistles and gasps and catcalls and pushing and shoving to get near her and touch her and get her autograph. "It's Kimberley Hudson, and she's so beautiful!" voices in the crowd said. Kim smiled and ate up every second of it, every whistle and catcall and gasp.

Kim said the next afternoon was one of the happiest of her life. Doc took her to lunch in Charlie's Café Exceptionale, which was her first meal in a truly distinguished restaurant. There she had her first glass of sherry and her first taste of wall-eyed pike and wild rice, the gourmet specialties of Minnesota. She saw her first real lake. (The Studio back lot had a fake lake with machines to drum up waves.) She saw several real lakes: Lake Harriet and Lake Calhoun and Lake Como and Lake of the Isles. He showed her the Mississippi River that more or less divided the Twin Cities of Minneapolis and St. Paul and the great, sprawling University of Minnesota. In St. Paul she saw her first state capitol building. Doc showed her Minnehaha Falls, her first falls, and took her on a quick guided tour of Walker Art Gallery, her first visit to an art gallery. Excelsior Park on Lake Minnetonk was her

76

first trip to an amusement park. There she had her first ferris wheel ride.

Driving back to Minneapolis, Doc said, "You know, the movie-making business can be a cruel one."

"Cruel?"

"In many ways. What I'm thinking now is you make a movie and get to be like a family. You're together day after day. Like in any family you come to feel close to some members and maybe don't like other members at all."

"I know what you mean," said Kim. "If I never see Tinker Wells again it'll be too soon."

"You can grow very attached to someone," said Doc, "and you don't want to let go. The thing that brought you together is finished but your feelings for that person aren't."

"I'm sure glad I got to know you," said Kim.

"That's just what I'm trying to say." Doc took one hand off the wheel and patted Kim's thigh. "We may never find ourselves working together again. But I don't want to lose touch with you."

The evening gave Kim another first. At the Bancrofts in Wayzata she caught her first glimpse of how the very rich lived and she wondered if she'd ever be rich enough to live like that. The imported French château stood nobly on a small elevation and was approached by a long, circling gravel roadway lined on both sides by Lombardy poplars. The Bancrofts had no visible neighbors. Their property stretched over hill and dale for acres and acres. To the rear of the house there were stables, a pond that swans glided dreamily across, a stream stocked with trout, tennis courts, a miniature golf course, and a deer park. There was also a big red barn to stock all the antique cars Mr. Bancroft was collecting as a hobby.

Kim counted eleven in inside help. There was a white-coated butler, cocktail waitresses, footmen, a governess, the kitchen staff. A large tent had been set up in the back yard. There the guests and their hosts ate from a buffet piled on tables that were about as long as airfield runways. Afterward everybody gathered in the enormous drawing room. Tinker took over the entertainment. He told Hollywood stories and slightly off-color jokes and did a lot of general mugging. At the bone-white baby grand piano he accompanied Margery Bancroft, who sat perched on the piano à la Helen Morgan, through numbers like "The Trolley Song" and "I'm Looking Over a Four-Leaf Clover."

Feeling shy and unsure of herself, Kim stayed close by Doc all evening. At one point when Doc excused himself to go to the bathroom, Tinker used the occasion to needle Kim.

"You're not teaching my father any dirty tricks, are you?"

"I don't know what you're talking about."

"I don't want you fucking him. Old Doc Baxter's supposed to be simon-pure and a nice clean old man."

"Stop pestering me, Stinker."

"Wanna fuck?"

Back at the Radisson, Doc said to Kim at her door, "Now I've got one more present for you. You go inside and I'll give you a little knock in about three minutes."

"I was going to give it to you when we got back," Doc explained, handing her a box, "but it's been such a perfect day I just . . . well, didn't want it to end. I wanted to keep it going a little while longer."

The box contained a flesh-colored satin nightgown with lace ruffles. "Oh, Doc, it's heavenly!" she cried. She embraced him and kissed him again on both cheeks. "I've never had anything like it. You should see the nightgowns I've always had. Mostly hand-me-downs from my mother. Ugly flannel things. But this!"

"I have only one request and it's a special one. I want to see you model it."

"Sure, Doc."

Doc got a surprise if he was expecting her to trip into the bedroom to change into the nightie, as she had done when she put on the chiffon frock and shoes he had given her. Innocently as a child she stripped right in front of him. But with a woman's cunning she let her visitor feast his eyes a moment on the raw flesh before she put on the nightgown. "Doc, it's just too marvelous!"

"You're such an eyeful I can hardly believe my eyes," said Doc. "But you're so much more than just beautiful. You're sweet and kind and so alive and bright."

"You're all those things too," said Kim. "And beautiful."

Doc's eyes misted. "Oh, Kim, Kim. Promise me, I'm not going to lose you now when we get back to the Coast."

"I promise."

"I think I must have been sleepwalking for the past four years. Until you came into my life I don't think I had any idea of how numb and empty I was. Just going through the motions of being alive. And one little girl changed all that. No, I mustn't say 'little girl.' One very special young woman brought me back to life."

"Oh, come on, Doc."

"No, it's true, it's true. Now I can feel joy and pain again. I can feel the pain of loneliness. Kim, dear?"

"Yes?"

"Do you know what kills me? Now that I can feel pain again? It's the thought of leaving you after this completely happy and wonderful day and having to go back to that empty suite where I'll be all alone again."

"Don't leave then, Doc. You don't have to leave."

Doc looked at her in unbelief. "I don't?"

"Of course you don't."

"Kim, just to be here, to sleep out here on the couch—"

"You don't have to sleep on the couch."

"Kim, I don't know how to say this. I—"

"You can say anything to me."

"I wouldn't want anything that could be harmful to you, my child." He paused. "You're not 'my child.' I shouldn't call you that. You're on the threshold of womanhood and there may never be a nicer time in your life. I couldn't wish for anything that would . . . how do I say it? . . . get in the way or interrupt your development and fulfillment as a young woman. I couldn't ask—"

"You can have anything you ask for, Doc."

"Oh, Kim." The mist in the old man's eyes formed into beginning tears. "God love you, darling. That's so much. I don't want much of anything, when it comes down to it."

"Tell me what you want, Doc."

"I want, I want . . . to not be alone. I don't want to wake up at three o'clock in the morning and be alone. I want . . . all I want is to . . . cuddle."

"Oh, Doc," said Kim, hugging and kissing him again, "I want to cuddle too. With you."

She took him gently by the hand and led him into the bedroom. "Beautiful as this nightgown is, I'm not going to wear it tonight, Doc, if you don't mind."

She slipped off the nightgown and got into bed. She turned modestly to the wall so Doc could undress in private. But when he approached the bed she turned around to welcome him. She took in the whiteness of his body, the deathly white skin that had no pigment of coloration from the neck down. His chest sprouted a few whitish hairs and the thin grove of pubic hair was almost totally white. He was soft but not fat. Crawling into bed beside her was a once handsome man in ruins.

Kim extended her arms in an embrace. "Tell me what you want," she whispered.

"Just this," said Doc, returning her embrace. "To hold and be held."

"Do you want me to do anything?"

"Just this," sighed Doc. "I'm an old man. Just this is . . . heaven."

"You're not old," said Kim. "I'll never think of you that way."

The man who had started out playing her father curled up like an infant beside her. Then she felt tears dropping onto her breast and a mouth working at her nipple like a suckling babe.

Chapter 10

When actresses like Kim and Judy Garland and Elizabeth Taylor and Shirley Temple and Deanna Durbin got to that awkward age between childhood and adultery, as they say, the problem was to find roles suitable for them. The public had adored them as children but now these ex-children were physically women. Still the adoring movie fans weren't about to accept them in adult roles. This was more true, of course, for Judy and Elizabeth and Shirley and Deanna than it was for Kim, who was hardly a household name at this time.

The Studio produced only family-type films. The first commandment of the Boss was that every picture had to be fit for the whole family to see. The second commandment was that it should always be a picture that the whole family would *want* to see. (Considering the shape the movie industry's in today, maybe the Boss should still be around.) So, using one of the sappy, saccharine bits of fluff that had been turned out by a best-selling novelist the Studio had hired to write scripts for $1,500 a week, suddenly a savvy producer put one and one and one together and got three.

The three were Mark Spencer ("the Giant") and Maura Anderson and Kimberley Hudson.

The Giant was big enough box office to carry any piece of junk single-handed, the high-priced thinking went. Then you throw in Maura Anderson, a raven-haired beauty fresh out of South Carolina who had every promise of coming across as a fantastic new sex symbol. For extra good measure you throw in a young actress who could develop into God knows what. Well, chalk up a winner! *The Kid Sister-in-Law*.

The story was soppy and stupid. Mark Spencer is married to Maura Anderson. She's a sensational young beauty he met when she was chosen Queen of the Azalea Festival in North Carolina. As an up-and-coming lawyer who's also president of the local Junior Chamber of Commerce, he presented the crown to Maura. One thing led to another and finally to the altar. For Maura it was a big hike up the social ladder because she came from a poor family of sharecroppers in South Carolina. About the third year of their marriage Maura's younger sister Karen (Kim) comes to spend the summer with them. Karen's just finished secretarial school and she's to work that summer in Mark's office relieving the other secretaries going on vacation. With the money she earns she wants to go North in the fall, to take up modeling in New York.

The obvious happens—and doesn't happen. Karen falls desperately in love with her handsome brother-in-law. But nothing comes of it. Mark, however, is really tempted. The girl is even more of a looker than her beauty-queen sister.

Things come to a head during the last week of the long, hot Southern summer. Tippi (Maura) is summoned home to South Carolina to take care of an ailing mother. This leaves Karen and Sam (Mark) under the same roof together. In their separate bedrooms, with their doors left open to catch any stirring current of air, they can hear each other's breathing and tossing for sleep. Karen is almost mad with desire for Sam.

One night, in her frilliest nightie, Karen goes downstairs and makes a pitcher of lemonade and takes it up to Sam, who's lying in bed in just his shorts. While Sam downs the lemonade, Karen gushes out her declaration of love . . . she didn't mean to do this . . . she loves Tippi and hates herself for betraying her sister's trust . . . but there it is, it happened . . . and, well, she's his, if he wants her, on his terms . . .

"Want you?" Sam cries. "I want you with every atom of my being. Why, you little fool, do you think it's just the heat that's been keeping me awake and pitching from one side of the bed to the other all night long? If you knew how I've had to fight myself to keep from going into that room to be with you! . . . I doubt whether anything more tempting will ever come my way. But, Karen, I'm going to keep on fighting. And I want you to help me . . . Tippi's everything I ever dreamed of in a wife and I want to try to be worthy of her . . . Sure, who's to stop us from losing our heads and getting away with it? Tippi need never be any the wiser. But you'd know and I'd know. It's just not the sort of thing you do when you got something so great going for you . . . and someday, Karen, I think you're going to look back and be glad you didn't let yourself be so cheap . . . You're such a warm person and you're becoming such a beautiful young woman you'll have half the men in the world panting for you. You'll have the pick of the very best around, and believe me, whoever the lucky guy turns out to be and however won-

81

derful he turns out to be, he won't be half good enough for you ..."

It's funny how life has a way of imitating corny movie scripts. Almost.

In *The Kid Sister-in-Law* Kim got third billing, just below Mark Spencer and Maura Anderson. But she got something that thrilled her even more. Her own portable dressing room. It wasn't much of a trailer and it was meagerly furnished, but it made her feel like a star.

"What's Mark Spencer like?" I asked a few days after the start of rehearsals.

"He's nice and polite. But he doesn't know I exist." She added brightly, "He will, though."

I didn't know exactly what Kim meant by that. But I had my doubts Kim or anybody else, no matter how beautiful and alluring, was going to get very far with Mark. Mark had a watchdog on the set in the form of his wife, the chewing gum heiress. She knew she had won a prize, she had a few years on Mark, and she didn't mean to let him out of her sight. Every day she accompanied him to the set and kept her eyes focused right on him. Between scenes they retired to his dressing room. They didn't socialize with anybody else. The new Mrs. Spencer explained her constant presence as prompted by the fact she was "so crazy, nutty in love with the whole movie-making business."

One part of the movie business Mrs. Spencer wasn't "so crazy, nutty in love with" was Maura Anderson. Maura was coming along fast, both in her career and sex life. Magazines were saying she "radiates sex with every breath and movement," and the Studio hacks were doing their best to put a silencer on her sexual favors. Some wag said she had one important thing in common with Will Rogers: she had never met a man she didn't like. Carrie Spencer had no intention of letting Mark become the latest of Maura's conquests.

"I think Maura's dying to get her hands on him," Kim told me, "but there's Carrie practically sitting there with a shotgun."

"How about you?" I asked. "Do you think he's all that special?"

"He's cute and I'm sort of stuck on him. I can see how millions of women would want to throw themselves at his feet. But I don't feel it that much. I like him and I'd like to get to know him. But I don't think I'd ever lose my head over him. He's nice to me and that's all and it's okay. I'm sort of stuck on him but not falling head over heels in love with him. It's just nice the way it is."

"Doesn't Mrs. Spencer ever get sick?" Kim heard Maura ask Mark breathily between takes.

"Not since I've known her," said Mark, straight-faced. "No, I'd say she enjoys remarkable health."

"Too bad," said Maura, smiling suggestively.

But Carrie Spencer's mother suddenly wasn't enjoying remarkable health. Carrie was called back to Chicago to wait out the death of an old woman in the last stages of lymph cancer.

Kim was amused at Maura's efforts to make the most of her opportunity. But Mark was wary. He knew that if he spent so much as five minutes alone in her company anywhere the news would be carried in all directions by the four winds. He smiled cagily when she suggested a drink in her dressing room. "Don't tempt me," he said, "I'm on the wagon."

"He's afraid of Maura," said Kim. "But he's not afraid of me. He never really looks at me."

"I doubt that," I said.

"I mean, not the way men usually look at women."

"But you're not a woman."

"I'm getting there fast," said Kim irritably.

"Do you still want to get friendly with him?"

"I want him to notice me. I want him to really notice me. Not just as somebody he says lines to."

Carrie Spencer was gone nearly three weeks. A day or so before she was due to return, shooting of the script had progressed to the climactic bedroom scene where Mark (Sam) tells Kim (Karen) their temporary infatuation with each other can't go any further.

"Mr. Spencer," said Kim, just before they went into their first take, "I find this so hard."

Mark looked at her quizzically. "You're embarrassed. You're a very nice, proper young lady and you've never seen a man in his shorts before. Or been seen by a man in a thin little nightie."

"It's not that," said Kim. "I wish there was a little time I could talk to you."

"We can talk."

"Not here," said Kim. "Maybe in my dressing room."

Mark Spencer followed her a few steps. But he hesitated at the door to her portable. "Kim, maybe this isn't the best of ideas," he said, smiling.

Kim, who was already inside, said, "Why not?"

"Well, because this sound stage has about a thousand eyes and half as many tongues. People would be only too happy to draw the wrong conclusions and start some shady stories going around about the two of us. We both have our good reputations to protect, remember."

Kim remembered what she had heard with her own ears the day he had been with Sarah Blandings in her dressing room. She also remembered that his name had been involved with about a hundred women whom he didn't happen to marry.

"Besides which," the Giant added, "you're still a girl yet and your tender years rate protection from anything anybody could twist into a slimy rumor."

"When does anybody stop being a girl? I'm almost eighteen," she lied.

"Are you? Well, well." He smiled at her again in that puzzled way, but not disbelievingly. "All right, we'll have our talk. If I can be of any help, it'll be my pleasure. Could I by any chance buy you dinner tonight?"

"That would be wonderful!"

"Tell you what," said Mark. "I'll pick you up at seven at the exit gate nearest here. That way I can get home and feed the animals and call Carrie before it gets too late out in Chicago. It looks like a beautiful night coming up. We'll drive up the coast a ways to a nice spot I like to sneak off to once in a while. You tell your parents or guardians or whoever's looking after you I'll have you home in good time for your beauty sleep."

Kim almost had to pinch herself to believe her good luck. She was having dinner with the Giant, the fabulous Mark Spencer! Throughout the world there must be a hundred million women or more who would give anything to be in her shoes.

"I don't know just when I'll be back," she told her mother. "I'm having dinner with Mark Spencer and his wife at their home. Mark has a lot of advice and suggestions he wants to give me on the scenes we still have to do. He said if it gets too late I can just stay in one of their guest rooms."

Kim's first surprise of the evening was to be picked up in a Pontiac. She was expecting something very sporty or expensive or exotic. But a Pontiac!

"You were expecting a golden chariot?" Mark asked, correctly reading her thoughts. "Well, I'll tell you, Kim. I get fed to the gills with all the star stuff. The most fun I can think of is to cut away from all the hokum and pass myself off as Mr. Average Guy."

In a minute Kim got the full impact of his meaning. They were driving up the coastal highway, past Santa Monica and Malibu, past clusters of beach houses and dumpy fishing shacks. The road turned away from the rolling sea and the traffic seemed suddenly to thin out. Mark stopped the car on the gravel shoulder.

"Oh, no," thought Kim. "We're not parking. He's not going to start something. *Here.*"

She was both thrilled and revolted by the thought. Thrilled that something might happen. Revolted to think it couldn't be anything more than the clumsy fumbling of a high school sophomore out on his first date.

Mark reached into the back seat and brought out a kit. Before Kim's amazed stare he pasted on a small black wig that covered up the widow's peak hairline that was one of his telltale features. Then he pasted on a pencil-thin moustache. He had some large flesh-colored fake ears to clamp on over his real, unusually tiny ears. An unbelievably real-looking fake nose gave his real nose a very different shape. To complete the disguise he put on a pair of amber-tinted horn-rimmed glasses.

"May I introduce you," he said to Kim, in a mild, colorless voice that was about an octave higher than his normal gutsy bass voice, "to Anthony Hogan, CPA?"

Kim was dumbfounded at the change in appearance. He looked and sounded for all the world like the prosperous, soft-spoken certified public accountant he was passing himself off as. His drab navy-blue suit, plain navy-blue four-in-hand, and white button-down shirt complemented the illusion.

"Who is Mr. Hogan?" Kim asked.

"He's the other me," said Mark. "No. Not the other me. Just me when I don't want to be sucked up to and pawed over and all that crapola."

Kim marveled not only over the change in appearance but that anyone could be so fed up with recognition that he'd go to such lengths not to be recognized.

Mark reached into the glove compartment and pulled out a pair of dark glasses and a babushka. "Do me a favor," said Mark. "Put these on and become Shirley Abramovitz, my new secretary."

"I'm not a star," Kim giggled.

"You'd be surprised how many people would recognize that puss the place we're going," said Mark. "It's a movie place. Anybody's seen a movie you've been in will never forget that face. That face and Mr. Anthony Hogan, CPA, somehow don't go together. They recognize you and for sure they'll start taking a closer look at me."

Kim, who had been almost no place that wasn't engineered by the Studio's PR department, knew this was true. She still couldn't believe that if she just showed up somewhere on her own, without the flacks beating the drums ahead of time, there'd be any commotion.

Flattered, she put on the babushka and dark glasses. "Just call me Shirley Abramovitz," she said.

Movie people really did hang out at the Holiday House. Why, there was Elizabeth Taylor with Michael Wilding. And a couple of tables away, Eleanor Powell and Glenn Ford. Kim saw at least a dozen other faces that looked vaguely familiar.

They got a warm welcome. "Good evening, Mr. Hogan," said the maître d'hotel. "It's been a long time."

"Tax return time," said Mark in his higher, unnatural voice. "Busy concocting dodges for a lot of VIPIs."

"VIPIs?" asked the maître d'hotel.

"Very Important People Indeed," said Mark.

The maître d'hotel seated them and allowed that the Columbia River salmon was "especially tasty tonight."

"Almost eighteen, is that right?" Mark asked. "Legally you're not allowed to drink. On the other hand, if you're the new secretary of the respectable Mr. Anthony Hogan ..."

Kim joined Mark in a daiquiri.

"This is one of the ways I get my kicks," Mark confided, "getting into this Anthony Hogan get-up and then coming to a place like this that's always full-up with industry people. Not once has anybody ever caught on. This is the first time I've done it since I've been married to Carrie. Carrie doesn't go for the disguise idea and her picture's been in the paper enough she'd be recognized."

Throughout the dinner, with a whole bottle of chablis to do justice to the salmon, Mark did almost all the talking. He talked a lot about himself. He told her how he had dropped out of high school when he was sixteen and run away to New York. He told her he had nearly starved there for two years in the Depression. Finally he met and married a theatrical agent fifteen years older than himself and she got his career started ... bit parts in straw hat theaters, then bigger parts in a couple of minor Broadway hits, then the call to the movies. He told her interesting morsels of Studio gossip. In some detail he described his famous run-in with the Boss, when he went in to demand a fat salary raise. He got every cent he asked for, Mark told her, but not until the Boss had cried and begged and cursed and threatened to run him out of Hollywood.

They were dipping into strawberry parfaits when Mark said, "You had something on your mind. You wanted to talk to me."

Kim panicked slightly. When she first said that to him, her

only thought was to have the chance of being alone with him. At the Studio almost anything about the picture would be excuse enough to want to talk to him. Now it had better be pretty good to justify his giving up an evening and taking her out to dinner.

"I think this is a dopey movie," she said, not knowing just where she was heading.

Mark laughed. "You're a smart girl. Now don't tell me you've just made this discovery."

"It's especially dopey the part we're at now."

"Our so-called bedroom scene?"

The cocktail, the wine, and a full stomach gave Kim the boldness to follow on this track. "I don't believe that's the way those two people would act in real life."

"Are you saying you don't think there's such a thing as marital fidelity?"

"No, I'm not saying that. But I don't think that man and that girl would act like that once they got into that . . . situation."

"You mean you think you should be crawling into bed with me or I should be crawling into bed with you?"

Mark had a twinkle in his eye. Kim felt herself blushing. "I know that can't actually be shown in a movie but there must be a way of hinting that's what really happened. Because I think that's what that man and that girl would do. They might hate themselves or each other afterward. But he wouldn't be making that silly speech and sending her away. I just don't believe it."

"If the scene played that way, you'd be letting the man and the girl in for a hell of a lot of punishment. Before the picture was over they'd have to be punished severely for their terrible sin."

"Is it such a terrible sin?"

"According to the movie censor it is. But I must say I find myself gagging on those god-awful lines they wrote for me to say."

Kim smiled, quivering with some nameless thrill of excitement.

Mark consulted his watch. "Almost show-time. The real reason for bringing you here."

He ordered brandies for each of them. When they came, he led her out to an enormous bar suspended over a cluster of foam-covered rocks. The last faint orange streak of sunset was slipping into the sea. Concealed floodlights lit up the rocks. Every thrust of the surf against the rocks brought thousands of flashes of silver, like a shower of coins.

"All those little silver things you see down there," said

Mark, "are fish. They're called grunion. They come here by the million to spawn. They do it at just a certain time. You can clock them just like the swallows coming back to Capistrano."

Kim was entranced with the pageant of sardinelike fishes washing up on the shore. She felt sorry for them when Mark told her that beach-dwellers waited eagerly for this spawning period and went out with canvas bags and buckets and scooped up as many as they could catch and would bring them home to fry them in butter.

"Right now," said Kim dreamily, "I'd like nothing better than to take off my shoes and stockings and let the ocean and all those sweet little fishes come rolling over my feet."

"I'm afraid you can't do it here," said Mark, "with all those rocks. But if that's what you'd really like to do I'll take you some place where you can do it."

They drove back down the coastal highway. Mark pointed out the Colony, which was a group of exclusively guarded beach houses at Malibu where some of the biggest stars lived. A little further on, he turned off the highway into a narrow beachside road that rolled around to a dead end. Mark led Kim down a catwalk to a rickety frame house that stood off by itself in almost scary isolation. It also stood on some stilts. It had dark shutters and a captain's walk.

Mark led Kim by the hand, his other hand carrying a flashlight to light the way. He flashed his torch on a nameplate just outside the front door. It read: "A. HOGAN."

"See?" he said. "I live here. I mean, Anthony Hogan lives here.

"Here, just leave your bag on the chair," he said, not putting on any lights. "Now come on and you can meet the grunion."

Kim took off her shoes and stockings. She was going to put them down in the sand but Mark reached out for them. It was an intimate gesture that thrilled her. She ran up and down the beach just inside the line where the surf was washing against the sand. A small crescent of platinum moon was on the rise. She thought it was all supremely beautiful . . . the shine across the sea, the feel of the icy water, and the tiny fish lapping across her feet, and Mark Spencer, America's No. 1 male heart-throb, alias Anthony Hogan, standing there holding her shoes and stockings.

"A goddess from out of the sea," Mark saluted her.

Inside he gave her a towel to dry her feet. With the lights on, she was a little disappointed to see that it was the beach cottage of an ordinary person and not a movie star. There were just a few basic pieces of white-painted rattan furniture outfitting a longish and thinnish living room and a smallish, square-shaped bedroom. There was also a tiny, functional kitchen measuring about six by three feet. A tile pattern of linoleum covered the floors of the entire cottage.

"Very plain, as you can see," said Mark. "Basically, Hogan's a very plain guy."

"How does Carrie like it?" asked Kim.

"She's never been here."

"I like it."

"Now I'm going to have one little nightcap," said Mark, "and then I'm going to take you home."

"I'd like one too."

Mark lifted an eyebrow significantly. But he poured her a small whiskey from a cabinet bar in a corner of the living room.

Kim knew that he meant to keep his word. He meant they should finish their drinks and leave. She also knew she would never "fall" for him. She liked him. She liked him a lot. Everything that had happened that night had increased her liking and respect for him. Even with Mark's disguise as Anthony Hogan she couldn't for one moment not be aware of the sexual attraction that reduced so many women to simpering idiots ready and willing to wash his feet with their kisses.

But as Kim always said about any of her love affairs, she knew from the very beginning—from the first date, her first sight of a man—whether it was going to build into anything. If she never saw Mark Spencer again in her life, she would always have a warm spot in her heart for him because he had been so kind to her. But she wouldn't remember him with a pining heart. And yet, and yet . . . she couldn't let it go. She was curious and tempted. Maybe, she said afterward, it was just being able to say she had something so many other women could only dream of having.

"I thought I was going out with Mark Spencer," she said. "And I've spent a whole evening with Anthony Hogan."

"Anthony Hogan's a nice guy," said Mark. "I was hoping you'd like him."

"I do like him. But not as much as I like Mark Spencer. Can't I see Mark Spencer tonight at all?"

"Can do," said Mark, "if that's what you'd like."

The Anthony Hogan trappings, the hairpiece and the moustache and the ears and the nose, dropped off and Kim saw the real face of her co-star.

"That's better," said Kim. "But Mark Spencer doesn't dress like that."

"Sorry," said Mark. "I don't keep any Mark Spencer clothes here."

Kim gulped her highball and said, "You can at least take off the Anthony Hogan clothes."

"Baby, you're something," said Mark, shaking his head. "Usually it's the guy who tells the gal to get undressed."

"I just said I wanted to see Mark Spencer without any of the Anthony Hogan stuff."

"You could be in for a big disappointment, you know."

The second he started taking his coat off Kim thought she was seeing an old movie. She thought she was seeing that old movie where Mark found himself sharing his room in an overbooked hotel with a young woman who arrived late and had no other choice but to move in with him or sit up all night in the lobby. The young woman thinks Mark'll play the gentleman by giving her the bed while he sleeps on the floor fully clothed. Nothing doing, sister. She watches him strip down to his jockey shorts and then turns her back and covers her eyes in horror. He stretches out on his side of the bed and wishes her a good night with pleasant dreams. She waits until he's asleep before lying down on the other edge of the bed. It's she who keeps all her clothes on. For added security she stacks her suitcases on the bed between her and Mark.

Kim had no intention of behaving like that ridiculous heroine.

In telling me about the events years later, she could have blamed it all on the considerable amount she had had to drink that night—that night was her real initiation into drinking—but she didn't put the blame on alcohol. Without a drop to drink she'd have done the same thing, she said.

Kim was always one of those females who could get out of her clothes faster than the hottest male. Mark was just unbuckling his belt when Kim stood before him naked as a jaybird.

"God alive!" Mark exclaimed.

He nearly strangled in his pants legs trying to get his pants off. Then he stood in the jockey shorts he had made famous. Not the same pair, of course. These were lighter, silkier, almost transparent. Kim had a fleeting memory of Cal Sommers as Mark approached her. She shivered with anticipation.

"This isn't the way the script goes," said Mark. "Are you sure this is what you want?"

"I told you the script was dopey," said Kim.

Mark took her in his arms and kissed her tenderly. She felt his hardness thrust against her and almost went faint in his arms. Mark kissed her again, this time full and firm on the lips. Then he scooped her up, bride-across-the-threshold fashion, and carried her into the bedroom. Gently he put her on the wide bed with its deep blue satin sheets. The touch of the sheets was exciting in itself. She lay there watching Mark opening windows and drawing blinds. He moved to turn off the lamp and climb in beside her.

"No," she said, holding his hand back from the switch. "Take them off first so I can see."

"Nosy little witch," he said.

He pulled off the distended shorts. She gulped at the sight of his magnificent maleness.

"They should call you Hercules," Kim giggled, "instead of the Giant."

When she got around to jotting down notes in her Little Lavender Book, Kim gave Mark her highest ratings. He took his time with her. It was as if there were all the time in the world and getting there was the end in itself. His fingertips sensitively explored the whole surface and all the orifices of her body. Then his lips traced the route of his fingertips. Fingers and mouth returned to the special areas of excitement. He whispered to her, sweet nothings at first and then the blunter language of sex. The raw words excited her shamelessly. "Say it again," she begged.

He said the words into her ear again and again with hot drafts of breath and tongue probings of her ear. Then all talk between them stopped. He stretched his body across hers and tongued his way into a deep exploration of her mouth. He rolled slightly from left to right, tickling her nipples with his chest hairs and pressing his inflamed member into her belly. At no point did he make any move to enter her.

"Now!" screamed Kim, breaking away from his mouth. "Fuck me!"

Kim thought she would go out of her mind during an interminable delay while he used his hand to guide the tip of his penis lightly, teasingly into her navel and then in slow, sweeping movements across her stomach and through her pubic bush. She was wet and close to ecstasy when she felt that huge head make its first tentative movement inside her.

"Oh, God!" she cried.

"I'm not going to hurt you." Mark whispered. "Don't be afraid."

"Put it all in! Fuck me!"

Two millimeters forward and one back, Mark slipped expertly back and forth, inching himself deeper and deeper inside. When he was completely inside her, he stopped dead still. He embraced her tightly, kissed her deeply on the lips. "I almost forgot," he murmured. "Just one second."

Kim almost wept as she felt him withdraw from her. She

91

watched him snap on a light. He took something out of a dresser drawer. It was a rubber sheath which he began rolling up over his penis like a pair of stockings.

"I hate these things," he grunted. "But it's better to be safe."

Kim watched fascinated, wondering how such a nothing little bit of rubber could be made to stretch over such an enormous thing as Mark's dong. But it did, stretching itself thin as a second skin.

On top of her again, Mark renewed his kisses and caresses. He guided the tip of his armored penis over her tummy again until she got so feverish she yelled for Mark to come inside her.

Mark entered, gradually and insinuatingly as before, thrusting forward and backward. When she had all of him, he kept up the to-and-fro motions, thrusting forward and moving back so far she feared he would leave her. Then he moved within a closer range, taking shorter strokes, stepping up the beat, stroking faster, faster, faster.

"Baby, baby, baby," Mark moaned into her ear. He went into a stream of alley words that fired their mutual excitement. He waited for her, sustaining the pace. When she was ready, he raced the tempo to join her in her moment of release. He covered her mouth to muffle her scream. Tears began flowing down her cheeks. Mark lapped them up with his tongue.

For a long time he held her in his arms saying nothing. Kim guessed she might have drifted off to sleep. She came alert when he smacked her lightly on the behind.

"Whew!" he blew into her ear. "That was beautiful."

"Yes," she agreed.

"Like they're always saying in those bad movies, 'Thanks, I guess I needed that.' Except it's always some hysterical dame who's just gotten a slap across the kisser who's saying it."

"You haven't done it with Maura . . . or anybody . . . since your wife's been gone?" Kim asked slyly in the darkness.

"Nope. I've been good as gold. No circuses for three weeks. Practically a record for me. Jesus, this is messy!" He jumped out of bed and Kim heard the ping of something being dropped into the toilet bowl. "If you could have seen how I filled my little loving cup," he said, as he flopped down beside her, "you'd believe I've been good as gold."

They dozed in each other's arms. Again it was Kim who was being roused. "It's late," Mark said softly. "All good things must come to an end. I've got to get you home."

"No," said Kim.

"Your mother will soon be calling the cops."

"At this hour," said Kim, "she won't know where she's at. Or care where I'm at."

"*I* should be getting home."

"No." Kissing him urgently on the lips, she said, "More."

Half-groaning, Mark reached out for her again. There was no more thought of getting home—or even getting much sleep—for either of them that night. Twice more Mark ravished her almost in the same way he had taken her the first time, carefully, gradually, wooing her again, and winning her completely. He showered then and returned to their bed smelling new and fresh and cleansed. Tactfully, he wanted to know if Kim would like to enjoy his body in some of the ways he had enjoyed hers. Oh, how she would! For the rest of the night, with Mark as her patient and painstaking teacher, Kim became a devoted student in the arts and techniques of pleasuring the body of a man.

"No place he didn't lick me," she said about that night of ecstasy with Mark Spencer, "and no place I didn't lick him."

With all they had been and done to each other that night, Kim had the courage in the darkness—between their rounds of lovemaking—to tell Mark that she had accidentally overheard him the day he visited Sarah Blandings in her dressing room.

"That's one dame I don't go for," said Mark, his voice rising. "That was the first day on the set. And it's the last time it happened, I can tell you. We had hardly been introduced when she said to me, 'You're supposed to be such a hot shot in the sack. I could do with some servicing. Then I'll tell you how good you are.' You'd have thought she was challenging me to a duel. I thought to myself, 'Okay, sister. You asked for it, but you're not going to like what you get.' She was trying to use me and I made up my mind I'd beat her to the draw. I made up my mind she wasn't going to have any fun out of our little rendezvous in her dressing room. It was going to be strickly 'Bam, bam, thank you, ma'am.' I'd finish my business before she hardly knew I was there. If you were anywhere around, you must have heard the screaming."

"I did," said Kim. Reaching out to draw him to her again, she said, "I thought that's the way it must have been. I knew if it wasn't going right it was her fault."

Once more, just as the light of day was breaking, they made love.

Mark had his hands clasped behind his head when Kim came out of the shower. He was gazing thoughtfully at the opposite wall. "Do you want to hear how that scene should go?" he asked her as she lay down beside him again in bed.

"Sure," she said.

"Well, of course, they sleep together—the girl and her brother-in-law. Not wild horses or all the commandments or codes of honor in the world could have kept them apart. It was just one of those things that had to happen under the circumstances. They both wanted it. They both enjoyed it thoroughly. They wake up with pleasant memories and no regrets. But he tells her that it probably can't happen again, and this must be their little secret. As long as it remains their secret, no one can get hurt. He tells her how deeply in love he is with his wife and what's just happened has nothing to do with that. He tells the girl how beautiful she is. He tells her what a gift for lovemaking she has. He tells her what a lot of giving and receiving of love she will have in her lifetime. He tells her she'll be able to have anything and anybody in this world she wants . . ."

Kim finally stopped his speech with a sweet kiss. She knew exactly what he was trying to tell her, pretending it was a script he was rewriting. He needn't have worried. She was absurdly happy because of the night he had given her. He had awakened her and brought her to life. She would love him forever without being the least bit in love with him.

Chapter 11

Kim always regarded the night with Mark Spencer as a special milestone in her life. It was the night that separated the girl from the woman. Afterward she always thought of herself as a woman—and free to act like one. And she owed it all to Mark.

The picture she made with Mark and Maura Anderson was a dud. But the reviews of *The Kid Sister-in-Law* pointed out that she was no longer a "kid" but a woman. A typical review read:

It's not much of a picture. But it doesn't have to be if it's got Mark Spencer. What it has besides Mark Spencer—in lieu of a script—is two of the most beautiful young women in films. It has Maura Anderson, Hollywood's newest candidate for the throne of reigning Sex Queen. It also has the unforgettably beautiful young Kimberley Hudson, who henceforth can never be mistaken for a youngster or even an adolescent . . .

Fan mail for Kim began arriving in great volume. The experience was so new to her that she demanded to read every letter. These weren't the awkward scrawls of kids who had seen *Wendy* and were writing in for a picture of her with the dog. Now she heard from everybody. Mature men and women—married and single—smitten young bachelors, adolescent schoolgirls who idolized her. And she got a lot of correspondence from the wonderful world of weirdos:

"I'm hung about as good as you're built. How'd you like to . . ."

"Would I ever love to fuck you! How about it? And I can come and come and come . . ."

Kim got a kick out of the form reply every writer got, no matter how filthy his letter might have been. It read:

Thanks for your kind expression of appreciation. I do wish I could reply individually to everyone who writes to me. I am sure you will understand that this is not humanly possible. But I do want you to know how grateful I am for your support. Having fans like you is one of the greatest rewards of working in pictures.

One day Kim found a letter that interested her. It wasn't gushy and it wasn't obscene. The writer of the letter said he was a senior at UCLA and captain of the swimming team. An enclosed snapshot of himself showed him to be a handsome, muscular, pleasant-looking young man. After a few low-key compliments he ended his letter with, "Don't tell me you already know how to swim. Would I ever love to teach you!"

Kim decided to answer this letter personally. "Okay on the swimming lessons," she wrote him, "if they're free." She gave him her phone number at the apartment.

Larry Scanlon really did teach Kim how to swim. No doubt he learned a thing or two from Kim, too.

Larry picked her up in front of her apartment house one afternoon in his old third-hand Packard touring car. He was something new to Kim. He was a very rah-rah college boy, full of enthusiasm for the simplest things. He could grow lyrical about how blue the sky was or the tacos at the Hacienda or the genius of a high school chemistry teacher.

He was eager to show off his college and his fraternity house and the pool where he trained. He was just as eager to show off his parents' home in Pasadena, which was a white rambling bungalow with red tile roof and a large swimming pool. He was even eager to show off his parents. Except for

95

the fact that Larry was an only child, they were a typical prosperous suburban family, with their easy manners and sociability. Larry was plainly the apple of their eye. As the four of them ate steaks on the patio, the elder Scanlons beamed with pride and wonder over their son, who had somehow used his abundant charms to wangle a date with a pretty young movie actress.

"Did you mean it?" Larry finally got around to asking her, when he was driving her home. "About wanting to take swimming lessons."

"Sure," said Kim. "I've never once in my whole life been in a pool or a lake or the ocean. If anybody threw me in the water, I'd sink right to the bottom."

Kim was marking time waiting to go into a long-forgotten B number called *This Sorry Angel*. In that one she played a girl whose father owns a secretarial school. She almost loses her virtue to the man who teaches stenotyping. Just in the nick of time she learns he's not single, as he told her he was, but has an estranged wife and three kids living in another city.

While she waited for *This Sorry Angel* to begin, she spent her days in the school room with Miss Bitters and checking in with Wardrobe and the publicity department. Late in the afternoon a couple of days a week, after his classes were over, Larry would pick Kim up and drive her out to Pasadena. Good as his word he gave her swimming lessons in the big pool. Afterward there would usually be a cook-out dinner with his parents. In the late evening he would drive her home again.

"He's cute," said Kim.

"Has he tried to get fresh?" I asked.

"Not yet. Maybe he just wants to be friends." She laughed. "He's sort of funny. The other day he looked at me in my bathing suit—we were in the pool—and he said, 'You know, I really think the breast stroke must have been named for you.' Then he blushed all over. Even his chest and legs got red. Like he'd said something real terrible."

One day Kim was wondering what it would be like to be married to someone like Larry Scanlon. "He's going to be a doctor. You just know he's going to be successful at it. He'll never have to worry about money. He'll be just like his parents. They're so normal they seem strange. I mean, it's so different from the nutty way I grew up."

"If he ever asked you to marry him, would you?"

"No. At least I don't think I would. That probably makes me a big dope. This thing here at the Studio is so crazy. They give you a seven-year contract but they can cut it off at the middle or the end of the year any old year. If it ends, then what? Being married to a doctor would take care of the money thing anyway."

I knew what she meant. At fourteen years old I was already facing a shaky future. In a couple of months our contract at the Studio would be up and there hadn't been a word said about any renewal. As far as the movies were concerned, singing sister acts were going out of style fast. The most likely bet was that if and when the Studio or any other studio wanted us for anything we'd be hired on a one-shot basis. Our West Coast agent thought our future was with clubs and records and television variety shows. Papa had finally pushed the daisies about a year ago. He left being sincerely mourned by maybe nobody except Mama. But Mama was still with us, thank God, and we still had to take care of her as well as ourselves.

"He's twenty-one," Kim said about Larry, "but he seems more like sixteen. I have a feeling he might never seem to be really much more than sixteen. No matter how old or successful he gets to be."

In fairness to Kim, she had rejected completely the idea of anything serious with Larry Scanlon before she got the call from Geordie Harmon. But the call from Geordie closed out the chapter on Larry a little sooner.

Geordie actually caught up with her just as she was leaving the Studio to meet Larry at the main gate outside. He traced her to the phone extension on the sound stage of the new Billy Baxter movie, where Kim had been kibitzing with Doc Baxter.

"Miss Kimberley Hudson," came the smooth, well-bred voice from the other end of the line, "where have you been all my life? Geordie Harmon here."

From all the Studio gossip, from a thousand newspaper fan magazine pictures showing him escorting the most beautiful women in Hollywood, Kim was well aware of who Geordie Harmon was. It crossed her mind for a second that the call might be a hoax.

"Hi, Geordie Harmon."

"I said, 'Where have you been—' "

"I thought my turn would never come."

"I bet. Well, I've been watching you. I got a pair of binoculars up here and I look out the window a lot. I've been watching you a long time. I've been waiting for you to grow up enough so I could take you out and not get arrested for picking up San Quentin quail. Know where you're going to be tomorrow night?"

"Not yet. I never plan that far ahead."

"They're preeming *The Death of a Star* at Grauman's Chinese Theater tomorrow night and I want you to be my date. We see the flick and have a spot of supper afterward. Okay?"

"Okay," said Kim.

"Go to wardrobe tomorrow and tell them to lend you some suitable rags. I know where you live. I'll pick you up at seven thirty."

Kim almost floated into Larry's car. Tactfully she gave him no clue to her head-in-the-clouds giddiness.

"My parents are off in St. Louis at a dentists' convention," Larry told her. "We'll have a lesson and a swim and go out some place to eat."

Kim had a feeling this would be the last time she had a date with Larry. But nothing in her high spirits that day could have given Larry the same feeling. She obeyed all his instructions with girlish glee. She even managed to keep her eyes open under water, which she had always balked at before. She did four consecutive laps of the pool, up and back and up and back again. At his command she finished them without once grabbing onto the rail at either end to rest.

"Now the great Olympic champion Larry Scanlon," he called out to her, "is going to demonstrate some diving feats. Stand back, fans."

Standing at the far end of the pool from the diving board, Kim wildly applauded his double somersaults and jackknifes and side flips. "Fantastic!" she shouted to him.

"Get ready for this, Kim. Come in a few feet. Now put your legs way apart. Right. Now watch."

Bounce, bounce. Leap. Flip. Plunge. A long, lean, muscled fish whizzed between her legs and surfaced behind her. It flapped its drenched fins on her shoulder blades.

"Terrific! Do it again."

At Kim's coaxing Larry repeated his trick. Again and again. He put the whole pool in motion. The motion was whipped up some more by a rising breeze in the eucalyptus trees that encircled the back yard. The soft massaging of the tepid waves on her legs and thighs and the warming flush of the falling sun worked like aphrodisiacs. The quiver in her groin was sexual yearning.

"Once more," she said to Larry.

"Gladly."

In the few seconds it took Larry to pitter-patter wet-footed across the concrete edging of the pool and scramble up the ladder of the diving board, Kim had flung off both her bathing cap and her bathing suit.

He stopped, paralyzed, at the tip of the diving board.

"What's the matter?" Kim asked innocently.

As if she didn't know! As if she didn't know the effect such a sight would have upon a college boy who for sure had done a lot more talking about women's bodies than looking at them. As if she didn't know he had never seen a body like this. As if she didn't know that last stain of sun was putting her in her best light, painting her white body with seductive pinks and golds and violets and sparking that great mane of copper hair with flickering fireflies.

"What are you waiting for?" she called to him.

He stood staring. "Aphrodite," he said, barely loud enough for her to hear him.

"Aphrodite?"

He shook his head, smiling.

"Jump!" Kim cried.

Larry jumped. This time she caught the long, lean, muscled fish. She caught it by the head. Swiftly she clamped her knees on its neck in a tight vise. She held fast for a moment, feeling its curly head bobbing against her rear cleavage.

She released him and he popped up behind her. She turned around and saw him staring, jaw agape. She also saw the rising bulge stretching the front of the brief nylon swimming trunks.

"Why don't you take it off?" Kim suggested.

Larry gulped. "It's sort of . . . embarrassing."

"No more embarrassing," said Kim, looking only at his trunks, "than leaving them on."

As he hesitated, Kim reached out and took hold of the top of his trunks. He put one of his hands there too. With their combined yank, he was quickly out of his trunks.

"You've got nothing to be ashamed of," said Kim.

Larry's penis had the long, sleek, straight lines of a book opener. Kim reached out to stroke it. It leapt upward out of her grasp. Larry wrapped his arms around her in a fumbling embrace. In an eager-beaverish schoolboy way he came all apart . . . fat, sucking kisses hitting off-mouth, hands wandering astray, his upended penis pressing randomly across the surface of Kim's belly.

"Let's get out of the pool," said Kim.

"Good idea."

He started to lead Kim away from the pool, toward the house. "No, here," she said. She spread herself down on the siding of the pool, still warm and sensuous from the afternoon sun. "Let's do it here."

The college boy went out of his mind. He charged into her immediately. He threw back his head and howled like a

99

werewolf. He pumped wildly for a few seconds and stopped short. "Oh, shit!"

"What's the matter?"

"I haven't got anything on." He lay flat and unmoving on top of her. "I'm ready to go and I haven't got anything here. I never thought this would happen. I keep my Trojans in a dresser back in the frat house. We can go back there. We can——"

"No," said Kim. "Now. Here."

"I love you till I'm out of my head," Larry gasped, starting his pumping again. "I'd marry you so fast if anything happened. I'd take care of you to the end of time. Aw, shit, you don't want that. Nothing'll happen, Kim. I'll pull out . . ."

At the moment it was frustrating. Later she remembered him fondly for his consideration.

"I'm sorry," he whispered. Not a second too soon he pulled out abruptly, dropping his seed beside them on the edge of the pool.

"I'm sorry," he repeated a moment later, lying beside her. "I'm sorry I didn't satisfy you. I just didn't want to take any chances. I'd love to have stayed in you and got you knocked up. But that's no way to get a girl . . ."

The next afternoon Kim paid Dr. Wetherbee a visit.

"I'd like to have one of those things," she told him, "you put inside you so you won't get knocked up."

"You mean a diaphragm?" asked Dr. Wetherbee.

"I guess that's what you call it."

"You don't need that yet, do you?"

"Yeah, I think it's about time."

Kim got a funny little tremor of excitement wondering what was going through Dr. Wetherbee's mind when he fitted her with the contraption.

"Come back in a week or two," he said, his jaw going dropsy. "I want to check that thing out. Sometimes it can be pretty irritating."

Even at fourteen I had so little understanding of sexual matters I could only be amazed at Kim's experiences and the things she knew about.

"Did you get that thing put in you," I asked nervously, "because you think Geordie Harmon might try . . . something?"

"Not the first night," said Kim. "But it'll be nice to feel safe all the time. You never know when something's going to happen. The motto of the Boy Scouts is Be Prepared. I don't know why the Girl Scouts don't have the same motto."

"I've been here five years and I never went to a premiere,"

I said. "Now I'll soon be leaving and I guess I'll never get to one."

"Oh, Gina, I'm sorry."

"I guess I'm still pretty young for anybody to be taking me to a premiere."

"I mean I'm sorry you're leaving."

She sounded sincere and I was touched. In the four years I had known her it seemed like I was always standing in her shadow. It was I who looked for her and it was Kim we talked mostly about when we were together. I knew she liked to come to our house when she could for Mama's home cooking and I knew she was genuinely devoted to Mama. When she told me about something naughty she had done, she'd always add, "Don't tell Mama." She confided in me and I knew in her own way she was fond of me. But there was always something cool and superior and apart about her. I couldn't remember that she had ever touched me. It was really something to hear her say she'd be sorry to see me go.

"Gina, I hope we'll always keep in touch."

"Of course we will."

"Gina, I just feel my life the way it's going so far will make a great book some day. You probably know more about me than anybody else. My life really started when I came here. Barton's already like something that never happened. If we keep in touch, you can write it all down some day—the story of my life—and make a million."

At the moment I was crestfallen. Later, of course, I realized that such egotism and self-centeredness were the hallmarks of a star.

Chapter 12

I can't wait to see Kim at the reunion. There'll be so much to catch up on. I'm dying to know what gives in the matrimonial department and what's between her and the new Mystery Man. Or whatever. Say this for Kim, there's hardly a dull moment in her life. If you've been out of touch with her for a month—let alone a year—there's a lot of catching up to do.

Our lives are such a contrast you wouldn't believe we've gone on being friends at all. But maybe in friendship, as in sex or love, *viva la difference!*

Days I'm in the A&P trying to decide between chopped

chuck or more Bumble Bee tuna ("Not tuna fish again, Mama!") it kills me to think she can pick up five hundred thousand clams by walking through some dog of a picture. It's not the mil plus percentage she was getting a few years back. But the business has changed. Nobody's getting it up front now. They get it when they've made it back for the big banking mucky-mucks.

All right, sing no sad songs for me. Not long ago I was almost at the end of my rope. But I'm alive. I've got my sanity. Slowly I'm crawling out. I'll be all right. If my present claim to fame is to write novels that "tell it like it is" and get called dirty, so be it. The thing is I'm alive. If you've got that much going for you, anything is possible. We should all remember that.

Thinking about Kim, I think: She can be in a clinic in Switzerland getting overhauled and recharged and stripped down from stem to stern. But if the reason for it is to try to pull the wool over the eyes of a young lover, forget it. If you've been in the public eye since you were a kid, you can never lie about your age. I don't care who you are. Kimberley Hudson or Queen Elizabeth. The whole world knows how old you are.

Kim is thirty-eight. She still has the face and the body that could launch a thousand rockets. But the thought of getting older terrifies her. "God, Gina," she said once, "how I'll hate to be forty!" Now that particular biggie is just around the corner.

There are times when Kim seems older than God. Other times she's more of a child than my Timothy, who is six.

For the most part Kim's life is yecchier than anybody else's I can think of. Including my own. Long ago *Magic Screen* came out with a screaming story about her called: "A Scandal at 20—A Legend Before She Was 30!"

By what funky throw of the dice people are thrown together—and cling together—I'll never know. One thing I do know Kim and I have in common is we're both survivors. Like me, Kim's been through the mill a dozen times and come out sawdust. Somehow we both manage to paste ourselves together again.

In spite of everything, I do love her. On my good days I remember only the dear things about her ... how much damn fun she can be when she's not breaking down ... her booming laugh and gutsy sense of humor ... her basic honesty ... the way she digs food and can eat up a cyclone ... her delight in gossip ... her sudden attacks of generosity ...

Those times I get a warm, protective feeling toward her and I want to shield her from all the crap in the world like she was one of my kids. I want to tell the press they don't understand the first damn thing about her. I'd like to cry thinking how much she seems to have and how she really has nothing at all.

When I'm down, I think she is a mean, selfish, self-centered bitch who is getting back about what she puts out. When I cry, I cry alone. When she cries, she always has a full complement of soothers. Including me. Where the hell was she when I needed her? Long time no see, no hear. Except for a couple of breezy transatlantic calls and a check one Christmas. ("Go stuff yourself and stuff the kids' stockings.")

Kim and I have this in common too. We both got married about the same time. Me for the first time. Kim for the fifth. ("I think my fifth will take," her little joke went, "considering how I take to a fifth of vodka.") We both thought this was going to be the supreme, enduring commitment of our lives. Kim, like me, has apparently lived long enough to learn better.

When the thing with David Glasgow got going, everybody called Kim a home-wrecker. They accused her of stealing a man from his wife and children. Well, that's garbage. No woman can get a guy who isn't ready to walk. Any more than she can hold a man who doesn't want to be held. As for David, he had the reputation of being a horny Scotsman who has screwed everything that would hold still long enough. Even a lamp post if you'd put a skirt on it.

They didn't stop there. They called Kim a ball-breaker. They said David Glasgow could have been the finest Shakespearean actor of his time, that he could have gone on to become one of the immortals of the English stage. But Kim broke him. She bastardized his talent and turned him into a movie hack who just went for the buck. She needed him to support the life of luxury she had got hooked on ... the spectacular jewelry and the mile-long yachts, the ski chalets in Switzerland and the haciendas in Mexico and the castles in Ireland, the restless roaming across the earth—always traveling flamboyantly deluxe. So they said.

But who really knows? The votes on Kim will never be in until she takes her last breath.

If Kim does have somebody else, I'm not surprised. In fact I'm surprised she stuck it with David this long. She has never been one to suffer humiliations gamely. You keep hearing about David's extracurricular activities. Not to mention his monumental boozing, which is common knowledge.

Of course I'm one to be speculating on other people's

shaky marriages. My own marriage turned out to be about as much of a mess as one woman and one man could make it. Well, one woman and one pseudo-man. By the time I discovered what Matt was, I had had it Up To Here with Tinseltown West and Tinseltown East and all the phony-baloney garbage of showbiz. All I wanted was out—and to take my kids with me. If I never connected with another man again, I couldn't care less. Oh, God, just give me a little peace, I prayed. Give me that and I'll never complain or hunger for anything else.

Say this for a lousy marriage. It makes a better story than a happy one. I wrote about my life and hard times with Matt in a novel called *How Gay It Was!* Would you believe there are people in this day and age who didn't "get" the title? There are still letters coming in from shocked and angry readers who must have opened the book thinking it was going to be a fun, romantic thing ... maybe the reminiscences of some hundred-and-two-year-old lady remembering her girlhood and coming-of-age in Gramercy Park in the 1880s.

How Gay It Was! had a modest success in the hard-cover version. Now it's in paperback and doing sensationally well. Nearly a million copies so far, according to my latest royalty statement. Which is a good thing, because when you're divorced from a smart showbiz lawyer who doesn't want to pay alimony or child support, you're really fucked. Just try to squeeze one penny out of the bastard. He knows all the ropes and disappearing acts. So when you've been living on the tab for five years, you have to "move a lot of product"—as they say in the book business—to get yourself out of hock with the butcher, the baker, the candlestick-maker, and everybody else.

My next novel will be about *us*—the child stars of yesterday—and what really happened to us. Seeing all us young innocents on the magic silver screen, who'd have dreamt so many of us could fuck up our lives so completely?

Nothing like us ever happened before. Or ever will again. We were the most famous kids in the history of the world. We were like *royalty*. We sat on the laps of presidents and we got patted on the head by kings and queens and grand duchesses. Millions and millions of poor wretches who hardly knew where their next plate of beans was coming from shook their piggy banks to get dimes or quarters so they could watch us be cute as hell up there on the old silver screen. We were like everybody's adopted kids. Everybody wanted to wrap us up, take us home, and smother us with love. *Us.* Well, we *did* come across as lovable. *Then.*

God, what a bunch we were! They're not making child stars the way they used to. In fact, they're not making them at all. Why? Is it because we turned out to be such a poor argument for talented kids? I mean, if we were an example of what you could expect, wasn't it better not to exploit the talents of children? Or was it because enough has come to light about us and the things that went on at the Studio so that nobody could ever again believe in the purity and innocence of kids who had been put through a meat chopper like that?

Thinking about the reunion, you have to think first about all the ones who wouldn't—*couldn't*—be there. You think about all the untimely deaths, the suicides, the alcoholics, and the junkies dying a day at a time in their separate hells, the jailees and the mental lock-ups . . .

Thinking about who wouldn't be there, you have to think first of one person. Sally Strickland. To recall Sally can reduce strong men to tears. Poor, dear Sally. She was only the most talented kid of us all. She could sing like nobody else. She could dance. She could clown. She could do soft-shoe and blackface and take pratfalls. And she could act her ass off. She was a natural. She was the little nobody born in a trunk, the weed that sprang up in the crack between the sidewalks, who could break you up one second and tear your heart out the next. The whole world loved her. She made the rest of us look sick. She was going to make show business history, become rich, get lucky in love, and live happily ever after. You know what happened. Always the pressures, pressures, pressures. The bouts of hard work, the bouts of hard play. The sex binges. Boozing. Drying out. Uppers. Downers. Finally, the tired old ticker conking out in a Cophenhagen hotel room as she slept in the arms of a new boy friend who would never become an old lover . . .

It's not much less depressing to think about survivors.

Except one survivor I'll lay you ten to one *won't* be coming to the studio reunion. "Missy" Arlen.

Everybody remembers "Missy" Arlen. For about three years back in the Depression she carried the whole damn Studio on her little back. Sixty pounds of sugar and baby-fat who lisped and sang and tap-danced and mugged her way into the hearts of half the world. Do you know that syrupy song she sang—"My Doggie's Going to Heaven"—has sold two and a half million copies of sheet music? And is still selling?

Here's a fact I'm pretty sure you *don't* know. Those darling blond curls came out of the bottle. Honestly. Her hair was straight as string and dark as molasses. I used to see

105

them "doing" her. First they'd strip the hair and it would come out this god-awful bright orange. Then you'd see one guy standing by with the coloring bottle and somebody else with the curling iron. "I just saw Miss Sun-Kissed getting her dye job," I remember Kim saying to me once. "I wonder if she's just as phony under the curls."

I never thought "Missy" was phony. I thought she was a fluke. She was just a little girl who got caught in the lens of somebody who saw her as something she could seem to be but was certainly not. She wasn't cut from the same bolt of cloth as the rest of us. Her parents never pushed. And they were honest. All her earnings went into trust funds for *her*.

"Missy" not only grew up rich. She married rich. A big orchard man in Oregon. She has four kids, you probably know, and they're all presumably healthy and happy. She couldn't care less that she was once the dimpled darling of millions. That's how I know she won't be coming. Now her big interest is ecology and saving endangered species. Any time she lets herself be interviewed or goes on a talk show it's to raise the red flag for the threatened condor or whooping crane or ivory-bill woodpecker. It seems so unfair that her own life is being threatened by a killer disease.

You know one jerk who will be there for sure? Tinker Wells. If he isn't in the brig. I could tell you any number of things Tinker's done that would get anybody else a good stiff jail sentence.

"You know," as one of the Studio lawyers said to the Boss, "you don't often come across a fourteen-year-old who's already one complete son of a bitch."

The Boss's answer became one of those classic quotes you still hear quoted in show business circles. "Yes," he said, "but don't ever forget he's *our* son of a bitch."

Yes, Tinker would be there. At fifty-two he was still trying to play juveniles. Apparently he hadn't seen the dirty joke time had played on him. Lately, I heard, he's been producing porno films. Not full-length features. But the old eight millimeter "loops" they show at stag parties and the sleaziest grind houses in Times Square. But you remember Tinker as that naughty-but-nice, full-of-Wheaties, oh-so-lovable boy-next-door in fourteen folksy Bobby Baxter movies that were all as wholesome as apples and milk.

Will Peggy Palmer show? If you remember Peggy, you remember her as the bitchiest, brattiest kid in movies. That's the part she always played. In real life she wasn't like that at all. She was soft and scared. No wonder. She had the stage

106

mother to end all stage mothers. Mrs. Palmer pushed, pushed, pushed every second of the day and stayed awake nights scheming. She made all the other mothers look like amateurs.

Peggy found her security blanket in dolls. She'd do her bratty, rotten kid bit and go home to feed and fondle her dolls. That was okay for then. But she's still "into" dolls. Now there's got to be something weird about a forty-six-year-old woman who's still playing with dolls. I read somewhere she took all the dough she made on that air freshener TV commercial and built a mansion on Doheny Drive that was an exact replica of the first doll house she had when she was a kid. I heard she had more than eight hundred dolls from almost every country in the world. She had names for all of them and kept up a personal relationship with each and every one of them. She'd sit and talk with maybe a dozen one day, chatting with them individually like parent to child. The next day she'd move on to another dozen or so. Peggy was married to somebody a long time ago—for about ten minutes. Whoever he was, he couldn't have stood a chance of competing with the dolls. They were the only real thing in her life.

Who else? "Cuddles" Malloy? Hal Harper? Bunky McAllister? Hattie Shannon?

Oh, no, not Hattie. If you read the tabloids, you know Hattie a couple of months ago was picked up in San Jose for hooking. Sad, sad Hattie. Her mother pissed away the bundle Hattie made in all those tear-jerkers where her horse was always dying or her dog was getting run over by a truck or she lived in such a filthy, falling-down shack that even the Avon lady or a drunken old Santa Claus wouldn't make a house call there. Broke, washed up, and carrying an alcoholic mother on her back, Hattie had fallen into a profession even older than make-believe.

No, Hattie wouldn't be coming.

It isn't all that important who will or won't be there. I'm curious, of course, but it's enough knowing Kim will be there.

"Indiana, it's me. I'm here!"

"Oh, Miss Spinelli. Welcome. How are you?"

Even over the phone I could hear the warm familiar rhythm of Indiana's voice, sounding a little too much like home. "I'm fine, thank you, Indiana," I said, and then rushed on, "Indiana, is she *there*? Can I talk to her?"

"No, Miss Spinelli. She isn't here."

"Not here? Indiana, that's impossible. The party starts at six and it's already after five."

"I know, Miss Spinelli. I thought she'd be here hours ago."

"And you haven't heard from her?"

"Not a word. Not since I talked to you. All I know is that she was definitely planning to be back for the party."

"Indiana, that's not like her. To say she'll be some place and not be there. Without explaining to anybody."

"It's not like her at all, Miss Spinelli. That's why I expect she may be along any minute. Her plane might have been delayed somewhere."

I consoled myself with the thought she might be cutting it as close to the bone as possible. She could be on a flight from Geneva that would be just late enough so she could make a late, late entrance at the reunion.

"Aren't you coming here, Miss Spinelli?"

I looked at my watch again. Five twenty.

"No, Indiana. I'm traveling light and I've got my party clothes on. I think I'll go straight to the Studio. I'll see you later. Would you please have Mrs. Glasgow call me the minute she gets in? She'll know where to call."

"I certainly will, Miss Spinelli. I'm sure you'll be hearing from her soon."

Soon. The word had a strange sound of foreboding. . . .

Chapter 13

Geordie Harmon was handsomer than most of the male stars of the movies. But he always said he had never had the slightest interest in acting.

When Kim met him, Geordie was twenty-six. He was tall and quite slim except for a beginning lardiness around his middle. His skin was pink and his eyes were royal blue. He had winged, wheat-colored eyebrows and eyelashes so long and sweeping that they almost looked pasted on. His nose and lips had an aristocratic thinness. His chin was dimpled.

The one thing everybody knew about Geordie Harmon was that he was rich. Stinking rich. He was the son of the vice-president of the Bank of America who was in charge of loans to film companies. Roger Harmon also happened to own an enormous hunk of shares of Studio stock. Roger Harmon was a force that even the Boss sucked up to with his toothiest smiles and sugariest flattery.

It was known that Geordie Harmon had grown up in the rich San Francisco suburb of Hillsborough. It was known he had gone to Choate and flunked out of Yale. After that Geordie's bio got a little confused and the stories conflicted. Depending on who you listened to, Geordie had either done a stint on Wall Street or an apprenticeship in a Madison Avenue advertising firm or a couple of years bumming around Europe.

Thanks to the weight his banking papa swung, Geordie at present was carried on the Studio payroll as a producer. He had as big and impressive an office in the Producers and Writers Building as any of the top-rank producers. As yet his credits were nil. He had that in common with a lot of other so-called producers in Hollywood. To date Geordie had not displayed any kind of talent around the Studio as far as anybody could see. The backbiters said his only visible talent was knowing how to raise his elbow and to take beautiful women out to dinner. They said he was usually either on the town or out of town on mysterious junkets that didn't seem to produce any results as far as movie-making was concerned. When he was in his office, they said, he spent his time cutting out paper dolls and standing at his window gazing at women through his binoculars. Much of the backbiting might have come from envy. Hollywood's always been a town of soreheads. Many of the poison tongues giving Geordie the shiv would also have given anything to change places with this handsome, well-heeled young fellow.

Geordie called for Kim in a long black limousine. He looked so beautiful and dashing in his midnight blue tuxedo with an Inverness cape thrown loosely around his shoulders. Kim's mother had everyone in the apartment house alerted to watch her daughter being handed into the back seat of this ritzy, chauffeured chariot by Prince Charming himself.

"You are the most!" He appreciatively took in all of her, her borrowed long kelly green silk gown and matching slippers, her long white gloves and the mink cape she was clutching as if somebody were about to steal it.

"I told you I've been looking at you for a long, long time," he said. "From up in my office. With my magic binoculars. I think binoculars are the greatest invention since the wheel."

"How do I look from up there?"

"Almost as sensational as you look from down here."

The way Kim looked that night can be researched in the files of the *Los Angeles Times*. In the next morning's edition she is pictured entering the theater in the glare of klieg lights and searchlights. She has her arm through Geordie's and she's smiling up at him.

They went afterward to Romanoff's for dinner. At the

door Geordie was ceremoniously greeted by the "Prince," who kissed Kim's hand when he was introduced to her.

"Who all's here?" Kim asked, looking around at the other tables.

"Who cares? You're here and that's all that counts."

He said it so matter-of-factly Kim felt her heart flutter. He never took his eyes off her. Still, Kim couldn't help but notice that Lana Turner and Lizabeth Scott were seated at other tables. She knew from the newspapers that each of them had been his date sometime before. She couldn't help wondering if all his dates got the same treatment she was getting.

Geordie downed two very dry martinis before he gave the waiter their order. And he asked for a third to be brought while they waited for their food. When he wasn't taking a gulp of drink, he talked almost continuously. His talk kept getting more open and warm.

". . . mostly trying to learn the business so far, how a picture is really made . . . finding out what everybody does, the directors, the writers, the cameramen, the cutters, the sound people, the lab technicians . . . got an idea for something that might shape up as a strong A movie and I have a writer working on a treatment . . . like to get my hands on a property that would be just right for you and I'd work like the devil to make sure every detail was just right . . ."

Geordie freely admitted he was where he was because of his father. The movie companies depended on the backing of the banks. It was a good investment of the Studio to have the son of a friendly banker on the payroll, even though Geordie's salary hadn't "paid off" for the Studio yet. Geordie knew that sooner or later he would have made it on his own, without his father. But as his father's son, he confessed, he had a lot of privileges even top-ranking producers didn't have. For one thing, he could come and go as he pleased. He didn't mind admitting he had used this privilege to the hilt. But coming and going he always kept his ears open. He was trying to learn how the public felt about movies in this time when the public for movies was shrinking and the industry was having rough going. He always kept his eyes open too. He was always on the look-out for promising properties. For instance, next week he was off to London. There he would take in a lot of plays in the West End with an eye to their suitability as movie vehicles. Oh, lordie, if he could just find something that would be great for Kim!

"You have got to be sensational!" Geordie exclaimed over an after-dinner Grand Marnier. "I wish I could say I discovered you."

In the limousine he went into a semi-doze, holding her hand.

At the door to her apartment house he kissed her on the cheek. "Wonderful evening," he whispered, "wonderful girl. You'll be hearing from me."

Kim stayed awake until after dawn in a state of excitement. It had been the most glamorous night of her life. After one date with him she would agree with anybody who called him the most eligible and desirable bachelor in Hollywood. He seemed to be everything she had ever dreamed of in a man. He was rich and handsome but he was also charming and attentive. And he was intelligent. She knew he could be somebody on his own. She wouldn't be surprised if he developed into the best producer in the movie business. Most important, she could imagine herself being very happy in bed with him.

He told her he was going to London. But one week went into another and the next. Still there was no word from Geordie. She didn't know whether he was back in town or not. As the weeks slipped by, she began to give up on him. She had had her fling and now it was time for Cinderella to turn into the pumpkin. Her relationship with Geordie was falling into the apparent pattern of Geordie's relationships with all his other dates—a one-night outing. From what she heard, he had never had a serious affair with anybody. A lot of starlets boasted they had been laid by Geordie. But that was typical starlet bullshit. None of the famous beauties he took out had ever been heard to say to even their closest friends they had been laid by him.

Kim couldn't put him out of her mind. She didn't know what to make of him and his behavior. Maybe he just liked to take out pretty girls and he hadn't found one yet he wanted to take out twice. Including herself. Luckily for him, in a town like Hollywood, the supply was almost inexhaustible. New "starlets" were arriving every day.

Kim thought it was likely Geordie had a private and heavy sex life going for him that was completely apart from his public appearances with beautiful women. He might have some homely-as-sin little nobody who could fuck like a rabbit locked up in his house, where he kept her barefoot and pregnant. Or these trips he went off on might be big sex binges.

A couple mornings after her date with Geordie Kim was summoned to the Boss's office. "What now?" she wondered. "Maybe he's heard about that kid from UCLA I was going with and he's going to lecture me about the risks of keeping company with 'civilians' and getting a 'reputation.' "

The Boss was oozing sweetness and light. "Kimberley," he

111

said, "it's that time again when we can tell somebody under contract that we want to drop them. I'm happy to tell you that's not why you're here. The crew and everybody else, I hear, like to work with you. I hear you're always on time and you take direction nice and you always know your lines. We appreciate that spirit and we're going to give you a raise. I think we made a little adjustment last year about this time. Now you're going all the way up to five hundred dollars a week."

Kim mumbled some thanks, in shock.

"Now you keep on being a good little girl," said the Boss, "and I'm sure we're all going to be happy we know you and you're here with us. You are being a good little girl, aren't you?"

"What's a good little girl?" Kim asked.

She had almost put Geordie Harmon out of her mind completely when she heard from him again. It was more than a month after the night of the premiere. She was into her third week of shooting on *This Sorry Angel*.

"It's me," he said simply. "I told you you'd be hearing from me."

He was calling from his office to the sound stage where she was working. Kim was too excited to say anything.

"Hey, are you there?"

"I'm here," she said weakly.

"You're there and I'm here. Perchance tonight the two bodies can meet for dinner. Perchance?"

"Perchance," echoed Kim.

He picked her up at her apartment house in a fire-red roadster, tootling a device that went off like a fire alarm. "Hello, you," he said, as she crawled in beside him. "Thought I forgot about you, didn't you?"

"Yes."

"Shows how much you know."

Kim had never seen anyone like him before. He looked so un-Hollywood. It must be how they dressed in the East. He wore charcoal gray flannel slacks, a white button-down shirt open at the collar, and a tweedy sports jacket with patches at the elbows. Over his open neck he wore a dark blue ascot with a figure of racing horses.

Kim had dressed her best for the occasion. She was disappointed that Geordie was not taking her to a fancy restaurant. Instead they pulled up in the parking lot of a dumpy-looking, out-of-the-way little Italian restaurant three blocks down a side street off the Strip.

But in Viareggio's it was the same as in Romanoff's. They knew Geordie and they knew he rated their best.

"First I went to London," Geordie said over his first martini. "Remember, I told you I was——"

"Tell me what London's like," Kim interrupted. To her, London was as remote as the moon.

"It's beautiful and charming and quaint. When it's being nice to me, it's my favorite city in the world. It wasn't very nice to me this time. Somebody dragged me into a gambling club and I ended up losing a couple of shirts."

"You were going to see some plays," Kim reminded him. But she didn't remind him that he had said he would be looking at them to see if there was one that could be made into a movie that would have a peachy part for her.

Geordie frowned. "I didn't see anything that would have a chance of doing any business if it was made into a movie over here. What people go for over there is usually a lot different from what American audiences go for."

He drank a couple more martinis before the food came. He told her about a couple of English films he had seen which he thought would be appreciated in the States if they were brought over.

"You drink a lot," Kim commented.

"But not too much. It all depends on how much you're used to and how you handle it."

With the veal Marengo and spaghetti came a bottle of Chianti. Over the food and numerous fillings of his glass Geordie told Kim what it was like to grow up rich outside San Francisco. He told her how little he had seen of his father when he needed him most. His father and his mother had scarcely spoken to each other since he could remember, but for God knows what reason—they weren't Catholics—their marriage had never wound up in the divorce courts, where it belonged if any marriage ever did. Geordie recalled being chauffeured to a fancy day school for boys in San Francisco. Then he went East to boarding school (which he hated). He deliberately let himself flunk out of college because he couldn't "see the point of it." He wanted to be doing something useful and creative in the "real world." He couldn't see how spending fourteen or fifteen grand of the old man's money to keep him in Yale was preparing him for that goal.

"I'm having real script trouble," he confided to Kim. "I had this honey of an idea for a picture. I outlined the whole thing to a writer but what he's come up with is a mess. One of the things I can't do is write or I'd write the damn thing myself. Now I'll have to put another writer on it. I'm dying to get into production with this one. It would be really giant BO. . . ."

"Body odor?"

"Box office, bitchy-witchy," said Geordie, leaning across the table to kiss her on the hair.

Through an after-dinner brandy and a couple of highballs Geordie made Kim the subject of conversation. How did she like where she was living? How did she hit it off with her mother? How was the new picture going? Was the script any good? How was she getting along with the director and the producer and the rest of the cast?

He came on so genuinely interested in her career and welfare, Kim volunteered, "I got a raise."

"How did that happen?"

"I don't know how it happened. I know when it happened. It happened right after you took me to the premiere and our picture was in the paper. The Boss and I really hate each other, I think. I *know* I hate him. But he called me in and said I was getting a raise because I had been 'a good little girl.' "

"So you went from what to what, if you don't mind my asking?"

Kim told him and Geordie slapped the table so hard the wine glasses tipped over. "That prick! That chiseling prick. Anything he offers anybody is half what it should be. You should be getting a grand a week right now if you're getting a penny. That prick knows you're going places and he knows what you're worth right now. Here's what you do. You go in there and hit him for a grand. Tell him Geordie Harmon clued you in. He'll get a note from me backing you up on this."

Kim's second date with Geordie ended much like the first one. He left her at the door, brushing her cheek with his lips. "Lovely evening," he whispered. "You'll be hearing from me."

Again Kim stayed awake hours thinking about Geordie. She recalled his handsome face. She wondered if the rest of his body was as pink as the high, healthy flush of his face. She wondered why he hadn't tried to take her some place, to his house or a motel. She'd have let him do anything he wanted. He must have guessed that. She fantasized about his body. The more she thought about it and tried to visualize it the more she wished he had taken her some place and made love to her. She got herself very hot thinking about him. In her excitement she did the thing she once told me she had accidentally discovered on her own. She inserted her middle finger and started moving it in and out. Faster and faster until she got her relief.

When she went to sleep, she dreamt about Geordie.

During the next two weeks she heard nothing from or about Geordie. "You'll be hearing from me" could mean anything.

A month or a year or even longer. Geordie might be off in London again or almost anywhere else.

While she waited to hear from him, she decided to take him at his word that he had dropped the Boss a note about increasing her salary. He couldn't have forgotten anything so important to her. She asked Morton Shapiro, the producer of *This Sorry Angel*, if he'd arrange an appointment for her to see the Boss about something "personal."

The Boss greeted Kim effusively. She knew it was her signal to be on guard.

"I saw your rushes yesterday," he said. "You're photographing very nice. I think your acting's coming along nice too."

"Did you hear from Geordie Harmon?"

"Geordie Harmon? Hear from him about what, Kim?"

"He said he thought I was being paid too little and he was going to get in touch with you about it. He was going to write you a note."

"Why, no, Kim. I haven't heard a word from him on that subject. Or any other subject."

Kim believed the Boss and she was furious with Geordie. That smooth-talking, would-be big shot! She might have guessed it was all big talk and no action from him. Now she might be on the spot in the Boss's office empty-handed, but since she was there she wasn't going to shrink away from asking what she wanted.

"He may be busy with other things. But I'm sure—"

"Geordie Harmon busy with other things?" the Boss sneered. "Geordie Harmon busy with *anything?*"

"I'm sure if he said he was going to get in touch with you he will," said Kim, not feeling sure of any such thing. "He said I should be making a thousand dollars a week."

"A thousand dollars a week!" The Boss rubbed the region of his heart and slumped back in his chair. Apparently he had just suffered a coronary arrest. "Kimberley, Kimberley, Kimberley."

Kim waited for him to get done with his dramatics. "That's what he said."

"Kim, Kim, Kim, we give you a contract when you're a very little girl that pays you three hundred and fifty a week. Then I see you've been working out nice and getting along with everybody and out of the goodness of my heart I give you a nice raise. Not once. But two times. Remember how I called you in here when it was option time and I said—"

"I remember," said Kim. "But Geordie Harmon said I should be up to at least a thousand dollars a week by now."

The Boss laid it on for Kim. She must know the rough

times the business was going through. It was touch and go whether the movie industry would ride it out. There had been a lot of good years. But now, with the competition from television, who knows? They had hired some "smart accounting fellas" from the East to come in and oversee operations. These accounting fellows said everybody on the payroll was being paid too much. The first thing the Studio must try to do was run a tighter ship.

The end of the essay on the hard times of the Studio had the Boss on bended knee before Kim. "You got a lovely future here," he said, waving his arms up to the roof. "In this town. But that's if the word's out you play fair and square and you're a reasonable little girl."

"Geordie Harmon says I've been a too reasonable little girl," said Kim. "He said I'm working for peanuts."

"When Geordie Harmon has to meet a payroll, he'll be a better judge of what people can be paid. And when he does his first day's work, he'll be a better judge of a lot of things."

The Boss went into some more theatricals designed to make Kim back down from her salary demands. He told her she would be in a much better bargaining position when her contract came up for renewal if she had been "cooperative," if she accepted the raises offered along the way instead of sticking her employers up. He hinted there were ways of dealing with people who were uncooperative. Suddenly he switched gears.

"Is that the stuff Geordie Harmon put in your head the night he took you to the premiere?"

"Not that night. The next time he took me out."

"You're lying. He never takes anybody out more than once."

"He took me out twice. It was the second time he took me out he talked about this."

The Boss eyed her suspiciously. "He never takes anybody out more than once. It's just once around the block with every beautiful babe. To get it on the record he took them out. Then on to the next broad. Pretty broads are a dime a dozen in this town. No problem snagging the next one."

"If I was out with him only once," said Kim, smiling fiendishly, "he must have told me the night of the premiere."

The Boss and Kim swopped eyes for a while.

Then the Boss said, surprisingly, "I think you're making a big mistake if you're seeing Geordie Harmon."

"Is that so?"

"Kimberley, he's not for you. I'm not going into why he isn't for you. Just take it from someone who's trying to be your friend, who looks out for you like you was his own daughter, he's not for you."

"Why?" Kim persisted.

"Now don't 'why' me. I'm telling you for your own good. Here's something more I'll tell you for your own good, little girl. You give me your word you're not seeing Geordie Harmon any more and I think we can come to some kind of adjustment . . . some kind of middle ground . . . about that little matter you just brought up."

"I think I'd just as soon keep on seeing Geordie Harmon," said Kim. "I might be even better off."

"You won't, you won't," hissed the Boss. "Believe me, you little aggravating cunt, you won't get to first base with him."

Kim went out of the office thinking she had lost that round. The Boss was probably right. She had gambled and lost. Her bluff had been called. She was furious with Geordie for getting her into this messy spot.

Two days later Geordie called her. She was so happy to hear from him she swallowed her fury. Nobody else sounded like him. He was so kind of la-di-da without sounding stuck-up or anything. It was fun just hearing his voice.

"Din-din tomorrow night?" he said airily.

"Sure."

On the phone he explained nothing about where he had been or what he had been up to. Nor did he ask her anything about herself. "Dress up," he said. "We'll go some place poshy."

He took her, in fact, back to Romanoff's. He didn't say anything about taking her back to the place they had gone after the premiere. Nor did she remind him they had been there together before. He might get embarrassed. That would mean there had been too many places and dates for him to keep them sorted out and he hadn't any real memory of where he had taken her.

He was such a mystery to her, so utterly fascinating. He tuned in and out of a conversation, jabbering away a mile a minute and then becoming silent for long spells of time. His mood would soar and dip. But he never let her out of his gaze. Not even when he seemed to be going back into himself and letting his attention drift.

Midway in his third martini, Geordie declared, "You got the most beautiful breasts!"

His head bent forward toward the objects of his admiration. For one puzzling but hopeful moment Kim thought he might kiss her breasts. At one of the best tables in Romanoff's!

"But you don't do enough about them," he added.

117

"Do enough about them? What should I be doing? Rubbing them with cocoa butter?"

"Naw, naw. They're there already. You don't need cocoa butter. They just need to be brought out better."

Geordie wanted her to go to Irenee Brossard, the Studio's top costume designer. He wanted Irenee to design a whole wardrobe for Kim that would "bring out" her best features and really look first-class. He was going to tell Irenee to design these clothes for Kim and send the bill to him. He wanted a whole wardrobe that would include outfits appropriate for every occasion. He wanted Kim to look just right if he was taking her out to an elegant restaurant or nightclub or to the racetracks or the beach or on a quickie trip to Las Vegas.

Kim guessed she'd see those clothes about as fast as she saw her raise. "You never got in touch with the Boss," she said, changing the subject.

"About what?"

"About that raise you said you were going to tell him I should get."

"I'm sorry," he said. "I didn't think it was that urgent. It wouldn't show up anyway until the next option time came around. I've been in Puerto Rico almost the whole time since I saw you last. Just got back the day before yesterday. I'll drop him a note tomorrow."

Kim wondered if he promised all his actress dates raises and new wardrobes. Why did he bother with promises he forgot about as soon as he made them? Dropping her off, he gathered her in his arms and kissed her lightly on the lips. Why did he settle for just that, she asked herself again, when he could have gone all the way? When he might have guessed that's the very thing she wanted?

Kim got two surprises the next day. One of Irenee Brossard's assistants called to tell her that Mr. Harmon wanted them to design some clothes for her and would she please drop around when she had some free time?

Then Morton Shapiro told her he had some good news for her. "The guys upstairs" in the front office had decided, on the basis of good reports they had been getting about her, that she rated a substantial boost in salary. When her option came up again, she would go to $1,000 a week.

Kim had to wait another three weeks before she had a chance to thank the one "guy upstairs" she knew was responsible for all the good things that had just come her way.

In his usual off-hand phone manner, Geordie asked, "Got anything to wear tomorrow night?"

Three weeks she hadn't heard from him and he's asking her what she's got to wear!

"I've got a beautiful new black dress with a plunging neckline. Thanks to you. My mother thinks I could get arrested if I wear it."

"Wear it. I'll put up bail if you do get arrested. Wear it tomorrow night and I'll check it out at the Troc."

At the Trocadero Geordie went into raves over the low-cut black dress Irenee Brossard had run up for Kim. He glossed over his activities in recent weeks. About all he said was that he had been in Europe "on a scouting expedition."

He was so handsome, so polished, so gentle, so attentive to Kim that she could not bring herself to quiz him on anything. She did ask him, leadingly, if he liked to dance.

"Are you a good dancer?" he countered.

"I don't know how good I am. I had to learn how for *The Kid Sister-in-Law.*"

"I don't like to dance. I'm so lousy at it. I guess that explains why I don't enjoy it."

That settled the question of being in his arms on the dance floor. But he took her in his arms again at the door and his lips lingered on hers. "Dear Kim," he said and was gone.

Again he left her frustrated, desiring him. Again in bed she did the thing her mother had told her "bad little boys do but girls who do it are worse than bad."

More pieces of clothing were fashioned for her by the hands of Irenee Brossard. Cocktail dresses, evening gowns, tailored suits. Everything was sculpted to show off the tantalizing terrain of her body, especially her 38C boobs. She was especially delighted with a pink jeweled chiffon strapless dress that Irenee said Mr. Harmon had practically designed himself for Kim. Hardly a day passed that she didn't come home to find a package from some Beverly Hills shop waiting for her. The contents might be a bag, a pair of gloves, a scarf, a necklace, a pair of earrings.

The gifts were in much greater evidence than the giver of them. Geordie Harmon was a mystery man. She thought about him all the time. Why was he doing all this when he didn't seem to expect anything in return? Irenee Brossard gave Kim the kind of looks that said she *knew* Mr. Harmon and his young friend must be having a great big thing together. Through Morton Shapiro Kim got the message that the Boss was most displeased at the idea of her having any hot romances. The Boss believed it was not in her best interests. She was too young for that sort of thing and it would hurt her image with movie-goers. If it only was a hot romance, thought Kim. If they only knew how little was going on.

"Wear the pink chiffon number," Geordie said, after another absence of weeks, "and I think you'll look great tonight in La Rue's."

Kim almost told him she had another date. Where did he get off just assuming she was sitting around waiting for him to call? But maybe this was the way that all the rich acted. They could buy their way. Anyway she was too deliriously happy at the thought of seeing him again to turn him down in the hope of teaching him a lesson.

With Geordie's example she was beginning to enjoy cocktails. Warmed and bolstered by a daiquiri at La Rue's, she said, "The Boss doesn't like me to see you."

"What the hell business is it of his?"

"He said he thought I was too young to go with anybody. He said audiences would be against it. But I don't think he really thinks that. Any time he says something is for this reason you guess it's for some other reason."

Geordie gave a horse laugh. "You're right, Kim. And you're sharp. I got the picture in focus. The Boss, as you may or may not know, doesn't have any daughters of his own. But he—"

"I do know," said Kim, recalling their first meeting when he dangled her on his knee, masturbating.

"But he does have a niece. His brother's daughter. He hates his brother but he's got him here producing pictures. Anyway, the Boss is crazy about his niece. When I first came here, I got the big fat hello from the Boss. He poured it on sweet and thick as honey. There were dinner parties out at his place and I kept being invited. By an odd coincidence I always found myself sitting next to his niece. Well, that niece has to be the turkey of all time. Teeth like a saber-toothed tiger and a mouth that just won't stop shooting off. I think the Boss long ago got the message on how much I went for that dog of a niece. But he still hasn't given up hope completely. As long as I'm in circulation, there's always the chance I'll come to my senses and discover her charms. It's not that he ever had any great love for me or thinks I'm the answer to a maiden's prayers. He's just foxy and scheming enough to know it wouldn't be a bad idea to have somebody connected with a bank in the family."

He was more talkative, more personal that night than he had ever been. Kim still couldn't begin to figure him out. But she got the feeling for the first time that he wanted to shed some of the mystery about himself, that he wanted to reveal himself to her. He told her he was still confused about many

120

things and groping. He told her he had been movie-crazy since he was five years old and saw his first Laurel and Hardy comedy. He told her what he thought was wrong with the industry today. He told her about the kind of pictures he wanted to make.

Looking deeply into her eyes, Geordie asked Kim a hundred questions about herself and hung on the answers. He asked her what kinds of roles she'd like to play and he told her he was going to make it his business to find them for her.

Saying good night to her he held her longer and his tongue slid briefly between her lips. "Next Tuesday," he said. "We'll have dinner at my place. Manuelo's no great shakes as a chef. But we'll get by."

"Wear that thing with the little plaits," Geordie told her on the phone the day of the dinner. "The one that matches the color of your eyes."

Kim was disappointed. That sounded like he was going to have other guests and wanted her to come looking dressy. But her hunch was wrong. They were going to be alone.

Geordie lived on Mulholland Drive. Outwardly the place looked pretty standard Beverly Hills, all cream-colored and red-roofed with pillars and a big, closely cropped lawn. But Kim thought she'd never live to see another house so strangely furnished. They ate dinner on a billiard table whose edges had been removed. The rest of the decor was all fun and games too. On her tour of the basement she counted forty-six one-armed bandits lined up against all the walls. There were even slot machines in what passed for the living room, along with crap tables and backgammon tables and card tables and roulette wheels and tables for blackjack and tables with cribbage boards. The carpets in his bedroom were in a gigantic checkerboard design so that you could have played checkers or chess on them. In his bedroom there was also a card table with the cards laid out for solitaire, and there was a backgammon table and a slot machine. The swimming pool was in the shape of a spade from a deck of cards.

"What do you think of it?" he asked her.

"It's strange," she said honestly.

"It's me, I guess."

She thought, "Yes, you're strange, so it figures." It was all so strange ... the place, sitting at this billiard table being served an Oriental dinner by a Filipino manservant who seemed to be the only other person in the house. And Geordie ... as strange and fascinating a man as she thought she would ever meet. Didn't that mean she was in love ... that she was so fascinated by a man that she didn't begin to understand?

"I like to play games, as you can see," Geordie explained. "That's what the whole movie business is about. It's game-playing. Taking chances. Gambling."

After dinner Geordie gave Kim her first lesson in back-gammon. In the library he helped her get the hang of throwing darts at the dartboard. He stood behind her, guiding her arm, almost embracing her. She hoped the next move was to the slot machine in his bedroom. And then . . .

"Come on," he said abruptly, "you're a working girl. You have to look dazzling before those cameras tomorrow. It's bedsy-bye for you."

He was leading her by the hand to his car. Kim realized, with a sickening sensation, that "bedsy-bye" meant her own bed at home. Alone.

At her door he held her and kissed her warmly. "The day you finish the picture we'll really make a night of it. What do you say?"

"I say yes," said Kim, kissing him on the cheek.

That day was still two weeks off. In the meantime Kim had only a couple of brief, breezy phone calls from Geordie. He was calling mainly to remind her of the celebration he was planning. He wouldn't give her any details about the celebration because he wanted to surprise her. She thought of him almost all the time, even when she was mouthing her foolish lines on camera. She could hardly wait for the magic night to arrive.

The day of the magic night a parcel was delivered to Kim's apartment. She opened it to find a dazzling chinchilla cape. The note from Geordie said, "Wear this tonight. You'll make the little rodents happy they died for you."

It was a night beyond her wildest expectations. But it didn't satisfy her fondest expectation.

Geordie picked her up at five thirty. They drove for miles through sections of Los Angeles she had never seen before. He wouldn't tell her where they were going. She got a romantic thrill not knowing. She was in his hands completely. He would take good care of her.

The mysterious drive ended at the Los Angeles airport. There a private plane—his own, Geordie later admitted—and a pilot awaited them. Kim had never been in a plane before. If Geordie hadn't been with her, she would have been terrified to be getting into a little plane (a Piper Cub, she learned) and flying off into the wild blue yonder to God knows where. But with Geordie it was an exciting adventure. It was even more exciting because he refused to tell her where the plane was flying.

The plane flew over a high ridge of mountains whose snow-capped peaks sparkled in the setting sun. Then it swooped over a vast desert, lowering as it approached a fiery blaze of lights and neons.

"Welcome to Suckertown," said Geordie. "Las Vegas."

A chauffeured limousine was waiting. Geordie directed the driver to take them to the Sands. Kim thought what a red face she would have checking into a hotel room with a man and not even carrying an overnight case. But at the Sands they went straight to a vast dining room. A man at the door greeted Geordie with a big hello and a bow. He led them to a table way down front.

"That's Kimberley Hudson!" Kim heard someone buzz as they followed the maître d'hôtel. It still amazed her that anyone recognized her, that people even went to the kind of pictures she had been making.

Geordie ordered a daiquiri for her and three martinis for himself.

"Three?" Kim asked.

"Three lousy ones here don't even add up to one good one. It's almost showtime and you can't get served once the show starts." He pointed his thumb at the large stage with drawn curtains.

Phil Harris was the headliner and it was opening night. Taking his curtain calls at the end of his act, he said, "Now we got some people out front who only came because they were promised they'd get a chance to stand up and be seen. (Laughter.) ... And down here, folks, a beautiful young actress from Hollywood who's really going places . . . Miss Kimberley Hudson! Will you please stand up, Miss Hudson, so everybody can get a gander at your gorgeous self? (Applause and gasps of appreciation.) And with her ..."

For the next couple of hours Kim got a whirlwind tour of the casinos of the big Las Vegas hotels. The Desert Inn. The Frontier. The Riviera. The Flamingo. People were milling around by the thousands in all of them and the activity was frantic. Everywhere they went, people knew Geordie and were calling out to him. Many of the people who greeted him were the men running the gaming tables, men in black suits with sticks. Kim was all the more impressed because they said, "Evening, Mr. Harmon" rather than "Hi, Geordie." She saw the men running the tables and the gamblers look at Geordie with interest and respect. She saw them taking her in too, their eyes going ga-ga. With all the noise and hubbub she

123

strained her ears to catch the admiring comments that were being passed about her.

"Not joining in tonight, Mr. Harmon?" two or three of the men in black asked Geordie.

"Just looking tonight," Geordie answered. "That'll make tomorrow a happier day."

"Don't blame you," one of them said, glancing meaningfully at Kim.

Geordie seemed to be so proud of her, almost as if he were showing her the casinos just to show her off. Just before midnight he escorted her into another big hotel room with a stage. Again they were expected, got the big welcome, and were ushered to a front table. Geordie ordered six highballs. "Might as well work off our minimum," he said, "and there's nothing in them anyway."

Jimmy Durante was the star of the show. At the end of his performance he startled her by introducing her to the audience and asking her to stand up and take a bow. This time the applause was much louder than at the Sands and there were whistles and catcalls. Now it was after two o'clock in the morning. But she felt as wide awake as if she had just had a good night's sleep. The only question was how wide awake Geordie felt. On top of everything else he had consumed that evening he had just polished off five Canadian Club and sodas. Had he made arrangements for their hotel room? Would he be good for anything besides going to sleep?

"Was it a great evening?" he asked her, guiding her to the waiting limousine.

"Perfect," she said. "I'll never forget it."

"I'm glad. That's the way I planned it."

To the driver he said, "Back to the airport."

On the return flight to Los Angeles Geordie took her in his arms. They were hardly aloft before he fell asleep. He slept deeply all the way to Los Angeles, his head buried in Kim's bosom. In Los Angeles he was wide awake and sober again. Kim was high from the lights of Los Angeles and nestling Geordie's head and dreaming that perhaps the best was yet to come. Geordie had his second wind. Anything might still happen before this fairy-tale night melted into day.

Geordie said nothing as he drove. But again the road led back to her house. "It's late," he said, letting her off, "and we're both bushed. I have something I want to talk to you about. But not now."

Chapter 14

If Kim was going to get a big pay boost, the Studio was going to get its money's worth out of her. Two days after her Las Vegas adventure she was told she would be going right into *Farewell, Arlington Street*. From the title, she assumed it was another run-of-the-dog picture.

The following Sunday Geordie asked Kim to go with him to the Santa Anita racetracks. All the way there, he talked heatedly about a horse named Four Seasons. He planned to "lay a bundle" on Four Seasons because he was positive that little Mexican jockey, Angelo Santiana, could ride him to victory.

At the racetrack Geordie was something to be with. He was a walking encyclopedia on horses and racing. He knew the history and pedigree of every horse running in every race. He explained to Kim about handicapping and the various ways of betting. He told her that as soon as he could break away from his duties at the Studio for a while he was going to assemble his own stable of racehorses.

His enthusiasm rubbed off on Kim. But her excitement really was the excitement of being with him, listening to him, and not hearing about a bunch of horses she had never met or watching them run around in circles.

How handsome Geordie was in that yellow linen sports coat and the white silk shirt open at the collar and his sombrero-shaped straw hat! She watched him more than she watched even the fourth race, which was the one Four Seasons was running in. She watched him work himself into a state of near-hysteria. He yelled to the horse. He yelled to the jockey. He kept jerking himself forward, as if that would speed up the horse.

Geordie's hunch was sound. Four Seasons came through by more than a neck. Georgie went wild. He screamed and threw his hat high into the air. He grabbed Kim in a crushing embrace.

"We did it! We did it!" he cried. "We did it, my beauty. You are my lucky star."

He held her close to him, kissing her on the mouth. Could it be her imagination? Was it something she just hoped was happening? Or was he becoming hard against her?

All through dinner at Scandia he did variations on a few

basic themes. It had been a marvelous afternoon, one of the best he could remember. Four Seasons was really a horse to watch, a comer. Kim was his good luck person. How great it would be when he had his own stable and was breeding horses.

It seemed a little silly to Kim that a rich boy could get so excited about winning a few thousand dollars he didn't need. The other night he had told her he wanted to talk to her about something. This must be what he wanted to talk to her about, horses and racing. It was such a letdown. For that he didn't need a girl. He'd have been better off with a man friend, who might have some real interest in the subject.

He was still in a state of exhilaration when he dropped her off at her door. There he gathered her to him in another close embrace. He kissed her hair and lips and again called her his lucky star. She stood blissfully in his embrace. Was it wish or fact? Again, did Geordie have a hard-on as he pressed against her?

"I told you after Vegas I wanted to talk to you about something," he said. "I wouldn't call it talking about something. It's just a question. Will you marry me?"

Out of a dream she heard him asking, "Do you have to think about it?"

"No," she said.

"No, you won't marry me?"

"Yes. I mean no," said Kim.

"Look. If you're thinking about your mother, don't. She can move into the guest house and she'll be taken care of in every way. If you think I want you to stop acting and stay home and have babies, you're crazy. You can have——"

"Stop it, Geordie. Of course I'll marry you." Through her tears, with a quaking laugh, she added, "I thought you'd never ask."

Geordie sighed, pressing hard against her. "How soon? And where?"

"Any time. I don't care where."

During the time Kim was having her on-again, off-again dates with Geordie Harmon, the Spinelli Sisters launched their nightclub act. We were playing the bottom of the bill at the Desert Inn in Vegas when I got an excited call from Kim.

"I'm marrying Geordie Harmon," she announced over the long-distance line. "Over there next weekend. Since you're there, will you be my bridesmaid or attendant or whatever you call it?"

Kim got some surprises in Las Vegas. The first surprise

was to learn that as Mrs. Geordie Harmon she would be the mistress of a house in Las Vegas. The house was a many-roomed, U-shaped, expensive pad a stone's throw behind the Flamingo Hotel. A bigger surprise was that Georgie built the house five years ago. Funny he hadn't shown it to her or told her about it that first night he brought her to Vegas.

The ceremony was performed by a justice of the peace in Geordie's house. I must say I was impressed as hell by everything. Starting with the house. But most of all, I was impressed by Kim. She was so radiantly beautiful in the amber-colored Alençon lace gown over snowy satin that Irenee Brossard had worked around the clock to get ready in time. Geordie was breathtakingly handsome in his white linen suit with the black piping and the royal blue shirt that matched the blue of his eyes and picked up his high coloring. They looked like a storybook couple getting married.

It was supposed to be a private wedding. It was supposed to be just us and Kim's mother and Geordie's parents. But it had all the razzmatazz of a movie premiere. News of the event must have been "leaked" by somebody. I suspect it was either Irenee Brossard or the PR director of the Flamingo Hotel. The driveway and grounds of Geordie's house were crawling with photographers and reporters. A police cordon surrounding the house kept them from getting inside to cover the wedding firsthand.

The inside of Geordie's house was about as crazy as anything else in the craziest city in the world. What would be a living room in any normal house was a miniature casino, complete with all the games of chance you'd find in any of the hotel casinos. Smack in the middle of all this gambling paraphernalia was where the sacred vows of marriage were performed.

For a change Kim's mother looked halfway decent and reasonably sober. Geordie's parents came from a different cookie cutter altogether. Geordie's mother was the snooty, tailored suit, tanned-from-golf, lean-and-mean type. She had steel-blue eyes and a novocained upper lip that could hardly crack into a smile. It took one split second to tell she wasn't happy to be here on this occasion. But I had the feeling she wouldn't be happy about any other marriage ceremony either if it starred Geordie as the groom.

Geordie's father was something else. Looking at him, you could see what Geordie would look like in twenty-five years or so. Not a bad prospect. He was fifty-five-ish and bronzed, with a few white hairs cropping into the blond hair brushed back from the temples. He looked like what he was, healthy and rich and sure of himself. Unlike his wife, he was obviously happy to be here, happy that this marriage was taking place.

As soon as the "I do's" were over, Roger Harmon was kissing the bride. "If there was ever a more beautiful bride," he gushed, "I wouldn't believe it if I saw her with my own eyes."

"Thank you, Mr. Harmon," Kim said, blushing.

"I can't believe I'm here standing up for Geordie at his wedding. I didn't think it would ever happen. That Geordie would finally pick someone and tie the knot."

"He's still very young," Kim said defensively. "Only twenty-seven."

"I know, I know. It was just a feeling I had."

"I hope you'll both be very happy," said Mrs. Harmon, sounding as if it was the last thing she hoped. She gave them each a token peck on the cheek.

A combo began playing bouncy dance tunes. But nobody moved to dance. Champagne corks started popping. A whole army of caterers came out of the kitchen carrying the food and dishes for an enormous buffet that was to be set up in the dining room.

I stayed only long enough to have a few sips of champagne. By that time it was eleven thirty and time to go back to get made up for our twelve fifteen show. Already Geordie had filled his glass several times and was feeling no pain. Mr. Harmon, I noticed, was becoming great buddies with Kim. Geordie seemed to be on fond, brotherly terms with his father and looked proud and happy that his father was digging his bride so much. Mrs. Harmon looked pissed off.

"Now promise me we're going to see a lot of you," Mr. Harmon was saying to Kim as I left.

Word had gone out to the press, which the police were still holding in check outside, that Geordie and Kim would come outside and talk to them at midnight.

The next day I woke up to find Kim's wedding was front-page news. The front page of the *Las Vegas Sun* had a banner headline:

HOLLYWOOD PRODUCER MARRIES ACTRESS HERE

At the newsstand downstairs I bought a whole bunch of papers from all over the country. All of them carried the story. Kim was famous for sure. The whole world must know her name by now.

Back upstairs I drooled over the accounts of the surprise elopement. Apparently all the old Hollywood gossip hounds had been scooped. Many of them frankly confessed their amazement. The desirable man-about-town who had been squiring Hollywood's loveliest lovelies—without showing any signs of having a "real crush" on any of them—had taken the plunge! And who had he picked after looking over the whole field? Not one of the leading ladies he could have had with a snap of his finger. He had picked somebody who was hardly a household name. A beautiful girl, yes. An up-and-coming actress, yes. But someone hardly in the league of stars who had always been his preference in feminine companionship. Say this for Geordie Harmon, he knows how to keep a secret and spring a surprise . . .

I was just starting to cut out all the clippings from the papers to send to Mama when the phone rang. It was Kim.

"Wanna hear all about it?" she asked.

Kim always sailed right into a phone conversation, never bothering to say who she was or what she was talking about. She just assumed the other person should know.

She could only be talking about her wedding night and I could feel myself getting squeamish. As dumb and curious as I still was about the whole business of sex, I was sure I didn't want to hear too many details about what Kim and Geordie had done in bed together their first night.

But she said, "Come on over," making it sound like an order.

She was waiting for me in that kooky living room that looked like a casino. A spooky character who reminded me of Mrs. Danvers in *Rebecca* let me in. She obviously went with the place. She looked like the kind of character who knew where a lot of bodies were buried, like she might have enough dirt on everybody in Las Vegas to lock the whole town up. Kim carefully waited until she was out of sight before even looking at me.

"Just leave us alone, Mrs. Anderson," Kim called after her. "We won't be needing anything."

I was shocked at the sight of Kim. Her eyes were red-rimmed from crying and there were hollows under them. I had never seen her so dragged-out looking.

"Where's Geordie?" I asked.

"He's left me," bursting into a fresh volley of tears.

"Aw, come on, Kim."

"You don't see him, do you?"

"He hasn't left you," I said consolingly. "How could he?"

She took off the giant sparkler Geordie had slipped on her finger just the night before and threw it at me. "Look inside."

Inscribed inside the ring were the words: "Together forever."

I waited for her to stop crying and tell me what had happened. I couldn't bring myself to push her into it.

"It's so crazy," she sobbed. "It's not my fault. But the way he took off it's like it was all my fault."

The story, as I could piece it together, went like this:

Everything seemed to be going so well. After I left, there were a few more toasts and glasses of champagne. Finally the caterers and the waiters and Kim's mother and Geordie's parents left. Then Geordie took Kim outside. They posed for pictures and chatted with reporters. Geordie was at his charming best, doing everything the photographers asked him. "Kiss her again." "Hold her close." He gave gay, witty replies to the questions called out to him. After about half an hour of this, he said, "Okay? Got enough?" The crowd thanked them for their cooperation and wished them much happiness and began to take off.

Inside, Geordie poured them each another glass of champagne.

"Mrs. Geordie Harmon," Geordie murmured, touching her glass.

"Hey, bridie," he said, "I'm going to sneak over to the lobby and get me a couple of long Havanas to celebrate. You make yourself comfy and I'll be back before you know it. Anything you want?"

"Just you," said Kim.

Kim went into the wild master bedroom. The big bed there was in the shape of a playing card diamond. In one corner was a pinball machine and against the opposite wall there were three slot machines. The walls were plastered with pictures of Geordie in restaurants and nightclubs in Los Angeles and New York and London and Paris and Rome with every girl he had ever taken out. There were also pictures of racing horses and autographed photographs of trainers and jockeys.

Kim quickly undressed and got between the pale blue silk sheets. She had always thought it was stupid for brides to be wearing nighties to bed on their wedding night. But maybe it was only in the movies that they did. She wore nothing to bed except the big rock he had put on her finger. She wanted to be ready for him the minute he climbed in beside her.

She waited and waited. The minutes dragged into an hour. An hour and a half. Where could he be? Had something terrible happened to him? She snapped on the light to see what time it was. Twenty minutes to four! In the darkness her fears overshadowed her desire. Something terrible *must* have happened. She turned on the lights again to look at her watch. It was almost five o'clock.

She was just about to call the police when she heard the front door open. Geordie bumped against the wall of the long corridor before finding their bedroom. Kim was almost sick with relief. Breathing evenly, she pretened to be asleep. How exciting it would be when he "woke" her up with his kisses and started making passionate love to her!

He undressed in the darkness. Losing his balance and crashing against one of the corners of a marble-topped card table, he cursed. Kim opened her eyes just a slit. She watched him pitch each piece of clothing in a different direction. When he got down to his underwear, she closed her eyes. She wanted to be surprised.

Geordie flopped into bed and moved near to her. She waited for him to touch her. He didn't. What was the matter? Was he being nice and considerate? Keeping his hands off her because he thought she was asleep?

Geordie's breathing deepened. *He* was going to sleep!

Kim put her arms around him and her lips found his. She kissed him and he limply returned the kiss. She kissed his harder.

"Not now," he murmured. "Let's sleep. I'm blotto."

His breath reeked of something stronger than champagne. Kim went on holding him and kissing him on the mouth.

"I'm so tired," he whimpered. "Let me sleep."

Kim wouldn't give up. Her fingertips gently stroked the back of his neck and then made little circles down his spine and came around to his stomach and poked into his navel and came circling up his chest to focus on his nipples. Then down, down, they rolled again until—could this be? He was still wearing his shorts!

Kim brought her fingertips down over his silky briefs and moved them slowly over the surface of his penis and balls. She went back over his penis. There wasn't even a quiver of life there.

"No," he said, brushing her hand away. "Not tonight. There's nothing there."

Kim snapped on the lights. "What's the matter? We're married. This is my wedding night. You're supposed to be loving me. Holding me, making love to me."

"I told you I'm blotto," said Geordie, shielding his eyes with his arms against the light. "I can't do anything tonight."

"Yes, you can. You're not that drunk."

"I tell you I can't. I had a few too many and I'm no good."

"You said you were going to get cigars."

"I got them. Then I ran into some old pals who wanted to shoot some dice and we ended up at the no-limit table."

Her frustration made her furious. "I don't believe it."

"It's true."

131

"You're telling me you were shooting craps when you should have been here fucking me?"

"We all have our little weaknesses. Gambling's one of mine. You should know that by now."

"You weren't shooting any craps," said Kim. "You ran into one of your old girl friends and you were fucking her when you should have been here fucking me. You thought you might as well get one more bang out of her because you could always fuck me. That's why you don't want anything now. People fuck when they're a lot drunker than you."

"Have it your way," Geordie groaned. "Just please let me get some sleep. Tomorrow's another day."

"It's already here."

"Not by Vegas time. Good night . . . love."

Geordie rolled over and slept like a log. Kim hardly closed her eyes. First she was kept awake by her fury and frustration. As the morning hours wore on, it was guilt that kept her awake. She knew Geordie liked to gamble and she knew he liked to drink. He could be telling the truth. Maybe he had meant to have just a few rolls of the dice and a drink with his friends and the thing had just gone on and on. It was certainly true, as Geordie said, that we all have our weaknesses.

By eleven o'clock she had decided to forgive him and apologize to him. Just before eleven thirty he turned around in the bed. He was facing her again but he was still sleeping soundly. Gently she pulled down the covers to look at his body. How beautiful he was! In his sleep he looked as sweet and innocent as a newborn babe.

She reached out and lightly brushed the faint blond down on his chest and his stomach. She pulled the covers down a little farther. Oh, thank God! The thing that was dead a few hours ago had come magnificently to life. She stared with delight at the thick stump with the cone-shaped top holding the flimsy jockey shorts up like a tent. It gave a throb now and then, as if responding to her gaze.

In one of its thrusts Kim reached out to take it in her hand. Geordie woke with a start.

"Hi," he said.

"Hi, darling," said Kim.

"Whew! Some night."

To her dismay Kim felt the stump going limp in her hand. Geordie took her hand away and held it away.

"Were you dreaming about me?" Kim asked.

"I don't remember dreaming at all."

"Your thing was so . . . hard."

"I always have a piss hard-on in the morning." He kissed

132

her sweetly. Glancing at his watch, he said, "My God, it's twelve thirty. I got to get cracking."

"You're not going somewhere?" she cried.

"Have to. I've got a one o'clock appointment. I can't keep everybody waiting."

"An appointment? Keep people waiting? Who? What about me?"

"I'm sorry, honey. But I made this date about a week ago to play baccarat with some guys."

He disappeared into the bathroom to shower and shave. In silent rage she watched him get carefully dressed. Madras jacket. White twill trousers. White buckled loafers. Around his neck he looped a maroon ascot.

"Where are you going?" she asked him.

"I told you. I'm going to play baccarat. It was a date I made before you and I suddenly decided to get married right away."

"You've got a date with some bitch," Kim hissed at him. "You were dreaming about her and that's how you got that hard-on. You wouldn't fuck me because you're saving it up for her. You wouldn't—"

"Kim, I've never heard you talk like that. You surprise me."

"Surprise you? What the hell do you think you hear hanging around a movie set?"

"I don't know as I go for that kind of talk."

"I don't go for you leaving me here. You should be here with me."

"Now, honey, I told you this date was made before—"

"Bullshit! When will you be back?"

"Expect me when you see me," he said, slamming the door.

She wept for hours. "Don't leave me, don't leave me," she begged in the empty bedroom.

"He doesn't love me," Kim said bitterly, the tears still streaming down her cheeks.

"He married you, didn't he?" I reasoned.

"But he wouldn't make love to me."

A sixteen-year-old virgin was hardly the one to serve as a marriage counselor but I felt I should say something comforting. "I've heard that some men get even more nervous than brides on their wedding night. Maybe Geordie's like that. If you just give him—"

"No. He's got somebody else."

The words were hardly out of her mouth when the doorbell rang. The spooky Mrs. Anderson came from somewhere in the back of the house to answer it. A minute later she handed Kim a package. "For you, ma'am."

In the box was a silver star with tiny diamonds embedded along the edges. I gasped when she held it up. Kim smiled for the first time. She read the card with it and brightened even more.

I love you. Wear this and look your beautiful best tonight. Be ready at 7:30 and we'll go out to dinner.

"See," I said. "He loves you and everything's going to be all right."

"Do you really think so, Gina? I sure wish I knew what was going on."

"How many brides get a ring like yours and another beautiful piece of jewelry the very next day?"

I had a rehearsal at four thirty. By the time I left, she was in much better spirits than I had found her. She was already rummaging through her closet wondering what she should wear. I was dying to know what would happen that night but I couldn't come right out and ask for a report. The next day was Sunday and I knew they'd be flying back to Los Angeles some time that afternoon or evening because Kim had to be on the set early Monday morning.

"Will you call and say good-bye before you go?" I asked.

"Oh, sure, Gina."

When she called the next afternoon she sounded cheery.

"I got laid," she announced. Giggling, she added, "Well, sort of."

By her account of the evening, Geordie had taken her to the Stardust to catch the dinner show. Their presence there caused a tremendous commotion and everybody was kowtowing to them. All through dinner, people came up to their table to get Kim's autograph. Geordie told her that now that she was Mrs. Harmon he would be taking an active interest in her career. He would see to it that she got better roles in better pictures and star billing. Of course there was no need for her to work at all but he knew she wouldn't be happy doing nothing like all those bored Beverly Hills wives who spend their days sitting around pools and shopping and going to hairdressers and psychiatrists and getting gynecological tucks.

Afterward they went to hear a singer in the Freemont and to catch the lounge act in the Riviera. The more he drank, the warmer and more possessive Geordie became toward Kim. It was two thirty in the morning when they left the Riviera and she thought they surely must be headed home.

Geordie swung the Bentley off Las Vegas Boulevard through a maze of driveways and stopped it in the parking lot of the Flamingo Hotel.

"Let's take a quick peek at the action," he said.

The casino was hopping and Geordie was in his element. Like a commodore showing off his yacht, he took her on a tour of the casino. This was a more detailed tour than he had given her that other night in Las Vegas. This time he told her exactly how each game was played. His eyes glowed as they feasted on the various gaming tables. Their mere approach to any table almost brought the action to a halt. Hands reached out to congratulate them and pieces of paper were shoved at Kim for autographing. Even the zombies at the slot machines stopped cranking long enough to stare.

"Come on, let's have a few giggles."

He changed some bills into two dixie cupfuls of quarters.

Before a quarter-eating bandit, he said, "Now you pull and I'll feed."

Kim pulled the lever. When the moving panels stopped, Geordie put another quarter in the slot. She was working a machine with transportation figures. On one pull she turned up three old locomotives. A clang of quarters came gushing out of the machine.

Geordie scooped them up and counted them. Twenty-six. He thumped her on the back as if she had won a fortune.

"Don't tell me. Geordie Harmon reduced to penny-ante?"

"Oh, hi, Robin."

Geordie introduced Kim to a tall, tanned, dark young man who looked as rich and elegant as Geordie himself. "Don't tell me it's come to this," said Robin. "Did you really get wiped out last night?"

"Not quite," laughed Geordie, "but I've got my bride on a very tight budget."

"Up to a roll or two?"

Geordie looked at Kim. "There are rolls and rolls. I don't know about your kind tonight, Robin."

The men laughed together. Geordie said to Kim, "How about it, honey? Let's just throw a couple and call it a night."

It was all a mystery to Kim what happened. They were over at a table in a fairly private corner of the casino. Geordie and Robin joined some other expensive-looking men around the table. Dice were rolling. The man in the black suit kept stretching out his long stick to scoop up red, white, and blue disks and pile them up in front of the players.

The other men were fairly quiet. But Geordie kept crooning a love song to the dice: "Baby, baby, baby, be my lover tonight . . . come to me and I'll be yours forever . . ."

135

In a trance, half-falling asleep on her feet, Kim was thrown up into the air. She came fully awake hearing Geordie yelling, "My lucky star. She's my lucky star."

He held her close to him and kissed her full on the lips. "One minute," he said, carting a big bundle of the red, white, and blue disks off somewhere.

It was nearly five o'clock when they got back into the Bentley. Home was only a few hundred yards away. Geordie drove with one hand, holding Kim's hand in the other.

"Know something, hon?" he asked. "We picked up forty-four big ones at that table. How about that?"

"Big ones?"

"G's. Grands. Forty-four thou."

Parking in the garage behind the odd U-shaped house, Geordie said, "Speaking of big ones . . . I wish you'd . . . well, put your hand . . . well, where you had it this morning . . ."

Kim eagerly put her hand on a thick stump that shivered in her grasp. She began to caress it.

"Easy, easy," he said, pushing her hand away.

In their bedroom he tore off his clothes like a madman. He came to her, fully erect. "Hurry up," he said. Hanging her dress in the closet, she felt hot, sweaty hands grasping her through her bra and the stump poking against her bottom.

Geordie scooped her up, screaming, "My bride, my bride."

He carried her to the bed and ripped off her panties with one furious yank. He embraced her fiercely. Then he was all over her with his body and his hands and his kisses.

"Oh, God, I love you, I love you, I love you . . . I can't stand it, I can't stand it . . ."

One sharp jab put him inside her. He took a deep breath and began driving . . . in and out, deeper and deeper, faster and faster.

"I'm going crazy," he moaned.

It was over before she began to feel much of anything.

"Oh God, oh God, oh God . . ."

He lay on top of her a long minute, almost dead-still.

"I'm sorry I shot so fast," he whispered. "You had me crazy."

He stayed where he was, holding her and kissing her, tenderly now, and with no urgency. While he rested, she fondled his back. She ran her nails ticklingly down his spine and over the ample mounds of his buttocks. When she felt no stirring inside her, she started moving her hips.

"I'm sorry," he said. "It won't work."

He moved out of her. Still holding her and kissing her, he put his finger inside her. His finger finally accomplished what his organ hadn't.

They fell asleep in each other's arms. It was almost noon when Kim woke up. Geordie was still sleeping but Kim saw that he was hard again. She held him there and ran her tongue along his lips.

Geordie woke up, smiling. "You're a naughty girl," he said, putting his hand on top of hers. But this time he didn't take it away.

"I think we could use a little eye-opener," he said.

He jumped out of bed and strutted nude from the bedroom. A few minutes later he came back with a pitcher of Bloody Marys and two glasses. The Bloody Marys were more Mary than bloody—mostly gin with a little tomato juice thrown in for coloring.

A few sips of it and Kim felt her scalp lifting. But Geordie drank in gulps and refilled his glass. He told her how much he loved her and she was the best thing that ever happened to him. Filling his glass again, he cradled her in his arms and told her he would try very hard to make her happy. He took off her wedding ring and looked at the inscription, "Together forever."

"Do you drink too much, Geordie?"

"I'm drinking to celebrate. Because I'm so happy."

By the time the pitcher of Bloody Marys was drained, Geordie was glassy-eyed. But he wanted her again. He lavished her body with hot impatient kisses and quickly mounted her. The thrust was frantic and ended abruptly. This time he fell into a deep sleep as he was trying to please her with his finger.

"Do all these gory details shock you, Gina?" Kim asked me.

"Not too much," I lied.

"I have to tell you because, remember, you're going to write that book about me some day. You'll sell so many copies you'll be able to live off it the rest of your life."

Chapter 15

Whatever might be screwy about the screwing she was getting, Kim dug her new status as Mrs. Geordie Harmon. She was an overnight sensation everywhere as the girl who had bagged the rich young man of the world that no other Hollywood beauty had come close to bagging. Newspapers and wire services and magazines from every corner of the world nagged their Hollywood correspondents to develop features on the glamorous newlyweds. It took the full time of two Studio publicists to screen all the requests for exclusive interviews and set up appointments and see that relations with the press ran smoothly.

Columnists were calling Geordie and Kim "Hollywood's most beautiful young couple." Fan magazines carried cover stories with titles like "What She Has Got None of the Others Had" and "Diary of a Storybook Courtship." One mag had a by-lined article by Geordie Harmon, "The Girl of My Dreams—I Found Her!" Another one plastered Kim's name on the cover as the author of a piece called "How I Knew He Was Mr. Right."

As Mrs. Geordie Harmon she was the lady of the house in Beverly Hills, nutsy as the inside of the house was. "If you want to change anything, honey," said Geordie, "just go right ahead." But how would you go about changing a decor of Gambling Moderne into Spanish Colonial or Louis XIV?

Kim's mother moved into the guest cottage with both a car and a housekeeper at her disposal.

Geordie said, "Open up charge accounts any place you want. Likewise in San Francisco when we go up to see the folks. They got some really classy stores up there. I don't want you spending any of your own money on anything. I want you to stash that all away in your own account. If I go broke sometime, maybe you'll lend me enough to get a bowl of soup."

And as Mrs. Geordie Harmon Kim suddenly rated chauffeur service to the Studio and back every day. She also rated star treatment, although actually she was still something less than a star. The director and the producer and the crew and the other performers deferred to her in little ways they never would have if she weren't Mrs. Geordie Harmon. It was somewhat embarrassing, but the experience of being Really Somebody was also so new to her she couldn't help enjoying it. Even the Boss came on the set one day to offer his congratulations and she managed to thank him graciously.

Mr. and Mrs. Geordie Harmon could have been the toast of the town. Invitations for dinner parties and cocktail parties and house parties and weekending arrived with every morning's mail. Some of these came from the biggest names in the film colony. They could have gone to almost any house. But they went nowhere. They declined all the invitations. Rather, Geordie declined them.

"Most of the people in this town," he explained to Kim, "are fucking bores. If you go to their houses, you're stuck. Thank God I can afford to buy my own food and booze."

Geordie, however, loved the café and nightclub scene. "You're around people and a little action," he said, "but you don't have anybody hanging on your neck."

Kim told herself that what he wanted was what she wanted. So many doors were opening, so many wonderful things were happening to her just because she was Mrs. Geordie Harmon. If Geordie said something was so, she would go along with it. She meant to be the kind of wife who adored her husband and backed him up.

Geordie preferred to take her out to public places in the evening, just the two of them, which meant he wanted to be alone with her, wanted her all to himself. So she told herself, in those early, baffling months of her first marriage, when she was still young and naïve enough to brainwash herself.

But he must have friends, she thought often. She couldn't be the one and only person in his life. And yet as long as she had known him, she couldn't remember hearing him talk about anybody in particular beside his parents. There were always people stopping by their table when they went out. And, in a way, Geordie seemed to know everybody. But everybody was just an acquaintance.

Most nights they got back home just in time to go to bed. Geordie, having drunk more than his share, would quickly fall asleep, but not before taking her in his arms, kissing her, and whispering like a broken record, "I love you, I love you, I love you . . ." And that was all. But on those nights affection was as good as passion. Morning came so soon, and Kim had to be at the Studio at six o'clock to get made up for the day's shooting.

The weekends, to her disappointment, were not much livelier. They would come home later than on "school nights," so that by the end of the evening Geordie would have had enough to drink to put him into a quick snooze. In the morning, waking, he would make a big pitcher of Bloody Marys or screwdrivers. When the pitcher was empty, he would mount her, coming rapidly, and fall back into a sound sleep. Then he would wake up again just in time to get dressed and take her chasing off to Santa Anita or down the coast to Del Mar.

One evening Kim came back from the Studio to find him waiting for her in a state of great excitement.

"I told Manuelo we'd eat in tonight," he informed her, "if that's okay with you." Over a shaker of martinis he told her he had "goofed off" from the Studio and gone to Hollywood Park that afternoon.

"And guess what, honey? They were running the Catalina Stakes today for three-year-old fillies and Bitch Goddess was the odds-on favorite. But I had a hunch about a little beauty

I had had my eye on for quite a while. Laura Belle. Well, Bitch Goddess was the quickest away and led around the first two turns and down the backstretch by lengths. Laura Belle left the gate slowly and went a bit wide on the turns. Then with about five furlongs to go, Bendotte switched her to the rails. The track was fast along the rails and Bendotte brought Laura Belle in by a nose. Sensational!"

"Sensational," said Kim limply.

Geordie's eyes held Kim's feverishly all through dinner. On the billiard table Manuelo served them prawns stuffed with sausage, hearts of palm vinaigrette, and pineapple ice. While they ate, Geordie told her he was sorting through properties the Studio owned trying to find "something juicy" for her to do after she finished *Farewell, Arlington Street*. He had an idea. Why didn't they take a run up to San Francisco the next weekend and see "the old man and the old lady"?

As soon as Manuelo had cleared away the dinner dishes, Geordie went to the bar and poured a crème de menthe for Kim and a hefty brandy and soda for himself.

"Let's go to bed," he said abruptly, leering at her.

He was undressed in half the time it took her to get out of her clothes. Sucking in his slight paunch, he stood before her, proud and beautiful and erect.

Instantly he was on top of her, washing her with his kisses, caressing her body with sweaty hands, entering her. Almost instantly it was over. As he went, he cried, "Laura Belle! Laura Belle!"

Kim held him there awhile, trying to recharge him.

"I'm sorry," he sighed. "I've got one terrific load and when it's gone, it's gone."

Kim went to sleep wondering if Laura Belle really was a horse. Or a girl Geordie wished he was sleeping with instead of her.

In San Francisco they stayed at the town apartment of the senior Harmons. It was a sumptuous twelve-room duplex out in Pacific Heights with knockout views of the Bay, the Pacific, and the Golden Gate Bridge. Mr. Harmon was there to welcome them warmly. He was spending the weekend in town, instead of out in Hillsborough, because Mrs. Harmon had gone East "to do a little shopping and see some theater."

Kim was overjoyed that she didn't have Geordie's cold mother to deal with. She doubted that she'd ever win *her* over. By her absence Mrs. Harmon was making it plain all over again she didn't like Kim or approve of the marriage. But Mr. Harmon made up for her. He was so warm and easy to talk to, so handsome and distinguished-looking, so smiling and charming, it would always be fun to be with him. She couldn't call him "Roger" but "Mr. Harmon" sounded too stiff. "Do you mind if I call you Daddy Harmon?" she asked him. "Call me anything," he told her, squeezing her shoulders, "as long as you call me."

Geordie's father took them to Ernie's for dinner. Before dinner was served, Geordie excused himself from the table long enough for Kim to start worrying.

"Do you think he's being sick?" she asked her father-in-law.

"Not on your Nellie," Mr. Harmon laughed. "If I know my Geordie, he's at the bar knocking back a couple of quick ones. The waiters are never fast enough to suit him when it comes to serving drinks."

"I think he drinks too much," said Kim.

"He maybe does. And maybe does some other things that aren't good for him either."

Kim waited anxiously to hear what those "other things" were. Mr. Harmon didn't elaborate. He said brightly, "But I think you're just the girl who can straighten him out."

"I wonder," said Kim.

In bed that night Geordie snuggled Kim like a teddybear and went right to sleep. In the morning he fended off Kim's coaxing for sex. "We better not start anything here," he said. "Dad might hear us and that would be embarrassing."

Mr. Harmon's bedroom was down at the other end of a long hallway and the rooms were all soundproofed.

Kim and Geordie flew back to Los Angeles late Sunday afternoon and had dinner at the Brown Derby. Kim deliberately ordered a second bourbon old-fashioned to loosen her tongue.

"Do you really love me?" she asked Geordie.

"Are you nuts? Of course, I love you."

"Then why don't you make love to me more?"

"I'm in love with you twenty-four hours a day," said Geordie, "but you can't expect me to be making love to you twenty-four hours a day."

"It isn't even one hour a week."

"The time spent making love doesn't have anything to do with how much I love you."

"When you do do it, why does it have to be so fast? Bang, bang, and you're done. Why can't you wait for me?"

"When I get the urge, it hits like a bolt of lightning."

"I wish the lightning would hit me too."

"I'll try to hold my horses, honey. Honestly, I'll try."

One night the same week they had just got to bed when the phone rang.

"Hey, Lars," Geordie boomed into the phone, "how's it going?"

Kim could hear that it was a man's voice but she couldn't make out what he was saying. Most of the talking was being done on the other end of the line. Geordie wasn't saying much more than "Uh-huh" and "Sounds good" and "Think I can do" and "I'll let you know."

"Who's Lars?" Kim wanted to know.

"A guy on the East Coast. It's kind of a business thing. He's in publishing and his house is bringing out a couple of novels he thinks might make hot movie material."

The next thing he said to her, "I'd better take a hop East and see what it's all about. The books aren't out yet but I can read them in galleys. He might just have something there. I'd snap up anything in a minute if there was a character in it that could be shaped up for you."

"How long will you be gone?"

"Shouldn't be more than three, four days. You're a working girl and you'll be busy. I'll be back before you even miss me."

"I'll miss you."

He called her after he had been gone four days. He was calling from Nassau. He had to explain where Nassau was to Kim, whose sense of geography was pretty dim. He sounded jubilant.

"What are you doing there?" she asked.

"Behaving myself," he told her. "But I wouldn't be if you were here."

He said "business" had taken him to Nassau. He was checking out a lead to an author who was writing a novel that could be something the Studio should buy.

"When will I see you?"

"Soon, soon," he assured her.

In the background Kim heard a man's voice call, "Come on, Geordie. Game's on."

"Who's that?" she asked.

"Oh, just some guy. We're having a meeting."

Kim wondered. He said he was going to New York but here he was in Nassau. The day after his call she received an insured package sent air mail special delivery from Black, Starr and Gorham on Fifth Avenue. Inside was a pair of eighteen-karat gold and diamond bracelets. The card, in Geordie's handwriting, read: "To the darling of my life."

‛t was almost a week after the call from Nassau before he
ome. He came back on a Tuesday, having been gone
‛kends in a row. On those weekends even the gift of

jewelry couldn't keep her from feeling lonely and neglected and resentful.

He greeted her with kisses and another present. This one was a coral ring and matching earclips set with gold wiring from Van Cleef and Arpels. He told her how much he had missed her. But he was glum and distracted.

"I should have stayed in bed," he said, "for all the good that trip did me. I didn't find anything worth bothering with. Well, better luck next time."

It took a two-year-old horse to get Geordie smiling again. The horse's name was Believe In Me. Geordie believed in her and she paid him off by winning the Chevalier Cup at Hollywood Park the next Sunday.

Manuelo had Sundays off. Still, Geordie suggested they go straight home and scrounge something up for themselves instead of eating out. Driving back to Beverly Hills, he stroked Kim's thigh sensuously. "Now," he said, "how about giving Junior a pat on the head?"

Kim didn't know what he meant until he gestured to his fly. He had a full-blown erection and he wanted Kim to fondle it.

Before even making the drinks, Geordie peeled off his slacks. He sat in his briefs while they drank their cocktails. Then he threw together cold cuts and a salad from the refrigerator. As far as Kim could see, he was in a state of semi-erection all through dinner.

The dinner dishes were left on the billiard table, as Geordie pulled Kim to the bedroom. He yanked his briefs off and nearly shredded Kim's clothes, undressing her. He exploded almost the second he was inside her. Exploding, he screamed, "Believe in me!"

Kim puzzled at the meaning of his words until she remembered they were the name of a horse.

She didn't try to hold him. She let him roll off. But she didn't wait for him to sink into a comatose sleep. Spreading his legs wide apart, she went down on him. She stuck her tongue first in his navel and twisted it around like a corkscrew. Her tongue moved south, through a thin strip of smooth belly and then across a lush forest. It licked down a moist, soft runway of skin.

Geordie clamped Kim's head in his hands. "You don't have to do that."

"I want to."

He let her go on for a while. She went at him fast and frantic. But the effort got nowhere.

Again he clamped her head between his hands. "Who taught you that?"

She shook her head free and went back to what she was doing.

"Who taught you that?" he repeated coldly.

"Nobody. It's just . . . natural."

"Don't," he said irritably, pushing her head away. "It won't do any good."

He was sweet to her, he talked to her, he showered her with gifts, he took her to fancy places. When he was in the mood, he fucked her. She might have thought Geordie's style and frequency of lovemaking was more or less normal if she hadn't kept remembering that wonderful night with Mark Spencer, when her love life had such a glorious beginning.

The Tuesday night after Geordie's luck at Hollywood Park they were awakened by a long distance call. The ringing of the phone startled and annoyed Kim. But Geordie seemed happy to be getting the call.

" . . . sounds tempting . . . yeah, I think I can make it . . . give me a couple of days . . . call you back tomorrow. . ."

"Just some guy in New York," was how he identified his caller to Kim. "A literary agent. We sometimes buy stuff from him."

"Does he always do his work in the middle of the night?"

"He has insomnia."

The following Friday Geordie was off again. He told Kim he'd be in New York. He didn't know just how long he'd be gone, but she'd be hearing from him. When she did hear from him, he was calling from London. But he must have been in New York at one point because she had just received an emerald-studded brooch from Olga Tritt on Park Avenue with a loverly card in Geordie's handwriting.

"You never know in this crazy business," he said, explaining his presence in London, "where the trail's going to lead."

He sounded "up," the way he had in Nassau. He told her how much he missed her and how he wished he had her in his arms that very minute. But it was ten days before she saw him again. While he put on a show of being glad to see her, he didn't rush her to the bedroom. He was obviously depressed again.

"Let's not discuss it," was all he wanted to say about his trip. "It was a dud. I didn't come back with a thing."

He suggested they "get the hell out of town" that weekend by "taking a run up to Vegas." At the gaming tables in the Flamingo luck was with Geordie again. High from his good fortune and from a steady ingestion of alcohol throughout the long night, he took Kim home and virtually raped her by the dawn's early light.

A couple of weeks later, another late-at-night call from another man took Geordie from her on still another "business" trip far away. When she heard from him next, he was calling from the Caribe Hilton Hotel in San Juan, Puerto Rico. She asked what kind of business it was that had taken him to Puerto Rico. "Oh, one thing and another," he replied vaguely.

She doubted that these trips were strictly business. But what were they for then? She dismissed the thought that he could be meeting with other women. If he had been doing that, the word would somehow have got out and got back to her, with the Hollywood gossip mills grinding away day and night. Since their marriage, there had never been a call from a woman—at least at home—nor had he received a single piece of personal mail from a woman. When he came back from wherever he had been, there were never telltale lipstick stains on soiled shirts or the odor of stale perfume clinging to his clothes. All the calls that sent him flying here and there came from men. She had heard those voices with her own ears. A horrifying suspicion crossed her mind. Could it be? Was it possible . . . ?

"Geordie," said Kim casually, "let's take Lonnie Braintree out to dinner some evening. He's always doing nice things for me."

"Lonnie Braintree, your fairy friend?" Geordie asked sarcastically.

"My very good friend," she corrected him.

Lonnie too had a role in *Farewell, Arlington Street,* and he made working in such a nothing picture fun. Kim and Lonnie had been friends from the very beginning, from when she first came to the Studio and he was the shy little boy fresh out of England who wanted so much to be liked and make friends. Most of the kids who were at the Studio had since fallen by the wayside. There had been no parts for them as they grew older. The Studio let their contracts expire and they faded away. Of the whole small army of one-time child actors the Studio had had under contract, the only ones the Studio had kept on the payroll as young adults were Sally Strickland, Tinker Wells, Lonnie Braintree, and Kim.

Kim loved Lonnie because he was witty and peppy, perceptive, gossipy, and unphony, and totally devoted to her. They were such good friends they told each other everything. When Kim was down, Lonnie pulled her up. If Lonnie was ever down, he kept it to himself.

Lonnie had discovered his sexual nature early. He never fought his inclination to swing a different way. Nor did he take any pains to hide what he was. Since he was sixteen he

145

had been living with—and largely supporting—a muscle builder he had met on the beach at Santa Monica.

"I just want you and Geordie to meet," Kim explained the idea of the dinner to Lonnie. "I think you'll like each other."

"You're on, ducks," said Lonnie.

If Geordie and Lonnie hadn't liked each other, neither one of them would have showed it. They were both too well bred. Also, each would have gone out of his way to keep Kim from being embarrassed. It all went very pleasantly, with everybody drinking a little too much and laughing a lot. Lonnie held the floor with his endless flow of anecdotes and slightly bitchy gossip. The evening ended early with Lonnie excusing himself so he could get back home and see what his "old man was up to."

"Lonnie," said Kim the next day on the set, "what did you think of Geordie?"

"If Geordie loves Kimmikins," said Lonnie, "then Lonnie loves Geordie."

It was always "Kimmikins" or "lovey" or "my sweets." Kim smiled.

"Lonnie, I have to know something," she said, "but if you repeat any of this to anybody, I'll——"

"No threats, sweet. You know me better than to worry about that."

"Lonnie, do you think . . . you know how you're always saying how you can always tell right away by the eyes, by the way they look at you, if somebody is like you . . . well, do you think Geordie likes . . . boys?"

"In a word, no."

"You really don't?"

"Not from last night, anyway. It never once crossed my mind. I think he's a chap with a pile of maggots eating away at his insides. But I don't think he's one of the boys. They say there's a bit of it in even the hetero-est of males. If he's got a bit of it, I'd daresay it's buried so deep you'll never find it."

Kim was grateful and relieved. But she was not altogether convinced. "Another thing you're always saying, Lonnie, is that your world is really a small world . . . how the 'fraternity' knows who all the other members are . . . could you, well—"

"Look and see if he's in the directory? Consider it a fait accompli, my imperishable beauty."

The day *Farewell, Arlington Street* finished shooting, Lonnie embraced Kim in the general atmosphere of celebration of the crew and performers. Then taking her hand and gently pulling her aside from the rest, he whispered in her ear, *"Parlez-vous espagnol?"*

"*Un poco*," said Kim.

"El esposo, according to the bead I took, is el straight-o. If he isn't it's the best-kept el secreto in Hollywood."

That was one thing to put out of her mind. Kim laughed with relief.

Chapter 16

Kim had three free days before she had to get busy with costume fittings and rehearsals for her first so-called A film. It was to be a Hollywood-kitschy version of a nineteenth-century English classic.

Two days before shooting began, Geordie left on another of his mysterious business trips. Before she heard from him she received a brooch from Cartier's. With it was the usual card inscribed in his handwriting. The first time he called her it was from London, then he called from Deauville in France. He thought he would be home in a few days. But a few days later he was calling from a place named Baden-Baden. When he told her Baden-Baden was in Germany, Kim burst into tears and hung up on him.

She called Geordie's father in San Francisco. "Daddy Harmon, I want to see you."

"That's the best thing I've heard all day," said her father-in-law. "I want to see you too. As often as you'll let me." He paused. "How about my son? Doesn't he want to see me too?"

"He's not here. That's sort of the problem. That's why I want to talk to you. I could fly up and have dinner with you tomorrow night and get a later plane back so I can get up and go to work the next day."

"You've got it."

At Amelio's the next evening Roger Harmon insisted that Kim try the snails. Good? What did he tell her? Now she must order the squab . . .

"All right," he said, finally, lighting up his cigar and taking a first sip of espresso. "You didn't fly a thousand miles just to eat snails and squab. And to eat them with an ugly old goat like me."

Ugly! That would be the day. Geordie would be lucky, at the rate he was going, to look this good even ten years from now.

"I don't think Geordie loves me," Kim blurted out. "And I don't know what to do about it."

She shied away from bringing up sex. If Geordie loved her, she wanted to know, why was he always leaving her for weeks at a time? He said it was business. But how come he was always calling her from some place that wasn't the place where he was supposed to be?

"Do you know where he is right now?"

"He called me yesterday from Germany. A town I never heard of. Baden-Baden."

"Oh-oh." He frowned. "I know what that means."

"Tell me. I sure don't know what it means."

"Kim, you must know Geordie well enough by now to know he has little . . . well, habits."

"Habits? You mean his drinking?"

"That, too. But I wasn't thinking of that so much as his gambling. You must know he's very keen on gambling."

"Oh, I've always known that. The first time I went to his house I could see that. Then the trips to Las Vegas and the horse races—"

"It's maybe worse than you think—more of Geordie's life than you think."

Roger Harmon explained to Kim that Baden-Baden was a famous health spa in Germany. But it was equally famous for its casino. The other "business" trips that had ended up in Nassau and Puerto Rico and London had ended up there for a good reason. They were all meccas for gamblers.

"That's not saying he's not trying to tend to business somewhere along the way," said Geordie's father. "But he's also indulging himself. Giving in to his . . . compulsion. And I regret that from the bottom of my heart."

Giving in to his compulsion? What did that mean?

"Gambling is a part of all our lives," Geordie's father observed. "Every important decision we make is a gamble. Am I really cut out to be a doctor? Is this the man or the woman I should be marrying? If I put my money here, how can I be sure I won't lose it? A man like myself gambles all day long. Let's just take one area you're familiar with, Kim. Every time I decide to invest the bank's funds in a movie production I'm gambling that it will be a movie enough people will want to see—and pay their hard-earned dollars to see—so that the bank will not only get its investment back but make a profit. In one way or another, we are all gamblers every day of our lives. We have to be. Life itself is a gamble. But there is gambling. And there is gambling. The kind most of us do is in the everyday game of life. Then there's . . . Geordie's kind."

Geordie's kind, his father said, was the kind that romanced gambling as a way of life for itself. People like Geordie would trade their own mothers in for a few extra chips.

Not such a bad idea, thought Kim, if you had a mother like Geordie's. She felt almost relieved to know what was behind Geordie's disappearances. At last some light had been shed on the mystery of Geordie. Now she could be positive of one thing. He wasn't leaving her to chase other women—or men. It wasn't that he preferred somebody else's company—or body—to hers. At least that was something.

"I guess it was naïve of me," Mr. Harmon was saying, "to think marriage could cure Geordie. Not even a marriage to the most beautiful girl in the world. Geordie's gambling is a sickness, a disease. I wish to God I knew how he contracted it. He certainly didn't get it from us."

Mr. Harmon didn't know how Geordie got his gambling fever. But he knew when. It was during a summer vacation father and son had taken together in Europe. It was really the first time they had ever done anything together. Geordie had always been a good student, but during his last year at Choate he had begun to lose interest in his studies. His grades plunged and he was in real danger of flunking out. His father flew East one weekend to give him a pep talk. He told Geordie that if Geordie would pull himself together and graduate, the two of them would take off by themselves for a month in Europe. It was pure bribery, of course. But it worked.

Beginning in Marseilles, Geordie and his father then traveled to Cannes, where they holed up at the Carlton. They sunned themselves on the thin, pebbly beach. So this was the Riviera! What was all the shouting about? The beach was a joke compared to the beaches of California.

Roger Harmon had in mind they would go directly from Cannes to Switzerland. First to Lugano and then to Zermatt. But, on the beach one afternoon, Geordie said, "Dad, we're this close, can't we have a look at Monte Carlo?"

"The big attraction in Monte Carlo was the casino," said Mr. Harmon. "The night he set foot in that casino—well, I never saw anything like Geordie's reaction. This was a Geordie I had never seen before. The quiet, withdrawn boy I had always known opened up like a sunflower. It was like he was being born again. This was his scene, his milieu. He was almost beside himself with excitement watching those roulette wheels and the chemin de fer.

"I let him bet a little. The money went like that. Do you think that fazed him? Not for a second. He was all for coming back the next night. He wished we could stay in Monte Carlo until it was time to go home. I told him nothing doing.

We still had Switzerland and London on our itinerary. What do you think knocked him out in London? Big Ben? Westminster Abbey? The Tower? Piccadilly Circus? We could just as well have skipped all the sightseeing. He took it all in in that nice, polite way of his. But Geordie's London was the London he discovered accidentally. I had an English friend—actually somebody I knew through business—and he invited us to be his guests at the Clermont Club, one of those fancy London sporting clubs. They've got every kind of gambling game going. Again I saw that same wild, feverish gleam in Geordie's eye. I let him have a little money to try his luck. But it was the same story. Just like Monte Carlo. Every last pound and pence down the drain. Do you think he was daunted? Not on your life. It was all I could do to haul him out of London . . ."

Kim found it hard to believe, but she knew it was true. How could a guy who had so much going for him wrap his life around stupid nothings like dice and cards and rolling wheels?

"That fall he entered Yale," Roger Harmon recalled, "and he had a darned good allowance. Geordie, you know, never wanted for much. Not in material things anyway. I kept getting letters and calls from him at Yale for advances on his allowance. There was a suit at J. Press he just had to have, or all his buddies were going off to Mont Tremblant for a ski weekend, and he needed an extra hundred dollars to go with them. I had a good idea the money was being blown in backgammon and poker games. Almost the day he came into his own money, he dropped out of Yale. That's when he really started to cut high, wide, and handsome. I guess he still is."

Mr. Harmon did have some grim comfort for Kim. If and when Geordie blew his whole inheritance, that would be it. There would be no handouts from Papa. Geordie would have to put his shoulder to the wheel and provide for himself. What they had would eventually go to Geordie. But that would be a long time in the future. Mr. Harmon was in excellent health and he was looking forward to a good many more years before pushing up the daisies.

"You know, it's such a pity and such a waste," he said, "that Geordie should be stuck with this goddamn thing. He's really a fine boy. He's—I guess I shouldn't be calling anybody twenty-eight years old a 'boy.' He's kind and sensitive and basically very decent. He's never done anything mean or underhanded in his life. All right, he fibs a little about where he's been and what he's been doing. But that's his pride. He's ashamed of himself. He's ashamed that he's a slave to this idiotic passion. Geordie's got a first-rate intelligence. If he'd only use it! He's got a real feel for the movies. He knows what's good and what's bad. He can dissect a picture better than any of those old moguls who've been cranking them out for a hundred years. He could really make his mark in this business if he'd put his mind to it."

"But why, Daddy Harmon?" Kim asked. "How did Geordie get to be like this?"

"I told you I don't have the faintest idea. I think only a psychiatrist could crack that nut."

The mention of a psychiatrist gave Roger Harmon an idea. Why didn't Kim consult a psychiatrist about Geordie? It so happened he knew the name of one in Beverly Hills who had worked with "a lot of the Hollywood crowd." He was supposed to be good. Would Kim please consult him and send the bill to Mr. Harmon? If the psychiatrist thought Geordie needed treatment—and if Geordie was willing—Geordie's father would foot the bill for that too.

"From all you tell me about your husband," Dr. Friedman said to Kim, "I think he is a very disturbed young man. The gambling and the drinking and the unsatisfactory sex performance are all symptoms of a serious personality disorder. I would say he's very much in need of professional help."

"If he came to see you, could you cure him of his gambling?"

"That depends. It would depend on his motivation, how much he wanted to change. But he wouldn't try to change anything head-on—the gambling or the drinking or the erratic sexual behavior. We would go back to the origins of his troubles. We would have to explore the earliest experiences of childhood and have a close look at the influences that molded him into the person he is today. Once you uproot the sources of the disturbance, the symptoms will disappear on their own."

Dr. Friedman was able to be a little more specific about Geordie's case. "We're a long way from knowing a lot of the answers," he said. "Why does one man at odds with himself turn to gambling while the next one will become a woman chaser and someone else will go out and become a tycoon? One thing we do know about the compulsive gambler. He is a man plagued with profound feelings of sexual inadequacy. Deep down he feels that he's no good—impotent. Gambling holds out to him the hope of proclaiming his manhood, his potency. When he wins, he feels good about himself. He feels masterful. He has the feeling he's a whole man, a powerful man. In the flush of winning, he even feels sexually sure of himself . . ."

151

In the flush of winning, he even feels sexually sure of himself.

These were the words of Dr. Friedman that took hold of Kim and wouldn't let go. In the middle of the night she woke up suddenly and couldn't get back to sleep. Why, of course! Now it all started to make sense. Geordie's sex urges all coincided with his winning streaks. The day at Santa Anita when Believe In Me came in and she could feel his hard-on pressing against her ... the night after their wedding night in Las Vegas when the dice were good to him at the Flamingo ... Laura Belle at Hollywood Park ... When he won, he was sexy and raring to go. When he didn't win—which was most of the time—he had no interest in sex. A hug and a kiss, yes. Geordie was always affectionate. But the hug and the kiss or the hair strokings had no fire behind them if Geordie hadn't won.

Geordie came home bearing the gift of a two-strand necklace from Tiffany's in New York. He tried to put on a happy face. But the usual glumness showed through. Kim was not to be put off by either the gift or his mood. She was going to have it out with him.

"Now you're not going to tell me you've been away all this time just on business?"

"No, I wasn't going to tell you that. Part of the time I was sleeping and I took time out to eat."

"Don't tell me you were doing business in Deauville and Baden-Baden."

"In this business, you chase any lead you get. Most of them turn out to be——"

"Don't give me that stuff, Geordie. Don't lie to me. I've got a pretty good idea of what you're doing on all these trips."

"What am I doing?"

"You're gambling."

"Oh, smarty-smarty. Big detective. So what if I do gamble a little bit here and there? I never tried to hide that from you. I told you right in the beginning gambling was one of my little weaknesses."

"It's more than a little weakness. I think you should see a doctor."

"A doctor? You're kidding. There isn't a damn thing wrong with me. I never felt better in my life."

"I mean the other kind of doctor. The kind who treats problems."

"You mean a shrink? What the hell are you talking about?"

"I think you have problems. He might be able to help."

152

"In the first place, if you'd ever seen any of these Beverly Hills shrinks, you'd know they were crazier than their patients. In the second place, there's nothing wrong with me. If I did have any problems, I could solve them myself."

"I don't think you can."

"May I ask what you consider my so-called problems to be?"

"Gambling. You drink too much. And the sex isn't very good. You almost never want to fuck."

"All right, I like to gamble and maybe I do drink a little too much. I never pretended I was the world's greatest lover. That's a knack some people have and other people don't have. It doesn't have too much to do with love. Some of the horniest cocksmen are mean SOB's. I think it's far more important to be loved than screwed."

"Screwing's important too."

The dice were good to Geordie the following weekend in Las Vegas. Kim again was the beneficiary of Geordie's lucky streak. He favored her with a screwing that was almost satisfactory. But he came before she was ready and there was no second time around.

When she was no longer married to Geordie, Kim wondered if things might have turned out differently if she had been more patient. Geordie did try to be a better lover. But what kind of love life could she ever have had with him if having sex depended on the throw of the dice or the outcome of a poker game or the fifth race at Hollywood Park?

In later times she joked about Geordie's peculiarity. "I could have had more sex than the busiest whore in Hollywood," she said, "if I could only have figured out a way to have the dice loaded and the cards marked and the races rigged so Geordie would always win. And then have my cot set up right beside the crap table or the card table or the racetrack to catch him at his peak . . ."

None of her tears or pleas could keep Geordie from running off with his pals to London or Marrakesh or Monte Carlo. Now at least it was out in the open. He didn't try any more to pass these off as business trips. It was the weekends she minded the most. If he wasn't there on week nights, she had dinner with her mother and went to bed early, going over her lines for the next day. But the weekends were lonely and empty.

"Geordie," said Kim after one of his long absences, "this isn't working out. Maybe it's partly my fault. But it's no good. It isn't working out."

"Of course it's working out. We were meant for each other. We belong together."

153

"But we're almost never together. Even when we are, it isn't so great. So why go on being married?"

"If you're talking about a divorce, I'll never give you one. You wouldn't have any grounds. I'm faithful to you. I've never lifted my hand to you or yelled at you. You and I married for better or for worse. I haven't got worse since we married."

"No better either."

He tried hard to be better. For the next two weeks there were no trips from home or weekends in Las Vegas or visits to the racetrack. His drinking tapered off. Most nights they had dinner at home, just the two of them. After dinner he rehearsed her in her lines for the next day. He told her how he'd have written this scene and that scene if he had been the writer, sharpening the dialogue and wringing more drama out of the situation. His father was right about him. How brilliant and knowing he was about the movies! If only the Studio would let him try his hand at producing a movie he believed in.

One evening he brought home a script he said had been "in the hopper" for two years. What a movie it would make! What a role there was in it for her! The script was adapted from a novel published in the 1920s by a famous writer who was now dead. The name of the screenplay was *These Murdering Children*. Geordie read it to her and she agreed with him that it packed a wallop.

"I've sent memos to all the powers that be," said Geordie, "but no soap. They all admit it's a good script. But they say it's too depressing to draw an audience. It makes you wonder why the dumb stupes bought it in the first place."

Kim thought those two cozy, homey weeks with Geordie were the happiest in her marriage. Geordie was there. He was sober. He was attentive and affectionate. He hugged and kissed her and went to sleep snuggled close to her body. It didn't seem all that important that there was no lovemaking between them.

"This is enough for now," she thought. "This is better than it's been. Soon I can bring up the subject of the doctor again. Maybe it would take just a few visits to solve Geordie's problems . . ."

Kim's happy, hopeful period ended abruptly one night. They were both asleep when the phone rang. Again it was some pal of Geordie's, who did most of the talking. But she caught the excitement in Geordie's voice. She heard Geordie tell his friend he would meet him in Miami the day after tomorrow. Kim began to cry. It was all as clear to her now as

154

if they were standing under the noonday sun. She and Geordie were through.

"Honey, that was Billy Breedlove," Geordie boomed into the darkness. "One of my best friends from Choate. Now I'm leveling with you. You know my little failings. I'm not denying anything. Honey, I've been good as gold and kept the home fires burning for a long time, you'll have to admit. Now I'd just like to go off and have a little fling with my old buddy."

"Where to?"

"Well, Havana. I'll tell you why Havana. George Raft is running a club down there called the Capri Casino. They've got a guy—Tommy Renzoni—who's the top baccarat 'pro' in the world. Baccarat hasn't really got going in Vegas yet. I just have to see how this Renzoni guy operates."

"I don't want to hear about it."

"It'll be just a few days, Kim. You'll be done with your picture then and we can take a real vacation together. You pick the place."

In his excitement—or guilt—he began kissing and caressing her. He took off his shorts and got on top of her. But nothing came of his good intentions.

"It's so late," he said, rolling off her. "We both better get some sleep."

Kim went through the next day in a mounting rage. How dare Geordie try to pull this on her! How dare he try to use that "I'll only be gone a few days" line on her again! She had been through his absences often enough to know that a few days invariably stretched into weeks. As the long day wore on, she made her decision. She knew what she would tell him when she got home.

He was waiting for her with a snack tray and a glass of cream sherry. She brushed aside his welcoming kiss.

"Geordie," said Kim, "I don't want you to go to Havana. Or any place else."

"Kim, we went all through this last night. I told you—"

"I don't care what you told me. I don't want you to go. At all."

"Honey, honey, honey," said Geordie, setting down his glass. He put his arms around her and rubbed his cheek up and down against hers. "You're not being very nice to me. You're not being understanding."

"You're not being nice and understanding to me."

"Kim, I am your husband," Geordie reminded her. "I think a husband has a little bit of say about what he does with his time and money as long as he doesn't leave his wife unprovided for."

"I don't need you to provide for me," Kim exploded. "I can provide for myself. I'm telling you right here and now: if you leave me again, I won't be here when you get back."

"Boy, oh boy, that calls for a real drink." Before he said another word he mixed himself a jumbo martini and took a couple of big gulps of it. "Kim, I can't let you do this to me. I am your husband and I can't let you threaten me. Any more than I would ever threaten you."

"It's not a threat. I'm giving you notice. I'm telling you what I'm going to do if you go away again."

"That's a threat. I can't have you threatening me. You are my wife and I am your husband. Husbands and wives don't threaten each other. At least not in my book."

"In my book," said Kim, "husbands don't keep running off for stupid reasons. If they do, they shouldn't expect their wives to be waiting for them when they come back."

"A good wife would understand."

"Then I'm not a good wife."

"Kim, believe me, I'm not testing you. But I just can't let you lay down the law to me. I have to be free to come and go as I see fit."

"I'm not trying to lay down any laws. I'm just telling you if you go I won't be here when you get back."

Geordie went. He went declaring his undying love for her. He went promising that he would be back in a jiffy and would be bringing her all kinds of exotic gifts from Cuba. Kim promised him she would not be there no matter how fast he got back or what he brought her.

She wept as he buzzed down the driveway, speeding off to the airport. Weeping, she called his father.

"Daddy Harmon," she wailed. "Geordie's left me."

"Kimmie, Kimmie," came the soothing voice on the San Francisco end of the line, "now just hold on. I don't know what's up, but I know my son Geordie well enough to know he hasn't left you. He's crazy, but not *that* crazy. He's my son, my flesh and blood. He couldn't be that idiotic if he tried."

"He's left me," she wailed. "And I'm leaving him. I told him I wouldn't be here if he went. But he did."

Roger Harmon let Kim sob herself into near-exhaustion. Then he said quietly, "Now, now, darling girl, it's not as black at you think. Everything's going to be all right."

"It won't be. Oh, Daddy Harmon, I'm so ... low. I don't know——" She broke off, crying uncontrollably.

"Kimmie," she heard her father-in-law saying, "if you'll just stop crying. I have an idea. But you have to stop crying ..."

He waited patiently. He didn't say another syllable until Kim had quieted and was ready to listen.

"Now you try to get a grip on yourself. And here's what I'll do. I'll fly down the day after tomorrow. I can do a little business down there, and then you and I will have dinner and talk out our troubles. Is that a date?"

Roger Harmon took Kim to dinner in the Beverly Wilshire, where he was staying. The sight of him did her so much good she almost forgot for a moment how unhappy she was. He kissed her warmly and held her in a close embrace. He and Geordie looked so much alike she could shut her eyes and imagine that he was Geordie, that Geordie was here with her and it was just a bad dream that he had gone off and left her again.

Kim ordered a second drink before dinner. She wanted to loosen up enough to pour out her whole bag of woes. The story she told him was pretty much the one he had heard when she saw him in San Francisco. The new development, as she saw it, was that Geordie had tried to change his ways and had failed. No matter what promises he made, she could never believe him. It was hopeless.

"Kimmie, Kimmie, hold on there." Roger Harmon put his hand across the table and rested it on top of hers. "I think you're looking through the wrong end of the periscope or something. I take a different view entirely. I look on it as a hopeful sign he was able to kick his bad habits for two whole weeks. He's trying. You have to realize these things take time. Any progress in human behavior never moves in a straight line. It's three steps forward and two steps backward. I want—I hope . . . for both your sakes, that you can be, well, the hardest thing in the world to be when you're young . . . that you can be patient a little while longer."

"I've been patient so long," she sighed.

Roger Harmon took her home in a taxi. She had loved being with him. He had tried so hard to buck her up. But nothing he said had changed her mind. He took her to the door and turned the key to let her in. She thanked him and kissed him and said good night.

He was getting back into the cab when, on sudden impulse, she turned and called to him, "Oh, Daddy Harmon, it's still so early. I don't want to go to bed yet. Please come back and have a drink with me."

Roger Harmon dismissed the cab.

Manuelo had the night off, so Kim asked her father-in-law if he would fix the drinks. They drank in silence. There didn't seem much more to be said. For Kim it was a comfort not to

157

be alone, to hear someone else breathing. She let him fill her glass again with whatever it was she was drinking.

During the dinner she had felt a little better. It was something just to have somebody to talk to. Now she was sinking again. Maybe it was just the liquor. She felt the tears coming.

"Daddy Harmon," she cried, "it's so terrible. I can't live like this."

"Now, now, Kimmie . . ."

"Before I married Geordie I was always alone. You can't count my mother. We just mumble nothings at each other. Then you marry someone and you know how lonely you've always been and you think it's going to be so different. But this is worse than before. I didn't know the difference then. I wasn't expecting anything then."

"Kimmie, you and Geordie have a million years to—"

"No! It has to be now. I can't live without love. And I want it now."

The words she had blurted out rang in her own ears. Their impact hit her like a bludgeon. How could she go on living and not have the thing she said she couldn't live without, which was love—her kind of love?

She felt so sorry for herself and gave vent to the feeling in a prolonged howl of misery.

"Kimmie, Kimmie, don't. Come here."

They had been sitting just inches apart on a loveseat. Kim moved toward him. His arm encircled her and brought her head to his chest. She flooded his shirt front with her flow of tears.

"Daddy Harmon, you're so nice to me," she sobbed. "Will you let me do something?"

"Sure. Anything, baby."

"You just said it. Will you baby me? Can I just curl up in your lap?"

Big girl that she was, Kim managed to curl herself into a ball against the protective warmth of Roger Harmon. He cuddled her so soothingly she almost purred. After a long while she said, "Don't go, Daddy Harmon. You don't have to go. Stay here with me. Keep me company tonight. Please."

As they undressed modestly in the darkness of the bedroom, Kim explained, "I just want to be in the same bed with somebody. I want to hear and touch and smell somebody in the same bed."

In bed they kept their distance from each other. They talked quietly. Mr. Harmon urged Kim again to be patient with Geordie. He confessed that the prospects of their being happy together seemed so much greater than they had been with him and his wife. He confessed that his marriage had been the biggest mistake of his life. Then why hadn't they divorced? Well, there were reasons why it had been "expeditious" to stay married and present the conventional united front. Also, the thing about having means, you could each go your own way without getting too much on each other's nerves. And that's what they had done. As for love, he could tell her in the darkness, well, he had taken his pleasures where he found them.

Kim reached out for him then. He would find his pleasure here because she would give it to him.

He held back for a long moment. "We shouldn't," he whispered. Then, with a groan, he stopped fighting. "Just tonight," he said, as he took her.

The ardor of Roger Harmon's lovemaking drove Kim up the wall. She thought, "He's just as starved for loving as I am. What a waste for both of us! We've both got such a need for loving. If only Geordie could be like this! Is it only older men—like Mark Spencer and Roger—who know how to drive somebody wild in bed?"

When it was over, she said to him gratefully, "I love you, Daddy Harmon. I'm going to do what you want me to do. I'm going to try to make a go of it with Geordie."

Out of gratitude she did something else. Their sex was over and it had been completely satisfying for both of them. She wasn't trying to tease or arouse him. She simply wanted to give him an extended good-night kiss. The kiss started on the bottom of his feet, tickling him. It worked up slowly and thoroughly—missing no part of him—until it ended with the lapping of a tiny baldish spot on the crown of his head.

Finally Kim gave him a demure kiss on the lips. Then she curled up against his body, fetus-position.

Just before he dropped off, Roger Harmon kissed Kim and said, "We might not make it through the pearly gates for this. Our only defense is, 'It's all in the family.' "

If it had not been interrupted, this would have been the soundest sleep Kim had had since she married Geordie.

"Wake-up time, my sleeping beauty! Your lover has returned."

Was it a dream? A nightmare? Was she asleep or awake? Did she hear a door banging? Someone calling out . . . running toward her? Could it be . . . ? Oh, God alive!

An overhead light snapped on. Kim kept her eyes shut. She waited a thousand years to hear him say something.

"Oh . . . no! Oh . . . no!"

The anguished cry woke Kim's bed partner. "Geordie!"

"Oh . . . no!"

"Geordie, it's not what you think—"

159

"God damn you to hell, both of you. God damn you to hell. If I had a gun, I'd shoot you both dead."

"Geordie," said Kim, sitting up and pulling the sheets up to her chin, "you don't understand. You don't—"

"Understand? What's there to understand? I understand too goddamn well. Only an idiot wouldn't understand."

"Geordie," said his father, "all right, all right. Things happen. Nobody plans them. They just happen. They happen and it's all over with. They don't mean that much."

"Am I dreaming? I can't believe it. My wife and my father! The two people—"

Geordie stopped. He slumped over on an ottoman, burying his head in his hands. For a long time he looked frozen, mummified. There was no movement or sound from him. Then the shoulders started to heave. It was a self-strangulating kind of cry. It lasted as long as it could without breath to keep it going. Then came a gasp for air. And a horrible, blood-curdling howl.

Kim watched, horrified. This couldn't be happening to her.

At the sound of Geordie's howl, Roger Harmon leapt from the bed. Stark naked. He clasped Geordie's cheeks in a gentle vise. He kissed the top of Geordie's head. "Geordie, Geordie, my son, my son!" he pleaded. "Don't."

He cradled Geordie's head and brought it to him. Geordie was still bent over on the ottoman. His father stood close beside him. In this embrace Roger Harmon's privates brushed against Geordie's cheek, against the locked fingers shielding his eyes. Neither one of them seemed to be aware of this strange, intimate contact. Geordie did not flinch from the hands that held and petted him. He was too lost in his grief to break away from this bizarre, innocent embrace. Had they ever been so close—confronted each other in such nakedness—as in this surprise encounter, this moment of betrayal and heartbreak?

Geordie cried himself out finally. Lifting his head, he brushed his father away with one thrust of his arm. "I thought I was coming back to a new life," he said quietly, not looking at either one of them. "I thought it was going to be a turning point. I met Billy Breedlove in Miami. It was good seeing old Billy again. We've had good times together. We flew to Havana and took a suite at the Nacional. We downed a few planter's punches for old times' sake and had some dinner. Then we went off to the Capri Casino. George Raft greeted us and introduced us to Tommy Renzoni. Tommy knows a lot about baccarat that's news to Vegas. For a while I guess I was fascinated. It was a new game, the way he played it. I won a little, lost a little. But it wasn't hitting me the way it usually did. It didn't seem to matter all that much. Something had gone sour on me.

"I left Billy there and went over to the bar and started drinking. Not in gulps, not to get high. Just slowly, thinking. After about the third rum and soda, some thoughts started to poke up to the surface. 'Is this what it's really all about?' I asked myself. 'Chasing all around the world to play some silly game? Is this what the rest of your life is going to be like? Cards and races and dice and booze? You've got a certain amount of talent and brains if you'll just knuckle down and use them. You're young and healthy, and you've still got enough dough left to make things damn comfortable and enjoy life a little bit. Best of all, you're married to one of the most spectacular-looking girls in the world—and she's crazy enough to still be in love with you. Are you going to fritter away all that just to end up some fine day a bum and a drunk—and broke to boot? All right, you've got some problems. You probably won't be able to solve them on your own. But what's so disgraceful about asking for a little help—even professional help?'

"It all became crystal clear. I was going to shape up and it was all going to be so good. My wife had told me if I went away she wouldn't be there when I got back. She maybe meant it. But she couldn't move out that fast. If I went back on the next plane she'd still be there.

"Well, I was right about that." For the first time he raised his head to look at her. He looked at her through reddened, tear-soaked eyes. "She is still here."

Those eyes paralyzed her into silence.

"You can go," he said to her. "You can have your divorce. You said it's what you wanted. Now it's what I want too."

Then Geordie turned to his father and said, "I never want to see you again."

Chapter 17

Geordie and his father left the house—separately.

Alone, it was Kim's turn to cry. She cried for Geordie and she cried for herself. She cried out of her shame and guilt, and out of self-pity. Now she would be alone again. It seemed far worse than being even one-tenth married. With all his failings, Geordie was a gentle man who honestly had loved her in his own way. And he wanted to change. He had proved that by turning right around almost after he got to Havana. Then to come home and find her . . .

Kim didn't need the alarm clock to wake her up in the morning.

The mid-morning call to her on the set was from Geordie. Just hearing him got her hopes up. Maybe he was calling to tell her he had changed his mind. He would forgive her.

"Geordie, let's just forget everything and start—" she began.

"I've moved into the Jonathan Club," he told her. "I'll go along with any way you want to handle things. You better see a lawyer, get some advice. Do you want the house?"

"Geordie, I don't want a thing from you. You don't have to give me a thing."

"Either way, there won't be any arguments. Just let me know what you want to do."

Kim couldn't miss the dry finality of his tone. His mind was made up and that was that. There would be no second chances for her. Their marriage was over. The day after her picture was finished, Kim flew to El Paso and crossed over to Juarez to pick up a quickie divorce.

News of the divorce rocked the movie colony, especially the Studio. On their last phone conversation Geordie and Kim agreed not to tell anybody anything except they had "differences that couldn't be reconciled." In the usual Hollywood fashion they "would always be good friends."

The Studio propaganda mills went to work, grinding out yarns about two people being pulled in different directions by the demands of their careers . . . the young actress-wife rising toward spectacular stardom and the producer-businessman whose activities kept him away from California and their lovely Beverly Hills home so much of the time.

Kim moved out of Geordie's house into an English-style "cottage" on Coldwater Canyon which she sublet completely furnished from a composer at the Studio who was going East to do a score for a Broadway musical. There was a guest apartment over the garage, which was the ideal setup for having her mother with her without having her in her hair.

Soon after the divorce Geordie sold his house and moved operations to New York. The Studio release said he had been named "East Coast executive story editor." He would also continue to be active as a producer.

Kim saw Geordie again only once. It was maybe ten or eleven years after their divorce, and then they only nodded to each other from almost adjoining ringside tables at the Copacabana in New York. It was at a Joe E. Lewis opening. She hardly recognized him, he had grown so heavy and florid.

His once lean, aristocratic features were all thickened and blurred.

A few months later he was dead from acute hepatitis.

Asked to comment on his death, she said, "I always loved him. He was such a lovely boy."

The "boy" just popped out. Just the way it had that day when Daddy Harmon said the word and thought he shouldn't be using it to refer to his twenty-eight-year-old son.

In the sublet house there was no Manuelo, no one to help her run the house, and Kim hadn't the ghost of a notion of how this should be done. An ad in the Los Angeles papers flushed out, like a miracle, Indiana Mackenzie. A tall, thin, proud and beautiful Jamaican woman, there was no telling about Indiana's age. She could have been thirty-five or sixty, and she was not the stereotyped sort of "help." She came bearing warm references from other employers but few details about her personal life.

Kim took only a minute to make up her mind. "Indiana," she said, impulsively flinging her arms around the black woman's neck, "I need you."

"Does that mean I'm hired?" asked Indiana, smiling.

"You're hired. I want you to stay forever and forever. If anything ever happens to me and I can't pay you—well, I'll just have to commit suicide."

Indiana smiled her wise, reserved smile.

With Indiana installed, Kim gave a sigh of relief. She seemed to be over Geordie. Could it be a housekeeper was every bit as desirable as a husband? Exit husband, enter housekeeper—same difference?

Between pictures and husbands, she was just catching her breath when a new man entered her life.

One day she was lounging around her pool when she got a call from a man who introduced himself as Jeff Varnum. "I'm calling for Charles Cramer," he told her. "He would like to meet with you."

Charles Cramer! *The* Charles Cramer? It was probably a gag, some nut on the other end of the line trying to trick her into a date.

"Why?" she asked.

"He would like to discuss your career with you. As you probably know, he's getting back into the movie business. He's just bought the A-R-N Studios and he really wants to get the company back on its feet. Put out quality pictures."

"Why does he want to discuss my career with me?"

"He doesn't think you're being used to best advantage. He doesn't think you show up as well on the screen as you could and he doesn't think you're appearing in pictures worthy of your talent."

"Why doesn't he call me himself?" Kim asked suspiciously.

"He's in New York right now."

"He could call from New York. He can afford it."

"You have to understand. That isn't the way he operates. He's got his little, shall we say . . . quirks."

To say the least. From all she had heard about Charles Cramer he was a dilly. He was a multi-multi-millionaire who went around looking like a bum. His money made the Harmon money look like peanuts. He owned an automobile company that made compact cars, but he had been movie-crazy all his life. As a very young man he had flown the coop from Oklahoma and his family's oil wells to go to Hollywood. There he made a flock of films, mostly lousy. He had dropped a fortune or two on movies starring his female "discoveries," whose main talent was their boobs. He was famous as a lover of beautiful women. Especially movie stars. But he had never married any of them.

"He's flying back tonight," Jeff Varnum was saying. "He'd like to meet you tonight."

"I'll be here," said Kim. "He can call me when he gets in."

"He's not coming all the way back. He'd like you to meet him at his place in Palm Springs. I'll drive you down."

"Okay," agreed Kim.

What did she have to lose? She trusted the voice on the other end of the line. It figured. Charles Cramer liked to have his turn with an actress as soon as she got divorced. For the last ten years the first name to be linked with every beautiful divorcée in Hollywood was Charles Cramer. Now it was Kim's turn. Why not? He must have something—besides money. At least it would be an experience.

Nothing was quite the way Jeff Varnum said it would be. He didn't drive her to Palm Springs. It was a chauffeured, long, midnight-blue Cadillac that brought her to Charles Cramer's place in the desert. It was not in Palm Springs but in Palm Desert. And it wasn't Charles Cramer's place. It must have been borrowed or rented. Kim could tell that with one glance at the living room. The grand piano with the whole gallery of mounted youngish mommy-and-daddy and kiddie pictures on top of it was a giveaway.

Her driver, who had let her in, said, "Make yourself at home. Mr. Cramer should be here any time now."

As Kim heard the car drive off, she went into a panic. How had she got into this mess? Here she was all alone in a strange house in the middle of the desert. What was she

164

doing here? What was going to happen to her? Was somebody coming to kidnap—or *murder*—her?

She picked up the phone. Thank God, that was in order. The minutes seemed to drag into hours. In the desert night there wasn't a sound. Her terror mixed with fury. She was about to phone for a cab—it was almost *midnight*—when she heard the car charge up the driveway and come to a crunching halt near the front door.

And there he was. Charles Cramer. Thin as a scarecrow and way over six feet tall. Handsome but weak-looking with his receding chin, pasty complexion, thick eyebrows and thick moustache, tousled, oily hair. He wore sneakers and suntans and a T-shirt. And immaculate white gloves.

"Hi," he said. "Bitch of a day in New York. You have to put up with the goddamnedest crap in that town."

"So do you right here," Kim said sharply.

"At this hour of the night," said Charles Cramer, "I don't need any more crap. Especially from someone I'm trying to help."

"At this hour of the night," said Kim, "who needs your help?"

"It would be a big help if anybody could see those tits the way I see them. I've seen every goddamn movie you've been in and I've never seen those tits the way I'm seeing them now."

"I came down here so you could look at my tits?"

"You came down here to do yourself some good, baby," said Cramer. "One way or the other."

Kim smirked. "It doesn't look like I'll be doing myself much good tonight. Any way."

"Hang on until morning. Your luck could change."

"I wouldn't bet on it."

"Sleep there," said Cramer, thumbing toward a bedroom. "I'm out of it. Catch you in the morning."

With that, her host disappeared into another bedroom, banging a door.

She slept until she heard his knock the next morning. He came in still wearing the same clothes he had worn the night before. In his white-gloved hands he was carrying a tray. "Straight from the orange's tit," he said, pointing to a glass of juice. The only other thing on the breakfast tray was a dish of seeds. "Sunflower seeds. You need them. Get this down and let's get going."

They got going in a lime-green Ford.

"How come Charles Cramer drives a Ford?" asked Kim.

"Simple. You think I want anybody to recognize Charles Cramer?"

165

"I like to be recognized."

"You may get over it," he sneered.

He drove fast and recklessly back to Los Angeles. He pushed the car up to a hundred miles an hour. Kim's heart was in her mouth. She was much too worried about whether she'd get back alive to think about making conversation. Charles Cramer said nothing the whole day.

The silence became embarrassing only when he swung into her driveway and kept looking straight ahead.

"Well, thanks for the ride," said Kim.

"I have a hell of a lot on my mind right now. We didn't talk."

"Except about my tits."

"I'll come by tonight."

He raced the motor as a signal for her to get out. He just took it for granted she had no other plans and she'd be there waiting for him whenever he chose to show up. He read her right. He wasn't like anything she had ever seen before. He was really an odd one. She was curious. And he was, after all, Charles Cramer, who was only one of the richest men in the world and who had had romances with at least a dozen of Hollywood's top actresses. Yes, she would be waiting for him.

He gave her a good wait too. Again she had given him up for a no-show. He turned up after eleven o'clock without any apologies or explanations. He didn't take off his gloves to shake hands with her.

"Why do you always wear gloves?" she asked him.

"Germs. To keep from picking up about ten billion germs."

"So the gloves pick up the germs—instead of your hands?"

"Your face is your fortune," said Charles Cramer. "And your tits could be another one. But they're just not coming through."

He told her he had spent a couple of hours that day composing a memo to a structural designer. The memo was all about a brassiere for *her*. He wanted the designer to come up with a brassiere that would show Kim's tits the way they ought to look on the screen.

"Your breasts just don't look natural," he said. "You see the stacking. But up front you get a rounded, flat impression. They look phony. Those breasts should come to a dramatic crisis at the nipples. The nips are just lost. I told the designer to try for a kind of very light, sheer half-brassiere with points built into them that'll look like real nipples pointing through your dress. You should be wearing a lot lower neckline. Let the customer see as much as the law allows . . ."

166

Charles Cramer went on very seriously and in great detail.

"I could do a hell of a lot more for you than the Studio's doing," he said. "They're not building you up the way they should be. They're not casting you in hot enough stuff. I'd like to buy your contract out if that old Shylock over there wouldn't hold me up by the nuts."

"He's a great friend of mine," said Kim sarcastically. "Should I say something to him?"

"No, no. Let me handle it. Right now I've got a hell of a good story I'm going to see if I can get you on loan for. He'll try to hang me up by the nuts even for that."

He stopped talking and yawned. "Christ, I'm tired. I've been at it ever since I left you. I must have stuck my finger in fifty pies today. I even forgot to eat. Could you scare me up something to eat? What I'd really like is a peanut butter sandwich. Have you got any peanut butter? The pure kind? Just the pure ground peanuts and none of that oil and crappy chemicals added to it?"

"It's whatever Indiana got from the grocery store. She just calls up and orders."

"You should have her go down to the Farmers' Market. You can get a few things worth putting in your stomach down there. Like pure peanut butter."

Charles Cramer wolfed down the peanut butter sandwich Kim made for him on pumpernickel bread. The only other thing he wanted was a glass of milk.

"Now I'm really bushed," he said. "If you have a shower and an extra toothbrush I could make myself comfortable right here."

"I have a shower and an extra toothbrush," said Kim, adding with a smile, "but I don't have an extra bed."

"Nobody asked about an extra bed."

It happened that simply.

Kim didn't put up much resistance to joining him in the shower. But she was a little surprised to discover he must think she was really dirty. He soaped a washcloth and rubbed her thoroughly from head to toe. He even asked her to lift one foot at a time so he could wash the bottom of her feet. He barred the shower stall, standing with his back to it, while he went over his own body just as carefully. Kim could hardly help looking at him. He was so thin and tall and ribby. Everything about him was long and thin, his legs, his arms, his thighs, even his penis. He was so thin his ribs stuck out washboardy. The hair on his chest and around his penis curled up in little black ringlets.

She watched the thin, long penis slowly straighten out and stretch upward under her gaze. He shut off the faucet and

167

reached for her. He took her right there while their bodies were both wet. She wouldn't have believed it could work so beautifully standing up soaking wet. Of course it wouldn't have worked at all if Charles hadn't taken a stool from beside the bathtub and lifted her onto it.

On the stool Kim towered over Charles. Grasping her to him, he ravaged the breasts he said weren't "coming through" on the screen. The fingers of one hand raced nervously up and down her spine and along her rear cleavage. His forefinger found the opening there and inserted itself. It tapped lightly but frantically, as if it were teletyping an urgent message.

Then that enormously long and thin shaft entered her. It gradually but firmly wound its way up and up inside her, like a corkscrew pushing into the cork of an upended wine bottle. He ground and ground, tapping and tickling, showering her breasts all over again with his kisses . . . until it was time for both of them.

"Wahoo!" Charles bellowed in their big moment.

He pulled himself out of her abruptly. He lifted her off the stool and turned on the shower again. Then he repeated the whole bathing ritual, going over first his body and then hers with the soapy washcloth, washing every cell of both of them.

"This is the best way for people to screw," he said. "It may be more fun in bed, but it's damn healthier in the shower. Even if you shower and go to bed you pick up a hell of a lot of germs walking across the bedroom floor. Even in slippers, which are just germ repositories."

Germs or no germs walking across the bedroom floor, Charles Cramer wasn't done with Kim that night. He took her again as soon as they were in bed. He was starved for her. He couldn't get enough of her. His hunger for her was like his all-day-long hunger to close on any of a hundred unrelated deals where he knew he'd be screwing somebody.

He took her over and over again. He had been with enough women to know what to do with them. He knew how to drive them to the ceiling without gushing sweet-nothings in their ear or pleading undying love.

"I don't always fuck everybody I'm interested in," he told her in the morning. "I've had girls under contract for years I've never met, let alone touched. I'd still be just as interested in you if we hadn't just screwed the night away. I can do things for you the Studio can't do. I got a hell of a picture for you. I want to present your real tits to every paying movie-goer. I'm working on that. Nothing's changed."

"I'll call you," he told her when he was leaving. "Move in if you want."

Kim moved in for a night and then moved out. Charles Cramer lived in one of the plush pink bungalows in the Beverly Hills Hotel. He bragged to her that he had the hotel by the nuts. He rented the whole bungalow at half-price. He told them he needed only one suite and he didn't want anybody living in the other suite. Wasn't it better to have half a loaf than none? Some of those bungalows were empty most of the time. Wouldn't it be smarter to have a steady tenant at half fare than maybe no tenant at all?

It figured. Charles Cramer expected to have his way in everything. And usually he got his way. The night she spent with him at the Beverly Hills Hotel he was calling people at all hours and in every corner of the world. Whoever he was calling was always there on the other end of the line. He barked orders into the phone and hung up abruptly. Between phone calls he ravished her.

He made love with the same self-assurance he talked business. He expected she was going to want it when he wanted it. Like most people who get their way, he had bargaining power. He was good at what he did. If you were connected with him in business, you were damn smart to hang on the phone waiting for his call. If you were his lover, well, he could screw a girl blind. He didn't offer undying love, just another screw, a roof over the head, and maybe some half-assed future in films.

Kim laughed aloud after each round in the Beverly Hills Hotel. After their third session, she said, "I was just thinking how cock-sure you are."

She giggled again and fell asleep.

In the morning Cramer told Kim he had to go to Indianapolis, where his automobile plant was. He might be gone nine, ten days. He'd call when he was headed back and she should be waiting for him.

Kim told him she didn't want to move in. She told him she'd like to hear from him and she hoped she'd be free to see him when he got back to town.

"You better be free," he told her.

Kim smiled to herself. He was trying to make it clear to her that she was his property, his "No. 1 girl." But he was free to whizz off on business and stay away as long as he wanted. She was supposed to be true to him while he was gone and waiting for him when he got back. What was there in it for her—except a good screwing if and when he was around?

While he was gone, she thought of something else there

169

might be in it for her. She made an appointment to see the Boss.

"What did I tell you about Geordie Harmon?" he teased her. "Didn't I tell you that would never work out?"

"I don't know what you're talking about," said Kim sweetly. "Who's Geordie Harmon?"

"All right. Why are you giving me the honor of a visit? What can I do for you?"

"I've been seeing Charles Cramer and he says—"

The Boss roared as if he had just heard the hugest joke of his life. "Don't let it go to your head. It don't mean a thing. He's laid every gorgeous broad in town. Laid and relaid 'em."

"Mr. Cramer is very interested in my career. He thinks I just get put in lousy pictures and I even look lousy in them."

"Let me tell you something, little girl. That son of a bitch wouldn't know a good picture if he went blind looking at it."

"He has a picture he thinks would be real good for me."

"I'm telling you he doesn't know shit about the picture business. He might have two billion dollars. But he doesn't know from shit. He made five of the biggest bombs in the history of the business. He goes off in fifty other fucking directions and he thinks he can come back here and make something out of that fucking, A-R-N jerk-off shit-house."

"He says he's got a good 'tits-and-sand' picture for me. He says 'tits-and-sand' pictures are the only things the public wants to see."

"If he thinks he's going to get you on loan, I'm going to hang him up from the skies by his nuts."

"That's just what he said you'd do."

The Boss smiled sweet as a saint. "Then I guess we understand each other all around."

"The other thing he said," said Kim, playing her trump card, "is he'd like to buy out my contract. He says he could do a lot more for me than you are."

"Bullshit! Listen to me, little girl. That son of a bitch doesn't know nothing about the picture business."

"He says not only do I get lousy pictures but I'm getting gypped to boot."

"Now you just look here. You're listening to the cheapest, chiselingest bastard on God's fucking earth. That fucker isn't about to give you anything—and I don't care how good a lay you are—unless he's thinking he can make a bundle off you. And have a lot of fun fucking somebody else in the deal."

Kim thought the Boss was probably right. He was such a bastard himself he should be able to spot another bastard when he saw one.

"I just don't know what to do," she said. "You may be

right about Charles—what he knows about the movies. But he wants to give me a five-year contract and pay me two thousand a week . . ."

Charles Cramer had never said such a thing. The Boss bore his eyes into Kim. She met them without flinching. He believed her.

"That's more than you're worth," he said finally, "but we'll match it. You'll be better off here than you will with that shit-hole screwball."

Again Kim found herself agreeing with the Boss. Nothing Charles Cramer could ever promise or give her would seriously tempt her to leave the Studio and put her future in his hands. She had a hunch enough about people and situations not to put her trust in him. But knowing him had paid off. If he was getting his fun cheap from her, she had found a way to use him too.

The day before Charles Cramer got back to town the Boss called to tell Kim he had a "fantastic" picture lined up for her. The name of it was *These Murdering Children*. By an odd coincidence, it was the very picture Geordie had wanted for her and couldn't get the Studio to go ahead with.

"It's a big A picture," the Boss drooled. "But we have to hold up for three months."

"Why?"

"Why? I'll tell you why, little girl. Your co-star is going to be Randolph Jahr. For Randolph Jahr you wait if he isn't ready. He isn't ready. He won't be ready for three months. Have fun with Charles Cramer and fuck him off."

Right-o, Boss. Check.

When he did phone, Charles Cramer asked if she'd meet him at the Players Club. This was the first time Cramer had ever really treated Kim to anything and she was greatly impressed by the three-tiered restaurant. It was a masterpiece. She had never seen such lavish decor or had such spiffy service or eaten such marvelous food in her life. In the middle of dinner she was startled by a big stage that began to rise right beside their table. Hydraulically propelled, Charles explained. On the risen stage a group of players assembled to put on a funny little skit.

After the performance Kim told Charles Cramer the Studio was putting her into a picture she was excited about for the first time. He said she was an idiot for not going with him. No matter how good the script or Randolph Jahr was, she had a better future with him than with the Studio. She didn't tell him about her fat raise.

Charles Cramer was almost tender that night as he screwed Kim. He did something she had always wanted him to do and he had always refused, saying it was unsanitary. He licked deep inside her ears.

Deep inside her ears he stopped licking long enough to whisper, "You're nuts if you stick with that fucking Studio."

Early in the morning he was gone again. He didn't tell her where he was going and she didn't ask. He said he'd "buzz" her when he was coming back to town again.

Kim found she got along without him very well. He was good in bed and he could keep going all night long. But as a person she had no idea what he was really like. He didn't open up and tell her much about himself. He had a great interest in her career—for what he might be able to get out of it, she thought. Otherwise he only wanted to show her off like a trophy and get her in the sack. He wasn't interested in what she thought or how she felt about anything. They were just two ships passing in the night.

Next to being in bed with him, the most fun she got out of the relationship was reading about it in the columns:

"The fabulous Charles Cramer has lost his heart to still another Hollywood beauty . . ."

"Charles Cramer has been hand-holding these nights with a brand-new glamourpuss whose initials are K.H."

"Tittle-Tattle: What playboy-inventor-industrialist has been spending his lonely evenings in Make-Believe Land with what up-and-coming screen siren?"

Three days later he was calling her from Seattle and telling her to meet him again at the Players for dinner that same evening. There, he announced he had thought of "a new tactic." She didn't know exactly what he meant until they got home. In bed they had hardly touched when he turned her around. He was already hard and she could feel him pounding at her back door.

"No," she said.

"Why not?"

"It'll hurt."

"Not the way I do it. I'll put Vaseline on and edge it in slow as molasses in January. You'll go through the ceiling."

He could be right. It could be the thrill of a lifetime. She had often wondered what it would be like. She had thought she might go for it a lot. But why should she make it so easy for him? Why should he get what he wanted, not even caring if it hurt her or gave her a big thrill?

"No," she said. "No Vaseline." She was glad that with her back turned to him he couldn't see her grinning. "I don't want any Vaseline up there. Just natural. You wet it with your tongue."

"Oh, shit," groaned Charles Cramer.

For the longest minute he didn't even seem to breathe.

"Come here," he said finally, leading her to the bathroom.

He took a soaped, wet washcloth and concentrated it on her rear opening. His thrusting fingers under the cloth poked so deep inside her she thought they might come out the other end. He dried her thoroughly. Then he started it all over again. The poking with a wet, soapy washcloth. The drying. He did this four or five times.

In bed he started to rub against her from behind again. Kim clamped herself shut. She had him, as it were, by the balls.

Groaning again, Charles gave in to her. As she felt his tongue go into her, Kim had a thought that almost made her laugh aloud. The publicists at the Studio were always asking her for items about herself they could feed to the columnists. She might say to them, "Last night I had Charles Cramer eating my ass."

Kim made him give her a good tonguing before she let him do what he wanted to do. Just as he was about to go into her, she said, "Now get the Vaseline."

"Bitch," said Charles.

He tried to excite her with his finger while he jabbed at the other end. But Kim didn't find this much of a substitute for the real thing. His jabbing from the rear certainly didn't send her through the ceiling.

"Well?" he asked afterward, when she didn't say anything.

"I'd say," said Kim, thinking of a pun, "it's not all it's cracked up to be."

Charles snorted. He was restless and in no mood to go to sleep. At one thirty in the morning he made a phone call. "Get your ass out of bed," he barked into the phone. "I want you there in an hour."

"Come on," he said to Kim. "Let's take a shower."

In the shower Kim tried to get him started again. "Not now," he said. "Get your clothes on and we'll go for a spin."

The spin was in a different Ford from the one they had come back from Palm Desert in. He told her he had a whole bunch of Fords and kept switching from one to the next. If he drove just one or two, people would start to recognize him.

Charles went into one of his moody silences as they drove at high speeds westward into the Valley. It ended in the darkened Van Nuys airport, where a pilot was standing beside a plane waiting for them.

Charles gave some orders to the pilot, ushered Kim into the plane, and banged the door to the cockpit shut. He didn't bother turning on any lights. In the darkness Kim could make out this wasn't like any ordinary plane. It had to be his private plane, fitted out to suit him. There was a bed, a huge desk with dictating machines, and a shower stall.

They sat side by side in two armchairs with seat belts until the plane was aloft. Then Charles grabbed her hand. "Get your clothes off."

In the bed he took care of the frustrations she had felt from the one-way sex trip they had taken earlier. She had no idea of where she was. Once she looked out the window and saw the ocean. Another time it was the desert. Who cared? Charles was keeping her mind on other things. He was so charged up he might never run out of gas. He was like a whole shipboard of sailors getting shore leave after months at sea.

It was almost dawn before they put down.

"Welcome to the Mile-High Club," said Charles, letting her off at her door.

"Mile-High Club?"

"You're a member if you've been screwed when you were 5,280 feet up in the air or higher. You were screwed that high up."

Kim was just falling asleep one night about a week later when the phone rang. It was Charles Cramer.

"I've had a bitch of a flight," he told her. "I just got in. From Toronto. I should be there in forty-five minutes. I didn't eat any of that poisonous garbage on the plane. Just fix me a peanut butter sandwich and I'll have a glass of milk."

Kim did a slow burn after putting down the phone. Who the hell was he to be calling her at midnight and ordering her around? What had he ever done for her except screw her? If he wanted a peanut butter sandwich, he could damn well make it for himself. If he wanted a screw, he could go some place else. She wasn't in the mood tonight.

She waited for him in the living room in her nightgown and robe. There he stopped dead, sniffing.

"Who's been here?" were his first words to her. "Who's been in this fucking room?"

"When?"

"When? Today, you silly—"

"Today? Well, let's see. Indiana dusted and vacuumed this morning. This afternoon Mother and I played a game of—"

"Does either your mother or Indiana smoke cigars?"

"Oh," said Kim coolly. "That was somebody else. But not today. Last night."

Kim had had a little adventure in Charles's absence, it was true.

In the darkness Charles came toward her. Kim stood up to face him.

"You two-timing little cunt," he raged. "Who was it?"

"A very nice writer," said Kim. "We had such a great time. I wish he was here now."

She did wish it. He had been so sincere, coming to her house late in the afternoon, wanting to do an "in depth" interview of her. He had taken photographs of Kim around the pool, gardening (which she never did), arranging flowers, pouring tea (which she never drank), and studying scripts in her study. He was so nice, with laughing eyes, that she asked him to stay for dinner, and then after dinner, she asked him to stay the night. Being in bed with him had been like being in bed with a live teddy bear. She had loved cuddling against him. He was so gentle and undemanding. Yes, she wished she were confronting him now. Not Charles Cramer.

When she looked up from her thoughts, she saw Charles coming at her. Suddenly he was squeezing her throat with his hands. For a moment she panicked. Would he choke her to death? His grip loosened. He threw her down on the sofa.

"You two-timing little cunt," he roared. "The second my back's turned, you're like a bitch in heat. Have to make it with the first nobody you can find. Some two-bit writer who couldn't buy his way—"

"Look, you don't own me. I'm not sitting around here waiting for you to show up. I don't owe you a fucking thing. What did you ever do for me? Except fuck me? Just the way you fuck everybody—one way or another."

"Shut up."

Getting to her feet again, Kim picked up steam. "You're just a machine. In bed you're a fucking machine. Everywhere else you're a machine that sucks people dry and then grinds them up into dust. You're so cheap you stink. You never even gave me a piece of junk jewelry I could throw in the garbage can."

Charles started for her again but she backed up to get in another lick. "You may have a trillion dollars," Kim jeered, "but you're not worth a shit."

Charles had her by the throat again. She was terrified that this time he really would kill her. Holding her by the throat, he flung her to the floor and began slapping her on the face, over and over again.

"No cunt ever talks like that to Charles Cramer," he said, slapping away. "You've got a lesson to learn and I'm just the one who's going to teach you."

Kim let him slap her until she had wiggled into a position where she could give her leg a terrific kick way up between

175

his two legs. She kicked him so hard in the balls he screamed and bent over, holding his sides. Kim scrambled to her feet and rushed over to the long table behind a loveseat. She dumped out the flowers from a porcelain vase and hurled the vase at Charles's head. She was on target. The vase crashed in a thousand pieces. He fell to the floor. A second later blood was gushing from cuts all over his head.

The sound of yelling and screaming and falling bodies brought Indiana to the scene.

"Miss Hudson! Oh, Miss Hudson! What's happened?"

"Not enough," said Kim. "The bastard's still alive."

"Oh, Miss Hudson, this is terrible. Look at him."

Whimpering, Charles Cramer had a handkerchief to his head, trying to sop up the flow of blood.

Indiana went to him and bent over him. "Do you want me to call a doctor, Mr. Cramer?"

"Doctor?" he yelled at her. "And get my name and picture in all the papers?" Without looking back at either of them or saying another thing, Charles Cramer stumbled out of the room, holding his handkerchief to his head. They heard him drive off.

"Go to bed, Indiana," said Kim. "Don't clean up the mess tonight." Sighing, she added, "That's all he is. A mess."

Chapter 18

Kim went down in history as the only one of Charles Cramer's "romances" who ever talked back to him. But better than talking back to him, she said, was not talking to him at all. He had been an experience. But it was so good not knowing him any more. God had blessed him with a lot. Money. Power. Brains. Success. Looks. Say this for Charles Cramer, too. He had balls and a cock. The only organ he was missing was a heart.

Kim was at loose ends. She still had two more months to go before the new picture would begin. She had never had so much time on her hands. She didn't know what to do with it. She was restless.

I really hadn't seen her to talk to and spend time with since Las Vegas. My first thought, as I laid eyes on her again, was, "It's got to stop. She can't keep getting more beautiful every time you see her. It has to stop some time and start going the other way."

In the commissary one day she saw Maura Anderson sitting by herself at one end of a long table. She asked if she could join her.

"Park your buns right there," said Maura.

Kim had always liked Maura since the time she had played Maura's younger sister in that dopey picture with Mark Spencer. Maura was no phony. She said and did exactly as she pleased. She didn't give a damn. She wasn't afraid to tell anybody off in language that would make a longshoreman blush. Even the Boss himself. She had been built up as the sexiest of the sex kittens. Off-screen she was busy living up to her image. She liked her fun, as they say. She was getting a big reputation. Hollywood being the home of wild exaggerations, she was supposed to have "had" everybody in town. The Boss tried to tell her to lie low. Maura said, "What kind of a sex kitten is it that doesn't go in for sex?"

"Jesus, I liked doing that one," Maura recalled, "with you and old Mark-o. Old Mark-o—one hell of a guy! There's one pair of britches I never did get into. God knows, I tried. I almost came out of my own britches, trying."

Kim smiled but kept her secret.

"Who needs marriage?" said Maura. "I've been having the time of my life since I dumped that bastard I was hitched to."

"How do you go about having the time of your life?"

"Oh, honey, it's there. It's there everywhere just waiting for you."

Kim looked puzzled.

"Honey, you should be playing the field like crazy," said Maura sympathetically. "A girl who's got absolutely everything. You can crook your finger and have every guy in the world panting."

"Oh, Maura," sighed Kim, "I'm not in your class."

"Do you want me to fix you up with somebody?"

"Well—"

Maura snapped her fingers. "I've got just the bird. Lance Sullivan. A beautiful hunk of flesh. He's a stud posing as an actor. He's doing a five-second bit on some D picture they're shooting on the back lot. He's never going to make it. Zero talent. His big talent is studding. He likes to make it with actresses who are more important than he is. Listen, *anybody's* more important than he is. The nice thing is it doesn't get sticky. You're not going to fall in love with him and he's not going to fall in love with you. He's so stuck on himself there isn't room for anybody else. But take it from your big sister, he delivers some lay! He's hung like a goddamn horse . . ."

Everything Maura said about Lance Sullivan turned out to

177

be true. He gave Kim a night to remember. She got his number for future reference. She couldn't imagine wanting to see him very soon again. Good as he was in bed, he was a complete bore out of it. A silly, preening, posturing ham-bone.

She called Maura to thank her for "fixing" her up. "Any time, honey," said Maura. "I've got a million of 'em. Ready for another whirl?"

With anybody else but Maura, Kim would have been ashamed to admit she was.

Maura lined up Kim with a whole series of satisfying one-night stands. It was just understood this was it—a single fling and that was the end of the line. Most of the men were bit contract players at the Studio or technicians of some kind. They were all good "performers." It was also understood they'd keep their mouths shut. It would be their necks if they started talking. They could be replaced. Their value to the Studio was nothing compared to Maura or Kimberley Hudson.

At Maura's suggestion, Kimberley started keeping count.

"For the record, Kim," said Maura. "Guys are always carving notches in their bedposts every time they get one of us in the kip. Why shouldn't we chalk up our conquests too? Wait till you see how I do it!"

It wasn't one of Maura's better suggestions. It got Kim into a lot of trouble later. If she had kept a "record," Maura's way, she might have been all right. Instead Kim came up with the idea of her Little Lavender Book.

It really was a Little Lavender Book. It had ruffled lace edges. It looked like the kind of book a proper Victorian lady might have used to jot down birthdays and wedding dates and other family remembrances. Kim's Little Lavender Book was a kind of love diary where she rated her lovers and made notes to remember them by. Sample listings:

M.S. (Mark Spencer) Greatest yet! Perfect lover. Strong, gentle, fun, sweet. Terrific dong. A-plus.

Doc B. Kind, fatherly. Perfect dear. Sucked nipples. No action below. Not fair to grade him. Too old.

G.H. (Geordie Harmon) Lousy. Gets it up only when he's won something or he's half-plastered. One-time Johnnie, shoots off in a second. Fat cock, knobby head. D-minus.

C.C. (Charles Cramer) *Prick*, with long, thin prick. Screws like well-oiled machine. Germ nut. Wish I had given him the clap. Real bastard. A.

Maura was so nice to Kim that Kim really began to think of her as her big sister, just like she had been in the movie.

178

All the men she lined up for Kim turned out to be just what she said they'd be. She never dealt her a dud. She never passed along anybody who was going to be bad news.

"I never thought this could be fun," Kim said to Maura. "Doing it with guy after guy and not caring if you ever saw any of them again. Just doing it and not getting lovey-dovey with anybody."

"You bet your sweet ass it can be fun," said Maura. "Take it from your great-grandmother here. It's a hell of a lot more fun than coming home every night to some bastard you'd like to kill."

If it weren't for the Little Lavender Book Kim might have lost count of just how many overnight lovers there had been. Sometimes, in a slight morning-after hangover, she had trouble recalling the face of the lover who had just left. As the haze lifted, she made her jotting in her book and checked in with Maura.

Kim's twenty-first birthday called for something special. Maura insisted on it. Maura insisted on being part of the occasion.

"Take it from your maiden auntie," said Maura. "Us'n two old maids are going to go out and have ourselves a time. On your maiden auntie."

Kim felt a warm glow of affection for her friend. Maura could be telling somebody to go fuck themselves out of one side of her mouth and talking love to somebody else out of the other side of her mouth. When Maura liked you, you really had a friend. Kim loved it when Maura came out with her "Take it from your big sister" or "Take it from your maiden auntie" routine. It sounded so warm. Maura was wild. She was a wild, beautiful girl who was going to be herself if it killed her.

Maura drove a flashy white convertible. That night she drove it to a little Mexican restaurant on a dark sidestreet just off Olivera in downtown Los Angeles. "Hell, we've both been to all the smarty-farty places," she said. "Let's go some place where we can have some fun."

Maura had obviously been there before. They all knew her and the place came violently to life. A bottle of tequila was rushed to the table. From the kitchen came a bowl of guacamole and tacos. The mariachis who were lounging around a big table in the back snapped to their feet and blasted into "Guadalajara"—Maura's favorite.

Maura's idea of fun was swilling down the tequila and tuning in on the blarey, brassy music. Then it was getting up and doing her version of the Mexican hat dance. She and

179

Kim both got half-buzzed from the tequila. Maura ordered chicken moles and enchiladas for them.

"See anything here you like?" she asked Kim.

"I like it all," said Kim.

"That's not what I mean. See anything you'd like to shack up with?"

There were just the mariachi players and a couple of seedy-looking customers at the bar, nodding over their drinks. Could Maura be serious? Were any of these Maura's speed?

"Okay," said Maura, "not interested. Choosy cunt."

She slapped down some money and they were away into the night.

"Let's just drive," said Maura, "and catch our breath."

Maura's driving was enough to leave anyone breathless. She raced up the coast highway, past Zuma Beach, Point Mugu, Oxnard, almost to Ventura, before turning back. She went at a speed that would have got her arrested if anybody could have caught up with her. On the return swing she zoomed the white convertible down Wilshire Boulevard.

"Do you go for dark meat?" Maura asked.

"You mean . . . turkey?"

Maura laughed. "I'd say rooster. Christ, Kimberley. Take it from your aging mother, who happens to be a virgin, you need educating."

Maura had in mind a jazz joint on Central Avenue in Hollywood. The musicians and the clientele were almost all Negroes. That's what she meant by "dark meat." Some of those "spades" could really give a girl a birthday present she'd never forget.

Maura was out of this world. A Southern girl—even an ex-poor white trash Southern girl—talking like this? She had a lot to teach Kim, as she had said. Kim was with her all the way.

But they never made it to the Cockamamie on Central Avenue.

Maura stopped for gas in Westwood.

A young attendant popped out of the station to fill her order. His eyes nearly popped out of their sockets when he saw who was sitting in the car. He was tall and skinny and blandly, blondly handsome. As he bent over with the gas hose, Kim saw that he had a chunky, well-rounded rear end that didn't seem to go with the rest of him. In later years she always described herself as an "ass-woman." She got turned on by men with ample back porches.

"Him," she murmured to Maura. "I want him."

"You got him, honey," said Maura. To the young man, she called out, "Hey, come here a sec when you're done."

© Lorillard 1974

King Size
or Deluxe 100's.

KENT

WITH
THE FAMOUS MICRONITE FILTER

DELUXE LENGTH

DELUXE LENGTH KENT

If you have
a taste for quality,
you'll like the taste
of Kent.

© Lorillard 1974

Try the crisp, clean taste of Kent Menthol 100's.

The only Menthol with the famous Micronite filter.

The young man was struck dumb as he looked into the car at so much beauty gazing right back at him.

"Do you ever put your nozzle in anything beside a gas tank?" Maura asked him in a purring, sexy voice.

"Uh?"

"I'll try again. How'd you like to go on a picnic?"

"Picnic?" he gulped.

"Yes, picnic."

"Tonight?"

"Yes, tonight," said Maura. "Now. Some picnics take place at night. And they're the best kind, believe me."

The kid looked like he was catching on but couldn't believe his eyes or ears—that this was happening to him. "Where?"

"Leave that to us," said Maura. "Get out of that grease-monkey suit and meet us up there."

She pointed to a dark garage that was open. It was about a hundred feet off Wilshire. It belonged to a semiresidential hotel that had just opened.

The kid was there about two seconds after Maura swung into the garage. He was wearing Levi's and a white T-shirt.

"What took you so long?" asked Maura.

"I had a knot in my shoestring," he came back.

"Jesus, Kim," said Maura, "he's not as dumb as he looks. Okay, we're not going very far. Sorry if that disappoints you."

They sure weren't going very far. Maura swung the convertible right back past the gas station. A little farther on, she turned into a quiet unlit street that didn't seem to be going anywhere either.

"Bottoms up," she announced. "From here we walk."

They were on the Westwood edge of the Los Angeles Country Club. Maura took a blanket out of the trunk and led them to the sidewalk. On the other side of the club was Beverly Hills.

Maura hiked her thumb to get them to follow her. She took them off to the right, into a wooded section of the country club. She spread the blanket under a big, broad-branched tree where the terrain was level.

"You first," she said to Kim. "It's your birthday."

The kid—they never did find out his name—had acted nervous as Maura led them into the pitch-dark grounds. Now he relaxed. He had the picture. He had shucked off his Levi's and T-shirt and was waiting for her on the blanket before Kim really knew what was going on.

My God, thought Kim, slipping out of her clothes, has Maura done this before? She must have. She must have been here on other nights with other lovers. Maura was incredible.

As the kid rammed into her, Kim heard the lilting, slightly Southern drawl of Maura somewhere off in the distance. "Birthday-baby," she called, "save me the bones. Bring something home in a doggy-bag."

Maura underestimated the kid. After Kim had her turn, there was plenty left over for Maura.

"Not half bad at all," she said to him appreciatively, afterward. "You'll be a man before your mother."

Back at her car, Maura said, "Don't bother to get in, buster. You're home." She pointed to the filling station, which had closed for the night.

Considering what the kid had done for each of them, Kim thought Maura was being a little rough. The kid must have thought so too.

"Jesus Kee-rist!" he marveled. "*Miss* Maura Anderson and *Miss* Kimberley Hudson. Wait till I tell the guys tomorrow I had them both in the same night!"

"Save your breath, stupid," said Maura. "They won't believe you. They'll just think you've gone around the bend."

"Yeah, I was a little rough on him," said Maura, as she drove Kim home. "But when you've been around as long as I have, you'll find a lot of these fresh-faced kids'll screw you the way you want to be screwed. And then they'll try to find some other way to screw you the way you don't want to be screwed. So the question is, whether the screwing you get first is worth the screwing you might get later."

It sounded plausible to Kim. Anyway, at this point, she was too grateful to Maura for this "coming of age" celebration to question Maura's wisdom about anything.

"I was thinking," Maura laughed, "how hard it is to get anyone into the movie houses to see the crappy pictures they're making these days. I bet there wasn't a person tearing down Wilshire tonight who wouldn't have stopped and paid a pretty penny to watch the little show we put on under ye spreading tree."

"Between the gas station and the two of us," said Kim, "that kid did a lot of pumping tonight."

"Which reminds me, we never did get that dark meat. Well, tomorrow's another night."

"Maura, you're delicious!" exclaimed Kim. As she started to get out of the car, she leaned over and kissed Maura on the cheek. "Thanks for a marvelous evening.

"*De nada.* Take it from your little sister, you'll do the same for me when I grow up and turn twenty-one."

Hollywood is such a fishbowl town. You couldn't hide there

if you wanted to. Not that many Hollywood folks are the hiding type.

It didn't surprise Kim that her so-called private life wasn't all that private. It didn't surprise her to read about herself in the papers.

"Sing no sad songs for Maura Anderson or Kimberley Hudson," one columnist wrote. "They may have shed their mates but they're not sitting home evenings moping. These two gay young divorcées are very much in circulation. Both of them are happily playing the field."

"Don't you love that 'playing the field' shit?" asked Maura. "What I'se calls it is 'sport fucking.' "

Another columnist wondered in print if Kimberley Hudson's fling with Charles Cramer was all over. The *Town Crier* called her "the brightest new adornment to light up the Hollywood night scene."

Kim let herself drift with the tide. One day dissolved into the next. Usually there was a new escort to take her to dinner and bed. On balance it was more fun than not. It was minus any responsibilities or headaches. She had earned this cutting-loose spree, she told herself. Soon she would be working again. Then she'd have to straighten up and be a good girl.

Not all the dates led to bed. Three of them were with Buck Fleming. She went on these dates as a favor to the publicity department at the Studio.

Buck Fleming was the newest feminine heartthrob at the box office. He was a strapping, handsome six-foot-two slab of rugged American manhood. If he hadn't made it in the movies, he looked like he could have signed with the Green Bay Packers.

"We're going to be in big trouble with him if we don't do something fast," Art Hoagland, the second in command in the PR department, told Kim. "He's shacking up on a houseboat with his lover-boy and going to parties in drag. If wind of this ever starts blowing across the land, we've got a dead duck on our hands. Now if you'd go to some restaurant with him we'd set up some pictures and push them out. Then Mr. and Mrs. America and all the ships at sea could jump to the false conclusion that Buck likes to go out with girls . . ."

On one of their dates Kim and Buck were snapped in her MG behind Ciro's. A waiter was serving them dinner in the car. The picture went out over the wire services. The caption said something about it being more romantic that way, eating dinner on trays in the car, than being with a lot of other people inside the busy restaurant.

"Thanks to that gas station jock," Maura said to Kim one

183

day, "we never did get that dark meat. Should we take up the hunt?"

Even if they didn't find any men, Maura was such good company Kim welcomed the night out.

Maura took Kim back to the same sidestreet Mexican restaurant in downtown Los Angeles. Lots of tequila, guacamole, and enchiladas. Mariachis serenaded them, and Maura did some wild solo dancing. Then they took off on another reckless ride through the night, this time in the direction of Newport Beach.

"This here is Richville," she commented. "Last year I had a little ding-a-ling here with a U.S. Senator." She told Kim his name.

Swinging around, Maura said, "Now that we've digested our dinner, could you go for some of that dark meat we've been waiting for?"

"Well—"

"Listen, little sister. I'm not going to force-feed you. If you don't see anything on the menu you like, you don't have to eat. But I think you might get a kick out of the joint. It's such a divey place. You like jazz, don't you? The combo they have there blows some great sounds."

There were no musical sounds to be heard in the divey little joint. It was Monday night—the musicians' night off. Maura swore so loud all conversation stopped.

"Oh, hell, we're here. Let's have a nightcap anyway."

It was near closing time. The only other patrons were three couples at a long table near the tiny stage and an old man dozing over a bottle of beer at the end of the bar. Kim and Maura drank their drinks sitting on torn leather stools at the bar, bathed in a ghastly blue light.

"I wouldn't have missed this place for anything," whispered Kim. "So many lovely gentlemen to choose from."

"My mammy always told me there'd be nights like this," said Maura. "When you strike out."

Outside, Maura said, "Come on. Let's put another cap on the night. I'll pour you one in my dump and drive you home."

Maura's "dump" was a bungalow at the Garden of Allah. She had lived there since the break-up of her marriage. The living room was a mess, strewn with Maura's clothes and magazines and records and empty glasses. She said she didn't even have a maid—and she didn't want one. When she was married to Bertie, they had lived in a big house crawling with servants. Having all those people around got on her nerves. You always felt they had their big noses in your business. It was a day's work in itself just to keep them out of your hair.

The moral of the story was never to marry a shorty. Shorties always had to prove themselves by putting on the dog.

"Well, here we are," said Maura, pouring their drinks. "It isn't the way I planned the end of the evening. You and me here drinking by ourselves."

"It's kind of nice," said Kim. "It'll be nice to wake up and not have to face anybody in the morning. Not even to say 'Be seeing you' or 'Get going.' "

Maura laughed. "I just had a thought. Here we sit. Two prize plums—by anybody's standards. We don't have to kid ourselves. There must be about ten million guys in this country who'd give their short arm if they could stick it in either one of us first. Now you lay all those short arms end to end. Mother of God! It must add up to about two million yards of cock. Think of it! There's two million yards of cock out there waiting for us and between us we can't even grab on to six inches of it."

"Oh, Maura," squealed Kim, "you are insane!"

"A girl has to be practical."

"Maura, the first time we had dinner, you told me I should keep track some way of the men I went out with. You told me you had a way of keeping track. But you never told me what it was."

"First let me freshen our cozies." Maura poured a long slug of bourbon into each of their glasses. "Now follow mother."

She led the way into a bedroom that was as messy as her living room. There were clothes all over the unmade bed and lipstick-stained glasses on the night table. Maura went to a closet and pulled down a large rectangular cardboard box.

"Here, my dear," she said, "are *my* impressions of the men I've known. In the biblical sense of the word."

Maura set the open box on top of the bed. In the dim light Kim could not make out what she was looking at. Maura snapped on a ceiling light. Kim was still mystified. There must have been fifty or sixty plaster figures in the box. They were all standing up, like trees in a forest. They all had more or less the same shape. But they varied considerably in height and thickness.

"Oh, Maura," Kim gasped, "they're *not!*"

"They are. A true-blue impression. Just so I'd have something to remember them all by. To hell with remembering their faces."

"How did you do it?" Kim asked.

"Well, that's mother's little trade secret. You can see it's plaster. You can guess what the plaster is molded on."

"Do they model for you?" Kim wondered incredulously.

185

"I'm no sculptress. I couldn't make these things up."

"Do you do it . . . afterward?"

"Are you kidding? *Before.* Some of these are one-time birdies that won't get flying again for another six months."

"Do they always let you do this?"

"Anybody starts balking, I tell him, 'No dippy the wickie, no fucky-wucky.'"

Maura started humming "Among My Souvenirs," as she held up samples from her collection for Kim to inspect. Into the base of each reproduction she had carved the initials of the model.

She put into Kim's hands a miniature pyramid that sloped from a wide base upward for eight or nine inches. "Would you ever have guessed that skinny little Wop singer had a dong like this?"

"How do you like this little fella?" Maura asked, holding up a thin, tiny stump. "And I mean, he's really little. Guess who?"

"Who?"

"Rod Butterworth, star of a hundred and forty-seven glorious Westerns. Six-three in his bare feet as he stands stroking his horse. And look how little he stands where it counts. Moral of the story: Some of the biggest pricks have the littlest pricks."

Maura's collection added up to an inside, under-the-pants guided tour of some of Hollywood's best-known men, single and married. As tour guide, Maura rocked Kim with her spicy commentary.

There was one model Kim recognized without being told who it was. Charles Cramer.

"That bastard's one-of-a-kind every way," said Maura. "He's the only one who always backed out of 'posing' for me. He raved and ranted and accused me of every damn thing. Like trying to castrate him and give him gangrene poisoning. But he saw I meant business about the no fucky-wucky without the dippy-wicky."

Maura snapped off the ceiling light finally and returned her collection to the closet, saying, "Well, so much for every little thing."

In the dim light Kim looked around the room, really for the first time. Over in a corner there was an odd, half-reclining chair almost as wide as a bed. It had stirrups and straps and leg props and switches and buttons all over it.

Maura said, "Hadn't you noticed? That's a fucking chair."

"A what?"

"A fucking chair. It's the one thing I insisted on getting custody of when Bertie and I split. Bertie was always going in for gadgets and contraptions. This thing is one of the few good ideas he ever had. He designed it himself. I don't know who he got to make it."

Maura demonstrated the workings of the "fucking chair." A couple could sit-lie side by side. A switch would throw on a motor which would create a sensation like a thousand needles pricking the flesh. Those needles could drive you out of your mind. Another button threw on a vibrator. A third started the chair moving up and down like it was having intercourse. The man could strap himself on top of the woman. Then he could enter her and just lie there, letting the chair do the work. The speed could be regulated. The couple could have slow motion or let 'er rip so much the strokes went fifty times faster than humans could have stroked. And no sweat. They both just lay there. The chair pushed the vagina into the penis at the desired pace.

"Wanna try it out?" Maura asked.

"I'll take your word for it." said Kim, shivering a little.

"If I was to drag out all my playthings, it would look like a sexual Disneyland. I wouldn't want you to think I'm anything but a nice, normal, old-fashioned American girl. However—"

Maura disappeared into a walk-in closet in another corner of the room and closed the door. A minute later the door opened a crack.

"Kim, darling . . ."

It was like someone else in the closet was calling to her. The voice was as deep and bass as any man's. Kim froze in terror.

"Kim, darling, in this life we play many roles. Sometimes, sometimes . . . we even cross over to the other side. We don't have to be just one thing or the other. We all of us have capacities we never dreamed of . . ."

The strong masculine voice spun theories, then slipped into sly innuendoes. Kim could pick up Maura's basic rhythms and accent. But it was as if she had been born again in that closet and come back as a man.

"Kim, you may not have known the depths of my passion for you . . ."

The door opened. Kim screamed.

Maura was wearing only a pair of men's shorts. They were boxer shorts. Protruding out of the fly was an enormous penis. It was in a state of erection. Maura stroked it sensuously as she came toward Kim.

"Kim, darling," she said in that scary basso profundo, "does this give you some idea of how I feel about you?"

187

Maura inched toward her, stalkingly. Kim screamed again.

"Oh, Kim, for Christ's sake!" Maura was speaking in her natural register again. "I'm only horsing around."

She jerked the penis out from her shorts and presented it to Kim. "Haven't you seen one of these before?"

Kim had never seen anything like it. Anything like it that wasn't the real thing. The object she held in her hand had the identical shape and look of a very well-endowed male organ. It was smooth to the touch, like ivory.

"It's called a dildo," said Maura. "It can be the best friend of the woman alone. When there's no man around the house, you makes do with what you has."

Marveling at the device, Kim almost unconsciously began to stroke it the way Maura had. "What they won't think up next!" she giggled.

"Come on, little sister. Rip off the rags. It's any-port-in-a-storm night. I'll show you just how this little lover operates. You'll like."

Almost hypnotized by Maura's urging, Kim found herself undressing. Maura dropped her shorts. The two young women briefly took in each other's exquisite body in the nude. Maura made balls of the clothes on top of the bed and pitched them into a corner. She smoothed the sheets and led Kim gently to the bed.

"You just lie back, angel," Maura instructed her, "and leave the driving to mother."

Maura lay down beside Kim on the bed. She teased and explored Kim with her finger and lubricated her before inserting the dildo.

"Now, honey, you just close your eyes and dream," she said. "Dream it's the man of your dreams. Or Tarzan. Or King Kong. Or whoever's going to get that darling little clit in a heat."

Kim closed her eyes and fantasized . . . about men she had had and about men she hadn't had—yet. A lover was thrusting deep and deeper toward her core . . . a lover's hands stroked her breasts, enfolded her nipples between two fingers and bent over to kiss them.

As her breath quickened, so did the lover's. The lover nibbled at her ear lobes and panted into her ears.

Close to the point of her fulfillment she felt the probing stop. The thing driving her delirious withdrew from her.

"No," she cried. "Don't take it away. Keep it in."

A sudden movement in the bed. The return of the lover . . . entering her now with a tongue that was probing the same route. This was even better. The tongue was more sensitive, more ravishing, hungrier. It worked itself into a fit. As it flicked and licked, hot gasps of breath blasted thrillingly all the way up the secret canyon.

Before her release came, Kim slipped into a giddy blackout. Where was she? There didn't seem to be anything under her. Was she going against gravity, floating in space?

She screamed for the third time that night. The scream anchored her somewhere. She could feel weight again. Above her and below her. Someone was lying on top of her.

"Was it good, baby?"

Maura. Oh, God. It was Maura who had done all that.

"Yes, yes," said Kim. "Wonderful."

"I'm glad."

Maura kissed her deeply on the lips. She rolled off and lay beside her.

Maura goes in for this, too, thought Kim. Maura was fantastic. No wonder she had all the guys in the world beating a pathway to her bed. If she could do this much for one of her own kind, what she must be like in bed with a man!

Kim felt the shaking beside her, heard Maura's moaning. She saw that Maura had the dildo inside her. Maura was shoving it in and out furiously.

"Do you want me to do that?" asked Kim.

"No, that's all right."

"Do you want me to do . . . what you did?"

"Thanks, baby. But I'm soon there."

When she got there, Maura threw the dildo into the same corner she had thrown the clothes. They lay side by side without saying anything. Kim remembered the way Maura had put it, "Any port in a storm." That was about it. Thanks to Maura, she had tried something new. Thanks to Maura, it had been enjoyable.

She knew this sort of thing was fairly common in Hollywood. You couldn't be around the Studio one day without hearing stories about famous actresses in love with each other or their maids or ballerinas or cocktail waitresses. Or whoever. Two of the biggest female stars were supposed to be "that way." Not about each other. Each one had her own female lover. Both of them were beautiful and feminine and talented and enormously popular at the box office. One was an exquisite Scandinavian *femme fatale*. The other was an aristocratic beauty from New England with strong opinions and high cheekbones.

Lots of times Kim had caught various women eyeing her in a funny-starey sort of way. She had guessed what their interest was. But so far no girl or woman had propositioned her. Now it had happened. Without anybody planning it. And it had been satisfying. Maura had made it satisfying. She had been seduced by one of the most beautiful and desirable girls in the world, and she had no regrets—no shame, no anger. Yet she knew it just wasn't her way. She had tried it with Maura. If you didn't want to be with Maura this way, you wouldn't want to be with anybody else of your own kind this way.

Kim nudged Maura. Maura was in a deep relaxation edging into sleep. "Maura, I've got to get home."

Rousing, Maura said frantically, "Oh, no, honey. Stay here with me. I can't let you go."

"I must. My mother'll be out of her mind if she—"

"You can't go. You mustn't. Please, please. I won't touch you. I promise. We'll get up in the morning and I'll have you home before your mother even wakes up. Please don't leave me . . ."

Maura was weeping hysterically and pounding the pillows with her fists.

"Maura, don't cry. I can't stand it. Please stop crying and tell me what it is. Please, Maura . . ."

It was so simple—and *unbelievable!* Maura couldn't stand to be alone at night.

Maura didn't know what it was. She wasn't afraid of the dark. But what was she afraid of? She could cope with any crap the day might dish up. Night was something else. She couldn't make it through the night alone. No matter how much she drank. Who would ever have guessed that this swaggering, hard-drinking, tough-talking, gutsy woman was such a frightened child underneath? Could you ever know anybody, Kim thought. Could you ever *really* know what gave with them—unless you were in bed together in the middle of the night?

Kim loved Maura for being weak and frightened in this nutty way. She felt a million years older than her older, worldly friend. Cradling Maura's head against her bare bosom, she said, "Of course, I'll stay."

"I love you, little sister. If you ever needed it, I'd cut off my right boob for you." Then just as she was dozing off, Maura said, "I told you I love you. I'm glad it's you . . . here. But know something? It could be anybody . . . *anything.* No offense, darling. But you do anything you have to do to get through the goddamn night . . ."

Kim woke up to the smell of bacon and eggs cooking. From the kitchen Maura was braying, "Come and get it. Get your lazy cunt out of bed. I gotta get going. I'm working in the grand-daddy of all pieces of crap." A pause. "I always say that. But the next time they always find a bigger piece of crap for me."

Kim smiled, stretching. Maura, dear Maura. The bluff, brassy, bawdy Maura she adored.

There was no mention of the night they had spent together.

Dropping her off, Maura said, "Hot damn. We still ain't got ourselves a chunk of that dark meat."

They never did. At least together.

Before noon the same day Spence Holmes called. Could Kim come to his office that afternoon?

Randolph Jahr was in town.

Chapter 19

Returning after all these years just for a reunion, I thought I could keep my cool.

But the mere sight of those Studio gates turned me all goose-pimply. The last time I saw them must be eighteen, nineteen years now. For maybe seven years before that the Studio was like my home. Before I was even awake in the morning I was carted here with my sisters. I worked here, ate here, went to school here. Often I was asleep before we got outside the gates at night. The house we lived in hardly seemed like home at all. I was never there except to eat dinner and go to bed.

"I'm Gina Spinelli."

"Yes?"

"I'm going to Sound Stage Seven. To the party."

"I'm sorry, ma'am. I'll have to see some identification."

That should cut me down to size. My name draws a fat zero. The guard is tall, blond, and handsome in the sort of dumb, lifeguardish style of healthy California good looks. He could be twenty-three. So he's never heard of the singing Spinelli Sisters. So he doesn't read best-sellers. What does he know from anything?

It took Laurie Ann's invitation *and* my ID card to clear the gates . . .

There! There it is. Ten, twenty, a thousand years slip away. There it is, just as I still see it sometimes in my dreams. This last corner of the once gigantic Studio. The old back lot 3. Now this final remaining hunk of Studio property had been sold to real estate interests. A year from now you'd probably find three or four junky high-rises on this very spot.

But today it's like it always was, except that it's deserted.

Not a man, woman, child, or beast. It could be the beginning of the end of the world. It's spooky. It's *haunting*.

A single glance can bring back ten thousand memories. In the good long-gone days, you should have seen the action! Magic-making was going on all over the place. Five movies were being shot at the same time. Right here on this back lot. Here's where all us Studio kids found our Disneyland. This is where we hung out when we weren't in front of the camera or in school or taking lessons in something. In our own way we too were "street kids."

It's like an outdoor museum. Or looking at an old family photo album. There's the railway station where Signe Johannsen died under the wheels of a train in that weepy old movie from the Russian novel. In front of it is the platform where beautiful women were always tearfully waving good-bye from train windows. Just around the corner is the bandstand where those two old operetta cornballs serenaded each other in *Springtime*. There's the jungle where Sonny Holtzman and all the other Garbons swung from limb to limb chasing wild animals away from Nan and Baby. There's the street where the great heartthrob Brock Nadel delivered milk bottles in one of his first movies. A little farther on you come to the cemetery where Jordan Russell carried the black bag with the severed heart in that ghoulish *Strange Night*. Right next to it is the prison yard where Johnny Dragon did time in *San Quentin Interlude*.

It's still standing! But just look at it. I'm talking about Dr. Baxter's house where Tinker Wells lived the ten best years of his adolescence in all those Bobby Baxter movies. If you remember the house and the block, be grateful you can't see it now. There are vines and scrubby bushes and tall grasses and crud growing over everything. It looks more like the setting for a Tennessee Williams play. Say, *The Night of the Iguana* . . .

Poking among the ruins, I become sadder and sadder. I also feel a million years old.

The opening of a door jolts me. To have life suddenly erupt in this mausoleum would jolt anybody. Out the door of Sound Stage 7 darts a slim, elegant man. He stops and gives me a surprised, puzzled look.

"Are you lost?" he asks.

The accent tips me off. It's Jason Walker.

"Oh, no. No, I'm not lost. I'm meeting some old friends here and I'm a little early."

"Oh. Well, I'm glad you're not lost."

Watching him walk swiftly down the street and out the gates and jump into his little red sports car, I felt a shiver of despair. If it hadn't been for his voice, I'd never have recognized him. He couldn't be more than fifty. But he had aged so terribly. He looked *old*. Old and gray and craggy. His face was like a beat-up washboard. The only youthful thing about him was his figure.

When the Studio was in its heyday, Jason had been a big star. A handsome young leading man then, who had just been imported from England, he breezed blithely through a never-ending succession of romantic comedies and musicals opposite all the beautiful women stars at the Studio. For years his career had been in the doldrums. How many chances are there for aging leading men who were never all that hot as actors? But I read that he was back doing a small bit in *Split Passions*, which would be the last film to be shot at the Studio. For exploitation purposes, the Studio had rounded up several ex-biggies to do walk-on parts in this final one. They had given a one-scene role to Jane Meredith, who had once been big box office as America's Favorite Young Wife in about forty forgettable drags the Studio ground out. They even tapped Pam Binford. You remember Pam, the chronic virgin-next-door in the Bobby Baxter movies. As soon as their scenes were shot, Jason and Jane and Pam would crawl right back into the mothballs. Sad.

Sound Stage 7: here is where it all begin. Yesterday. Forty years ago. The great golden era of movie-making.

It could be the inside of an abandoned airplane hangar. Not a breath of life stirring. Stacked like decks of cards around the sides are the sets of countless classics. Peel them off like the layers of onions and you'll discover the backdrops for *South Sea Island Madness*, *The King of Nome*, *Last Ferry to Mozambique*, *Love from Leningrad*, and a hundred other gems. Against the sets, hanging from the walls, dropping from the ceilings, east side west side all around this spooky warehouse . . . loom the stills. Stills of everybody who ever helped turn a buck for the Studio. Stills of every starlet who ever screwed her way into feature billing in a two-bit clinker. Of course there's one of Kim taken from her very first movie, with the golden retriever jumping up on her. The place is also littered with lots of junky furniture with "Sold" tags on them. "Sold" at the auction, no doubt, and now the buyers are having second thoughts about picking the junk up. Stacked almost to the ceiling are tons of moldy, smashed-in stuff I guess nobody would want even if the price was right (free).

Smack in the center is a big table about as long as a runway. It's covered with white tablecloths and from one end to the other it's a nonstop lineup of chafing dishes and tureens and crocks and pots and platters and ice buckets with champagne bottles sticking out. There are twenty or so funeral parlor chairs parked around it. At each place is a name card. Guess who's sitting at the head of the table. A dead woman! Sally Strickland. Guess what's on her seat. Her famous red slippers! Somebody's sick mind must have been at work here. Whose? Tinker Wells's?

The place card next to Sally's on her left reads "Scotty Barlow." Scotty Barlow? The name means nothing to me. But the name next to Scotty's does. Miriam Love. Underneath Miriam's name there is a big "?". They haven't heard from Miriam and don't know if she'll be coming. Are they kidding? Miriam won't be here. She's been in hiding for years—for good reason. You wonder what gets into somebody like Miriam—besides about a ton more of food a week than she needs.

Miriam looked like such a winner. She was so bright and pretty and she had the voice of an angel. She was only eleven when she made *The Fiddling of a Maestro* with that horny old symphony conductor. Wouldn't you have bet your last dollar she'd grow up to be an opera star and have a fantastic career at the Met? God knows why she blew it. The summer she was seventeen she took off for Europe and never came back. The story is she married a car salesman in Nice and has been eating merrily ever afterward. Once about three years ago she was in Rome and one of the paparazzi got a picture of her coming out of a restaurant. The picture appeared in papers all over Europe and got reprinted in *Newsweek*. Miriam looked enormous. Alongside her, Kate Smith would have looked like Twiggy. No, count Miriam out. It would take a blimp to transport her.

Next to Miriam is Hal Harper. That makes two empty seats side by side. He won't come. I hear he never leaves his apartment.

Remember Hal Harper? The gung-ho collegiate guy in all those Tom Adams at Yale movies? In the last second of play he was always making the touchdown that won the game for dear old Eli. Hal has fallen on rough times, so I've heard. Washed up in the movies and getting his kicks from booze and boys. Add to that he has a germ phobia. Which is why he never leaves his apartment in Marina Del Rey. The boys who go there get hosed down and fumigated and disinfected from head to toe before Hal will touch them.

Whoever arranged the table has a real sense of the macabre. Sally Strickland's not the only dead comrade being "honored." About every third seat is assigned to someone who couldn't possibly occupy it. Above the name on the place cards is written "In Memoriam." There's even a place for D.D. Jones, who's been dead since 1958. D.D., the big cult hero of the 1950s. So talented and troubled . . . and so self-destructive. He must have known you can't gulp down a fifth of Jack Daniels and go tooling down the Monterey Peninsula on a motorcycle unless you want to wrap yourself around a giant cypress. Which is precisely what D.D. did.

Four funeral chairs down the table is where April Todd should be sitting. Isn't it hard to believe something terrible was eating away at the hilarious little girl in *The Guru and the Bobby-Soxer?* April's tragic fate has been well chronicled. One fine day in May, April —only nineteen and going on ninety-one— wasn't feeling too good. She went to see that North Hollywood Dr. Feelgood who had been making her feel so good with some specialty of the house he shot into her behind. The shot and the little bottle of take-out goodies he gave her that day got her feeling so good she must have said to herself, "I've never felt better in all my life. I never want to come out of this one." So she never did.

If April could be here she would be sitting straight across from Lance Detweiler—if *he* could be here. Probably nobody knows what was bugging Lance, either. But say this for him. He went out in style. Hanging from the shower rod by a Countess Mara tie . . .

All of this is only yesterday. It's also way back in the Bronze Age. Reality and fantasy. Where am I? How long have I been here? Here in this dark, empty graveyard?

Am I just waking up? I am no longer alone. Has all this activity been suddenly orchestrated and synchronized . . . the caterers and waiters and bartenders bustling around, the soft-rock combo plugging in and warming up with "I'll Be Your Baby, Mother," that middle-aged woman approaching me?

Is it really *her?* So she's here!

"Peggy Palmer!"

The frumpish figure jumped. The doll almost slipped out of her arms. So it is true about Peggy and her dolls.

She looks for all the world like a late-fortyish version of the bratty kid we all remember. Bangs and ponytail (streaked with gray now) and pursed lips. The thick goggles are new. Through them she blinks quizzically at me.

"I'm Gina Spinelli."

"Oh, yes. Yes . . . Gina Spinelli."

"Thanks to you, my place always smells like heather-on-the-hill."

"Oh, yes . . . the commercial."

"I'm Kimberley Hudson's friend," I said helpfully.

"Yes, I do remember," she cries. "I remember. Where is Kim? Laurie Ann told me she's coming. I came just to see her."

"So did I, mostly."

"She was always so kind to me," said Peggy. "I don't care what other side there may be to her. I don't believe everything I hear and read. She was always kind to me. Whatever else they say she might be, I *know* how kind she can be. That's what I'll always remember about her."

"Yes, she can be kind," I agreed. For Peggy's sake I didn't add Kim could be kind when the whim suited her—or when she was out to get something.

"She gave me Lorelei." Peggy stroked the doll's long flaxen tresses. Behind the thick glasses I could see tears starting. "That's why I brought Lorelei tonight. I wanted to thank Kim in person and let her see what a pretty girl Lorelei is growing up to be. She's almost seven now. Kim found her when she was in Munich making *Duel in Bavaria*. Lorelei's changed so much I wonder if Kim will even recognize her."

Poor, dotty Peggy looked like a plump Dresden fraulein doll herself in her ruffly white dress with the pink satin sash around her wide waist. On the human chess board all moves are possible. Peggy's move away from people into a world of dolls might seem kooky. But don't knock it. If that's what makes a life for Peggy, that's okay. If she finds dolls a lot easier to live with than people, she just may have a point.

"I almost never go anywhere," Peggy was saying. "I seem to have a hard time getting out of the house. There's always so much to keep me busy right there."

"You do have your hands full," I said. "With almost a thousand kids to feed and take care of."

Peggy flashed me a grateful smile. Her "kids" at this very minute were probably in the custody of some doll-sitter she didn't trust. No wonder she kept glancing at her watch.

"If she'd just come," said Peggy tensely, "I'd say 'Hi' and 'Thanks' and be off."

"Kim wouldn't be Kim," I said, "if she didn't make the grand entrance. That means coming after everybody else is here."

But I was just mouthing some empty words.

It was almost seven thirty and I had a sinking feeling Kim wasn't going to show.

Chapter 20

The first time Kim met Randolph Jahr was in Spence Holmes's office.

Extraordinary, she thought. He's common as an old shoe.

He wore a rumpled denim suit, scuffed buckskins, and his legs were slung over the arm of a large maroon leather chair. He twisted around to watch her coming through the door. Innocently as a child, he stared. His eyes didn't roam over her legs and breasts like a horny stud's. They stayed topside, trying to lock her into an eyeball-to-eyeball grip. He spooked her.

Cheeks on fire, she concentrated on the model of the *Kon-Tiki* perched on a high marble stand in a far corner of the office.

"How are you?" There was a tremor under his eyes. His lips quivered, twisting up slightly in the shadow of a smile.

Was that all there was? Had she waited a thousand years to hear him ask, "How are you?"

You think the famous and/or rich are different from me and thee? Not at all. That's how they met, the famous young Broadway actor and the beautiful young Hollywood actress: "How are you?" "I'm fine."

Kim is hopelessly romantic. It's one of her most endearing qualities. She keeps believing that romantic love is the cure for whatever ails her, no matter how often she gets burned. The next love will be the really good one that was worth waiting for, the one that solves all problems and resolves all miseries. That's how she gets by. By being a hopeless romantic. But there's only once when she's been on record as saying she believed in love at first sight.

It was that day—that *second*—she connected with Randolph Jahr.

There he was, sprawled across that leather chair. Randolph Jahr, the hot-shot Method actor from New York. He was hauntingly beautiful. His face had the perfection of a delicate porcelain vase. Those staring eyes, boring right into her soul, were a deep violet. They were like the waters of a cavernous pool, holding the promise of such tenderness. They were hooded by long sweeping lashes and the oddly heavy, straight black slashes of eyebrow. His nose was a flawless blade that might have been sculpted by Michelangelo. That haunting face—so gaunt, so beautiful—a face that somehow could look hungry and wounded and sexy all at the same time.

He might have been twenty-six at the most. Whatever he was, she felt two thousand years older. She wanted to scoop him up in her hand like a fallen bird. But he also scared her. His eyes wouldn't let her go. It made her want to run.

"Well, I presume you two have already met—"

It was Spencer Holmes. Spencer Holmes apologized for not being there to greet them. He had been in a meeting. Kim had never laid eyes on him before. She was never so glad to see anybody in her whole life.

"Kids, we got a picture here I believe in with all my heart. It's different. Off-beat. A downer, even. But honest-to-God, I'm high as a kite on this thing. I honest-to-God think we can bring it off . . ."

Randolph Jahr hardly acknowledged Spence Holmes. He still stared at Kim. And Kim, too, glanced only for an instant at Spence Holmes, before returning her gaze to Randolph Jahr.

"Only one week of rehearsals?" Randolph asked whisperingly.

The question was put to Spence Holmes, who nodded. That neither looked at him had not escaped him. Spencer Holmes was pleased. *These Murdering Children* was off to an excellent start.

"You must make her . . . *live*," Randolph told Kim at the first rehearsal. "She must be . . . *alive*." He spoke so . . . hesitantly, breathlessly. Every word sounded like it could be his last.

The plot was as clean and lean as a Greek tragedy. A young man and his dumb-cowish wife come to work as servants of a big summer house in Southampton. The young man and the rich young daughter of the house are immediately attracted to each other. The attraction builds into a blazing love affair—the first for the girl. The wife wises up to the situation and threatens to blow the lid. The problem is what to do about her. The only solution seems to be murder. The young man brutally hacks his wife to death in her sleep, buries her body deep in a remote woods, and claims she walked out on him for parts unknown. Eventually the body is discovered and the crime is pinned on the young man. He's sentenced to death in the electric chair. His beautiful accomplice, who planted the seeds of murder in his head and helped him bury the body, goes free. If the picture had a message, it was: the poor burn and the rich find mercy.

"You've got to get inside her," Randolph said to Kim, "really inside her. Play her from the inside out. That way she'll

198

be so ... interesting. Not just a rich-girl type. Not a silly, surface debutante. Or just a mean, snotty spoiled thing. She has to be ... *complicated*. Nobody comes through real, *really* real, unless they're complicated."

Randolph Jahr himself was complicated.

Kim had never met anyone so complicated. She didn't know exactly what a Method actor was. The way he tried to explain it confused her even more. What did phrases like "conceiving outward" and "external thrusting" and "projecting from the core" mean? Who was Stanislavsky?

To Randolph Jahr (and, by now, almost everyone else), it was inevitable that Kim was headed for big stardom. It wouldn't have mattered what kind of pictures she was in, or how good a performance she gave. She just had that certain inborn something that belongs to only a happy few. You had it or didn't have it. If you didn't have it, a lifetime in acting schools wouldn't give it to you. But Randolph wanted more than just glitter.

Kim always said Randolph Jahr lit a fire under her. He was the one who changed the way she thought about herself. He encouraged her to take herself seriously. He was the one who told her that if she worked hard and concentrated on her craft she might become an actress instead of just a star. He made it clear he thought it was so much more important to be excellent than to be dazzling. She was selling herself short if she just gave her face and body to the cameras, and not her talent.

"The key to everything," he kept telling her, "is concentration."

"I had been sleepwalking until I met Randy," Kim said later in an interview. "I knew the pictures weren't any good. I was always playing the ingenue and I got to wear pretty clothes and have nice layouts in the fan magazines. I guess I thought it was a pretty pleasant and painless way to make a nice fat living. Then they finally threw a good script at me. I knew it was good when Geordie read it to me. But I was doubly sure when they got Randy to come out from New York to do it. He hated Hollywood and looked down his nose at the movie business. He was so honest and independent they couldn't have got him if they'd promised him the moon if he hadn't believed in the picture. It was Randy who taught me all I really know about acting. He worked so hard with me and I worked like a dog to be good. I would have died of shame not to live up to his expectations of me. We did have a director but I don't think I heard a word he said. For me, Randy was the director and one of the few real directors I ever had. Most of them, let me tell you, are nothing more than high-paid traffic cops. Their idea of directing a picture is to keep the actors from bumping into each other. I was in a trance the whole time I made *These Murdering Children*. I just followed Randy. From the second I first saw him I was so blindingly in love with him I'd have followed him into Hades . . ."

They weren't ready for Randolph Jahr in Hollywood. He wouldn't "go Hollywood" one inch of the way. He didn't rent a house with a pool and tennis courts. He rented one small, tatty room in the Hotel Charmont on the Strip. He didn't go out to restaurants and nightclubs. He wouldn't give interviews, even on the set. He turned down all invitations to parties. He didn't seem to have any friends and didn't want to meet anybody. He dressed like a bum, using this as a defense against social encounters. (See? He didn't have a thing to wear.) He didn't even own a car. ("Rent him something!" screamed the Boss. "He can't be seen hanging around street corners waiting for buses and taxis." "Save your money," said Jahr. "I can't drive.")

He rated chauffeuring back and forth to the Studio, but he preferred to ride with Kim, who also rated chauffeuring. And she preferred to tool back and forth in her Robin Hood green MG—with Randy.

To the Hollywood *mavens*, he was snooty and self-involved. Kim knew they were at least partly wrong. Mostly he was shy and terrified. He was shy even with her. In the car going to work she would ask a simple question and wait forever for the answer. Turning to him, she'd catch his eye for a fleeting second. He looked so vulnerable, so frightened. But what could he be scared of? Her? This strange country? Quickly he'd look away from her. The answer to her question came so softly she could hardly hear it.

It took her weeks to learn anything about him. He was born in Winnipeg. His father had been a grain broker, who drowned one summer day in the Lake of the Woods, when a sudden howler blowing in from the western prairies capsized his outboard motorboat. Randy was four at the time. The family was well fixed. Mrs. Jahr sold everything they owned in cold Winnipeg and pulled stakes for New York.

They moved into a cooperative apartment on Park Avenue.

Randy didn't know where the acting bug came from—himself or his mother. From the time he was eight years old he had spent more time in and around the theater than in school. In the beginning, it was just running around frantically from audition to audition whenever there was a casting call for a young body. He was nine when he got his first part on Broadway. Luckily, the play was a long-running one. He got good notices and a lot of attention. After that, he worked more or less steadily, even during the awkward adolescent years, when he was neither boy nor man.

He went to Collegiate, and then he enrolled in the American Academy of Dramatic Arts, which seemed to make more sense than going to college. And he was lucky. He had some good runs on Broadway and some good reviews. Bye and bye playwrights were sending him scripts they had written with him in mind. There were movie offers, but he always turned them down. Nothing had been really "right" for him until this one. Now he also had his other reasons for wanting to try his luck in Hollywood. Kim asked him what the reasons were. He smiled painfully at her without answering.

"You don't like to talk about yourself," Kim observed.

"I'm nobody," he said. "I don't have any personal identity. Really. I'm an actor."

The day shooting began he didn't respond to his call. Kim was not in the opening scene. But she wouldn't have been anywhere else but on the set. She was there to watch the man she worshipped make his debut before the cameras. But where was he? She ran off the set and banged on the door of his trailer.

"Randy, they're waiting. Are you all right?"

Hearing nothing, she said, "Randy, I'm coming in. Okay?"

She found him slumped over on the edge of a cot, script spread across his knees, shaking. He looked up at her like a wounded doe.

"Randy, what's the matter?"

"I'm not . . . *feeling* it. My conception is so o-o-o—"

"Oh, Randy, stop it! You're just nervous. You're the very last person who should be nervous. You can act circles around all of them. They've never seen anybody half as good as you out here . . ."

In the end, she literally led him to the set. He walked behind her, his moist, trembling hand hanging on to hers like a lifeline.

It never got much better. He always came onto the set shaking. He was always sure he had not got deeply enough "inside" Clifton (the young wife-murderer). He was sure his shallowness would come through. Kim persuaded Randy they should look at the daily rushes. Anything to be near him! Anything to help Randy see how good he really was!

Every day the front office people cheered in the projection room. But their cheers didn't calm Randy's jumping nerves. He could see a thousand things wrong with his performance. If they could only junk everything that had been shot that day and shoot it all over again tomorrow! Then he'd really be ready.

One afternoon the Boss himself turned up. He saw rushes of the scene where Randy and Kim first discover each other. Randy is repairing a flat on her bicycle tire. He's on his hands and knees and she's tapping her foot impatiently. He keeps sneaking glances at her until their eyes finally clinch.

"You two kids," boomed the Boss, "magnificent! Both of you. That's really acting. I got my doubts about the picture. If the public's going to buy it—anything so depressing. But I got to hand it to you. You two make a wonderful team, the way you act together."

"Since we make such a wonderful team," said Kim to Randolph, trying to sound casual, "why don't we go some place and have dinner?"

He looked upset. "Oh, no. I couldn't do that. 'Tomorrow and tomorrow creeps in this petty pace . . .' "

The next day he explained to her (1) "tomorrow and tomorrow" was Shakespeare and (2) he hadn't meant to be rude. But he was so drained and nervous by the end of the day all he could think about was getting back to his room. There he ate a tuna salad sandwich, crawled into bed, and worried about the next day.

That was his life? Being nervous and tense all day at the Studio and being nervous and tense all night back at the hotel? With only a tuna salad sandwich to keep him going? Kim believed him. But it was so strange . . . this getting into such a frenzy about acting, this total sacrifice to work. It was so *monkish.*

Would he ever notice her? Would he ever notice that she was falling hopelessly in love with him? That it took all the willpower she could call up to keep from smothering him with kisses and embraces? Every time she caught that wounded, startled deer expression on his face she ached to gather him up in her arms and say, "There, there, it'll be all right. I'm here."

Of course he did notice her. She was all he really did notice. Between takes and scenes he talked to her about her role, the scene they were playing . . . how to think and feel herself into a situation, how to dig into her very soul. He noticed her beauty and was awed by it. But he also saw it as a trap.

"Make them buy the whole thing," he said to her. "Not just the beautiful wrappings. There's so much underneath, inside. Make them buy the whole package. You're not just another face and body to be exploited. You must be seen in depth."

Kim feasted on these words. It wasn't somebody grabbing

her and declaring passionately, "I love you." But wasn't this another way of saying "I love you"? When someone gave you unselfish advice? When someone cared enough to help you day after day to discover things you never knew about yourself, to make you come off looking your very best?

Yes, this was love. It wasn't all she wanted from Randy in the way of love, but the rest could wait. She could see how much the work was taking out of him. This was his first picture and he was maybe taking it too seriously. Or it might be just his nature to get overemotional about things. But one fine day the picture would be finished. And then—

When you're in love, you believe what you want to believe. Kim believed that Randy not only loved her but it was the first time she had been really loved for herself. He could give and give of himself without making demands on her. Wasn't this the truest test of love? To care about somebody else without caring if you got paid back right away—or ever?

Kim began to enjoy the waiting . . . the postponement of their real coming together. Now there was something to look forward to. Looking forward to things, she already knew, could be better than actually having them.

Maura Anderson called once to suggest a double date, but Kim turned it down. She wasn't even tempted. And that was because of how she felt about Randy. There had been no love lost on all those other dates . . . the one-night stands with so many men whose names and faces and bodies she would never remember except for the Little Lavender Book. That certainly wasn't love—that fast grab in the night and good-bye. Fun, maybe, but not love. Kim couldn't imagine any more such quickies now that there was Randy. It was more fun waiting for him.

"You spark me," he said to her one day. They were playing Ping-Pong in the basement of the Southampton mansion. All you could hear was the sound of the paddles slamming the ball back and forth across the net. But their eyes held each other's.

"What does 'spark' mean?" Kim asked, her hopes skyrocketing.

"You . . . get my juices going. Set my fires. You make me give everything I have to give as an actor."

If only he had said, "You make me give everything I have to give as a *lover*."

She had no idea what he did with his weekends. He never told her. One Friday evening, as she dropped him off at the Hotel Charmont, he asked her, after a lot of hemming and hawing and silences, "Would you . . . I don't suppose you'd be interested in doing . . . seeing . . . something?"

With him? Anything. It was all she could do to keep herself from hollering, "Yes, yes, a million times yes!"

"It's tomorrow night. That's maybe too short—"

"I'm not doing a thing."

"A couple of kids" he knew from New York were connected now with the Pasadena Playhouse. They had the leads in a production of *A Doll's House* and he'd sure like to see them in it. He thought Kim might enjoy seeing the play too. There was almost no theater in Los Angeles. It might be good for her to see some real theater.

"What time should I pick you up?" she asked.

"Oh—" He stopped, blushing furiously. "You don't have to drive. I can hire a car. We can go—"

"Randy, I have a car and I like to drive. What time?"

"That isn't why I—I—I asked you," Randy stammered. "I was inviting you. I wasn't looking for a driver. I wanted you to come. I don't—use people."

"Oh, Randy," sighed Kim. "You'd be about the last person I'd ever accuse of that."

Kim had never seen a play before. She had never been inside a real theater. It was an exciting experience. She thought *A Doll's House* was a marvelous play. She wondered why things like this weren't made into movies. Randy told her how much he admired these actors. They were so much more dedicated than he was. They would rather starve to death acting in something good than pull down twenty-five hundred a week doing junk on Broadway. And as for the movies! Randy almost dreaded the thought of meeting his friends afterward.

His friends were Marcy and Phillip Granger. In real life they were husband and wife just as they were in the play.

The Grangers met Randy and Kim at a little Italian restaurant not far from the Playhouse. They both reached out for Randy and practically squeezed the life out of his frail body in a communal hug.

"Oh, I know you," exclaimed Marcy, turning to Kim.

"That's funny, I didn't," said her husband. He whistled. "But for Christ's sake, I wish I did. Good God alive!"

"This is Kimberley Hudson," Randy introduced her.

"Jesus, Randy, where did you find her? I sure haven't run into anything like her out here."

Amazing! Phillip Granger wasn't kidding around. The name meant nothing to him and the face wasn't familiar. Where had he been? Not at the movies for sure, or reading fan magazines. And Randy hadn't bothered to tell them who he was bringing. Anybody else she could think of would have dropped her name just to show off. Randy didn't need that. Randy didn't "use" other people, as he put it.

"Christ, Kimberley," Phillip said to her, "with a face like that 'you oughtta be in pictures, you're wonderful to see' as the old ditty goes. What the hell do you do?"

"I'm just a private secretary," she replied, smiling. "It might be fun to be in the movies. But I like my work and it's quite interesting. I have a nice boss, too. You maybe haven't heard of him but he's really quite well known. His name is Dwight D. Eisenhower and he's President of the United States."

Phillip didn't get the full gist of the joke. But Marcy and Randy howled.

"Touché!" Randy cheered. He leaned across the table to hug Kim and gave her a juicy kiss on the brow. It was the first time he had touched her away from the cameras.

Most of the talk left Kim out. The three friends talked of New York. They talked of plays and acting techniques and mutual friends. Kim was happy to sit back and listen. She had never seen Randy so relaxed before. Now he was in his element, talking theater with old friends from the East. It was a pleasure—and a relief—to see that he had an easier side to him.

"Well, here we are," said Phillip, twirling a gob of spaghetti on his fork. "The three old comrades. Two still true to their art and one sell-out."

"I didn't sell out," said Randy, turning red.

"Come on, come on," said Marcy. "Don't be sensitive, Randy. Phil's just pulling your leg. The truth is we'd both like to sell out too. If we could only find any buyers."

"Yeah," said her husband.

Randy looked at them both warily.

"How's Robbie?" Marcy asked lightly.

Randy gave her a funny look. "He's okay, the last I heard." On the way home Kim asked, "Who's Robbie?"

Randy took his time answering her. "He's a boy back in New York. A very poor boy from Harlem. He's an absolutely brilliant dancer. Or he will be with training. He's got more talent in his left toe than I've got in my whole body."

"I doubt that," said Kim.

"It's true. Anyway, Robbie's somebody I met and I'm trying to help a little bit. That's one reason I'm out here. To make enough money to help Robbie and various others who could use a boost. The Players Stage, for one."

"How did you meet Robbie?"

Another long pause. "Oh, you know New York." (How could she, never having been there?) "You meet everybody in New York. It was at some mad gathering somewhere."

It was after three o'clock in the morning when she pulled up in front of the Charmont. Late as it was, she hoped the night was not over. Tomorrow—today—was Sunday. They didn't have to be back at the Studio until Monday morning.

Randy brushed the back of his fingers against her cheekbones—a second touching in the same evening. "I love you, you know. You must know that."

Then he was running into the hotel without a backward glance.

"I love you, you know. You must know that." Those nine little words kept Kim from getting any sleep the rest of that night. She hadn't begged for them. He said them on his own. He told her he loved her. That's all she wanted to hear. Long after dawn the words were still ringing in her ears.

In her fantasies she romanced Randy in a hundred different ways. They were the screen's newest lovers. When *These Murdering Children* was released, pictures of them together would appear everywhere. Their marriage would be *the* event of the year. They would try to escape to the most secret, remote place in the world for their honeymoon. Some place like Madagascar or Tasmania or the South Pole. But wherever they went, the press would be waiting for them. They were just too "hot"—as stars and lovers—to duck the world. They belonged . . . to the world. Realizing this—reluctantly—they would cut short their honeymoon. They would go back to Hollywood and on to New York and London. They would become one of those famous performing couples like the Lunts and the Fredric Marches or Ginger Rogers and Fred Astaire . . .

In the hard glare of the morning sun the romantic images focused into realistic wonderings. What would it be like with Randy in bed? Would he be as exciting in bed as he was on camera? What would he look like with his clothes off? For the first time—consciously—she tried to focus on his nude body. Would he have hair on his chest? Would the hair down below be crawling up all over his belly? How big would he be? Would his balls be little marbles or big fat hangers?

She didn't care how big he was or how he was hung. All this stuff about size—size of cocks or balls—was crazy. She had had enough good times to know it wasn't what a man had. It was how he used what he had. She still couldn't stop undressing Randolph Jahr in her imagination. What would he look like . . . *be* like? The mid-morning sun, clearing the Hollywood Hills to the east, blazed on her. She hardly knew it was there. It wasn't the blazing, mid-morning sun that was giving her this hot, restless throbbing . . .

She *must* get some sleep. But how could she ever get to

sleep? When she was in a state like this? When all she could think of was Randy?

She blamed it on Randy. He had reduced her to this. Because he wasn't there, she went for the substitute. She did the thing she hadn't done since she was trying to get to sleep with Geordie Harmon on her mind. As she did it, she remembered that thing Maura had used on her the night they spent together. If she had it here now, she'd have used it on herself. She'd have talked to it—and called it Randy.

Monday morning Randy asked her in his trembling, tentative way, "Will you do me a big, big favor?"

"Anything," she said, and bit her lip to keep from adding, "I'd do anything in the world for you—even bad things."

"Would you . . . teach me how to drive?"

"Oh, Randy, I'd love to! You taught *me* what I know about acting. Compared with acting, driving's a snap. Look at all the idiots who drive cars."

"I think I'd better learn. If I'm going to be out here—"

"Randy, you're going to stay out here?"

"I didn't say that. I haven't signed any contracts. And I'm not going to. It'll be strictly on a picture-to-picture basis. But if a good script comes my way, I'll do it."

For one who hated Hollywood; he had certainly changed his tune. Kim was in highest heaven. She just knew she was one of the big reasons why he had changed his tune.

Randy approached the driving lessons with the same intensity he brought to his acting. Those long summer evenings and Saturday and Sunday afternoons Kim drove him out into the Valley so he could practice on quiet roads and streets. He learned too fast to suit Kim. She anticipated—correctly—what would happen. As soon as he passed his tests and got licensed, he got a car. Actually, he rented one.

Kim missed driving him back and forth. The Studio was equally unhappy about his new skill. The great Randolph Jahr should be seen in something far grander than a rented Volkswagen.

"I can't keep leaning on you," Randy said about the rented car.

If you only would lean on me, she thought. Forever!

She went from day to day in a state of suspended happiness. To be near Randy all day long, working together, talking together, sometimes embracing and kissing in front of the cameras . . . this was happiness. She dreaded the day the picture would be finished. She had a dread of what would happen.

"The way I've got it planned," Spence Holmes announced

one morning, "we should call this a wrap by Thursday lunchtime."

"Great!" said Randy. "I'll be on the first plane back to New York."

It's what Kim had dreaded. She was stricken.

"Don't get your hopes up," Randy said to Kim. "You're not rid of me. I'm coming back. I'm signing on for *An Autumn to Remember*. They sent me the script a couple of weeks ago. It's a beauty."

"Randy, we must have a celebration before you go. Celebrate the end of the picture. And celebrate your coming back."

"Absolutely. But no place fancy. I don't even own a suit."

"We'll have dinner at my place. The unfanciest place I know. I'll even cook for you. But watch out. It'll be the first meal I ever cooked in my life."

Kim called Mama Spinelli. "Oh, Mama, I need your help."

Mama was ecstatic to hear from Kim. She was alone now so much of the time, with Papa dead and the Spinelli Sisters usually on the road somewhere. She said, "It's the big movie star calling me?"

"No, it's not the big movie star calling you. It's just a girl in love."

Kim told Mama about Randy and how she had invited him to dinner and she was in a panic because she couldn't cook. Would Mama please tell her what to serve and how to make each dish?

"Mama, I remember the first time I asked you how you made something and you said you made it with love. I want everything in the dinner to be made with love. Give me some real love recipes."

Mama laughed and laughed. "Kim, honey child, I don't have any recipes. I cook by-love-and-by-golly. I never write anything down or read anything when I cook. I feel my way along. A pinch of this and a little bit of that. Kim, let me cook for you. Let me cook a nice big meal for you and your young man."

"Oh, Mama, would you? I'll love you to Doomsday if you would."

Mama would if she could come the night before to get her sauce started for the rigatoni. After picking her up, Kim set her loose in the Farmers' Market. She came out with enough food to feed the whole commissary.

Randy caught the odors the moment he set foot in the house. He did a mock-fainting act. He went through everything like a refugee from a concentration camp. Months of tuna salad sandwich dinners had put him in a state of semi-starvation.

Taking his plate to the kitchen for a refill of the veal milanese and risotto, Kim put it to Mama, "What do you think of him, Mama? Isn't he wonderful?"

"He's a lovely, lovely boy," Mama reassured her. "But he's so thin. That's no good. We have to put some fat on him."

"Oh, my," Randy groaned, when he had put away the last bite of zuppa inglese. "I've never been through anything like this."

He got up wobbily to pay his compliments to the chef. In the kitchen he hugged Mama Spinelli and pressed his cheek against hers. "Mama Spinelli," he declared, "you are a magician and an artist and a wonderful woman all wrapped up into one."

Mama basked in his holding hug and his flattering words.

"Now, come on," he said, "it's been a long day for you, and the boy actor has another morning to go. Come on, I'll run you home."

He kissed Kim on the cheek. "Good night, my love. Parting is such sweet sorrow . . ."

It was for her, anyway. But she knew it had to be. Even now he was getting a case of nerves about that last scene. In the morning he would be the doomed man being led to the electric chair for the murder of his wife.

"It was a wonderful evening," Kim told herself. "He's coming back. "He'll be gone only six weeks. Then he'll be back. He'll be more relaxed then. Maybe he'll even move in with me . . ."

Kim herself moved during the six weeks Randy was in New York. The composer whose house she was subletting came back. She found another furnished house for rent way up on top of Tower Hill Road. The house was called "Eagle's Aerie." It was a Spanish-type house that jutted out from a mountainside. Its best features were the fantastic views—and a guest cottage for Kim's mother fifty yards away from the main house.

Kim also moved into another ho-hum picture. A clanking thing set in medieval times. She did it in good humor. *These Murdering Children* was not in release yet. What could she expect but more junk from the Studio? But just wait till they saw how the public and the critics raved over her in the good picture. Then they'd promote her out of the junk stuff.

During that same six weeks Lonnie Braintree came to town.

Kim was beside herself with joy to see her dear, dear friend again.

It had been such a long time. More than a year. Lonnie had gone back to England, for the first time since he had come to the States as a little boy. He had gone back to do a show in the West End. It was one of those silly, frothy comedies the English like so much. Not surprisingly it turned out to be a big hit.

Lonnie was full of his success. During the year in London he had, to hear him tell it, lunched and tea-ed and cocktailed and suppered and weekended with every Englishman/Englishwoman of any importance. He rattled on about Larry and Vivien and Noel and Rex and Bea and "Willie" Maugham. He had houseboated on the Thames with Peggy Ashcroft and her husband. He had even taken tea at Clarence House with the Queen Mother and Princess Margaret. He was full of witty, malicious gossip about famous people.

Dear Lonnie! How she had missed him! He was her eyes and ears on the rich and the celebrated. He was such good fun. He always kept her laughing. He also made her feel important. Lonnie didn't like to be with people who were only so-so successful. If he spent time with you, you could feel that you were already important—or you were someone he had pegged to become very, very important.

"You, ducks," said Lonnie. "You look scrumptious. You're absolutely glowing. I've never seen you look so yummy. Is there some special reason?"

"I'm in love."

"That figures. Anybody I know?"

"I don't think so."

"Ah-ha. Not talking? Not naming names?"

"No."

"Playing games? Want me to guess? How many guesses do I get? Two million?"

"You don't have to guess, I'll tell you. I'm in love with Randolph Jahr. And I think he loves me. He told me he does."

All the lightness and gaiety went out of Lonnie. "How serious is this? How deep are you into this?"

"All the way. I'm head over heels in love with him. He's all I think about."

"Oh, duckie, duckie," sighed Lonnie.

"What does 'Oh, duckie, duckie' mean?"

"Not good, not good."

"Lonnie, you don't even know him. For God's sake—"

"Forget about it. Forget him, ducks."

"Forget him? It would be easier to forget my own name!"

"Sad time, sad time." Lonnie hugged her and kissed her on top of the head. "You've got to forget about it."

"Don't torture me like this, Lonnie. If you know——"

"It's no good, ducks. Remember when you asked me to take a bead on old Geordie?"

"Yes."

"And I did. And I reported back he was el straight-o."

"I remember."

"Not so lucky this time, ducks."

"Lucky? Oh, Lonnie, what are you saying?"

"Ducks, he's one of the brotherhood. Or sisterhood. He's one of us. He's my kind. Queer as the proverbial. Queer, queer, queer."

Chapter 21

Kim wouldn't speak to Lonnie for weeks. But she knew he had told her the truth. She felt it in her bones. After pushing and kicking at the truth with all her force—after grabbing at every straw in the wind—she gave in. It had to be true. It made all the pieces fit together ... his hands-off policy toward her even after he must have known she was his for the taking ... his rushing back to New York the second the picture was finished ... Robbie, the dancer from Harlem he was "helping" ... the way he had blushed at the mention of Robbie's name that night in Pasadena ...

Giving in to the truth, she went into a state of shock. She sleepwalked through the picture she was making. She was like a mechanical doll who had to be wound by someone (presumably the director) before she could move and speak her lines. Gradually the numbness wore off and she began to feel again. She felt sharp pain. She felt she was trapped in a no-end nightmare.

She tried to read up on homosexuality. But she found almost nothing had been written on the subject except the Kinsey Report. It was no comfort for her to read that one out of three adult males had had some homosexual experience. What about the male whose experience was all homosexual? Could he be cured? If he could, how?

I had reason to know just how desperate she was. We hadn't spoken in months when she caught up with me one middle-of-the-night. It was three o'clock in the morning— Framingham, Massachusetts, time. The Spinelli Sisters had a week's gig in a Framingham club so stinking in every way I refuse to mention its name. If you name a place and knock it

211

in every way you can think of, there are enough crazies around who'd go there and pay out their good money just to see if it's as lousy as it's cracked up to be. That's why I won't name it. My sisters and I were almost robbed and raped there one night in our suite by some thugs. We're all convinced we were set up for it by the management.

Just like Kim. No how-are-you's or how-are-you-doing's. You shouldn't expect idle chitchat and you should know what she was talking about. If she referred to "these things" you should know what these things meant.

"Gina," said Kim, "being around nightclubs and singers and musicians and comics all the time—well, you must run into a lot of funny people. I mean queers."

Wow! Just like that. Leave it to Kim.

"Did you ever know a queer who got over it? I mean is it possible to change if you are queer?"

She was asking me! I could be about the last person to ask. I was nineteen years old. But I could still be the greenest nineteen-year-old on any block. Sure, I knew what being queer meant. Maybe a couple of my best friends were queer. But as for having a cure . . .

"Why don't you ask that doctor," I suggested, "you saw that time about Geordie?"

"Oh, Gina, I think that's a marvelous idea," she said, sounding very excited. "Why didn't I think of that?"

Kim put the question to Dr. Friedman: "If somebody is homosexual, can he be cured?"

"That all depends," said Dr. Friedman. "It depends——"

" 'That all depends,' " Kim mimicked him, interrupting. "Is that your answer to every question? That's what you said the last time I was here. When I was asking you about my husband."

"It's a pretty honest answer," replied Dr. Friedman. "Because that's what it comes down to, when you're dealing with serious personality disorders. It all depends. Does the person—patient—really want to change? How hard and long will he fight to change?"

Yes, he told her, there was hope for the homosexual. Particularly for the young homosexual . . . a homosexual as young as the man she described. The big factor was the will to change. That will was almost always lacking. He had heard of miraculous cures for homosexuality. Shock treatments, hypnosis, group therapy. Maybe they worked in some instances. But he distrusted them. He would say to her again as he had said before. Any weird behavior pattern was just a symptom. Whatever it was—gambling, alcoholism, impotence, homosexuality—the cure came from treating the causes.

"Have you ever cured anybody?" Kim put to him. "A real out-and-out homosexual who wanted to be cured?"

"No," he said. "But I never had anybody come to me who really wanted to be cured. Yet."

Late at night—very late New York time—Randy called her. Night after night. He sounded lonely and longing. He never said mushy, gushy things. But he called. He called because he missed her and longed to be back with her. She knew that for a fact.

It was so simple. Once he got back, she would have a chat with him. She would tell him she guessed something about him. If it was true, it didn't matter in the least to her. The past was the past. The future was something else. If he wanted to change, Dr. Friedman would help him. It might take only a few sessions.

It wasn't that simple.

To celebrate his homecoming, Kim asked Mama Spinelli if she'd cook another "love" meal. Mama didn't have to be asked twice. In the wild excitement and happiness of seeing Randy again, Kim pushed away the thought of getting into anything heavy. But relaxed and numbed a little from too much wine, she found a way of easing into the subject.

"Randy, I know you have an apartment in New York. But you've never told me what it's like."

He told her what it was like, the seven-room duplex he rented in a run-down, cockroachy brownstone in the East Sixties.

"Seven rooms! For just one person? Randy, you don't live there all by yourself, do you?"

"No."

"Do you have a . . . roommate?"

"Yes."

He was being close-mouthed so she made a special effort. "Oh, who? Tell me about him."

"Just somebody who needs a roof over his head. A kid who's broke right now. I let him live there free in exchange for sort of looking after everything while I'm gone. With all that room—"

"Robbie?"

He looked at her cagily. "You didn't have to ask. You already knew. Who told you?"

"Nobody told me. I didn't know. I just guessed when you said it was somebody who was broke. The night we were out in Pasadena you talked about Robbie . . . how talented he was but he hadn't made it yet and he was still poor."

"You don't forget anything, do you?" asked Randy, still suspicious.

"I would never forget anything *you* say. Most people I don't even hear what they say. So there's nothing to remember."

"That's a very pretty compliment. Is that all you're trying to do? Pay me a compliment?"

He had her. He was so smart—and suspicious.

"No."

"What are you driving at, then?"

"Randy, please, please, please promise me you won't get mad at me if I ask you something. Maybe it's none of my business but I can't help being curious."

"Maybe you shouldn't ask it. If you're so worried about my reaction."

"No. I've gone this far. Randy, it's a crazy question—something that just popped into my head—but is Robbie, well . . . something more than a roommate?"

Randy had that stricken animal look, as if a rifle were being pointed at him. "What made you ask such a thing?"

"I don't know, Randy. Who knows how things pop into your head?"

"Your intuition is pretty sharp. Yes, Robbie and I have been more than roommates. To spell it out, we've been lovers."

"And still are?"

"Yes. But it's not so hot and frantic as it was in the beginning. He's there and I'm here, aren't I? I think we're more friends than we are lovers now. Next question?"

"Is this the way you . . . are?"

"It's the way I've always been."

"Is it the way you want to go on being?"

"I never thought about it much. Until lately. I don't know that I have any options."

"That's not so, Randy. You could do anything you wanted to do. You could change anything. I have this friend—right here in Beverly Hills—and he knows somebody who had always liked boys and then he met a girl he really wanted to love." She was making all this up as she went along. She hoped he wouldn't see through her. She hated the idea of fibbing to him. But if the fibs could give him ideas—that he could change if he really wanted to—maybe they were worth telling. "He found a psychoanalyst right here in Beverly Hills. And he changed. He married the girl and they're as happy as they can be."

"I'd have to see that to believe it," said Randy. "I mean, maybe he wasn't all the other way. He could have been a little iffy. AC-DC, as we say." He turned away from the intent, exquisite face bent toward him, hanging on his every word. "Anyway, psychoanalysis is out."

"Out? Why—if it could help?"

"It might not help. What I know is it would destroy me. Creatively. You're dead as an artist once you begin asking yourself why you do what you do—what it all means to you. I'm reasonably convinced acting is one of the most neurotic professions going. I don't think many—if any—sane, healthy, balanced people would ever want to become actors. Serious actors, I mean. I'm not talking about Lotusland out here where a no-talent with no training can make an easy fortune if they've got a face or a personality that 'clicks' with the masses. I'm talking about actors who work like dogs to perfect their craft. Actors who couldn't imagine any other life but acting, even knowing how nuts and childish the profession is."

He had said all this without looking at her. Turning his anguished face toward her, he went on, "This is all I've got that I can count on. My work. It's the spit and glue that holds me together. I have to protect it. I'm sure as hell not going to let some head-quack sitting on his fat can in a plushy office on Roxbury Drive take it away from me. 'What does acting mean to you, Mr. Jahr?' 'Can you recall when you first started to fantasize yourself as being somebody else . . . the conflict or provocation that made you retreat into imaginary worlds?' I'm not going to let a fat-ass fat cat like that put pins all over me. And pay him fifty or seventy-five bucks a throw for the privilege. Those guys don't have any of the answers. They're just on to the best con game the law allows. They're hucksters who have the built-in hostility hucksters have for creative people. That's why they try to knock the creativity out of any creative person stupid enough to put himself in their path."

Kim had never heard Randy get so wordy and worked up on any subject. So she could not talk him into a visit with Dr. Friedman—or any other doctor. He couldn't have told her anything more depressing. It made everything seem so hopeless.

What was there to say? She couldn't think of a thing. Everything had been laid out on the table and there wasn't going to be any way to pick up the pieces.

He was too tuned in to her not to catch her down mood. "Back East I heard a couple of interesting things," he said softly. "I heard there's a doctor in Philadelphia who's getting great results with people like me. Group therapy. Five, six, seven guys who really want to change join up with him for a

215

couple of sessions a week. It's supposed to be working wonders. I'm just waiting for some guy to write up his experiences for the *Reader's Digest,* 'Confessions of an Ex-Queer.' I also heard they were using hypnosis in England. Patients are hypnotized into feeling good if they think about girls. They get electric shocks of pain if they think about men. That's supposed to do the trick. That I'll believe too when I see it."

Jumping into his rented Volkswagen, he said, "Psychoanalysis is out. But I want to try to beat this rap. Any other way." He rubbed her cheek again with a soft brush of the knuckles. "I told you I love you. I do love you. I thought about you all the time I was gone. I'm back. I'm here. That must mean something."

To Kim, the dreamer of dreams, it meant everything. He had made his choice. He was back here because of her. He loved her more than he loved the boy in New York. Now all he had to do was to find a way out—an escape from his trap—and he would be hers. It couldn't be psychoanalysis. But any other way. She would think of a way. Something that could happen here. Something that didn't have to wait until he could go to Philadelphia for group therapy or to England for hypnosis.

"How do these things happen?" Kim wanted to know.

"You tell me," said Randy. "It's not a matter of choice, I can assure you. By the time you know, there's no turning back. You're hooked. Only you don't think about it like that. You're in love. It's maybe even more exciting that you're in love with somebody of the wrong sex—your own sex. It has the excitement of forbidden fruit—if I might coin a pun at my own expense. First love is first love and you can't imagine it could be nearly so good if it was anybody else in the world. There are no regrets."

First love came to Randy when he was thirteen. His love was reciprocated. The object of his affections was a classmate at Collegiate. A big, husky, budding football star named David Buchanan. After school they would go to Randy's room in the apartment on Park Avenue. Presumably they were going to do their homework together and listen to Bix Beiderbecke records. At the first sound of Bix's horn from the record player they were hugging and kissing. That led to more sex play. Then they were taking off their clothes—"and doing everything." Sometimes Randy almost wished they'd be caught. If his mother had barged in on them, he could have shown off his trophy to her. "He's mine," he'd have told her. "He loves me."

It was only a passing moment, an adolescent love, in David's life. The next year David was fourteen and was infatuated with a pretty young thing going to Miss Hewitt's Classes. Randy was heartbroken. He thought of committing suicide. What saved his life was work—a new play on Broadway. He played the fifteen-year-old man of the house in a family drama set in wartime England; the absentee father was off fighting the Axis as an RAF captain.

Randy began meeting men, both in and out of the theater. He went to bed with them. Mostly these were one-nighters. For years he carried a torch for David. Robbie was the next—and really the only other—lasting love he had ever had. He had been busy, thank God. This had kept him from making love—or what passed for love in the homosexual world—become the be-all and end-all of his existence. He had never let himself think too much about the future. It was too depressing. This kind of love didn't seem to have any future. Being in the theater, where there seemed to be so much of this, he had seen—met—a lot of older homosexuals. They came across as a sad lot, lonely, bitter, bitchy. They weren't much of an argument for Same Sex Love.

"To get back to your question," said Randy. "Where does it start? Why me and not him? I've read all the literature on the subject. How much do they really know, the head specialists? They all join voices in a chorus. The parents are mismatched. The mother was strong and aggressive and the father was weak and passive. The boy identified with his mother. He and his mother are locked together in an unholy grip. It's a love-hate relationship in which they're both frustrated. She manipulates him to gratify her emotional hunger. He despises her for what she's doing to him. But he has nowhere else to go. She's the source of any good thing that comes to him. It's a cat-and-mouse game they play. When she's ahead, she's a queen bitch out for the kill. But if he just once gets the jump on her—if he just once makes one pitiful little sign of trying to assert his potential manhood—she retreats at a gallop. Suddenly she's all milk and honey. It takes two to tango, remember. He must never get away. They're in this thing together. She's just clever and charming enough to bring it off. If she were an out-and-out witch without any cleverness or charm, she wouldn't get away with it. A boy could escape from a monster. But she's too shrewd for that. Her antennae tell her when enough is enough and she should yield. She goes back to her gambit of being submissive and seductive. She has him where she wants him. Comes a time when he puts up one last little whimper of fight. She honeys him out of it and that's the ball game. They settle into an arrangement or accommodation of sorts. When you come down to it, they're really sisters under the skin. They belong to

217

each other for life. They may live the rest of their lives ten thousand miles apart. But they're so deep into each other's bloodstream, it's like they're still under the same roof. Neither one of them will ever be able to share the other. At least, that's the script according to the psychiatrists."

"Is that the script," Kim asked, "according to you?"

"More or less, I guess, to be honest. If somebody was to ask me right now how I feel about my mother I'd probably say, 'I'll never in one million years ever forgive her—and I can't bear to think of the time when she won't be here.' "

"Oh, Randy, but . . . what is it—I don't understand—what is it that makes you, turns you——"

"Turns you against the opposite sex? It's your guess—your theory. Does son finally identify so much with mother they become like sisters . . . two girls—women—frustrated women . . . without men, looking for men? Or does he hate her so much for what she's done to him . . . practically castrating him . . . that he never wants to go near another woman again? And if he doesn't want to go near another woman . . . well, by the simple process of elimination, there's only one sex left. Which theory do you buy? Take your pick."

Kim rushed on. "Randy, tell me something . . ."

"Tell you something? Something more? After all you've heard—"

"Tell me. If this hadn't happened to you, how would you feel . . . about me?"

"Feel about you!" Randy cried. "Don't you know? Is there any mystery? How I feel about you?"

"Tell me, Randy."

"I go to sleep on you. You are my magnificent obsession. You are so . . . so special to me. I think about you all the time. When I was gone, I kept seeing you. It was spooky. You . . . you are my *passionate* friendship."

"Then I don't scare you and you don't hate me?"

"I love you. I want to be with you all the time."

"I wish you'd move out of that awful hotel and live here. There's plenty of room, as you can see."

Randy smiled his pained smile. "I'd better not—right now. That awful hotel room is good for me. Just because it is awful. It lets me concentrate. I can blot out all the gunk and junk in that room and concentrate. It's like a monastery. I can be a 'priest to my art,' quote unquote."

He had told her what she wanted to hear. She didn't scare him. He didn't hate her. Putting one and one together, Kim drew an important conclusion. She didn't remind him of his mother. Everything was possible. Hopes soaring, she hatched out a plan.

Randy's "secret" was known to her. There was nothing any more to hide or protect from her. She had heard the worst and she still wanted to be with him. Nothing had changed. He relaxed even more around her. She was the only one he wanted to see. He didn't bother to reply to any of the invitations that poured in through the mail. And he told the desk at the Charmont not to put through any calls unless they were from the Studio, Miss Kimberley Hudson, or New York.

Saturday and Sunday afternoons he tooled up to the Eagle's Aerie in his rented doodlebug. He was a weekend painter. From what she had seen, Kim thought he was a marvelous one. She was flattered pink when he insisted that he wanted to paint her portrait. Those long weekend afternoons she posed for him in a white chiffon dress and an emerald necklace, sitting perfectly still by the hour while he painted. Under his concentrated, admiring gaze, she felt warm and loved even though he hardly spoke to her. Mama Spinelli was always there to cook the nights Randy stayed for dinner. Mama loved Randy. She couldn't be subtle if her life depended on it. She made it loud and clear there were two things that could make her very, very happy. She would like Randy to put on a few pounds. She would like to see him and Kim married and living happily together ever after.

Randy always drove Mama Spinelli home when he was ready to leave. This made her happy on two counts. The great Randolph Jahr was driving her, Serafina Spinelli, to her very doorstep! That wasn't all. He insisted on coming in with her and putting on the lights. He wanted to make sure everything was all right before he left her. Such a lovely boy!

It made her happy too because it proved Kim wasn't the kind of girl all that mean, jealous gossip painted her out to be. Kim was acting like a lady and Randy was the perfect gentleman. They weren't doing anything they shouldn't be doing. She couldn't ask that her own daughters would be better behaved. Kim was going to wait until she was married— just like any other decent girl—before she started acting like a wife to Randy.

Over Mama's sincere protests, Kim always slipped a wad of bills into Mama's purse. Frankly those fat tips came in handy. The Spinelli Sisters weren't doing too hot at the time. It was often a strain to be sending Mama anything at all for living expenses.

One Saturday morning Kim called Mama and said, "Mama, you get a vacation today. Randy's so tired from working too hard he's just going to sleep through. I'll call you in the morning. If he can make it, I'll come early and get you."

"Mama can't make it today." Kim told Randy when he arrived. "The girls are working in a club in Atlantic City and they wrote her to be sure to be home at six o'clock her time. Because they'd be calling her long distance. But don't worry. We'll get fed. Indiana said she'd whip up something."

Randy and Kim lingered at the table long after Indiana had cleared away the dishes. Sipping brandy, saying very little, they looked sleepily and contentedly at each other in the candlelight.

"Randy, it's late. Stay here tonight. Don't drive all the way back to that crummy hotel. Stay here."

"I couldn't do that," said Randy, rousing suddenly from his torpor.

"Yes, you could. And can."

"No. I must get back."

"Randy, I've been thinking so much about what you told me the other night. About . . . your problem. It seems simple. It's something you can work out yourself. You don't have to go to Philadelphia or London or anywhere else."

"I'm listening."

"I shouldn't say by yourself," Kim corrected herself. "But I think . . . with a little help."

"Tell me."

"If you really wanted to do something," she began, "and you didn't even try to do it, it must be because you're afraid of it." She hoped the pink glow from the candles would keep her blushes from showing. "If you didn't know how to swim and you wouldn't even try to learn, there must be a reason. Because you know swimming is fun and it's good for you and it could save your life. There must be a reason you won't try to learn. It must be that you're afraid to learn. If you had to get somewhere in a hurry but you wouldn't go on a plane, there must be a reason why. You're afraid to fly. You'll never learn to swim if you won't go in the water. You'll never learn to fly if you won't get on a plane. I don't think you can stop being afraid of anything unless you face right up to it. I think it's the same with your problem. I think you can get over this easy . . . as soon as you see there's nothing to be scared of. That you won't die or get killed if you go to bed with a girl."

Randy looked amused. "You think it's all that easy, do you? I just go out and pay a prostitute to——"

"Not a prostitute, Randy! Never a prostitute. They're business women. They don't have time to be teaching." Her face

220

must be as bright red as if she had stuck it in an oven. But she had to finish her idea. "Let *me* help you Randy."

Randy's smile quickly faded, He was the caged bird again, desperate for escape, "I . . . *couldn't*. I love . . . respect . . . you too much "

"That sounds so silly. You *love* me so much. You're a boy and I'm a girl. We're both young and healthy. But you *love* me too much to think of being in bed with me!"

She told him how much it would please her if he stayed here tonight. If he would share her bed with her. The bed was big. Nothing would happen. She didn't expect anything from him. She wouldn't even expect him to try. They would just sleep together in the same bed, like brother and sister. In the morning he would wake up as safe and sound as if he had slept in his own bed.

The next time could be just the same thing all over again. But by and by his confidence would build up. He might get curious. He might want to experiment. If it didn't work the first time, who cared? They had all the time in the world. She would rather wait for him, no matter how long it took, than to make out with anyone else before he was ready. For him she had a bottomless well of patience. Just being with him was enough. It would always be enough, as long as he kept trying . . .

"Oh, baby, baby, baby," he sighed. His eyes misted and the fright had gone out of them. "You are something."

"So that's agreed on," she cried happily. "You just see. It'll work. You'll be surprised."

Randy shook his head skeptically. "I think your proposition calls for a fat slug of Scotch."

The fat slug of Scotch weakened his resistance. He let Kim lead him into the bedroom. Tactfully she turned out all the lights so they could get undressed in the dark. In bed she kept her bargain. She didn't come near him. They talked easily and drowsily for a while. Just before dozing off, Randy reached shyly for Kim's hand under the bedding. He moved close enough, for a moment, to kiss her lightly on the lips. "Good night, my love," he murmured.

Early in the morning Kim was awakened by a little tap on her bare shoulder. Randy was lying on his side on top of the covers, gazing at her.

"Hey, good morning."

"You've been feasting on my boobs," she joshed.

"What a breakfast!"

"They're getting to you, Randy. I just saw something down there give a little twitch." She pointed to his crotch, which was swathed in black nylon jockey shorts.

"It'll take more than a little twitch to turn me into a lover." He laughed nervously. "Hey, I got to get out of here. I got to get into the guest room before Indiana's up and poking around."

"Indiana knows I'm no angel."

"But she still thinks *I'm* one."

There were a lot of other nights like that, Fridays and Saturdays. Randy was spending his whole weekend up at Eagle's Aerie. It was fine even with Mama. She could see that he had his own room and it was better for him to be up there with all the space and fresh air and sunshine and good food than cooped up in that hotel eating sandwiches. Wedding bells would soon be ringing and then he would move in to stay.

Indiana kept her thoughts to herself.

Then came that fateful Saturday night.

After dinner—and taking Mama home—they played canasta. They sloshed up the Scotch pretty freely. Finally it was Randy who said it was "bedsy-bye time." It had always been Kim who led the way.

At Randy's insistence they undressed with the lights on— for the first time. Also for the first time Randy stripped off his shorts. A little woozily, under the brilliant light cast by a cluster of ceiling bulbs, they beheld each other's nude bodies.

His thin, pale, bony body was almost as smooth and hairless as a woman's. The sight of it filled Kim with longing . . . and the urge to grasp him to her in a tight, protective embrace and never let go. Down below he was on the tiny side with two smooth, smallish globes dropping like miniature golf balls under the small mauve head of his penis.

"My God!" he gasped. "You're fabulous, fantastic."

In bed. with the lights out, he immediately reached for her hand. "Let's just kiss," he whispered, "and hold each other."

She moved slowly, dreamily towards him. She mustn't scare him with any sudden lunges or gropes.

"My darling, my lover," she whispered, as their bodies touched. She put her arms around his neck and waited for his lips to find hers.

It was more a meeting than a kiss. Finding her lips, his stopped motionless and rested there. She waited and counted to a thousand before gently dipping the tip of her tongue between his lips. She waited another eternity before trying to press her tongue between his clenched teeth. He held firm a moment, then unclenched his teeth. Kim took it as her cue to move her tongue inside. Swiftly but gently she explored his gums, the roof of his mouth, and deep into the cavity of his throat.

"No!" he screamed, brushing her away. "Not so fast. I need another drink."

He poured them each a healthy Scotch, which they both drank in gulps, with the lights off. When she heard him put down his glass, she reached for him again. But she didn't try to kiss him.

"You're tied up in knots," she said. "Turn over on your stomach and I'll massage you."

Randy obediently turned over. Kim kneaded his neck and shoulders and ribs. He murmured his bliss. Kim flicked her tongue into each of his ears. "My darling, my lover," she whispered into each ear.

Then her tongue began to caress him . . . slowly, slowly . . . caressing the lobes of his ears, behind his ears, back of his neck, across the planes of his shoulders, under his armpits, down his spinal column, down, down . . . slowly but unerringly to the edge of the divide . . .

"Not there!" he cried. "You don't have to. Not there."

"Why not?"

"Because. Because I don't want you to . . . degrade yourself."

"*Degrade*? How can I degrade myself . . . loving the body of my lover? Trying to please him?"

Over his whimpering protests, her tongue found his rear portal and slipped in. She probed that dark passage gently at first, then more insistently, penetrating deeper and deeper. Suddenly Randy bucked and yelled. He leaped from the bed and rushed to the bathroom.

He must have come! He had come in bed with her. He had come because of her. He *was* changing. She was so happy she cried.

In the bathroom Randy was throwing up.

He had bolted the door and wouldn't let her in. He wouldn't even answer her. All she could hear was his quiet sobbing. After a long while she heard him gargling.

Before he came back to bed, he poured them each another powerful Scotch. He drank his down in three fast gulps. She left hers untouched.

She started up quietly again . . . a touch of the hand, a light brushing kiss on the cheeks, the quick thrust of tongue between his lips and teeth, then that exciting trip south, this time by a different route . . .

Over and over again she roamed that most private compound, his limp penis and the twin marblelike spheres. At last she took the lifeless tip between her moist lips. Her lips pushed back smoothly over the vessel, her tongue stroking its underbelly. Back and forth she went, picking up speed while her tongue slithered up and down the netherside. There wasn't a sign of life to encourage her. She tried harder. She must, she must bring him to life. She *must*. If it took all night.

He broke free of her abruptly, and stumbled back into the bathroom. There she heard him vomiting again. After a long time he came out, and in the darkness she could hear him filling up his glass with another Scotch. He sat on the edge of the bed, drinking.

"No good," he mumbled. "You're barking up the wrong tree. It'll never work. Never, never, never."

"You're wrong, Randy."

"Never. It won't work."

"No, Randy. You're wrong. You did it. You did it once tonight. You came."

"No. I didn't come with you."

"Well, you came. And aren't I the only other one in the bed?"

"No, Robbie was here too. Robbie likes to do what you did. I imagined it was him doing it to me. That's how I came. I was so disgusted with myself afterward I got sick to my stomach. I upchucked and made a decision in there. In the bathroom. I'd come back here and really try. If you made love to me again, I wouldn't let myself think about Robbie. Or any other boy or man I ever made it with. Or wanted to make it with. Every second I'd force myself to remember that I was here with you. I stuck to it. And you see what happened. Nothing. Zero. That's why I got sick again and upchucked. It's no good. It won't work. I desperately wanted it to work. I never wanted anything so much in my whole life."

"You're wrong, Randy. This is just the beginning. You have to give yourself a chance. Give yourself—"

"No. I know. It won't work. You better get yourself a man. A real man. I can't do you any good."

"Don't say things like that. You are a man. A real man. And you're the only man I want."

Snorting, Randy filled his glass again. He began fumbling and stumbling into his clothes.

"Why are you getting dressed?" Kim asked.

"Gotta go. Gotta get home."

"Please don't go," she begged him.

"Gotta go," he repeated. "Gotta think. Concentrate."

"You won't be doing much thinking tonight. Don't go," she pleaded.

"Have to."

"Then will you promise to call me the minute you get back

224

to your room? So I know you got home safe? You shouldn't be driving after all that drinking."

"I know every turn in the road between this place and the hotel. But I'll call you. Don't worry."

The phone rang long before Randy could possibly have finished the trip. Kim picked up the receiver in a state of terror. She knew whoever was calling had bad news.

"Miss Hudson? Is that you, Miss Hudson?"

"Yes."

"There's been a pretty bad accident—"

Chapter 22

It was horrible. So bad his rescuers didn't know who he was.

Kim shrieked at the sight of the Volkswagen. It was wrapped around a telephone pole like a pretzel.

"We heard him crash," they told her. "He was still lucid. A miracle! He whispered your name and number."

It looked like the steering wheel had slammed against his face. The dashboard was smashed. So was the windshield. Shattered glass lay in shards and splinters all over his head. He was bleeding so much there wasn't one area of his skin that wasn't bloodied.

A scream—louder than her own—rent the night. The sirens of police cars. An ambulance. White-coated men delicately lifted him out of the mangled car and laid his battered body on a stretcher.

Arms held her back. She screamed hysterically until one of the white-coated men came to her.

"He's alive, miss," he said.

As they lifted Randy into the ambulance, she broke free of the restraining arms and jumped in beside him.

"It would be better if you didn't come along," one of the attendants said to her.

"Try and stop me. I'm Kimberley Hudson. This is my dear, dear friend Randolph Jahr."

Later she remembered this was the first time she ever used her name to bully others.

All the way to UCLA Medical Center she held Randy's head. At her touch he seemed to come to. He moaned and whispered her name. Her dress and hands and arms became blood-drenched, but she took no notice. She just looked down

225

at the face that had been so beautiful and fought back more screams. Now it was just a banged-up bloody pulp.

At the hospital they wheeled him into the emergency ward. An orderly was directed to drive her home.

"Get some sleep," somebody said. "We're going to put him under deep sedation. We'll call you in the morning as soon as we have any news."

But Kim didn't wait for them to call her. A few sleepless hours later she called them.

"There's not much change, Miss Hudson. He's been given blood transfusions. He's still way under. His condition is stable and he seems to be holding his own . . ."

God, she thought, what's all that shit mean? It means they don't know anything. But he's alive. Randy's alive! Everything's going to be all right. It has to be.

She wondered how he could be alive when she got the inventory of his injuries. Ruptured spleen. Contusions of the spine. Broken vertebras in the neck and back. Concussions. Fracture of the skull. Some damage to the fibula. Most serious of all, a destroyed face that would have to be rebuilt.

The Studio suspended production of *An Autumn to Remember*. In press releases they said they were prepared to wait as long as it took for Randolph Jahr to recover from his injuries. There was only one Randolph Jahr and there could be no thought of a replacement for him.

It was three weeks and three operations later before Kim was allowed to see Randy. All that time he had been under heavy sedation. He still had two more operations to go on his body. After that, they would start on the really big job—putting his face back together again . . .

He was in Intensive Care. She found him behind some meshed white screens in a dimly lit room. He was slightly propped up.

She put her hands to her mouth to stifle a gasp. There were tubes running out of him. His head was completely bandaged except for two small openings at his nostrils and mouth.

"Hi," he welcomed her.

"Hi," she said, reaching for his hand. It was the only part of his body that wasn't bound or bandaged.

"Meet Humpty-Dumpty."

"Hi, Humpty-Dumpty."

"I can feel you shrinking with horror."

"Randy, how can you say that?" she lied.

"Think of all the Boris Karloff pictures you've seen. You survived them, didn't you? Maybe you'll survive me."

Through the narrow slit, so many teeth were missing that

his speech was weird-sounding. His laugh was even weirder. It had a bitter edge to it.

He was alive, yes. But look at him. A zombie.

She felt as guilty as she was horrified. A lot of this had to be her fault. If he had never met her ... if he hadn't been at her place ... if she hadn't tried to change him ...

"What do the doctors say?"

"They said I'll need both Max Factor and Russ Westmore to make up my puss when the bandages come off."

"What did they really say, Randy?"

"They said I should be crossing myself and lighting candles every day. Nobody should expect to come out of a wreck like that alive."

"What else do they say?"

It was terrible not being able to see his face, especially his eyes. It made it harder to know how to take anything he said.

"Do you think I'm blind?" he asked her. "Is that why they won't give me any slits to look through?"

"Randy, I'm sure you're not."

"Thank God! I don't think I'd be any good at selling good luck charms or newspapers."

"Randy, stop teasing me. What did they say?"

"They said the operation on the leg might leave me with a slight limp. Very slight. They said I'll probably need plastic surgery. To make my mug look beautiful again."

"Anything you need, Randy ... you must have the best. Don't worry about the cost. I'll help——"

"They're way ahead of you, silly. The Studio. They're bringing this Dr. Grierhaus fellow over from Switzerland. You know who he is. Plastic-Surgeon-to-the-Stars. Does lifts and eye tucks and the whole works. He's supposed to be tops."

"Is the Studio paying for it?"

"Silly girl, of course they are. Not out of any great love or compassion for Randolph Jahr. They've got an investment to protect. They can't let the star change faces halfway through a picture."

Kim insisted on being at the hospital when they took off the bandages. The staff tried to talk her out of it. They warned her it might not be a pretty sight. Just for that reason, she argued, she had to be there. She would hold his hand and tell him everything was going to be all right. There must be no mirrors in the room. She would be his mirror. If she held his hand and kept calm—no matter what she saw—his morale would get a lift. He too would believe everything was going to turn out fine.

227

He had taught her really everything she knew about acting. Now—for his sake—she must be prepared to do her best action job to date.

She gave the performance of her career that day. Anybody else would have found it completely convincing. But this was Randy, with his supersensitive antennae, she was performing for.

She ached and winced along with him through the whole ordeal of unbandaging. He squeezed her hand, moaning, as each bandage came off. She squeezed back to reassure him. Bit by bit, like pieces of a jigsaw puzzle being fitted into place, the naked face began to appear. She tried to steel herself.

But who could have been ready for this . . . ghoulish nightmare?

She didn't scream. She didn't even put a hand across her mouth to stifle a scream. She even managed to smile as that last bandage was peeled off his eyes.

His face was in hideous ruins.

The eyes were the most terrifying. One eye had an Oriental slant to it and the other—now grayish and mucousy—was distended, as if it were about to fall out. Across his left cheek was a horrible deep gash in the shape of a comma. On the right side of his mouth was another scar that seemed to be pulling his lips down. The cheekbones were out of line and the whole set of the face was out of joint, fiendishly lopsided.

"Now we know, don't we?" Randy said grimly.

"Know what, Randy?"

"I'm blind. Half blind."

He pointed to the drooping, discolored eye.

"Oh, Randy. Maybe it can be—"

"And we know this too, don't we?" He ran his fingers over his face. "We know I'm a . . . freak."

"No, Randy. Please don't, Randy."

"Bring me a mirror."

"No."

"Bring me a mirror."

"No. Not until you get all fixed up."

Randy pressed a button and a nurse appeared. "Bring me a mirror."

"No," Kim commanded the nurse. "Absolutely not."

The nurse said, "I do think, Mr. Jahr—"

"All right, you're both as good as a mirror. I can see myself in your faces. I've turned into a monster."

After the nurse left, Randy buried his face in his pillows. "I want to die," he moaned. "I want to die. I want to die . . ."

"Oh, Randy, no, no, no! It's going to be all right, darling."

228

She patted the back of his head and kissed him on the gruesome scar.

"Don't touch me. I'm loathsome. I loathe myself. I'm . . . a leper. Just bring me some pills or poison."

Then Randy lapsed into a silent, rhythmic, weeping convulsion. Kim stroked his head and kissed him. Her own tears washed both her cheeks and his. He was alive, that's all that mattered. There wasn't any accident that could make him ugly enough for her to stop loving him. Smashed up as he was, she would always see him as beautiful.

Dr. Grierhaus worked what miracles he could. Bones were reset. Skin graftings covered—mostly—the scars. The eyes were straightened. Vision could not be restored to the eye that was blind. But another eye was put in to match the color of the sighted eye. However, the replaced eye had no mobility. It just stared straight ahead. The face had more or less its original shape and dimensions. But it didn't begin to look the same. It had a pasted-up, plastered, unlifelike look. It looked grim. Grim bordering on ghastly.

The Studio showered Randy with "love" while Dr. Grierhaus worked him over. There were flowers, phone calls, daily visitations from hacks in the publicity department and assistant directors and producers. Even the Boss got into the act. He sent—at carefully spaced interludes—a watch, monogrammed cuff links, huge baskets of fruit, and finally a telegram. The telegram read: "Congratulations on your sensational progress. We're all counting the days until you return."

"You can bet they're counting the days," Randy said sourly to Kim. "Counting the days, counting the losses, weighing their options . . ."

"They're counting the days, all right," Kim agreed. "They need you. The show can't go on without you."

"Or *with* me."

As it turned out, Randy was right.

Both the director and the producer did a double-take the day he reported back to the Studio. Filming was supposed to resume. It didn't. The problem was Randy's face . . .

Makeup men worked on it way into the afternoon. Then Randy was called to the set and asked to say his opening lines from the next scene. He stood there by himself while the camera panned in for a close-up. He was told that would be all for the day.

That evening the director called him at the hotel and told him they wouldn't be filming next day. Randy should take the day off and enjoy himself. The director would call him the following evening.

This ritual went on for nearly two weeks. Each night the

director called to say there'd be no work the next day. No reason was given. Randy should take the day off and "have fun."

Then came the last call.

"Randy, I have to give this to you straight," said the director. "We're going to have to ditch the film. You're not being replaced. Hell, where do you find another Randolph Jahr? But the point is, we've lost the Randolph Jahr we had. With all due respects to the plastic surgeon and the makeup men, this just isn't the same face we have in the earlier footage. Not that it's ugly or anything. The blind eye—not moving—is a little disconcerting. But the main thing is you can't change heroes in mid-picture. And that's what it would be like, going on with the picture. I can't tell you what a disappointment this is for me because I think we were on the way to something great. For whatever consolation it's worth, you'll get paid in full. . . ."

Randy got the message. He was washed up in pictures. His whole acting career was maybe washed up.

Kim used the occasion to storm into the Boss's office and tell him what she thought of him and the Studio.

The heartbreaking irony was that *These Murdering Children* had just gone into release and critics from coast to coast were hailing Randolph Jahr as the most important new male film debut in years.

For the moment Randy had no financial worries. Numbed and stunned, he stayed on at the hotel. He slept almost around the clock.

The day the news broke that the Studio was abandoning production of *An Autumn to Remember*—"spokesmen for the Studio declined to give a reason"—Randy got a wire from New York. An off-Broadway producer wanted him for the lead in a Chekhov play.

The wire roused Randy from his deathlike slumber. "They may not want me when they see me," he told Kim. "But I won't know that until I get there."

The hardest, most unselfish thing Kim ever had to do was to give her blessings to his leaving. He was even more beautiful to her now, damaged and rebuilt. The beauty came from somewhere behind the face and bones now. Without him, life here would be so empty and lonely. He was all she thought about.

"You must go," said Kim. "You'll be great in *Uncle Vanya*." She had never heard of *Uncle Vanya*. Inside she was falling apart. But it was the only thing she could say.

"I'll call every night," she went on, "to see how it goes. Nine o'clock here's midnight there. As soon as I get through this dumb thing I'm in, I'll come out. I already told you. I've never been to New York. You'll be my guide. Oh, Randy, everything's going to be . . . beautiful."

She didn't have a chance to call him. The next night Randy was calling her.

"I've been keeping him!" he screamed. "And this is my thanks."

Randy sounded hysterical. Kim guessed he had been drinking. She waited for him to go on.

"He's stupid. He's stupid to act like this . . . to piss on the best deal he's ever had."

She got the story thickly and haltingly. Randy had arrived home around nine o'clock in the evening. He hadn't given Robbie any advance notice that he was coming. But naturally he assumed Robbie would be there. Robbie was not there. It worried Randy that he was not there. Robbie was always in bed early and it could be that something terrible had happened.

Randy sat up waiting, wondering what he should do. He was on the verge of calling Robbie's mother in Harlem—yes, even at four o'clock in the morning—when he heard Robbie's key twisting in the door. Robbie was not alone.

"I was under no illusion Robbie had been leading a monastic life while I was gone. I didn't care whether he was or wasn't. That's not the point. It's the way he treated me."

There was a scene.

"Oh, it's you," Robbie greeted him. "Or is it?"

When Robbie got a closer look, he let out an ear-splitting whistle. "Look at you, mother. I knew you had a little accident. But I didn't know you ran into a Mack truck."

Some greeting, eh? Randy had to ask who his "friend" was. Robbie introduced him as "Chipper." Chipper looked like a male prostitute straight off Third Avenue.

"I think you better tell your friend to go," Randy said.

"Under the circumstances," said Robbie, "it might be a good idea, Chip. Call me here around noon."

Randy hadn't been expecting a tender love reunion between him and Robbie. Nor had he wanted it. But he hadn't expected—or wanted—this kind of welcome either. Robbie was not glad to see him back. He was cold and resentful and sarcastic.

"Where do you get off being rude to my friend?" Robbie asked.

"Your friend's a little piece of trash," said Randy, "easily expendable."

"That's probably what you think about me, too."

"I never said that."

231

"Not to *me* you haven't. But I can hear you telling your friends. 'Boy, it's true what they say about niggers. I got me one from Harlem and can that kid ever fuck.' "

"Robbie, I don't understand. I never, never—"

"I don't understand, either. You always said this was my home too. But just let me try to bring a friend home."

"Robbie, I'm sorry. Maybe it's just that I'm tired. Tired after that long flight from the Coast—two hours late. And now waiting up to see what happened to you. It's so late."

"You're right about that. And I'm tired too."

Without saying good night, Robbie went off to his room and gave the door a loud bang shut.

The homecoming was so different the first time Randy came back from California. They were no longer the hot, inseparable lovers they had been three years ago. But Robbie had been waiting for him with open arms. Robbie had given him a memorable night of loving.

Later it had come out that Robbie had been having his little dalliances. Nothing serious, he assured Randy. Just bodies that passed in the night. Randy didn't reproach him. He didn't even put on a show of jealousy. Three thousand miles away from Kim, he thought about her incessantly and counted the days until he would be back in California.

Still, after his first return from the Coast, Randy slept with Robbie every night. Many nights they didn't make love. Randy would curl up inside the long, powerful, black arms and legs that entwined him and feel safe and loved. Out of bed there were still strong ties of affection that bound them together.

Randy decided he had been wrong to be so snide about Robbie's friend. But Robbie had no business bringing street tramps like that up to Randy's apartment. There were things of value there. From Robbie's own standpoint, it was a stupid thing to do. You took your chances when you consorted with rough trade. You could be murdered.

Randy was shaving when the phone rang the day after his return. He was in the nude and the bathroom door was open. Robbie picked up the phone. The call was for him. Probably Chipper, thought Randy.

Before he began to talk, Robbie came to close the bathroom door. He saw the scars on Randy's backside, where skin had been removed for the face graftings.

"Oh, mother!" Robbie flung at him. "They've even carved up your ass. That ass that used to be so beautiful."

Kim heard him out with a sinking heart. She was a whole continent away from him. All she could do was listen. So she listened. Night after night. Through the thick fog of alcohol she heard his anguished cries. Robbie was being rough on him. He hardly ever spoke to him and never had a civil word for him. He would disappear for days and explain nothing when he got back. He went out of his way to avoid Randy, to avoid *looking* at Randy when their paths crossed. It was unnerving in the extreme.

"He finds me *repulsive*," Randy cried. "Oh, why do I go on about him? You're the only one I care about. But you're there and I'm here."

Robbie as Robbie wasn't important to Randy any more. True. But the rejection was devastating. It shattered what little confidence he had in the new version of himself. If a black boy from Harlem who had once loved him was treating him like this, what could he expect from the outside world?

The only solution was not to go outside. He never left the apartment. He had everything sent in. He cancelled his tentative commitment to do *Uncle Vanya* downtown. Better to cancel than to be cancelled. He spent most of the hours of his day, he told Kim, in his Meditation Room ... thinking, arranging the developed films from California, finishing his portrait of her.

Kim heard him out with increasing dread. She feared it had been a terrible mistake for him to go back to New York. She had praised it as a smart move, the thing that would put him back on his feet. She knew now she had been wrong. Her guilt kept her awake nights. If she could only be there with him! She poured out her love for him over the long distance wires. But how much good could that do? He so desperately needed someone right there holding him and caring for him.

"Randy, Randy," she said to him one night. "Just hold on. I'm coming. I'm coming the second they call it a wrap. And that's soon."

"It's the bleeding end," he burst out the next night. "He walked. That fucking, ungrateful nigger walked."

Randy's story took a long time to unfold. He sounded very drunk and nearly incoherent.

Robbie had come home earlier that evening and gone straight to his room. Randy heard him moving around in there and banging drawers. He came out with two packed suitcases. He put them down and looked at Randy, without saying anything.

"May I ask where you're going?" Randy finally put it to him.

"I'm leaving."

"Just like that?"

"Oh, didn't I tell you? I've been accepted in the Calvin Morley Dance Company."

"What's that got do do with it?"

"The Calvin Morley Dance Company's up in Harlem, in case you haven't heard. So I guess I'll just get my black ass back uptown. I'll be seeing you around."

"Wait! You mean to say you'd walk out of here just like that?"

"What were you expecting? A farewell fuck?"

"I think you might have thanked me for my hospitality."

"Thank you?" Robbie jeered. "You want to be thanked for taking in the little nigger boy and letting him give you your kicks in bed? For letting the little nigger boy build your ego up and make you feel like the Great White Father and Heap Big Liberal? You walked out on me when you had a chance to gather the gold dust. I didn't hear you say anything about taking me out there with you. I didn't even get a penny post-card both times you were out there. And you'd still be out there if they hadn't canned you. Now it's my turn to leave. And, frankly, mother, I can't stand your New Look. It voo-doos me."

Kim's efforts to calm Randy failed. He didn't argue with her that Robbie was a good riddance. It was the way the thing had ended. It was the cruelty of Robbie's farewell. It was being left alone at a time when he was badly shaken and floundering.

"Randy, will you just this once listen to me?" she pleaded. "And do just as I say? Don't drink another drop tonight. Try to eat something. Then get some sleep. Here's what I'll do. I'll fly out for the weekend . . ."

Kim never got there.

The next day was the longest day of her life. She went through it in a trance. She could think of nothing but Randy. It took all her self-control to keep from calling him during the day. But she mustn't let him know how terribly anxious she was about him. That would only make matters worse. By the time she got home and put through the call—it would be nine thirty New York time—she was in a panic.

There was no answer.

She called every five minutes for the next hour.

Randy's mother was in Europe, he had told her. So Kim couldn't call her. And she didn't know the name of the married sister who lived on Long Island.

In desperation, her heart beating so wildly she thought it would carry over the phone, she called the police.

She gave them Randy's name and address. Would some-body go there immediately and see if he was all right? He had been very sick, she explained, and he might be in need of help. She gave her number and asked if somebody would call her back collect if Mr. Jahr wasn't there or couldn't call himself?

"Who did you say this was calling?" the police sergeant asked.

"I didn't say. I'm . . . a friend."

She hung up and began her vigil.

An hour passed. When nobody called, her mood lifted. The police had gone to the apartment and found nobody there. Randy was out somewhere—maybe to dinner. She only hoped he wasn't trying to find Robbie.

Her optimism quickly faded. No, no, he wouldn't be out to dinner. Or anywhere else. He hadn't left the apartment since he got back to New York. He had to be there.

She hadn't eaten all day but food was out of the question. So was sleep. She turned to Randy's solution. She poured herself a stiff Scotch. When that was finished, she poured another. And another. It was liquor that eased the pain and got her groggily through the night.

The call she was waiting for came at five o'clock in the morning. But it wasn't the police—or Randy—calling. It was Stanley Kellerman, the Studio's chief of press relations in New York.

Sleepless and drink-drugged, Kim was startled into alertness and sobriety by the ringing of the phone.

"Sorry about the hour," Stanley apologized. "Have you . . . heard?"

"Heard what?" she screamed.

"Now hold on, hold on. I called Dan—Dan Greenway, your producer—and he said I should call you. I know it's only five o'clock there. It's eight here. Anyway, he'll be coming over as soon as——"

"Heard what? It's Randy, isn't it? Something's . . . happened . . . to Randy?"

"Yes. He's dead."

"How?" she managed to ask, before collapsing into hysterical tears.

"It looks like suicide."

He waited patiently for her shrieks and wails to subside. "Now, Kim," said Stanley finally, "get a grip on yourself. You do want to hear what I can tell you, don't you?"

"Yes," she sobbed.

"It's coming over all the newscasts now. But just bulletins. The first I knew was when I picked up the *Daily News*. It's the front-page headline there: ACTOR FOUND DEAD."

Stanley read her the story inside:

235

Summoned to a duplex apartment in a plush East 63rd Street townhouse by a mysterious phone call from the West Coast, police early this morning discovered the body of actor Randolph Jahr, 29, an apparent suicide.

The distinguished young star of stage and screen was found in a small room at the rear of the lower floor of the apartment. He was clad in a silk paisley dressing gown. He was slumped over in a captain's chair, before an easel. There was an empty whiskey bottle on the floor beside his chair.

Police surmise Jahr may have been dead as long as 24 hours before his body was found. But pending an autopsy report, no official cause of death has been given. Recently Jahr had suffered severe injuries in an automobile accident and had undergone plastic surgery that had significantly altered his appearance. The room in which the once-handsome actor was found could provide some clues to his strange death.

It was "spooky-looking," as Patrolman Walter Dumbrowski described it. "Like some shrine to a lady friend who might have jilted him." The walls of the tiny, windowless room were covered from floor to ceiling with photographs of stunning Hollywood actress Kimberley Hudson. (Jahr co-starred with Miss Hudson in *These Murdering Children* and the two had become very close.) The portrait on the easel, which may have been painted by Jahr himself, was easily identifiable as Miss Hudson.

A suicide note addressed "To Kim" was found in the lap of the dead man. Contents of the note have not been made known.

Jahr's obvious obsession with Miss Hudson led police to suspect that the call sending them to the scene of the tragedy may have come from the actress herself. . . .

Randy took his life by ingesting a strychnine pellet.

Strychnine pellets are not all that easy to come by. You just don't go to your connection or your friendly neighborhood druggist for a strychnine pellet. He must have planned his end carefully. Not for Randy the leap from a back window that might leave him alive with a broken back. Nor swallowing a bottle of barbiturates only to wake up to the pumping of his stomach.

Randy went out with a quick, idiot-proof killer.

For her own sake—to clear her of any dark suspicions or

rumors—Kim was persuaded by the Studio to share Randy's note with the world.

To a few insiders who knew Randy or knew about him, the note was perfectly clear. To the rest of the world, the note raised more questions than it answered.

His last words to her:

My darling—

The miracle we both hoped for—*tried* for—can never be. Without that miracle, life—for me—is an unbearable farce. For a sweet second we were both beautiful, you and I, in an ugly world.

Now you are alone in your beauty. You are imperishably beautiful. Inside out.

But I am ugly in the same old ugly world.

I'd rather be dead than ugly.

Above all, I'd rather be dead than not be able to share with you . . . what you tried so hard to give me.

But we both know—since we are both honest—that it can't be. It is just not possible.

If there should be another world—and I have to be honest even now, in my last breath, and say I don't think there will be—you are the only one I'd want to share it with.

My beloved, my exquisite one, how bleak my life would have been if I had passed this way without knowing you!

Good night, sweet princess. Perchance to dream . . .

Your lover manqué,

R.

Chapter 23

Count Randolph Jahr among the missing tonight. There isn't even a place setting for him. Odd, considering how many dead nobodies are assigned seats. Eight thirty-four.

You can be sure if Randy was alive and well and aboard, Kim would be aboard by now—if she was alive and well and not otherwise detained.

"Hey, Spinelli! Miss Gina Spin-elli!"

Oh-oh. That voice I'd know anywhere.

"Author, author." Clapping of hands. "Let's hear it for the lady author. Only you ain't no lady, Gina. No lady would write a book like that. You know what you are? You're one dirty broad. That's damn near the dirtiest book I ever read."

"I only told it like it was, Tinker."

Is there anyone more revolting than a revolting ex-juvenile gone to pot? Look at him. Fat as a pig. Hangdog jowls. A huge paunch bulging out over his belt like a canopy. Bald as a bat. Five deep gulches running across his forehead.

"Well, you sure shocked the jockey shorts off my short arm. But on second thought, it's damn nice to let the little guy go free. Hee, hee, hee!"

That'll be the day, when Tinker's shocked. You name it, he's done it. If it's true he's making XXX films, he's only fulfilling the sweet destiny God laid down for him. Thank God he's *making* them instead of performing in them.

Behind his sappy grin Tinker's eyes were sharp and shrewd. "Where's that busty buddy of yours? I heard she was coming."

Laurie Ann must have dangled Kim as bait to whip up attendance at this Auld Lang Syne affair. Without the promised presence of Kim, would any of us be here?

"I really don't know," I said. "I know she's supposed to be here. When Kim says she's going to be some place, she usually gets there. Sooner or later."

"Kee-rist, it must be eighteen, twenty years now. I can't wait to lay eyes on that puss and those boobs."

That's all he'll ever lay on her, you can be sure. "If he was the last man on earth," I can remember her saying, "I'd renounce sex and get me to a nunnery."

"When she gets here," he droned in, "I'm going to make her an offer she can't refuse. Have I got a proposition for her! She'll clear twenty M's the first year without even moving her butt . . ."

Doesn't he know? Is he blind? Did he never get the message? Did her unadulterated loathing never get through to him?

Pleading the need for a refill, I drifted away from Tinker.

I had already had too much to drink, so much that all the faces were blurring and blending into a kind of pasta-mist. . . .

The only other face I could give a name to was Arthur Morgan's. And I had no intention of making contact with Arthur Morgan. He was even fatter and balder and uglier than Tinker Wells. Andy, by latest report, was getting his kicks these days from speed and thirteen-year-old girls. He was also said to be scooping up on a string of juice bars from San Diego to Santa Barbara. The only way anybody can scoop up on juice bars, as any idiot knows, is to charge five bucks for a squirt of juice and play blind to what the kids are dropping into the juice.

Arthur was also supposed to be dealing to the Hollywood crowd. Right now, by any bets, he could have enough stuff on him to hang a hundred ghetto kids if they were caught carrying it.

I hate calling the shots on anybody who was once one of America's dearest darlings. The Imp beat a pathway to the hearts of everybody who went to the movies in the Depression years. Only someone made of stone could have resisted the homeless little waif swathed in rags and sleeping in doorways. Thank God for old bums like Maxie Brophy. Big boozy old Maxie was always stumbling along to fish the Imp out of the gutter. Well, then was then. Today, the Imp is something else and I don't dig it. . . .

Kim, Kim, where are you?

Chapter 24

Kim said she wished she could die too. Now that Randy was gone, her life was over.

And she damn near did die. She gulped down some pills a doctor had once prescribed for nerves, but which she had never taken. Hoping they would put her to sleep and she would wake up to find this had been a bad dream, she downed half a dozen. An hour later she was being rushed to the hospital in an ambulance. Her face had swollen up like a pumpkin and she was gasping for breath.

She was taken into emergency where her condition was diagnosed as allergic bronchitis.

Mama and I—and Kim's own mother, when she was sober—stood vigil at Kim's bedside during the week she spent at Cedars of Lebanon.

Allergic bronchitis, the doctor explained, was a form of asthma. It may have been dormant all these years. Kim used to sneeze occasionally and she would break out after eating strawberries. But the asthma was news to her as well as to the rest of us. The doctor thought the pills plus the shock she had been through had brought on this severe reaction. He warned that she must always be very, very careful about any drugs she took. The wrong ones could be fatal. They should be carefully checked out against her allergies.

This was the beginning of Kim's long medical history, the

239

first of the many illnesses that would shut down production and have everybody in a turmoil.

You look at somebody like Kim, so beautiful and radiant and well-put-together, and you assume they must be strong and healthy. You never guess their whole insides can be a mess. But you name almost any ailment going, and Kim's had it.

Mama cried to see her in that hospital bed. She longed to scoop her up and take her home and love her back to health.

"No, thank you, Mama," said Kim. "I'm going to be all right."

When she was on her feet again and back at work, she said she wished they had let her die in the hospital.

I believe she believed what she said.

The Studio made the most out of the situation. It exploited the hell out of the picture Randy and Kim made together. The picture was already doing the kind of business that didn't need any extra boosting. But Abe Fleischman, the VP in charge of advertising-publicity, figured a good thing could always be blown up into something better.

Out came new over-lines for the newspaper ad copy:

"See them together—for the first and last time!"

"As star-crossed on the screen as in life!"

With one picture—and his death—Randy became immortal. Millions of movie-goers felt some kind of special connection with him. Women, young and old, mourned him. Young women cried for him as the perfect, poetic lover lost to them forever. Older women wished they could have protected—*mothered*—the poor, vulnerable boy. Then he wouldn't be dead! Young men made him a cult hero. They admired his cool. They identified with his victimized, one-against-the-world situation. Young men who wanted to be actors looked to him as their model. Man, that was acting! So clean and deep and straight, with all the fat cut off.

Kim disappointed the world by refusing to say anything about Randy. In silence she became the tragic, grieving, romantic heroine deprived of her great love.

Beyond grief the legacy Randy left her was the picture they made together. Now she was more than a pretty face, more than a star. Now she was a star who could act. Poised on the threshold of ripe womanhood, she was a star who was going to soar and shine for a long, long time.

Luckily for her she was back on her feet working. She had to get up in the morning. There was some place she had to go. Something was expected of her. Even though the picture was a dog and she could walk through it, she should know

240

her lines. Should do her best. She should make an effort to be pleasant to her fellow performers and the crew.

On the last week of filming, the Boss asked to see her. "How about this?" he said, showing off his newly redecorated office. He had been "redone" completely in white upholstery. Even the ceiling was in white upholstery.

"Nice," murmured Kim.

"Look over there." He pointed toward a door in the far right corner of the room. "Bathroom Number Two. Know something, Kim?"

"What?"

"I'm the only mucky-muck in the business with two bathrooms."

Kim smiled, thinking to herself, "You *need* two bathrooms —anybody as full of shit as you are."

"Kim, you've suffered a great loss. I know you're going through plenty. Lucky you're working. I always say work's the best cure for anything that ails you. I wish we had something here right now for you to go into soon's you finish up what you're in. But we don't. Nothing that's up to your standard. So here's——"

"The thing I'm doing now isn't up to *anybody's* standard."

"It's no great shakes, but it'll do all right, all right. You got into that one, remember, before all the bands started playing for *These Murdering Children*. Now we have to be careful how we show you to the public. You're a real star now and the public wants to see you in things worthy of a star."

"So I get a vacation?"

"No. It's best like I say—best for you—for you to keep on working. Keep busy. There's a dandy little picture over at Criterion they're dying to have you in. A picture that'll be good for you. So I'm going to loan you to them. Maybe they can loan me somebody sometime for something we're doing here. I'm doing them a big favor. But the point is it'll keep you busy when it's so good for you to be busy."

Big favor, my ass! she thought. Pretending he was thinking about her. What a phony bastard he was! Even an idiot could figure out what he was up to. He was loaning her out for a fat hunk of dough. She'd get her weekly salary and he'd pocket the difference.

"I don't care what the picture is," she said, "I don't want to do it."

"Don't want to do it? What does that mean?"

"I don't feel up to it. If it was here, okay. But going to another studio where everybody's a stranger——"

"No problem. You'll get the big treatment from everybody. The best hairdresser, best makeup men, best cameramen. Best of everything."

"I still don't want to do it."

"Well, now, just hold on, young lady. If you want to hear the truth, I don't give a good fuck about what you want to do or don't want to do. I've made a deal. You're going to take your sweet little tush over there. And you're going to make that picture."

"And what if I say I won't?"

"Suspension. No pay. Not until you come back to your senses."

"You prick," she said.

Her fury with the Boss was the first thing she had felt since Randy's death. It kept her awake until almost midnight, which was the latest she had been awake since Randy's death. Being awake so late, she felt the stirring of an old hunger. There were other ways of getting through the night besides drinking yourself into early oblivion. . . .

Kim started dating again.

It started with Wex Merriman, the handsome young second lead who *didn't* "get" her in the cruddy picture they were doing.

"You look like you could do with a little recreation," he said to her a couple of days before they finished filming. "Off the reservation. How about dinner tonight?"

"Why not?" she said impulsively.

She propped herself up with too many drinks before dinner and too much wine with dinner. Wex looked handsomer and sexier and sounded more interesting each time her glass was refilled. He did all the talking. He obviously was out to amuse her. He'd finish a little story or anecdote and lean toward her, smiling and waiting. It was her cue to laugh, though she had been only half-listening to what he said. It must have been as plain to him as it was to her they'd end up in the sack together that same night. But he was crazy if he thought this was the start of anything. It was strictly a one-nighter.

In the morning she wouldn't have remembered what he looked like if she hadn't faced him again in front of the camera.

She had a hard time remembering what he had *been* like in bed. For the record she wrote in her Little Lavender Book:

W.M. Efficient, mechanical. Clean. Puts deodorant on his short ones. Not circumcised. No hair on his balls. Comes too fast. (I *think*!)

The publicity man assigned to the picture at Criterion was a sweet young guy who followed Kim around like a puppy dog. His soft spaniel eyes held her in a worshipful gaze. He made it clear she had only to ask for anything under the shining sun and it would be hers. If he could swing it.

The second week into shooting Kim decided to throw him a crumb. "Sol," she said, "why don't you take me to dinner some place tonight? It doesn't have to be any place fancy."

Sol Pitman was incredulous. His racy imagination, he told someone later, went wild dreaming up the scenario of the evening. He titled the script "My Turn with Kimberley Hudson."

It was just a fantasy. Sol never got his night with Kimberley Hudson. He just got to be her dinner-mate a few times.

At Scandia, over their third daiquiri, Kim saw a man sitting alone at the bar. He looked attractive. He was probably waiting for his date to show up. But what the hell . . .

"Sol," said Kim, "be an angel. Go over and tell that man at the bar I would like to meet him. Invite him over to the table to have a drink with us."

"Kim, I really don't go for that."

"Sol, don't be silly. And don't be jealous. You and I can always go out together. He looks cute. And I might never see him again."

"I'm not thinking about myself," said Sol. "I don't think it's good for you. In a place like this you don't know how many people will be watching your every move and ready to jump—"

"I should care."

"Yes, you *should* care."

"Sol, go get him."

"You're much too handsome," Kim greeted the stranger, "to be drinking all by yourself at the bar. Drink with us."

"I'm not alone," said the young man. "Alone—yes. Over there. Right now. But I was waiting for . . . somebody."

He was so flustered at the company he found himself in he didn't know what he was saying.

"In that case, we'll have to have our drink some place else, won't we?" Kim purred. "Why don't you tell the bartender to tell your girl friend you were called away on a big emergency?"

To Sol, Kim said, "You settle things here, Sol. And thanks for being an angel."

Sol soon gave up the notion his "turn" was ever going to come. He must have guessed as well as Kim knew that she was using him. He was her liaison to any stranger sitting at a bar or another table who might catch her fancy. The more

243

she drank the more relaxed her standards became. The evening never ended with Sol having to take Kim home. There was always someone else seen or met along the way who would make do.

Sol's job, beside settling up, was to make the introductions and to smooth over the appearance of things. If anyone asked questions, Sol could say Kim had just run into a dear old friend and wanted to go somewhere and have a tête-à-tête with him.

Sometimes a pickup didn't get the message. He thought the relationship had a future. In the morning he would start to woo her like a guy who had got a girl into bed with a lot of phony promises and then woke up to discover he wanted to keep those promises.

"Once is fun," Kim would say, yawning in his face. "But twice is too much."

"You know what I am," said Sol Pitman to her bitterly one night. "A goddamn pimp. That's what you've turned me into. A goddamn pimp."

They were at Perino's. She was on her third Margherita and her eyes were glassily scouting the prospects.

"I've never been in a spot like this before. With any of our prima donnas. Where I'm just a common pimp hustling dates for my dinner companion."

"Well, you're in that spot now," said Kim sweetly-acidly. "So stop bitching."

"I shouldn't be here at all."

"Well, you are here. And you'll be wherever I need you when I say I need you there." She gave him a syrupy smile and directed his attention to a table for two in the far corner of the room. Two men at the table had been staring at her all through dinner.

"The curly-headed one is beginning to look awfully fascinating," Kim said to Sol. "I'm going to order another Margherita. I think by the time I get it down the hatch he'll look like one of the world's most fascinating men. Go get him, Sol."

She watched Sol advance upon the table. He stood there longer than he usually did. There seemed to be quite a dialogue going on. The curly-headed one lifted his glass and waved it at Kim. She gave him a low wink.

"What was all the chitchat about?" Kim asked Sol, when he got back.

"I was trying to get a reading on him. I can tell you this much. He's one bird I don't go for."

"Well, that's beside the point, Sol. What's holding him up? I don't see him getting over here very fast."

"I didn't exactly extend an invitation. I said you *might* feel like asking him over to the table for a drink. I said I'd come back and let him know. You're not committed—"

"I told you to go get him. Now what's the problem?"

"I'm trying to tell you I don't like his looks. I haven't been exactly smitten with a lot of your other 'conquests' either. But at least I didn't have the queasy feeling I have about this number. He's on the make. Unemployed actor 'with a lot of good leads.' Not queer, basically. But the guy he's with obviously is. And is keeping this one. So until those 'good leads' come in, our boy will make his bed where he can find it. Not for him the odd jobs of waiting tables, modeling, crewing on somebody's yacht—"

"Oh, for Christ's sake, Sol. I'm not interested in your opinions or impressions. You're not getting paid to psychoanalyze people. You get paid because of people like me. I told you to go get him. Go get him."

Kim knew that she had had too much to drink and that liquor was not one of her good friends. It brought out a nasty streak in her. She was just sober enough to know that Sol was trying to advise her for her own good. And she was just drunk enough to insist on having her way, whatever the consequences.

He was swarthy and sallow and introduced himself as Jonathan Merriweather.

"Oh, shit, that's not your name," Kim sneered. "Your real name. If you want a phony name, get one that fits you. My name's phony. But at least I look like Kimberley Hudson."

"What name would you suggest?" he asked, smiling unctuously.

"Lemme think." She appeared to give the matter great consideration. "Maybe Mickey Parchesi. Or Smiley Consky."

Jonathan's mouth kept flashing its toothy smile. If she had been more sober, Kim might have caught the twitch under his eyes. Sol caught it. But Sol was dismissed by Kim before he could catch much more. He paid the bill and gave her a worried look in parting.

Kim remembered that she had several more drinks at home. And that Jonathan sipped at one highball. He wanted to talk. She wanted to get to bed. She drank so much because she was bored. She drank to make Jonathan and what he was saying *seem* more interesting.

He was an actor. He knew he was just on the verge of making it big in the movies. All he was waiting for now was that important break that could get him flying. He wasn't a type. He was an original. There was a place for him in the movies because there wasn't anybody else like him in the movies. He really had something to offer. Once he got a foot in the door, his future was made.

Didn't Kim agree? He had good "ins" at all the other movie studios. But for some odd reason he had never made any connections at the Studio. If Kim thought he had possibilities, maybe she could put in a word where it would count . . .

"You don't interest me as an actor," she said coldly. Her head was swimming so much from drink she could hardly see him. "I got actors coming out the woodwork. I don't give a fuck whether you can act or not. I don't give a fuck how you're going to show up on a screen test. All I care about is how you're going to show up in bed. How you're going to show up in my Little Lavender Book."

"Your Little Lavender Book?"

"My Little Lavender Book."

Mention of the Little Lavender Book got Jonathan off the boring discussion of his career hopes and the sly, insinuating digs about what she might be able to do for him. How many names did she have in the Little Lavender Book? Who counts? she snapped. Were there any real big names in it? A hell of a lot bigger than his. Did she really go into detail about . . . well, about what everybody did? As much as she could remember, she yawned. Had anyone ever seen the book?

"None of your goddamn business," she said peevishly. "Oh, for Christ's sake, knock it off."

An evening of steady drinking had made her increasingly irritable. And sleepy. At this point she didn't care if anything happened. She was almost sorry she had started the whole thing. Sol was right about Jonathan. She didn't go for him either.

"I'm ready for the sack," she announced, giving her glass a couple more fingers of whiskey. "Care to join me? If not, there's the door."

Jonathan joined her.

To the best of her memory he gave an okay performance. She couldn't quite remember whether she had been there or not.

Waking groggily in the morning, she took a while to focus.

Someone had gone to bed with her. But there was no one in the bed.

Jonathan. He was gone. Thank God! That was a switch. At five-thirty in the morning they were usually sound asleep. Or if awake, giving signs of digging in for a siege. Her first chore of the morning was getting rid of them.

246

Her relief at finding Jonathan gone soon gave way to panic. The bastard had probably stolen her blind!

Not so. She took a total inventory of her jewelry. Everything was intact. The cash she kept in the right drawer of her dressing table hadn't been touched. A quick check of the dining room showed the silverware was all in place. Whew! A creep but not a thief. Good-bye, Jonathan.

How would she remember him in her Little Lavender Book? Her memory of what happened was so dim she might have to make up something. Yes, she might have to use her imagination. But she'd better jot down something before she forgot his name. Or that there had been such an evening in her life.

She opened the left-hand drawer of her dressing table.

The Little Lavender Book was gone!

Jonathan. That slimy, stinking piece of garbage. He *was* a thief. That's what he had stolen. That's why he had taken off while she was still asleep. He thought that little book was the valuable most worth stealing.

She wasn't even dressed before the call came.

"Hi," he cooed. "Remember me? Maybe not."

"I remember you. There isn't enough liquor in the world that could make me forget."

"I've been reading something *awful* fascinating. Egad, it's better than *Gone with the Wind*. One of those books you absolutely cannot put down."

"You stole it too soon. Another day and you could have read all about yourself. 'Shit. No talent—in bed or out. Goes to the top of the Drop Dead list.' "

"You're being even nicer to me stone sober," he said, with a nasty laugh, "than you were last night."

"Get to the point. What do you want?"

"I've been thinking. Something like this should be insured. It should be insured against loss or theft. Or even fire. It's highly inflammable, you know. For the moment, it's in safe hands. You're lucky. But luck has a way of——"

"How much?"

"How much? Well, personally, I've always believed a person could never have too much insurance. My daddy always thought that way too. Daddy was poor and broke all his life. Half the time he wasn't even working. But he always kept up his insurance. He said it's the one thing he could do——"

"How much?"

"How much was daddy's insurance? Why, if I remember right, and this is going just according to what my mammy told me, why it was one hundred thousand dollars. Of course I could be wrong or she could've been——"

247

"You're out of both your fucking heads. I don't have money like that."

"What kind of money do you have?"

"Nothing. Pin money. Everything comes in goes out. Mother, the help, clothes, rented house, car, doctors, lawyer, Indian chiefs. You'd have been smarter to lift my jewelry."

"Jewelry, hmmmm. I should think jewelry could be converted into insurance."

Kim put out her harsh, cackling laugh. "Not paste jewelry."

There was a long pause on the other end of the line. "In that case, maybe I should peddle my insurance policy some place else. Now let me see. Give me a minute while I go through my files here and see just who might be in the market——"

"Do yourself a favor," Kim cut in. "Anybody you see in that book who looks like a sitting duck, forget it. Every last one of them is more man than you. You start anything cute and they'll tear you limb from limb."

Another long pause. "We were so friendly last night. A few hours later you're out to bury me. I thought we were friends. You tell me we aren't. Now I have to think who might be my friend. I can't help thinking I'm sitting on top of a best-seller. I can't help thinking somebody would jump up and down at the chance to publish——"

"If you're thinking you can sell this to any columnist or fan mag," Kim broke in, "you're even more of an amateur than I took you for. In the first place, they wouldn't put up that kind of dough. In the second place, they wouldn't touch it with a ten-foot pole if you fed it to them free. Who do you think keeps them in business? The industry. Just let one of them try to fuck the industry with any juicy scoop that'll sour the public and they're dead."

"I see," said Jonathan thoughtfully. "Well, I'll just have to put on my thinking cap. I must think of somebody who'd like to take out an insurance policy on this, this——"

"Nobody's going to pay you a dime for it. You can be the life of the party for the next five years flashing it everywhere you go. But nobody's going to pay you a goddamn dime for it." She waited for this to sink in. "The only person it's worth anything to, when you come down to it, is me."

A deadening silence on the other end of the line.

Kim tried for a note of lightness. "A lot of living has gone into that book. I'd really like to have it back. It'll always be a reminder of what I was up to when I was young and beautiful. It'll be something to show my grandchildren."

More silence.

"Tell you what, Jonathan. Give me back my little diary and the next two paychecks get signed over to you." She laughed what she hoped came across as a high, careless laugh. "For good measure, I'll even take you out to dinner. And I'll promise to stay sober. So I can enjoy any good thing that might turn up afterward. Notice I said 'up.' "

"Hmmm. Mighty interesting."

"For extra added good measure I'll even see if I can't wangle a screen test for you at the Studio."

"Say this for it," said Jonathan. "It's the second best offer I've had today."

Kim knew he was bluffing. Who would he be talking to before dawn? That five grand and the vague promise to try to get him a screen test would bring him around. Where else did he have to go? She had the jerk by the balls. She waited gleefully for him to cave in.

She stayed home that night, expecting his call.

She never did hear from Jonathan again.

The call she *wasn't* expecting came from the Studio. The Boss.

He called her at Criterion. "Get your cunt over here," he roared, "as soon as you're done there today."

"What a fucking little tramp you turned out to be!" he yelled at her as she came into his office.

"Thank you," she said. She smiled demurely, as if she had just been paid a tremendous compliment.

"Wipe that smile off your face. You may not realize it but this could be your ass. We got a little thing called a morals clause in all our contracts. We could dump you on the morals clause."

"Now what have I done?" Kim asked sweetly.

"What have you done?" He snorted. "You not only've been fucking everything with a cock on it, you have to be such a goddamn idiot to write it all down like a fucking newspaper reporter."

He opened a desk drawer and threw something at her with all the steam of a major league pitcher. Her Little Lavender Book hit her in the left breast. "Do you know what it cost me to buy that piece of dynamite?"

"One hundred thousand dollars."

"You got it! And you're not worth it."

"But you paid it."

"That fucker had me by the nuts. And he knew it. Look, little girl, I'd like to bust your fucking cunt for you."

"And I'd like to bust your balls—if you had any."

"You haven't got the morals of a pig. That filthy thing

there makes Mary Astor's diaries look like *Rebecca of Sunnybrook Farm.* You're worse than Fatty Arbuckle."

They were a match for each other, the Boss and Kim. The Boss fuming and frothing. Kim, outwardly cool and composed.

The story that spewed out of the foam from the Boss's mouth was this:

Jonathan Merriweather had got hold of someone in the press relations department. He said he had in his possession something that would interest the Studio. A "hot" item involving one of its stars. He said just enough on the phone to get across the idea this was not some crackpot calling. He had the goods.

The guys in PR took one look at what he had, whistled, and got him a fast appointment with the Boss.

"We have ways of disposing of little fuckers who come in here and think they can give us the finger," said the Boss. "But this little fucker was no dummy. He knew what he had and nobody was going to muscle it out of his hands. He had made a copy of your filth. He said anybody would believe it was a copy of the real thing. He told his roommate where he was going—in case anything happened to him on the way home. He had called the city desk of the *Los Angeles Examiner.* Naming no names, he asked if they'd be interested in the red-hot sex diary of a beautiful young movie star? Would they! Would they be willing to cough up for it? They would. The fucker told them he'd have to let them know."

A hundred big ones just to buy some rotten filth that shouldn't be on paper in the first place! Anyway, he had settled that bastard's hash. He made him bring the copy and hand that over with the book.

"If you got another copy and that gets out," the Boss had told him, "we'll have a messenger find you and rub you out. And ain't nobody ever going to find out who done it. And another thing, you crummy creep, you'll never work in this town as long as I'm alive. Call yourself Johnny this or Schmucky that. I'll remember the kisser. And, buddy-boy, you've had it."

"I guess I should thank you," said Kim, tucking the Little Lavender Book in her purse. "I didn't know I was worth that much to you."

"You aren't worth shit to me. You're a piece, a thing, a property. We got an investment in you. This crap comes out on you, we're dead. Kiss of death. Murder at the B.O. Three pictures not even in foreign distribution yet! You think we're thinking about you? Sh—i—i—t!"

"Well, thanks for setting me straight. For a second I thought you had turned into a pussycat."

"Pussycat? Sh—i—i—t!"

"You know something? I trace my downfall to the day you loaned me out. Seems like things just went——"

"You cunty bitch. You were born garbage."

"Will that be all?"

"One thing more. You're going into *Her Uncle Gave Her Away*. We bought it for a bundle from Broadway. We're bringing the guy out who did it on the stage. Grosvenor Forbes. Very classy guy. Get next to him. Maybe some of his class'll rub off on you."

Her Uncle Gave Her Away was the movie that put Kim into the top ten box office attractions.

It was a silly bit of fluff but it had a certain style and wit. It had had a long run on Broadway. It was a comedy about a young girl who half-falls in love with her uncle just as he's about to give her away in marriage. She hadn't seen him since she was a child. He had been running a coffee finca in Brazil all these years. Her father was dead so his brother was sent for to give her away. He's so handsome and charming and elegant in a kind of exotic way he almost sweeps her off her feet. Overnight she has second thoughts about the young man she's about to marry. When the uncle sees what's happening, he has a nice fatherly-type talk with his niece and she "sees the light." In the last scene they exchange knowing winks as he waltzes her down the middle to meet her groom.

Her Uncle Gave Her Away introduced Grosvenor Forbes to the movies.

It also introduced him to Kimberley Hudson.

Grosvenor Forbes was what used to be known as a matinee idol. For nearly twenty years he had been titillating the ladies in one light frothy comedy after the other on Broadway. He was so suave and sophisticated and aristocratic-looking the ladies from Larchmont and Darien and Far Hills and Oyster Bay nearly creamed in their panties. He was the nearest thing to a debonair Rex Harrison-type Englishman the American theater had produced. It probably figured. He was a Proper Bostonian. Beacon Hill, St. Mark's, Harvard (Fly Club), Somerset Club and all that. He had been practically disinherited when he decided to become an actor. The story went that his seventy-nine-year-old mother had yet to see him perform, though most of his plays had tried out in Boston before coming to New York.

Grosvenor Forbes, according to the poop sheets, was forty-four when he hit Hollywood. You automatically add three. At forty-seven, give or take a couple, he was a magnificent specimen of middle-aged manhood. Tall, slender, ramrod-straight, high cheekbones, a pencil-thin moustache, electric blue eyes, and a great mane of silver hair parted in the middle and flowing back in billowy waves. And blade-thin lips that seemed permanently set in just the suggestion of a sneer.

Grosvenor Forbes exuded self-assurance like garlic. He seemed unflappable. He had the air of having been everywhere, having seen it all. Nothing could surprise him. He sighed with world-weariness.

"You must forgive me, my dear, for not being familiar with your work," he said to Kim in his courtly fashion. "But the awful truth is I never see films. It may be just a bad attack of sour grapes because this is the first time I've been asked to appear in one."

"And I'm not familiar with your work," Kim came back. "Never having been to the thea-a-tah in New York."

"I daresay we've both been culturally deprived." The sneery lips curled into a smile of sarcasm.

"I daresay," Kim repeated after him, conscious this was the first time in her life she had ever used the word.

Grosvenor Forbes fascinated Kim. He seemed so wise and solid and strong and really worldly. And so la-di-da. She hated to agree with the Boss. Grosvenor really was class goods. He knew who he was. He had a foundation under him. He looked with ironic detachment at all the goings-on in Tinseltown. The showing-off and the pushing and the backbiting and the lying and the frantic bids for attention. He didn't choose to be involved.

"I find it amazing," Kim said to him one day when they were lunching in the commissary, "you aren't married. Such a . . . charming and eligible man as you."

"I find it amazingly lucky of me, too," Grosvenor agreed, "as one who has been a three-time loser in the matrimonial steeplechase."

Kim was calmer than she had been at any time since Randy's death. She was having fun making this goofy comedy. And she had lost all interest in helling around. Or what Maura Anderson called "sport fucking."

She credited these changes to the stabilizing influence of Grosvenor Forbes. Even though she hardly knew him. And he showed almost no interest in wanting to know her. On the set he was always polite and correct and cooperative. Sometimes, when she was putting herself out to please him, his usual reserve would break down a little. He'd act then like a real-life uncle, indulgent and amused. Off the set he went his own way. Into his trailer. Grosvenor was a reader. He actually read *books*—the first such person she had ever met in her life.

Grosvenor had three ex-wives and six children scattered somewhere between Sun Valley and Mykonos. Nobody knew the alimony he had seen. That much Kim pried out of him. She gathered that was why he was in Hollywood—for the quick loot. She also gathered that three times burned, he was forever shy.

"You're not very sociable," she chided him.

"My dear child, my experience has taught me I have very little talent for socializing. I've had to pay such a price to learn that lesson. Improving my mind—and my body—keeps me out of trouble. And it's a relatively inexpensive discipline."

When he was not reading, Grosvenor was doing push-ups or running in place in his dressing room. Often he stayed there and drank a quart of carrot juice or ate a container of yoghurt topped with wheat germ and honey instead of going to the commissary for lunch.

Grosvenor was renting a cottage at Malibu. There he jogged on the beach and swam and read all weekend long. And apparently saw nobody.

Kim's fantasy machine went to work on Grosvenor. Maybe he was just what the doctor had ordered for her. He was so much older and wiser and more learned. He was elegant and worldly. He was the voice of experience that could guide her. He could shape her up and give her some sense of discipline. He could provide the firm but loving support of the father she had never had. Being so much older, being so much the man-of-the-world, he would surely be a thrilling lover. Oh, in a million ways, he was just what she needed.

"You are something different," she remarked one day near the completion of the picture. "Usually the leading man makes some kind of grab for me."

"My darling child, I'm *not* your leading man. I'm your *uncle*."

Kim was sure she detected a certain curiosity. Cool and aloof as he was, she saw the signs of interest . . . of dawning desire.

"I never had an uncle," she said. "You make me wish I had one."

"If I may say so—and no offense intended—I think you're a bit long in the tooth to be yearning for an uncle."

"Wouldn't you like to have a niece like me?"

"My ravishing beauty, who would want you for a *niece?* Unless it was some psycho with proclivities toward incest?"

Kim closed her eyes blissfully.

"You're right," she said after another long fantasizing interlude. "I don't need an uncle. What I need is ... a husband. Will you marry me?"

Chapter 25

"You're proposing to an antique?"

"You don't look like an antique to me."

"Dear, dear child. Believe nothing of what you hear. And very little of what you see. What you see is late autumn masquerading as early autumn."

"I like what I see."

"Withered bones, dried-up marrow ... a sere heart?"

"I never know what you're saying," said Kim. "That's why I think it would be so fascinating to live with you."

"My sweet seductress," countered Grosvenor, "if you could hear yourself talk, you'd know how sadly in need you are of a course in basic logic."

"There's this, too. I wouldn't be like your other wives. It wouldn't cost you a penny if we ever broke up. I seem to have a pretty good-paying job."

"A credential not to be dismissed lightly."

"What do you think?"

"It's a little early in the day for me to be thinking. However, I can tell you categorically it's the only proposition I've had all morning."

Oh, yes, he was the one for her!

Two days later when he had not given her an answer, she said, "Well, how about it?"

"How about what?"

"That attractive offer I made you."

Grosvenor Forbes laughed his dry, brittle laugh. "You *are* a little necrophiliac, aren't you?"

"Whatever that is."

"Someone with a taste for the dead."

"You make fun of yourself. I like that. Everyone around here is so busy blowing themselves up. That's because they don't really believe they are any good. It's the opposite with you. You can make fun of yourself because you know you really are somebody. You pretend you're old and tired because you know you're young—in body and mind anyway—and in good shape."

Grosvenor smiled noncommittally.

"So?" she pressed.

"Am I to believe you're serious? Darling girl, don't you know you could have the cream of virile young manhood—"

"I've already had them. But I didn't want any of them for keeps. I want someone who can take me in hand. Someone I can look up to."

"Well, I *am* a bit taller than you—"

"Quit stalling, Mr. Forbes. I just want to hear one little word. It's spelled y-e-s."

"Promise always to call me Mr. Forbes? Did you mean it about the alimony waiver?"

"Both! I'll write it in blood."

"Oh, Gina, have I got a man for me!" she trilled into the long distance phone. We were doing a club date in the Venetian Room at the Fairmont in San Francisco. For half an hour, without once asking me how I was or how we were doing, she babbled on about the charms and wonders of Grosvenor Forbes.

"He'll pull me up to his level and straighten out my mess of a life," she predicted. "I think about him all the time. But my heart doesn't start pounding like tom-toms every time I see him. And that's good. For once in my life I seem to be using my head."

I hope this was true. But I had my doubts.

"We're going to tie the knot here Sunday. In Santa Monica. No church wedding or anything like that. We'll just stand up in front of a justice of the peace. Will you be my witness?"

I knew she was calling for some other reason than a chitchat. I told her I'd be pleased and flattered to fly down for the occasion.

"Don't be flattered," she laughed. "The truth is I don't have any close girl friends. From the time I first discovered men, I've never been much interested in women. Oh, I love Maura Anderson. But with the kind of life she leads, I don't think it would be too hot an idea to have her standing up with me at a wedding ceremony. Of course, I'm hardly one to talk."

No two people ever agree totally about a third person. But I could hardly believe Grosvenor Forbes in the flesh was the same person Kim had been raving about on the phone. Naturally my opinion of him was colored by the way he treated me. Which was almost as if I didn't exist. Even if he had been more civil, I'm sure I'd have written him off as cold and smug and superior. A real Boston snob. There's only one worse kind. And that's the English snob. Both varieties know their blood is running thin and time is running out on them, which is probably what makes them so insufferable.

But there was something else about Grosvenor Forbes I couldn't quite put my finger on. It was a hazy suspicion that he could be conniving. And cruel. Even sadistic. I couldn't help feeling he wouldn't marry Kim just for herself and her beauty. It would have to be something else he saw in her too. Was it her success? The hope that he could ride on the coattails of her success?

How long will this one last? I wondered, as I toasted the newlyweds. I gave it a year.

It lasted five years. When it was over, Kim said in her blasé way, "I did a five-year stretch with Grosvenor Forbes. Freedom! It's great!"

But not for long. Kim doesn't go for the man-less type of freedom.

The thing with Grosvenor Forbes probably wouldn't have gone five years if Kim hadn't been so distracted. First with career, then with trying to become a mother.

During the first couple of years of her marriage to Grosvenor I saw more of her than I had at any time since we were kids.

The Spinelli Sisters had broken up as an act. First, my oldest sister, Anna, got married. To a jerky kid we had known back in Brooklyn who was now a nothing in a two-bit music publishing house in Tin Pan Alley. Then we were three. For about five minutes. Then my next oldest sister, Rosa, eloped with the drummer in the house band at the Stardust in Vegas. That left just Angelina and me. We decided to throw in the towel. An easy decision since nobody was exactly screaming to hear me and Angelina as a singing twosome. Angelina went to try her luck in New York and I went home to Mama in Los Angeles.

I was twenty-one and felt like a has-been. I was marking time. I didn't know what was going to happen next. Who or what was going to rescue me from Deadendsville.

Kim's star was shooting. It made me sick sometimes to watch it.

After *Her Uncle Gave Her Away* came two more smash successes. Kim was way up there with the biggest. She was famous now from one end of the world to the other. Her face was as recognizable as President Eisenhower's or Queen Elizabeth's or Khrushchev's.

She finagled a fat new seven-year contract at the Studio.

"I broke that bastard's ball," she said, meaning the Boss. "He's got only one, you know."

Her honeymoon with Grosvenor Forbes—a long weekend in Acapulco—was like a dress rehearsal for her real honeymoon with fame and fortune.

"Gina, I bought a house!" she announced one day excitedly on the phone. "The first one I've ever owned in my life."

I caught the first person singular. I wasn't surprised. I knew damn well who'd be footing the bill.

It was a Mediterranean-style villa off Benedict Canyon. For a good twenty minutes she ticked off all its attractions and unique potentialities. "The owners sold us a lot of their furnishings," she said. "But of course they didn't want to part with their best things. They did leave us, though, an inventory of everything that had been in the house. Oh, Gina, everything was done just to the nth degree. That's the way I want it to look again."

She stopped and I waited.

"Gina, I was thinking. I could really use your help. If I gave you a list of the things I want and places where you might find them and had Walter drive you around, you could help me put the place into tip-top shape. And, Gina, I think it would really be great for you. It would give you something to do and keep your mind busy now while you're in this in-between period . . . not working . . ."

Typical Kim. Asking for favors and making it seem like she was conferring them.

How was life with Grosvenor? Sheer bliss. *Quiet* bliss. And could she ever do with some quiet bliss! Being around Grosvenor was an education in itself. He was getting her interested in reading for the first time in her life. He was giving her tips on grooming. He was teaching her about health and diet and making her do exercises. He was gradually weaning her away from hard liquor and developing her appreciation for fine table wines. She had never felt better in her whole life.

Grosvenor's motto was "Moderation in everything." He said it came from the wise, ancient Greeks who strove for the golden "mean." The golden mean, I gathered, meant moderation in sex. Another way of saying not much sex.

I wouldn't have dreamed of asking her anything about their intimate relations. But then I didn't have to.

"Grosvenor's a very good lover," Kim volunteered. "Especially for somebody his age. He's in terrific shape. And that makes all the difference. Once he gets going, he's really like an athlete in bed. I still want it a lot oftener than he does. But he's gradually knocking some sense in my head about

257

that. As Grosvenor says, 'Look, do you want to be a slave to your passions? Man is supposed to be a thinking animal. Even dumb beasts aren't always thinking about copulating. They couple only in mating season . . .'"

I got the picture. Grosvenor was operating on low voltage. And he was trying to make a virtue out of his disinclination.

The success of his first picture—though it was really Kim's picture—made Grosvenor Forbes a semi-hot property. He didn't want to sign any contracts with anybody. But the offers of a hundred and fifty grand a pic looked pretty good. In six weeks or so he could scoop up the kind of loot it would take him a year to earn doing eight a week in a long-running Broadway hit. He was willing to condescend to the vulgarities and cultural desert of California as long as the offers kept coming.

They kept coming. Three pictures in fast succession, all dogs. Grosvenor Forbes might knock the matinee ladies dead. But he wasn't killing 'em at the Orpheums and Lyrics and Pantages around the country.

As Grosvenor slipped, Kim kept soaring.

I saw more of her in that period than I ever had. Or probably ever would again. And that's when I learned not to envy anybody. No matter how much anybody has, they never have it all.

If you could just have the fame and fortune and let the rest go! If you could just be loved and adored and admired and at the same time keep everybody at their distance. Keep their greasy, cotton-picking hands off you. If you could just have all the privileges and the freebies and the kowtowing and the red carpet treatments. Period.

It's never the way it works.

The whipped cream curdles. Under the cream is all the garbage . . .

The human garbage. All the creeps and bums and con artists and spongers and blackmailers and leeches and crazies and jerk-offs and bloodsuckers out to milk her dry. Some of them put on the face of friends and/or lovers. Others came on as would-be agents, managers, financial consultants, dress designers, script writers, public relations geniuses, biographers, lawyers, accountants, gardeners, cooks, butlers, chauffeurs, hair stylists, social secretaries, bodyguards, spiritual guides, dieticians, interior decorators, playwrights, landscape artists, architects, diction specialists, makeup advisors, dog breeders, horse trainers, travel agents, dance instructors, gurus, palm readers, brokers, psychologists, marriage counselors . . .

Like moths around a flame they came . . . a whole army of

258

hokey hangers-on. They all made their pitch. Oh, what they could do for her! How she needed them!

There was one whole bundle of aggravations she lumped together in what she called her "Do this—come here—help, help!—call-write-cable immediately or I'll kill myself" file. A whole nutty world was trying to tap her for love, money, friendship, advice, comfort, employment, and a host of other unlikely benefits.

"The human race is sick," Grosvenor said loftily, with his sneer.

Many of the pleas and pressures had some kind of professional basis. Whether to give this interview and duck that one. Whether to talk to this columnist and not take the calls of that one. Whether to make this personal appearance and skip that one, to answer the cable from Melbourne and ignore the one from Capetown, to go on this publicity junket or not to go . . . Whether. Whether. Whether.

"The only thing that's really fun is the obscene mail and phone calls," she said. "I've given strict orders at the Studio to put through any obscene calls that come for me. Fuck anybody else that might be calling.

"Sometimes they get me kind of hot and sweaty," she explained. "They're nuts and freaks, I know. A lot of them don't say a goddamn thing. They just breathe and pant. But they're a pleasure to do business with. They don't want anything, really. Just to know you're on the other end of the line. They don't make any demands. They're not out to suck you dry like everybody else. They're harmless. Sickies. But they are excited. And they get you excited. Just all that breathing and panting and dirty talk. If you called their bluff—if you said, 'Come right over, smooth talker'—they'd hang up so fast and loud it'd break your eardrums. I kind of like egging them on to keep telling me more . . ."

Yes, if she could only have had the cake *and* the frosting! And none of the garbage.

"I feel like a goddamn pie!" she cried petulantly to one Associated Press interviewer. "Being carved up into thirty-six pieces instead of six. A sliver here. A sliver there. Little pieces of me going in all directions. And not one little piece left for myself."

"The price of being a *femme fatale*," the interviewer remarked.

"Is that what I am? Gee, I guess I am. That's the nicest thing I think I've ever been called."

"You know you have wit as well as beauty."

"Beauty," she sighed. "Who needs it?"

"We all wish we had it. When the gods lavish such a disproportionate abundance of it on one person, the rest of us earthlings can only gaze upon her with awe and envy."

"Beauty," she repeated. "Why should anybody want it?"

The interviewer smiled. *She* could ask that. How many others would you ever catch asking that question?

"Do you know what I want? What I really want?"

"I can't wait to hear."

"I want a home. I know, I know, I've got a home. But I want a real home that's the center of my existence. A quiet place somewhere where nobody knows my name except the butcher and the grocer and the guy who owns the corner drugstore. I'd like to have a home where I could just hang around all day looking like a mess and cook and bake and putter about the garden and have a husband who came home at regular hours and we'd have nice long evenings together talking over the little events of the day. And there wouldn't be any lines to learn or fan letters to answer or hectic phone calls."

The interviewer smiled again. He had heard that story before. He had heard it from other women as untypical as Kim. These women wanted these things because they were things they had never had.

"Millions of women have that," he pointed out to her, "and they're miserable and discontented. They think life is passing them by. There isn't one of them that wouldn't give her left tit to be Kimberley Hudson for a day."

"I'd change with them in a minute." She added, with a giggle, "Providing, of course, I didn't have to give my left tit to do it."

"Don't ever part with that, whatever you do."

"They can have it all. The whole Hollywood glamour scene. All the razzmatazz. Who needs it? The only thing worth having is a little quiet and peace of mind. And a husband who has the time and devotion to give himself to your needs and little quirks and changes of mood. And do you know what I really, really want?"

The interviewer could hardly wait, already knowing the answer.

"Babies. Oodles and oodles of babies."

"You can have babies here."

"Hollywood's no place to be having babies and bringing up children. Not with all the pressures. All the hassling with agents and managers and producers. All the dealing and double-dealing. And all the endless talk about money, money, money. Some time soon I'd like to retire and get away from here and anything that has to do with show business."

The interviewer had heard too many movie queens giving

out the same line to take her seriously. So he was surprised—and so was everyone else—when Kim announced she was quitting Hollywood.

She was going to New York with Grosvenor. Grosvenor was going back to resume his career on the stage. Kim made it plain she had no intention of seeking a theatrical career for herself. All she wanted was to keep house for Grosvenor and have babies.

It maybe wasn't all that romantic and impulsive on Kim's part. The handwriting was on the wall for Grosvenor. He wasn't setting the movie kingdom on fire. After five or six movies—each one worse than the one before—nobody was making him any offers. Kim had the choice of staying on alone or going with him.

She was pretty convincing in her insistence that this was the very thing she wanted. To go East and become a housewife and mother. Subordinate herself to her husband's career.

Methinks she protests too much, I thought.

Her decision cost her the wrath of all the biggies at the Studio. The Boss called her everything in the book and put her on suspension.

"The eagle just stopped shitting," he informed her. "You won't get a glass of cold piss out of this studio till you get your ass back here. See how long that snotty, washed-out Boston beanpole can support you in anything like the style you've been enjoying. Thanks to us. It could've been anybody, you know. Any dumb little cunt in the world. We could've taken any dumb little cunt off the street and done the same thing to her as we did to you. You didn't have a fucking thing to do with anything that's happened to you. We made it happen. We can take any dumb little cunt off the streets and make her into anything we want her to be."

"The eagle can stop shitting till the end of time," she shot back at him. "I'm going to start living. Living like normal people. Having babies and being able to call my life my own."

Grosvenor cast a frosty eye on the babies bit.

"Sniveling little snot-faces," he said of children. "Born ingrates and hellions. Insufferable parasites who'll give you tired blood and bleed you for everything they can get. And then fly the coop without a backward glance."

"*Some*, maybe," Kim conceded. "But no child of mine."

"You should listen to the voice of experience. In the children department, I am a six-time loser."

"You were married to the wrong women. With me as the mother, you'll have a fabulous child."

She fantasized almost obsessively about that first child. It would be an extraordinary child. Whether it took after her or him, it would have to be beautiful. She would make it the center of her life, showering it with love and devotion. How could it help but grow up into a sunny, strong, secure person who would return love for love forevermore? With Grosvenor's blood running in its veins, how could it help being a thoroughbred?

Destiny had brought her and Grosvenor Forbes together. Subconsciously she must have been looking for the perfect father for her children and known, from the first instant, she had found it in him. The breeding her children would inherit from their father! The grace, the intelligence, the fine bones, the athletic body, the aristocratic manners!

It didn't matter that Grosvenor was cynical on the subject of children. He might say he didn't want any more of them. But once the babies started coming, he would soon be singing a different song. These children would be different from his others. They would be magnificent. They would turn him into a proud, beaming father.

Kim didn't exactly burn all her bridges behind her. She got rid of the Chinese houseboy, the cook, her personal secretary, and the gardener. But she didn't sell the Benedict Canyon house. She said she had to have some place for her mother to live. There wouldn't be room in New York.

She left her mother and the house in the custody of Indiana.

In New York they moved into a rented, marvelously quaint house in Macdougal Alley. Like its neighbors, it was the former stable house (slightly glorified) of the Washington Square North house it was attached to. It was three stories high and had a circular staircase winding from the street-level kitchen to the top-floor bedrooms. It also had two balconies overlooking the Alley.

This was Greenwich Village chic at its chic-est.

Kim loved it at first sight.

The house was charming and the situation was sublime. The park was just three steps away but the Alley was so safe and cozy and tucked away. Their neighbors were in the "arty" professions. A famous abstract expressionist. A best-selling novelist. A show business lawyer. The lyricist for a string of hit Broadway musicals. A set designer and his male roommate who, as Grosvenor put it, "wore four hats—housekeeper, secretary, friend, and lover."

The day after they moved in, Grosvenor went into rehearsals.

Alone all day, Kim set about exploring her new neighborhood.

Wearing dark glasses and a kerchief over her hair, she found she could go anywhere and not be recognized. Or was she recognized? And this being the Village, nobody blinked? God knows, the Village had been home to enough of the great ones to be able to take a movie star in stride.

She discovered Balducci's, where she bought armfuls of fresh produce and exotic cheeses. Daily she trekked to Sutter's, where she loaded up shamelessly on the best pastries she had ever in her life tasted. Who cared if she put on a few pounds? The infernal cameras were no longer grinding on her face and figure. Besides, pregnant women always tacked on weight and looked the better for it.

Only she wasn't pregnant.

Invariably her strolls took her through Washington Square. For hours she would gaze with trancelike fascination at the mothers and nannies pushing tiny tots on the swings and playing in the sand piles with them.

Soon, soon, she would be there too. . . .

But almost from the time Grosvenor had reluctantly agreed to give her a baby ("Oh, hell, let's have a shot at it"), the chances of their having one seemed to diminish. Their sex life suddenly tapered off.

It was true the long hours of rehearsing left Grosvenor drained of energy. Kim tried to be understanding. Many times she would snuggle up to him in bed and try to get something started only to have him say, "Not tonight, darling. Papa is bushed. Come here, and we'll have just a little good-night smooch and call it a day."

But there were other nights when Grosvenor initiated sex and put a great deal of energy into it. These nights were after days when he had been rehearsing just as long and hard. It was curious.

The play rehearsed five weeks in New York. Kim went with Grosvenor to Boston for the three-week tryout at the Colonial. They stayed at the Ritz-Carlton. The reviews of the play were enthusiastic and Grosvenor was in excellent spirits. Chances were he could look forward to a good long run when the show came to Broadway. That meant no financial crunch for any foreseeable future.

Grosvenor was also very much of a celebrity in his home town. He was much courted by fans and old friends and played up to in the papers. In his arch, mocking way he seemed proud to show off Kim to his old friends. The likes of Kim was not often seen in Back Bay by a group of middle-aged Harvard grads.

The fans and old friends and the press were eager to embrace Kim. But she liked staying in the shadows. It was so nice not to have to cope with all the interviews and phone calls and requests. It was so nice to sit back and "let Grosvenor do it."

Kim loved Boston. At least the Boston of the Ritz-Carlton, the Commons, and Beacon Hill. She half-wished it were possible for them to live there. It seemed like a much nicer place to bring up a family than New York. But New York, of course, was the only place an actor could make a living.

Two things puzzled her during the weeks they spent in Boston.

Grosvenor's mother lived on Chestnut Street, only a few blocks from the Ritz. Grosvenor went to see her three or four times but never said a word about taking her along.

"I'll be over at Mother's for a couple of hours," he said. "You'll be able to amuse yourself until I get back."

She thought it strange Grosvenor's mother wouldn't be demanding to meet her son's new wife.

"I'd like to go along," Kim said to him the third time he was setting off for Chestnut Street. "I'd like to meet your mother."

"No, you wouldn't."

"Sure I would, Grove. She's my mother-in-law, for Christ's sake. And I should think she'd be curious to meet me."

"Mother's curiosity centers on things like stained-glass windows and genealogies and old cemeteries. Not my wives. She met my first one and didn't like her much. I haven't bothered to introduce the others to her. Believe me, my angel, you're better off gazing at the ducks down there in the Gardens. At least they're much tamer ducks than that old mummy of mine."

The pattern of their sex life also continued to mystify Kim. There wasn't too much of it. But what there was, was satisfactory.

There was no predicting when it might happen. It could happen at the least likely times. He might want her on a Wednesday night after he had done both a matinee and an evening performance, at a time when he should be all tuckered out. On a Sunday, when there was no performance, he might have no interest at all. "Have to shore up my energies for the coming week," was his explanation.

His batting average since they left the Coast had been no more than once every fifth or sixth night. Then there had been three dry spells of about ten days when he hadn't touched her.

She mulled it over and over in her mind. A suspicion be-

gan to take root. And, yes, the mystery was beginning to un-
ravel. She began to hate him.

Very clever. And cruel. She would never have guessed he
was capable of that kind of trickery and cruelty. At the earliest possible moment, she would leave him.

The moment she got out of him what she wanted.

Chapter 26

She had been duped. He had led her to believe if a baby
was what she wanted, well, then, that's what he wanted too.
Anything to make her happy. At the same time he was taking care to see that she wouldn't have a baby, that she
wouldn't have the very thing that would make her happiest.

She could be understanding about their infrequent sex. It
didn't take much sex to get pregnant. It did, however, require
sex at the right time.

If he had used contraceptives, he would have been giving
himself away that he didn't want that baby. Instead he used
the sneakier approach of cutting off sex completely each
month during the time when there was the slightest chance
she could conceive.

Her discovery made her furious. But she held her tongue.
She couldn't charge him with anything. She mustn't let on
that she had seen through his strategy.

Once again her skills as an actress were put to the chal-
lenge. If it killed her she would go on playing the adoring
young wife, the happy homemaker who wanted more than
anything to please her husband and lose herself in his interests. No matter how much she came to hate him, she wanted
a child by him. A healthy, handsome intelligent child with the
great Boston name of Forbes. The moment she got it, she
would leave him.

Yes, Grosvenor Forbes had to be the father of her baby.

How she was going to pull it off was the question.

The Inconstant Lovers opened to warm praise from the
New York reviewers and a healthy advance sale at the box
office. Everybody said it would run two years at the very
minimum.

Thanks to Grosvenor and his attraction for the suburban
ladies, the matinees for the next four months were sold out
before the play opened.

Kim waited out Grosvenor's performances in his dressing room to keep any of his fans from letting their enthusiasm get out of hand. With Grosvenor rationing his sex activities, she wasn't going to let any of his favors get out of the family.

She whiled away all those hours at the theater reading the books he gave her to improve her mind and broaden her cultural horizons.

Grosvenor did not seem to have friends in New York or want them. They did almost no socializing. They went to the theater, ate dinner in restaurants where the celebrity crowd *didn't* go, and went back to Macdougal Alley. It was a strange, unreal, marking-time period in Kim's life. She had always been pulled around like a marionette. Now she was waiting for something to happen that she must make happen herself. If she was putting this part of her life into a script, she wondered how she'd make it happen.

Shopping and fittings and poking around the city passed the hours pleasantly enough for Kim when she wasn't at the theater.

And there was Ryder Downey.

Ryder Downey was the lover-friend-housekeeper-secretary of the set designer who lived two doors down from them in the Alley. Ryder reminded her a little of Lonnie Braintree. Like Lonnie, he was bright and funny and brimful of delicious gossip. There the similarity ended. Lonnie was sweet and cuddlesome. Ryder was the bitchy fag with a nasty, biting edge to everything he said.

Kim drew Ryder's eyes like a magnet. She could rarely slip out of the Alley without Ryder's rushing out to overtake her. Didn't she have time for one quick beer in the Jumble Shop? He had something *perfectly gorgeous* to tell her. Ryder ditched the dirt about everyone in the Alley. Some of the stories were eye-openers. Kim didn't much like Ryder, but his chatter could be spellbinding. It was fun to listen to as long as everybody else was the subject. She wondered what he said about her when he had somebody else for an audience.

"I'd stay away from that particular bird of passage," Grosvenor warned her. "I find him about as wholesome as a cobra."

Grosvenor continued to perform well in bed when he performed at all. But those occasions were rare. He kept careful track of her period and kept away from her for several days on either end of the time zone when she might have conceived. The bastard.

Kim went on playing sweet and dumb. Frequently during the "wrong time" she would try to coax him into action.

266

"Oh, darling, you're trying to whip dying embers into flame," he protested. "It won't work."

"There was plenty of fire the other night."

"But the fire flares seldom now. You must remember I'm not a young whippersnapper like you. I'm a tired old man."

"You're only fifty," she retorted. "There are men going at it hot and heavy into their seventies. So I'm told, anyway."

Then he surprised her. "I do know one way of banking that dying fire," Grosvenor said, giving her one of his mysterious, ironic glances.

"How?"

"I seem to respond quite well to discipline. I always have. It's perhaps the Boston Brahmin in me. Descending no doubt from a long line of Anglo-Saxon warriors."

She didn't have the foggiest idea of what he was talking about.

"Fetch me my walking stick, if you'd be so good."

She got from the closet the walking stick he sometimes carried when they took Sunday afternoon strolls. It was a slim, elegant ebony stick with a sterling silver handle.

"An inheritance from my dear, dead father. That walking stick always did double duty in our family. Father carried it on fine days when he walked back and forth to his offices on Marlborough Street. He also used it as a chastening rod. When my brothers or I got out of line, we were asked to go to our room and drop our britches. Presently Father would be there with his walking stick. Then, wham! A dozen or twenty or fifty hearty thwacks across the bare bum. Whatever the crime merited."

Kim shuddered. Whatever the failings of her mother, she had never once lifted her hand to Kim. Charles Cramer was the only person who had ever struck her. And he had got it back in full measure. As would anyone else who ever tried that one on her.

"Do you know something? I rather enjoyed it. I must have. Oh, it hurt and stung and there'd be welts on my bum. But I'd also have a terrific erection. I'd lie there across the bed until Father had left the room so he couldn't see the state of excitement I was in."

He reached for her hand. "Come."

He led her to the bedroom, brandishing the walking stick.

"Get undressed," he instructed her.

He practically tore off his own clothes. "Somehow I have a feeling I've been very, very naughty. I don't quite recall my misdeed. I don't think my Puritan conscience will feel right until I've been properly punished. Take the walking stick, my dear, and apply it to me old bum."

Grosvenor flopped on his stomach on top of the bed. He patted his fanny. It was her signal to begin applying the cane there.

Kim was shocked and appalled. She had no idea he went in for this sort of thing. She certainly didn't. The time might come when she wished him dead. But not if she had to beat him to death. The thought of violence for the sake of kicks—whoever got the kicks—sickened her.

"I'm waiting, darling. I've been a very naughty boy. 'Spare the rod and spoil the child.' "

As she hesitated, he urged her again, practically pleading. God, it takes all kinds, she thought. But if it was a means to the desired end, why not? In his own way he was being cruel to her. Why shouldn't she get back at him with a few blows? Especially since he was begging for them?

Kim delivered a few strikes across his backside. But they didn't pack much wallop.

"Harder!" he commanded. "The stick won't break. Neither will me bum. They're both tough."

She bore down a little harder.

"Harder! You can do better than that. Darling, you're a strong woman. You have to be if you're going to be the mother of my child."

The mention of the child got her so mad she was able to whack Grosvenor the way he wanted to be whacked.

"Wonderful!" he screamed. "Marvelous. Keep it up!"

He flung himself around finally. Tears streamed down his cheeks. He reached for her urgently and made voracious love to her. Repeatedly.

When she came back to earth again, Kim marveled that she could be so transported by someone she detested.

"Did you like doing what you did to me ... disciplining me?" he asked her shyly.

"If it pleases you," she said. "I am your wife."

Grosvenor went on to commit little crimes that cried out for disciplining. Deliberately he would tip over a full glass of wine on the tablecloth. Or "accidentally" kick Kim under the table. Or say something snappish or sarcastic to her. "How naughty of me!" he'd exclaim. "Get the stick, my dear. I've earned a good caning."

But Grosvenor somehow never provoked a caning during the time that would have suited Kim's purpose.

One evening, when she thought the time was right, it was she who brought up the suggestion of punishment. "I think your attitude has been lousy all day. Mind if I give you twelve rough ones across your sweet little ass?"

"I most certainly do," he protested. "On the contrary, I've

been most civil to you all day long. I don't object to being flogged when I'm guilty of some wrong-doing. But not when my behavior's been exemplary."

Kim managed to hide her frustration. You smart-ass bastard, she thought, I'll get you yet.

"You'd make a terrible headmistress or prison matron," he told her one night. It was after he had confessed to a misdemeanor, taken his medicine, and given her an hour of riotous screwing.

"Not that I ever wanted to be a headmistress or a prison matron," she said, "but why?"

"Because I know you instinctively hate to administer corporal punishment. You're too sweet and gentle and permissive."

She let that sink in without comment, waiting.

"My darling child, knowing how much this goes against the grain—your grain—I had a thought. I think it's essential to my character that I go on . . . being disciplined. And since it's distasteful to you, perhaps we could hire professional disciplinarians when the occasion warranted."

Now what was he talking about? Did he mean people would be hired to come in and thrash him? And afterward there would be a big gang-bang? A pile of bodies on the bed, arms and legs entangled like a mechanical puzzle, everybody sweating and moaning, and Grosvenor thrusting into every opening like a bull in mating season?

Perish the thought! No, no, he specifically and categorically meant no such thing.

"Think of them only as servants," Grosvenor advised her. "Trust in me. Your receptacle will be the sole beneficiary of any ejaculations that I might muster, little mother."

They called themselves Tiger Lily and San San. One was Chinese and the other was Japanese. They were precisely what Grosvenor had ordered. Integration applied to the Orientals, he explained to Kim, as well as to the black and whites. After all the strained relations in the Far East dating from World War II, it would be nice to see a Chinese girl and a Japanese girl working together so "intimately."

Grosvenor ordered the girls from Madeleine Dandridge. Madeleine Dandridge operated the classiest call girl operation in New York. There was no taste or yearning so kinky Madeleine Dandridge could not find someone to satisfy it.

Tiger Lily and San San were both young, fragile, and exquisite. Neither one could be more than twenty-two years old. Tiger Lily could have been the direct descendant of emperors. San San might be someone trained in the civilized graces of the geisha ... or a young matron blushing behind a fan in some teahouse in ancient Kyoto.

Tiger Lily and San San each wore lovely silk dresses with a high slash going up the left side. Kim and Grosvenor welcomed them in dressing gowns. The hour was well after midnight.

They sat in the second-floor drawing room drinking tea from a samovar, speaking almost in whispers, teacups tinkling. The girls giggled and blushed demurely.

"Come, come," said Grosvenor. "Not fair to take up your time with our tiresome twaddle. We're all working folk. And you've got miles to go before you sleep."

He led the entourage to the bathroom off the landing below the third-floor master bedroom. It was the bathroom with the Jacuzzi whirlpool bath. He started the water running.

"Off with the duds, girls," he said, "and in the tub."

The girls were "pros." They knew an instruction when they heard one. In a flash their dresses and undies were off and they were facing each other in the whirlpool bath.

"Observe, my bride," said Grosvenor to Kim, "it's not true what they said about Oriental girls. Prejudice is such an odious thing. It always distorts and slanders. Observe, my bride. Our Oriental guests are essentially no different from me or thee. Correction. No different from thee. ..."

Grosvenor pressed Kim's head closer to the bath.

"Observe that, my bride. Doesn't that set to rest once and for all a vicious rumor? Their luscious little pussies go the same direction as yours. They're not slanted at any ridiculous angle."

Grosvenor dug his fingers into her shoulder blades, riveting her attention.

"Now, girls. Down to work."

This was what he wanted from them? This was what he had ordered?

Kim watched, hypnotized. ...

Tiger Lily and San San were into their scene.

Tiger Lily had taken the lead. She was kissing and lapping at San San. Tiger Lily rolled her tongue around San San's purplish nipples, then took them between her lips. She kissed San San in the cleavage between her firm, strong tits. Her tongue worked down and down San San's almond-colored body to the patch of springy hair.

"Eat her up, baby!" Grosvenor yelled. "Get your tongue way in there."

San San squealed as she climaxed. She caught her breath and leaned forward to go to work on Tiger Lily. While she devoured Tiger Lily's body with her kisses, Grosvenor stroked himself under his dressing gown. Kim felt her own excitement mounting.

"Eat her good now," Grosvenor panted to San San. "Make your tongue come out the other end."

Tiger Lily's explosion left Grosvenor nearly breathless.

"I'm sorry, girls," he apologized. "That was wicked of me. Pushing you into that tub and forcing you into an unnatural act. Your turn to get back at me now. Follow me."

Grosvenor took Kim's hand and led the way up the stairs to the master bedroom. The two nude girls followed, dripping a trail of whirlpool bath.

In the bedroom Grosvenor threw off his robe. He was wearing nothing underneath. He was totally erect. He motioned Kim to stand aside. He gave the walking stick to Tiger Lily. To San San he gave a shillelagh that had been hanging on the wall over the fireplace. He flopped on the bed, backside up.

"Now spank me for being such a bad boy."

Tiger Lily spanked him on his buttocks and San San spanked him higher up. They spanked hard. Kim guessed they had been through this scene before. With Grosvenor. Though they had pretended they were meeting him for the first time.

"You're killing me!" he cried. "Stop!"

They stopped and put down their weapons.

"Your money's in the envelope over on the table," he gasped. "Get dressed and get out."

Turning over, he presented to Kim his joyous, tear-drenched face. And his inviting erection. He held out his arms to her.

It was almost morning before he finally calmed down.

"And you call yourself an old man?" she asked.

"There's nothing like a good spanking to shape me up."

Kim thought it had been a pretty weird scene. But she had to admit she liked the aftermath. She almost hit the roof when she learned the two Oriental chicks picked up two hundred bucks for their services—which didn't even include screwing the client!

Still, she didn't discourage other visits from Tiger Lily and San San. She had a hunch that just possibly something really good might come out of them.

"Who were the pair of slant-eyes I saw tripping out of your place about two-thirty A.M.?"

It was Ryder Downey. He caught her on the way to a dentist's appointment. My God, he didn't miss a trick. If the night had a thousand eyes, so did Ryder.

She had to think fast. "Well, you know—or maybe you don't—how interested Grove is in everything Oriental. Now one of his hobbies is learning how to cook Chinese and Japanese food. Those girls give cooking lessons."

"Uh-huh. And I'm a translator at the United Nations."

One Wednesday Kim purposefully stayed away from the matinee. She told Grosvenor she was going to see her gynecologist. He looked worried.

"Oh, nothing's wrong," she assured him. "Just a checkup."

She didn't go to see any doctor. When she met Grosvenor for an early supper at Sardi's, she put on a brave smile.

"Everything all right?" he asked her.

"Yeah, I guess. Except he doesn't think the chances are good for me to have a baby."

"What's wrong?"

"Nothing, really. Certainly not with you, God knows. Since you're already a father six times over. And not with me, either. I've been visiting him for months and he still can't find any reason why I *couldn't* have babies."

"Then what's the problem?"

"He says some women are just like that. There's no physical reason why they *can't* get pregnant but they just never do get pregnant, no matter how hard they try. He went over my whole life history and he said, 'Look, how can I be encouraging? You tell me neither you nor your sex partners have ever used contraceptives and you've had extensive sexual contact over a period of almost ten years?' "

What a crock that was! No matter how drunk she had ever been, before she went to bed with a guy, she knew that she was going to wake up safe. Thanks to the magic little device that dirty old doctor at the Studio had fitted her out with years ago. She would have committed suicide before submitting to the knife of an abortionist. Hollywood was full of dumb broads who were always getting knocked up and having to get an abortion. She was never going to be one of them. The operation must be sheer hell. If you had to have it, it stamped you as such a dummie.

"What conclusion can we come to?" the doctor said. "That all the men in your life were sterile? Not very likely. No, Mrs. Forbes. You'll just have to face the facts. You may be one of those women who are physiologically capable of becoming mothers but who for some mysterious reason never manage to get pregnant. It can be a heartbreaking situation. You could go on trying and hoping for years and never have your heart's desire. I do think if you are this set on having a child, you might do well to give some thought to the idea of adoption."

272

"To hell with that," snapped Grosvenor. "We'll just keep trying."

Oh, you don't know how much we will, thought Kim.

"Then he brought up the psychological thing," she said, pausing.

"What's the psychological thing?"

"He says a lot of women think they want babies with all their hearts. But subconsciously they don't. Way down deep they're afraid for some reason to have them. They're afraid of childbirth itself. Or it'll mar their beauty. Or come between them and their husbands. Or interfere with their careers. Many reasons. And the subconscious, he said, is a powerful factor. It has the power of killing the semen before it hits the egg."

"I don't go along with any of this psychoanalytical bilge," said Grosvenor scornfully.

Now he was playing the sympathetic husband, the loving partner whose own hopes of fatherhood were being shattered. He thought he was being so clever. Just wait. He'd see.

"You know, Grove, it set me to thinking." She pulled on a sweet, sad, philosophic smile. "He just might be right. Way deep down is this what I really want? I thought it was what I wanted. But maybe it was because it was something I didn't have and everybody else seemed to have. But I wonder if I'd want it all that much if I had to give up what very few other people have. I wonder if that's not what a little voice deep inside of me hasn't been saying."

"Personally, I think you'd make a wonderful mother."

"I wonder. I wonder how wonderful I'd be. I'm so immature myself. It might be like a little girl being given a doll to play with. Anyway, I guess I don't have to worry my pretty head about that. It's something that doesn't seem to be in the cards. . . ."

She had never left home really.

The Studio had been on her back the whole time she was in New York. Phone calls, telegrams, letters. When was she coming back? What an idiot she was to walk out at a time like this! Just as she was really reaching for the top.

Kim worried about her mother. She knew Indiana was looking out for her. But she still couldn't help worrying about her. And being a little homesick for her. This was the first time in their lives they had ever been separated.

It was also the first time for almost as long as she could remember that she hadn't been working. And earning. She missed the soothing rhythm of the weekly paycheck coming in.

In the first month in New York she had been too dazzled by New York and Grosvenor to read the scripts the Studio kept sending to her. Without opening them, she'd file them in the garbage.

The scripts kept coming. Now she opened them. And lay awake nights reading them. One of them looked pretty good. She called up the next day and talked about it with Sy Raskin, who would be producing.

"Grove," she said that night in his dressing room at the Broadhurst, "I've come across something I'd sort of like to do. I think it might be good for me to get off my ass and back to work for a while."

"How long?"

"They said it had a shooting schedule of seven weeks."

"When?"

"Whenever I'm ready, I guess. It might be nice too to pick up a few bucks I could call my own."

"You don't have to, you know. One way or another I'll always be able to support you. Though it might not be in the style you've been accustomed to. Or would like to get accustomed to."

"There are other reasons too. I'd better check up on the house. And my mother. It's easier going out there to see her than trying to bring her on here."

"I want you to do what you want to do," he said. "But you must know how much I'll miss you. I do love you, you know."

He spoke so sincerely she was touched. Yes, he did love her. In her obsession to have a baby, she had lost sight of that fact. All she could see was that he seemed to be standing in the way of what she wanted most. He loved her and in so many ways he was a remarkable man. Maybe in time she would recover the first rapturous feeling she had felt for him. Maybe a couple months' separation would rekindle her feeling of love for him.

Especially if she got what she wanted.

For a couple of weeks the atmosphere was charged.

There were all the phone calls from the Coast. Endless discussions about casting, wardrobe, changes in the script, the choice of a director, a starting date. In due time it was announced that Kimberley Hudson was returning, after a lengthy absence from films, to make *A-Hunting We Will Go*.

The announcement brought pandemonium. The rumors started flying. Was she headed for Splitsville with Grosvenor Forbes? Editors, fan magazine writers, radio and television impresarios, and gossip columnists clamored for interviews with her.

"I want to scotch one rumor," Kim told Earl Wilson. "I am not—repeat not—separating from my husband. I am going out to Hollywood to make a picture. Period. As soon as the picture is finished, I am coming right back here to be with Grosvenor. I don't think any marriage can survive if two people have careers that are going to keep them apart much of the time. It's a matter of priorities. My first priority is home and husband. Acting—being a movie star—will always come second . . ."

Earl twinkled as if he had heard that story before.

With the time approaching, Grosvenor wanted to know what day she would be going.

"Probably Tuesday," she said. She did her utmost to sound casual. It was vitally important that he shouldn't be put on his guard. "My horoscope says that's the day I 'should be receptive to an opportunity that might involve a long journey.' You know I don't go much by that stuff. But all the same, if it's between one day and the day before or the next one . . ."

"Tuesday's a sensible day to travel," said Grosvenor. "Usually quiet. You miss all the hustlers and drummers buzzing off Mondays to set the world on fire. Dreadful types."

She was over the first hurdle. He didn't suspect a thing.

"I think Monday night we should have a little farewell celebration."

"Under the circumstances," said Grosvenor, "I should think that would be quite in order. Any suggestions?"

"How about a not-so-quiet evening at home?"

"Elucidate," he said, with his charming smile.

"I thought we might invite down our dear old friends Tiger Lily and San San," she said lightly.

"I had no idea you found them so enchanting."

"I don't." She gave him a sultry wink. "But I find *you* enchanting when they've been here."

"Thy will be mine."

Whew! She had cleared the second—and crucial—hurdle.

Now if she could just be sure of her timing . . .

For Kim's farewell party, Tiger Lily and San San poured all their energy and enthusiasm into the flagellation scene.

Grosvenor got the spanking of his life.

As she yielded herself to Grosvenor's frantic embrace, Kim saw something like a crack of lightning flash through the curtained east window.

She heard footsteps following the click-clicking spiked heels of Tiger Lily and San San.

Please, God, make this the night!

275

Chapter 27

She had to admit it was nice to be back again. She had missed so many things . . . the California sunshine and palm trees . . . her mother and her friends . . . the beaches . . . the abalone and the Mexican food and the salads . . . the free and easy ways . . . "the business" itself . . .

In the commissary, her first day back, she got a standing ovation. On the menu there was a Kimberley Hudson salad.

And that was nice too.

Don't get her wrong. She loved Hollywood.

But . . .

Her place was with her husband. That's where she wanted to be. She was just going to do this one picture. The day it was finished, she would hurry back to him in New York.

Like a good wife she called Grosvenor every night. "See how I'm behaving myself," she said. "Nine o'clock and I'm home and ready for bed."

"Is anybody ready for bed with you?"

"My purple past is behind me," she assured him.

She always had newsy little tidbits of the day to report: "The Boss is purring like a pussycat. He's visited the set three times. He treats me like a little girl who went astray but has come back to her senses.

"He thinks he's so subtle. Today he said they wanted to build a bungalow for me on the back lot. My permanent dressing-room. What kind of decor would I like? Get it? I'm being a good girl and I'm back to stay."

One night she put a question to him: "Lonnie Braintree wants to take me to a party tomorrow night. He says there'll be a lot of VIPIs there. That's Very Important People Indeed. Do I have your permission to go?"

"You certainly do," he laughed. "With Lonnie Braintree as your escort I shan't worry too much about your conduct."

The next time she called, she reported on the party: "I met that wild producer Marty North. Actually I had met him a couple of times in the commissary. But never really to talk to. He's like bottled lightning. He came charging at me like a crazy man. He said he had me in mind for something spectacular. I told him whatever it was, no thanks. It was probably to work for a dollar in some picture. You've heard, haven't you, he's conned all those big names into working for nothing in that epic thing he's making called *Christopher Columbus Discovers America?*"

"You sound so happy and bubbly," Grosvenor observed. "Is it because you're away from me?"

She *was* happy and bubbly. But not because she was away from him. She couldn't tell him the reason. She'd wait until she was sure.

The next day her hopeful hunch was confirmed.

"Are you sitting down?" she asked him. "Well, get a good grip on yourself. Have I ever got some news for you!"

"Tell me, tell me."

"Guess what? I'm pregnant."

There was a dead silence on the New York end of the line.

"Are you there, Grove? Have you fainted?"

"I'm here. Are you sure?"

"Sure I'm sure. I only go to one of the best doctors in Bevrly Hills."

There was another deadening silence.

"Now don't start getting any funny ideas. I can just hear you thinking to yourself, 'Is it mine?' Well, it is, I swear. Since I met you no one else has been near me."

She didn't tell him how carefully she had plotted it. That farewell party the night before she left New York, featuring Tiger Lily and San San, was planned for the time when she would be right on target to conceive. Grosvenor knew her calendar as well as she did. But he had probably dismissed the danger thinking she wasn't the conceiving kind. So she had told him the doctor had told her.

"Well, that's wonderful!" he said at last.

He sounded as if he really meant it! As if this were the very thing he wanted as much as she did.

"Now you've got to get back here at the earliest possible moment," he said. "The facilities are superior here and I insist on supervising your pregnancy. This will be my seventh. None of my progeny so far have developed into dreamboats. But, by God, every last one of them entered this vale of tears as superb specimens of healthy babyhood. Thanks, in no small measure, to the no-nonsense regimens I've enforced."

Kim felt a surge of relief and warmth. He did care. He really was concerned for the well-being of her and their unborn child.

But she was into her fifth month of pregnancy before she got back to New York.

On the heels of the first picture, the Studio had a second property they wanted to rush her into. It wasn't much of a property but it could be shot in six weeks and her name on the marquee would be enough to carry it. She was promised a whopping bonus if she'd agree to do it in view of her "condition." What's more, the "blessed event" clause in her contract would be liberally interpreted. The Studio would keep her on the payroll—at full salary—through the rest of her pregnancy and for a reasonably extended time after the child was born.

Kim didn't tell them that after her child was born she never intended to come back.

Her last Sunday in California she took Mama and me for a long drive up the coastal highway. Her pregnancy didn't show yet. But she was absolutely radiant. She glowed as if she were already holding the newborn child in her arms. I had never seen her so soft and ingratiating. She was going all-out to be pleasing.

During lunch at the Biltmore in Santa Barbara she asked me questions about my career. For the first time I felt she was sincerely interested. She knew things hadn't been going so hot for me. As a single I wasn't burning up the nightclub circuit. One-nighters in two-bit clubs in towns like Fresno and Bakersfield and San Jose weren't exactly the big time.

Kim wondered if I had sent the demo to that agent she had recommended back East. I had. And I had heard nothing. Gosh, she ought to be able to push her weight around at the Studio to land me something. Especially when you considered all the no-talent singers they kept sticking in pictures. And all the leading ladies who couldn't sing but got put in musicals and needed somebody to dub for them behind the scenes ...

"If we could just marry you off to somebody rich," she sighed.

Mama beamed at that suggestion.

"I've got nothing against rich men," I said. "They just don't seem to be beating down the door."

"Gina," said Kim brightly, "I can hardly think about anything but my baby. I've got it all planned. You're going to be the godmother."

"Me?"

"Yes, you. You're my oldest girl friend. And practically my only one. Except Maura. You'll probably be having about ten kids of your own any day now. But I know if anything ever happened to me you'd look after mine like it was your own. I think you'll be a marvelous, warm, loving mother ..."

She bubbled on about my qualifications to be the godmother of her child. It was all music to my ears. I was thrilled and flattered nearly out of my skin.

"And Mama's going to be the honorary godmother. And Lonnie Braintree's going to be the godfather. Oh, I know he's not some people's idea of what's manly or what a father should be like. But I love him and he loves me. And that's what it's all about. If anything ever happened to me and Grosvenor, I know I could count on Lonnie. He's such a wonderful person."

Her spirits kept soaring, lifting me up too. I never saw her so happy again.

"Mama and Gina, I want you to fly East for the christening. Lonnie's coming to. I'll send you the tickets. They'll be in first class too. Nobody flies tourist to see Kimberley Hudson's kid get christened. This'll be the event of the century!"

We didn't make it to the christening. There was no christening.

"Let's see what you got in the oven," Grosvenor greeted her. "Take off your clothes and let's have a look at you."

Kim preened before his admiring gaze.

"Nice," he said, patting the tummy that was just beginning to swell.

He got down on his knees and brushed his cheek against her stomach. He kissed tenderly the whole surface of the swollen area. Embracing her by the buttocks, he swept his tongue upward. Round and round it encircled each breast, sweeping in smaller and smaller circles until it was lashing the rim of her nipples. With a hot gasp he took a great gulp of breast into his mouth and sank his teeth gently in the horizon of soft flesh.

Then his tongue was bushwacking downward, down, down over the budding embryo and into her core. It dug deeper and deeper into her.

God, how hot he was! How starved for her he was!

"I've missed you," he panted, coming out for air. "Or did you gather that?"

"I'm getting the general idea."

"To the boudoir we will go. It's perfectly safe. For junior, I mean," he added, patting again her slight protuberance.

"Be careful," she cautioned him coyly. "A girl could get pregnant."

Except for the times when Tiger Lily and San San had been there, it was the best sex she ever had with Grosvenor. He might be fifty but he was twice the cocksman of a lot of guys she had had who were only half his age.

Grosvenor meant it about supervising her pregnancy.

"I want you to do what your doctor advises you," he reassured her. "My regimen begins where they leave off. The

279

medical profession—at least in this country—is incredibly inept."

Grosvenor said okay, okay, to all the milk-drinking and the vitamin supplements and the not overdoing and the no-smoking and moderation-in-alcohol consumption and the standard exercises prescribed.

But this was not enough.

It didn't say no to her cravings.

She must put herself in his hands, listen to him.

Kim gave in happily. It was heaven to feel helpless and cared for in this most important time in her life.

"Darling, you mustn't feed on those loathsome sweets," he scolded.

He was referring to the goodies from Sutter's she was practically addicted to . . . the rhum babas and napoleons and cheesecake. He objected even to the breakfasty brioches and croissants and French bread. They were starchy and just as full of carbohydrates as the sweets.

For Sutter's he would substitute Brownie's. Brownie's was a long-established health foods restaurant a soybean's throw from Union Square. There in off-beat hours they would run into such luminaries as Danny Kaye and Bea Lillie and Carol Channing and Gaylord Hauser. There he introduced her to carrot juice and Tiger's Milk cocktails and eggplant steaks and kelp salads.

"Now eat up—like a nice knocked-up princess," he cooed.

"These bends and stretches and pushes and what-nots," he scoffed, "they tell pregnant women to do are totally inadequate. The expectant mother requires vigorous exercise."

Kim wondered what he meant by vigorous exercise.

"Walking briskly. Jogging."

It was insane.

He put her through her paces around the reservoir in Central Park. Running a few steps, walking a few. Then running again, more walking. Gradually extending the running lengths. Keeping her going until she was breathless.

Five times a week they took a cab to 86th Street. Soon she was going a quarter of a mile before she had to slow down to a walk. Grosvenor told her she should set a goal. She should tell herself that by the time she was in her eighth month she would be doing one whole lap around the reservoir (1.6 miles) at a good jogging clip.

A terrible suspicion crossed her mind at the beginning. He still didn't want the baby. He was trying to bring on a miscarriage.

"Are you sure this is good for me?" she asked him. "All this bouncing up and down . . . this heavy exercise?"

"The best thing in the world for you," he declared emphatically. "My mother happened to be a close friend of Eleanora Sears. Eleanora in her heyday was perhaps the most illustrious long-distance walker in America. When Mother was carrying me, she accompanied Eleanora on a walk from Boston to Salem. Which is perhaps twenty-eight or thirty miles. The girls did the journey in a day, stopped with some friends there, and returned via foot the next day. Would you say I'm any the worse for Mother's athletic feats?"

Kim's doctor gave his grudging support to her exercise program.

"You seem to be in tip-top form," he said. "Obviously the jogging isn't doing you any harm. Who knows, it could be doing you a lot of good. At this point I see no reason to forbid it."

"What did I tell you?" Grosvenor gloated. "The medical profession is about the laziest, unhealthiest occupational group alive. If they only practiced what they preached! If only a few more of them would get off their gluteus maximuses, they'd not only be a lot healthier. They'd be extolling the virtues of strenuous exercise. For everybody. Including pregnant women!"

Kim listened to him, obeyed him blindly.

There were no complications. Junior kept swelling and swelling. Shouldn't a pregnant woman coming close to her "time" be feeling lousy? She had never felt better in her whole life.

How she had misjudged Grosvenor! He may not have wanted this child. He had maybe done everything in his power to prevent it. But now that it was coming, he wanted it just as much as she did. He wanted it to come into the world as strong and healthy as possible.

She lived only for the coming child. She saw nobody but Grosvenor. And the inevitable Ryder Downey, who always seemed to be lying in wait for her every time she took a stroll out of the Alley.

On the surface he was all friendly concern about how she felt. But he made her uncomfortable. His smile was close to a leer. It said that he knew something . . . either something she didn't know or something she didn't know that he knew.

"The quintessential creep," Grosvenor called him.

Her preoccupation with the growing infant inside her excluded any interest in sex. She wondered if it was the same for other women. Could it be that all the frantic sex activity in her past had been undertaken because she subconsciously hoped it would result in a baby? Even though she had taken precautions against conceiving? And now that she was going to have a baby, sex had played its role and shuffled off into the wings?

Grosvenor was not pregnant. Uninterested as she might be in sex, she could not ignore his needs. He gazed at her ballooning figure with rapture. To him, she could see, she had never been so beautiful. Or desirable.

When she was undressed, he stroked her protruding belly. He put his cheek against it, kissed it, and listened for interior sounds of life. His admiration/adoration of the madonna gave way to sexual excitement. Her heart was not in it. But Kim did the best she could to satisfy him. Everything she had read was confirmed by her doctor. There was no reason why sexual relations could not go on almost all the way through pregnancy.

"Let's have a party tonight," she suggested impulsively one day within weeks of the birth of her child.

"Party?" Grosvenor said. "Who on earth would we invite?"

"Tiger Lily and San San."

"At this delicate stage of your life? Are you quite serious, my dear?"

"As long as they don't start beating *me*," said Kim, "what does it matter?"

Her suggestion made Grosvenor very happy. Tiger Lily and San San gave him a thorough thrashing. Then they paid hasty compliments to Kim. They wished her and her baby every blessing. They dressed quickly and were gone. Grosvenor ravished her gently. The big swelling that brushed against his stomach was a sacred growth. It must be treated like an eggshell. It was so much more important than any of the quickie returns he might get underneath.

I came to New York ahead of time. Long before there could be any christening. It was still days before the baby was due.

I came early because someone else was picking up the tab for my flight. United Air Lines. First class yet.

The Mick Gordon Show was doing a two-part series on once well-known show business teams you didn't hear much about any more. It was to be one of those "what ever happened to———" kind of things. Comedy duos. Composing teams. Singing sisters acts. Et cetera. My sister Angie and I were to represent the Spinelli Sisters.

I got transportation plus scale plus two nights in the Waldorf.

"Oh, Gina, I'm so glad you're here!" Kim chirped into the phone. "I'm so glad you're here before anything's happened."

"Well, yeah," I said. "It's not like I'm a midwife or anything."

"I know you're not. Even so, it's nice to know you're here."

"It's nice to be here. When do I see you?"

"In the hospital. It can't be more than a couple of days. Look, Gina, I want you to stay. Stay on me. The Waldorf can bill me. This is such a secret baby. Nobody but nobody knows when or where I'm going to have it."

"That I find hard to believe," I said.

"I mean it. It's too important to me. For once in my life I'd like to have a secret. I don't want my baby to be a circus. One more thing for the flacks to kick around. I swear, the Studio doesn't even know when or where I'm going to pop."

"I'm the only one, besides Grosvenor and the doctor, who knows . . . when and where?"

"Honestly." She laughed. "If you don't count the creep who lives a couple of doors from us. Ryder Downey. Believe me, I don't count him."

For weeks the weightiest—and maybe the only—thing on her mind had been the choice of a name. After thumbing through books of names and mulling over all the possibilities, she narrowed the list down to three choices for a boy and three for a girl.

There was more soul-searching before she finally threw out Jennifer and Millicent. And Michael and David. If it was a girl, she would be named Melissa. A boy would be named Randolph.

Kim checked into Klingenstein Pavilion at Mt. Sinai Hospital almost twenty-four hours before her baby was born.

Her nurse was a pretty, laughing West Indian woman named Dahlia.

"She was just lovely," Dahlia told me. "We get some of them in here who give themselves all kinds of airs and drive you crazy with their demands. But she wasn't like that at all. If you didn't know who she was, she could be just Mrs. Jones. Between her pains she was always joking."

But behind the kidding Dahlia could tell Kim was as tense and scared as any first-time mother-to-be. She could tell from the things Kim said and asked.

"You are going to knock me out, aren't you? So I won't feel a thing?"

"You don't have a thing to worry about, Mrs. Forbes."

"I don't understand those natural childbirth mothers. I think they're nuts. I want to be knocked out cold. And I

283

don't want to wake up until it's all over. And the first thing I want to see is my hairdresser and somebody from Elizabeth Arden coming in to make me up. Then I want to see my husband arriving with some really expensive bauble from Tiffany's or Cartier's. And then I might consent to have a peek at my baby."

"First things first, Mrs. Forbes. You've put everything in the right order."

"Oh, Dahlia, I do like you. Promise me you won't leave me while I'm knocked out."

"You'll be in good hands."

"How long will it be before I can see my baby?"

"It shouldn't be more than ten or twelve hours."

"Ten or twelve hours! Why so long?"

"It'll take that long for the drugs to pass out of the baby's body."

"What drugs?"

"The same drugs that'll be in you. The injection they give you to put you under. The baby will still be part of you when they give you the injection."

"Oh. Well, I guess we can both wait ten or twelve hours to meet each other. Dahlia, promise me something. If I give birth to a little two-headed monster—and it would be just my luck—I'm going to roll over on it. There's no future for little two-headed monsters in this world. And I want you to swear the little monster just stopped breathing. Or else I'll spend the rest of my life in jail for murder."

"That's gruesome, Mrs. Forbes. This is a time when you are supposed to be thinking nice, sweet thoughts."

"Dahlia, what happens if a baby is born dead or—well, deformed?"

"I don't think you should be thinking about these things. Or talking about them. Because they almost never happen. And they're not going to happen to you."

"But I insist on knowing."

"All right. Stillborns—children born dead—are taken to the lab. If it is the wish of the parents, an autopsy is performed to determine the cause of death."

"What do they tell the mother . . . at first?"

"The doctor and the husband usually tell her she has lost her baby."

"What if the baby comes out misshapen?"

"Those babies go to a room at the third floor rear. And she sees the baby when the doctor thinks she's . . . up to it."

"Does she have to see it?"

"*Have* to? No, I don't think she *has* to see it. Oh, but Mrs.

Forbes, this is such depressing talk. You shouldn't be thinking about such things."

"I know I shouldn't. I should be thinking about that damn enema you're going to give me."

"That's right," Dahlia laughed. "Only let's call it a laxative. But that is something that really is going to happen."

Somebody once said war is hell. So are hospitals. Even the best of them. They're chock-full of stories with tragic endings.

Every experience I've had with one has been excruciating.

There were even complications when I was having each of my children. With Timmy I got toxemia and it was thirty-six hours before I could see him.

I went with Grosvenor to Mt. Sinai. Kim gave birth to a baby boy in the middle of the afternoon. But it was almost midnight before she came out of the grog.

By that time the horror had sunk in. And we had rehearsed our script.

Grosvenor had gone off and done his show while I stayed in the room with her. He was back by the time she came to. He was reading the *World-Telegram* with great concentration. I was busily changing the water on the flowers.

"Grove?" said Kim croakily.

"Yes, darling?" He reached out and took her hand in his.

"What happened?"

"What happened? Why, you gave birth to a baby boy. You're in remarkable shape and you're going to be out of here before you know it."

"Where's the baby?"

"It's downstairs. Resting."

"Gina?"

"Yes, Kim."

"Where's my baby?"

"Kim, it's downstairs. Resting. Like Grosvenor said."

"You're both lying. Tell the truth. It's dead, isn't it?"

"Kim!" we exclaimed in chorus.

"Then get it. I want to see it."

"Well, darling, you can't just now," said Grosvenor. "For both your sake and the baby's. You're still woozy and should get a good night's sleep. And the baby needs his rest too."

"Where's Dahlia?"

"Dahlia's off-duty. She looked in just before she went off. She was pleased to see you resting so comfortably."

"Grove, Gina?"

We said "Yes" in chorus.

"I wish one of you would tell me the truth. Something is being held back from me."

Grosvenor and I exchanged glances. I let him do the talking.

"The little fella's having a few problems. He's got a mucous condition. There's some irregularity in the heartbeat——"

"Is he going to live?" she interrupted him.

"Yes. Yes, he's going to live."

"Is he going to live, Gina?"

"Of course he is," I said reassuringly. "Grosvenor wouldn't lie to you."

"I think you're both lying." She turned over on her side, yawning heavily. "I want to sleep until I can see my baby. Get somebody to bring me something to make me sleep."

She didn't look at either of us or say anything while we waited for the nurse to bring some pills.

"Just put them there," Kim told the nurse when she came, motioning to the night table. "Good night, Grove and Gina."

We were dismissed. We told each other that her mood was understandable. We also agreed that whatever her suspicions were, she did not suspect the worst.

In the morning she would be rested and feel stronger. She would be in much better shape to confront the truth.

Kim was wide awake when we left. She didn't take the pills until much later. She waited until she knew we were out of the building. She got out of the bed, woozy and wobbly. The easiest thing would have been to fall back on the bed. If she did, she might not get up again. It seemed to take her an hour to stagger to the closet. She threw a robe around her and poked her head outside the door. Time was on her side. It was one o'clock in the morning. The corridor was deserted.

It might take her the rest of the night to get there. It might be the longest journey she would ever make. But she must make it and get there. . . .

She inched her way down the long corridor. It stretched on and on, like a runway to the moon.

From Dahlia, she knew where she must go. It was not to that big room with the picture window where all the proud papas peeked in at their newborn, each one tucked up in its bassinet with the neat nameplate identifying it. No, that was not where she would find her son. She would find him in that third-floor rear room—without the picture windows—where "the others" were kept.

It took her half a lifetime, stumbling a million miles, until she reached that red light Exit sign. Leaning heavily on the bannister, she slowly and painfully made her way down two flights of stairs.

She opened the door just a crack.

There it was. That must be the room.

There was a window. But it wasn't a picture window. This was no showcase for beautiful, healthy newborn babies. These were not the babies any hospital would want to show off.

Through the window Kim could see a nurse bustling around. She also saw two tanks that looked like aquariums. Incubators obviously.

She closed the door and fell back on the railing to get her strength. Then she opened the door a slit again and watched. She repeated the process for what seemed like an eternity.

It must have been nearly dawn when she saw the nurse take one last glance all around the room and leave. Through the slightly opened door Kim watched her walk briskly to the bank of elevators halfway down the corridor. She waited until she heard elevator doors closing on the nurse. Kim took a deep breath and made it across the narrow hall in four or five quick steps. She opened the door into the room of "the others."

The light was dim. It was a smallish room. Not like the big nursery where thirty or forty babies might be on display. Here were the incubator babies . . . and "the others." The freaks.

There he was. Forbes, Randolph . . .

Oh, my God!

Its head was huge. The face was round and pressed flat as a nickel. Out of that flat nothing a nose twisted up like a pig's snout. The eyes were enormous. Bulging, thyroidal, and they were open, staring at her with a ghastly intensity.

Under the covers lay a stumpy, distorted body with a club foot.

Kim put her hand to her mouth. But her shriek penetrated to the far ends of the floor.

A nurse—a different one—was there in a flash.

"What's this all about?" the nurse cried. "Who are you? You don't belong here. What are you doing here? You get out of here—"

Kim raised her head from the bassinet to the nurse.

"Oh, Mrs. Forbes, I'm sorry. I didn't know it was you. I'm so terribly sorry. I'm so terribly sorry about   everything."

"Tell me one thing. What is . . . *this*?"

"Haven't they told you? Oh, Mrs. Forbes, I am so sorry."

"Stop being so goddamn sorry and tell me what this goddamn thing is."

"It's—*he's*—a Mongoloid, Mrs. Forbes. And I'm sorry."

"I've seen it," Kim greeted us when we came in the next morning

"Oh, Kim," Grosvenor and I both said together. We were like a Greek chorus.

"I've seen it," she repeated coldly. "And I never want to lay eyes on it again. I don't care what you do but get rid of it. There must be places—institutions—that take care of such babies. Find one and tell them to come and get this one. I don't care how much it costs. This . . . thing came ouf of me. I'll be responsible for it. If I had to scrub floors or go on the streets hooking, I'll see that it's cared for as long as it lives. Or I live. But I don't ever want to lay eyes on it again."

The day she was to leave the hospital Kim had a surprise and unwelcome visit from Ryder Downey. He came bearing a large box of chocolates from Blum's.

"Well, you're looking marvelous!" he cooed. "I'm dying to see the little heir—or heiress."

"It's a boy. But I'm afraid you can't see him now."

"I'm so disappointed. Why not?"

She thought fast. "He seems to be having some breathing difficulties. He's in a special contraption. It may be an asthmatic condition."

"Uh-huh," said Ryder, with his mocking smile.

Chapter 28

Randolph Forbes must be twelve now. Closer to thirteen. Kim has never seen him. I doubt that Grosvenor has either. Her son could be dead for all she knows firsthand. How she knows her son is not dead is that the monthly bills from the Verde Desert Home in Lost Valley, Arizona, keep coming in.

Kim's bills are all paid by her accountants. You can be sure the accountants know the boy is alive. The kind of accountants people like Kim hire get paid to check such things out. They don't plunk out for goods unreceived or services unrendered. One way or another Berkwith & Berkwith of Beverly Hills have satisfied their curiosity that the boy is alive. Kim pays them for that curiosity. It is a curiosity she herself does not share.

The subject of Randolph Forbes never comes up. The accountants know better. Interviewers with long memories know better than to bring up the subject.

Movie-goers with long memories dimly recall that Kimberley Hudson had a child years and years ago. Wasn't it a boy born with a severe respiratory problem? So severe he had to live in a special climate—Arizona?. And didn't they read somewhere that Miss Hudson always rushed off to Arizona the moment a picture was finished? Scratch a star and you find just an ordinary, flesh-and-blood human being. . . .

That poor woman! That poor suffering mother!

"Your child is a statistic," Dr. Lacey told Kim. "Once in so many thousand births—six, eight, ten, I can't tell you precisely off the top of my head—a child is born . . . this way. And that's all it is. A statistic. It just happens and there is no rhyme or reason to it. It could happen to anybody—under the best of circumstances. And it does. There's no way to forecast such a baby. Even hindsight there's no way you could have seen it coming. It's just a slip-up in the cosmos . . ."

Kim pulled the pillows around her ears, drowning him out.

"Kim," I pleaded. "Please say something to me. There isn't anything in the world I wouldn't do for you. Please, please, tell me something I can do."

"Go home."

"Hard cheese, my poor darling," said Grosvenor. "But not the end of the line. We'll have more babies."

"No. There won't be any more babies. With you. Or anybody else."

For three months she was in Catatonicsville.
Alone.
In the guest room in Macdougal Alley.

It was years before she could talk about that terrible time in her life.

I doubt that she ever talked about it more than once.

But on that occasion the circumstances were just right. I was awaiting the birth of my first child. We were having lunch at my house on Doheny Drive. (I had moved up in the world, thanks to a no-thanks marriage.) The next day Kim was flying to join David Glasgow in Mazatlan. Under the circumstances, she was happy enough to be able to talk about that deeply unhappy, traumatizing experience.

She was also tipsy enough, after a second martini, to have a loose tongue. I wouldn't have had to be there. She spoke in

289

a soft, low monologue: "I hope I'm done with hate in my life," she began. "I lost a whole chunk of my life just hating. I could hardly open my eyes. I couldn't eat. The trays went back untouched. I couldn't bear the sound of anybody's voice. I sat in that back room. And I hated. I hated so much I was paralyzed. That's what hatred you don't spit out will do for you. You go into a depression that drains the life out of you.

"Hatred is such a cancer. Once it gets started it spreads everywhere. All I had to do was to think about somebody and I'd start hating him. But my thoughts didn't go much beyond Grosvenor and me. God, how I hated us both! I was on a seesaw trying to figure out who was to blame, who was the one I should be hating with all my heart. Grosvenor or me. I kept zigzagging back and forth. There was such a good case against both of us.

"The case against Grosvenor was easier to live with. It was a mistake to marry anyone that much older. He didn't want the child. So we were rewarded with a child no one would want. All that exercise he made me do was a fiendish mistake. It scrambled up my insides. He was decadent, perverted. That wanting to be beaten by whores. Just watching it—especially when I was seven months pregnant—must have done violent things to my nervous system. Oh, it was easy to find Grosvenor guilty and hang him.

"Too easy. My mind, simple as it is, wouldn't buy it. Maybe I should look closer to home for an explanation. To myself. For the first time in my life I thought maybe there is a God. And this was His punishment for the messy life I had lived. Or maybe it was His way of setting the scales straight for all the shoddy values the Hollywood scene promotes. I thought also maybe I got what I deserved for tricking Grosvenor into the pregnancy. I even thought the jinx came from wanting to name the baby for Randy, who was just about the most jinxed person I ever knew.

"While I was at it, I even hated Dr. Lacey. The day after—after I had seen what I had seen but he didn't know I had—he came into my room and sat on the edge of the bed and launched into this nice sweet philosophical chitchat. About how sometimes babies weren't born to the exact specifications of their mothers. Sometimes they even had obvious defects that would require lots of special attention. There was no predicting how mothers would react to such babies. Some mothers wished the babies had never been born. But there were other mothers who clasped these babies to their bosoms and loved them more passionately than they would a baby who could win a beauty contest. Blah, blah, blah.

"I think I hated Dr. Lacey because he dumped in my lap

the hated image of myself. I wasn't one of those mothers who could love the freak more than the cherub. I wouldn't let the freak shit on my—quote unquote—beauty by even acknowledging its existence . . ."

Hating and depression.

This was her life, day after day stretching into weeks. She kept to her room, spoke to no one. She watched the soaps on television without seeing them. She drank bourbon steadily, from waking to oblivion. And she brooded.

She must leave here, leave Grosvenor. But how? When? It would take so much strength. So much concentration. And she was fresh out of strength and concentration.

"My dear bride of Heathcliffe," said Grosvenor one day, barging in on her privacy. "Enough is enough."

Who was Heathcliffe? she wondered foggily. Who was Heathcliffe's bride?

"I think I have been patient perhaps longer than is consistent with good judgment," he went on. "To use a corny line from everybody's favorite Grade Z movie, 'We can't go on like this.' "

Exactly! Thank god, *he* was bringing up the subject! Of course they couldn't go on like this. He was asking for a divorce. He wanted out as much as she did.

"Now I'm not saying you're loco or anything like that," said Grosvenor. "But I do think you are overreacting to . . . well, a less-than-fatal tragedy. I am going to insist that you do one thing. Think of it, if you like, as a favor to me—perhaps the only one I'll ever ask of you. I am going to insist that you keep an appointment I have made for you. It's with one Dr. Feinberger on upper Fifth Avenue. He's a psychoanalyst. One of the best. He should be—at a hundred bucks a clip. I think an hour with him will do you a world of good. It's all arranged. I've hired a Carey limo to pick you up and wait for you. . . ."

So he *wasn't* asking for a divorce. He just wanted her to get straightened out. And a shrink was supposed to work this miracle in one fifty-minute hour.

It was easier to give in than to argue. She didn't have to look at him or say anything.

Grosvenor was waiting for her when she got home.

He held out his arms to her. She sailed past him.

"My darling," he said, "I do think you owe me some minimal account of your dialogue with Dr. Feinberger."

"Gladly," said Kim. "I'll tell you about Dr. Feinberger. He's full of bullshit. A hundred bucks an hour for bullshit. 'Now, Mrs. Forbes, do you have any clue to why you're reacting in such an exaggerated fashion . . . ?' Bullshit. They're all full of bullshit. It's the last time anybody ever gets me to talk to one of those bullshitters. Not even if they pay *me!*"

"Hold on, dearest," said Grosvenor. "I think we're getting somewhere. I think Dr. Feinberger has earned his fee. Do you realize something? You're talking again. The cat that got your tongue has been caught. Caught and charged with grand larceny. And made to return the tongue to its owner."

"Now that I have my tongue back," said Kim, "I've got a message for you. I'm leaving you."

"I should never have married Grosvenor," Kim said to me that day. "He played my uncle in the movie and I should have let it go at that. He'd have made a good uncle or a wise, older friend. My life story always reads like a lousy movie script. One of the reasons, I think, is I can never tell where a movie stops and real life should pick up. I let one slop over into the other. I never know where to get off stage."

The news that was heard around the world was heard first in the Alley. By Ryder Downey.

Who else?

Kim received a note hand-thrust into their mail slot.

"Sweetikins," it read. "Congratulations! Must see you. Have I got a getting-divorced present for you!"

Kim ignored the note.

The next day Ryder came down harder.

"Imperative that I see you! *Before you go.*"

She tossed the second note into the circular file.

Half an hour later Mrs. Harrison, the housekeeper, told her Mr. Downey was at the door, begging to see her for just a few minutes.

Oh, hell, Kim thought. Might as well see him and get it over with.

"Well," said Ryder, "the Queen is receiving. We haven't seen you in many a moon, have we?"

"I guess not, Ryder. I haven't been going out much."

"And now you'll be saying bye-bye to our little corner of the world."

"It looks that way."

"I told you I had a little lagniappe that just demanded to be delivered into your lily-whites."

He handed her an envelope he was carrying. "Open."

There was a picture of Tiger Lily and San San coming out the front door of the house in Macdougal Alley.

"How on earth did you get this?"

"I took it with my own little Baby Brownie. About two

thirty one morning when those Asian charmers were tripping out your door."

Oh-oh. She could remember the night. The thing that seemed like a crack of lightning as it flashed through the curtained bedroom window was Ryder's camera. The footsteps she heard in pursuit of Tiger Lily and San San's clicking heels must have been Ryder's.

Kim had a sense of foreboding doom.

"Our cooking teachers," she said lightly.

"Cooking teachers, my ass. Don't tell me I can't spot a couple of hookers when I see them."

"What their other talents might be, I can't say. I know we engaged them——"

"Sweetikins, don't play games with your Uncle Ryder. He's been through the mill enough times—and come out sawdust—to know the score. You might also be interested to know the girls were in a talkative mood that night. I asked them if they would join me for a nightcap in the Jumble Shop. I flashed a fifty-dollar bill in their faces and said that it could be theirs if they'd join me. It looked pretty good to them. It was money under the table, so to speak. They wouldn't have to split it with the madame. And they wouldn't have to turn a trick with each other or anybody else to get it. All that was wanted was their sweet society and a bit of civilized conversation. Well, Mrs. Forbes, some of the beans that were spilled that night!"

"What do you want?"

"That's something I'd like to explore with you. I tell you what I *don't* want. I don't want to write that story for *Confidential* magazine on how Grosvenor Forbes and Kimberley Hudson got their jollies. Even after Mrs. Forbes was well along in her pregnancy. But can you imagine how wild *Confidential* would go if they were offered such a juicy morsel? Nor would I ever want to speculate in print *anywhere* about the whereabouts and disposition of Mrs. Forbes's child——"

"My child is a severe asthmatic. He's in Arizona. He'll always have to live in a dry climate."

"Sweetikins, he may be in Arizona. But not because of asthma. It's an awfully convenient place to stash away a Mongoloid."

"Really, Ryder, you don't know what you're——"

"Don't tell me I don't recognize a Mongoloid when I see one," he cut in. "A nurse reluctantly showed a 'dear old friend of the family' young Randolph Forbes on being assured that Mrs. Forbes had granted her permission. No, I don't want to exploit either situation. The visits of the Asian girls and the nature of their services. Or the unfortunate trag-

293

edy of young Randolph Forbes. I've always had a loathing of anything that smacked of blackmail."

"I'd like to know what you call this."

"Not so, not so. Untalented people traffic in blackmail. If you've got anything on the ball, you don't have to stoop to that. I have talent. Talent that I think could be extremely enhancing to you and your career. You're going back now and I predict you're going to be the biggest, hottest thing in the business. I think you ain't seen nuttin' yet. The kind of success you'll have. The kind of trouble you'll attract. You need an experienced trouble-shooter, an all-around personal press relations specialist. Someone who can have you coming up smelling roses whatever mess of garbage you fall into. You need the kind of special, personalized, full-time attention no studio can give you. You need *me*. I honestly think I'm your man. . . ."

Ryder Downey indeed turned out to be her man.

He became the first of a more or less permanent entourage that kept growing and growing. Eventually there were thirteen personal retainers, one of whom had no other responsibility than to keep tab of Kim's jewelry.

None of them was more devoted than Ryder Downey.

Ryder came to absolutely adore—*worship*—Kim.

Three years ago, when Kim turned thirty-five, Ryder thought it was the milestone that called for a biography. And who was better qualified to write it than himself?

If you've read *Kimberley* by Ryder Downey, you get my point about his devotion.

It's what the book publishing business calls "an authorized biography."

If you've read it, you know what I mean. I mean, that book dripped honey and goo from page 1 to page 237 (the last page). If Kim is anything less than a saint, if she isn't ripe for canonizing, if she has a teeny-tiny shortcoming or ever did anything that was less than righteous, you'd never guess it from reading *Kimberley*.

Ryder has served his mistress well.

The day the news broke—about her divorcing Grosvenor Forbes—Kim got a wire from Marty North.

"Must see you," it read. "Told you when we met I had something spectacular for you."

Chapter 29

Marty North, riding a high crest of success, was at his cockiest. His *Christopher Columbus Discovers America* had opened all around the country to rave reviews and smashing business at the box office. In a town where you're only as good as your last picture, now he could write his own ticket.

Marty's career had had its ups and downs. But even when he was scraping the bottom, nobody doubted for a moment that he was a born showman. When he flopped, his creative spark still shone through. Nobody conceived things the way Marty North did. Maybe being short was one of the reasons he always thought big. He was conceiving spectaculars before the word was invented.

Marty North was born Hyman Hirshberg on Rivington Street on Manhattan's Lower East Side. As Marty told it, he never finished the third grade. He was the sole support of his whole family by the time he was ten years old. He got his background by sneaking into all the Yiddish productions on Second Avenue as soon as he could talk.

Bluff and bravado had carried Marty a long way ... from burleycues in Passaic, New Jersey, to slick "girls and garters" shows that toured all the army camps at home and abroad during World War II to a big Broadway smash and four bombs to a string of low-budget flicks that got panned by the critics but found an audience via word-of-mouth because they had moxie and energy and flair.

And then to the grandiose *Christopher Columbus Discovers America* that had many of the highest-paid talents in the business doing cameo bits for free. Fast-talking Marty snowed them into believing they'd be appearing in *the* picture of the century.

Which *Christopher Columbus* might yet turn out to be.

Marty bought a gargantuan mansion on top of Beverly Hills with breathtaking views that swept from Old Baldy to the Santa Barbara Islands to Catalina. He gave out interviews modestly admitting he was "the greatest," and if you thought *Christopher Columbus* was a masterpiece, "you ain't seen nuttin' yet."

Kim called him the day after she got back to the Coast. If he had her in mind for something "spectacular," she wanted to see him fast. Getting back to work again, after all the months of not working and the sad news and the blah-ness, might be pretty exciting. Especially if she would be working with the hottest producer in the business.

"Come back to me, little *shiksa,*" Marty North oozed into the phone. "How fast can you get your little *tushy* over here?"

Shiksa? Tushy? Oh, God, somebody else she couldn't understand.

"Tomorrow morning."

"Not any sooner?"

Marty North sat at a desk about twice the size of a billiard table. He was in shirt sleeves, chomping on a cigar. He wore fire-engine red suspenders and a black derby tipped forward jauntily on his brow.

He signed something with a wild flourish and sent the pen rolling across the huge desk.

"So," said Marty. "We come together. The union of the greats."

"We've met before," Kim reminded him.

"Foreplay. We meet. Now. To make spectacular music. Together."

"I'm not very musical," said Kim.

"*Shiksa,*" said Marty. "With me you're gonna hum and sing and pluck strings of the most expensive Stradivarius in the world. We'll make heavenly music."

"Do you have a score?"

"Baby, I *am* the score. *Pardonnez.* You and I will be the score. We'll score together."

He wasn't the least bit handsome. He was short and plump. He had straight, thick bushy eyebrows that jutted out like canopies over bright black dancing eyes. His skin was sallow and soft and flabby and when he looked down he had a jowly look and two well-developed chins.

Even though Marty North was not young—he must be way over forty—he shot off sparks. He breathed excitement. He charged the air with electricity. Kim remembered the phrase she had used to describe him to Grosvenor the night she met him at a party: bottled lightning. He was lightning and what was she doing in the path of lightning?

"Those are beautiful cuff links," Kim said nervously.

"They should be. I designed them myself."

She still didn't have the foggiest notion of what he wanted to talk to her about. He was too busy proclaiming his greatness, pointing to plaques and prizes all over the room. He was holding up sheafs of reviews and reading her the latest *Variety* figures on the grosses of *Christopher Columbus.*

"I can see I'm in the presence of genius," Kim finally interrupted him. "But I always knew you were a genius. So can you please tell me precisely why I'm here?"

"You're here because I got something big to talk to you about and I haven't got time to go into it now because I'm getting a call any second from New York and I've got to take it and so our business will have to wait until tomorrow when you join me on my yacht for a sail and a *nosh* and some sweet-talk. I'll have James pick you up at eleven. It'll be nice, nice, nice. No phones. So nobody can get at me."

"Or *me*," said Kim. "And if you hadn't taken up so much time talking about yourself, we might have got to what was on your mind."

"Touché, shiksa."

Kim hooted when she saw him on the *Santa Maria*. He was all decked out like a commodore. The short, squat figure was sheathed in white and he wore a white, braided cap cocked at a jaunty angle.

Kim hooted from nerves as much as the sight of Marty North. Even the yacht unnerved her. It must have been more than a hundred feet long.

"Nice little canoe you have here," she said.

"Yeah. I designed it myself."

The *Santa Maria* (he would have to take a name out of *Christopher Columbus*!) began to move after she came aboard. But where it went she couldn't have said to save her life.

Commodore North sat them down at a table for two topside.

Something with tequila (not a Margherita because the filler tasted like papaya juice) was poured by a steward into tall frosted glasses.

"You didn't know why you were in my office yesterday," Marty said. "I did. But I was too busy. I'm hotter'n a cannon, you gotta realize. You gotta realize when you got something going, you ride her like a bitch."

"I realize," said Kim, smiling sweetly. "I also realize something else. You're full of crap. You're up to your eyeballs in crap."

He doffed his cap to her. Saluting her, he pushed his knees forward to touch hers under the table.

Jesus, God, she thought, what's he doing? What's happening? Don't let it happen. Where am I? Where in hell are we drifting in this goddamn boat?

"Touché, shiksa," he repeated.

His knees brushed against hers.

The sky reeled and the calm Pacific seemed to be roaring into wild rollers that would wash over the deck, engulf her, and suck her down, down, down. Oh, no. Oh, no. Not now. Just when she was beginning to breathe again. She mustn't go under, down.

"You know why you're here, don't you, *bubeleh?*"

"I don't," she said, laughing shakily. "Give me just one guess and I'd say you were trying to lay me."

"What a way to go!" Marty cried, tossing his skipper's hat into the air. "I couldn't think of a better way to go *schlepping* between Long Beach and Oceanside. But I got something even bigger in mind for me."

"Do tell me," said Kim.

"You're going to marry me, that's what."

"No," she said.

"Oh, yes, you are, little girl-chick. You might not know it but you are. I'll tell you something else. I'd write out a check for a mil right on the spot to be honeymooning on this yacht right now. But no hanky-panky until we get the knot tied. You don't catch me opening my Chanukah presents in August."

"You're crazy."

"Maybe. But determined too."

His knees brushed against hers again, more insistently this time. She went dizzy from the contact. She closed her eyes. Let him think it was the sun . . . or that she was drowsy from the food and drink.

Let him think anything—as long as he didn't see how hard she was trying to hold on to herself.

NO!

Please, God, let me have just a little peace and quiet.

It mustn't happen.

Marty North coming on like a ton of bricks was mostly the reason Kim jumped at the chance to go to Texas. The picture was called *Land of Kings*. It was going to be a big one about some big people in the biggest state of them all. Everything about it was going to be big. The size of the cast, the budget, the shooting schedule (five months).

They wanted Kim to play Amanda Delderfield. In the beginning of the film she would be a beautiful twenty-one-year-old bride. She was to age until at the end of the film she was a ninety-year-old great-great grandmother and the grand matriarch of the whole Delderfield clan.

"So I end up old and ugly?" Kim said to Tony Crespin, the producer.

"It'll give you a chance to show your stuff as an actress,"

he said. "And don't worry. Who's going to forget for one second after the movie's over that Kimberley Hudson is still young and exquisite? But they'll go out of the theaters saying, 'Jesus Christ, what an actress she turned out to be too!' "

To Tony Crespin's surprise, Kim didn't need much urging.

Kim wasn't surprised much that Tony Crespin's predictions all came true. *Land of Kings* turned out to be a blockbuster. The reviews of the picture were overwhelmingly favorable. The reviews of Kim's performance were almost universally enthusiastic. Typically they read:

We should be contented to gaze upon someone so blindingly beautiful as Kimberley Hudson. Apparently Miss Hudson is not contented to be blindingly beautiful. In *Land of Kings* she has had the courage to assay a role that shows her in the unglamorous poses of extreme age. In daring to do so, she has added immeasurably to her stature as an actress. No longer can we look at her as a beautiful face determined to show only that beautiful face. . . .

Why did she bury herself for five months in Texas during a long, hot summer, everyone wanted to know.

"It was a good script," she replied. "By this time, I do know a good script when I see one."

"Was that the only reason?" somebody asked.

"Look," she laughed. "It wasn't even the main reason. I went to Texas to keep Marty North out of my hair."

"Kiddo, you won't get away from me," Marty told her before she started the film.

"Yes, I will. I'm going to Texas."

"I'll be there."

"No, you won't. If you dare come, I'll walk. If I walk, production stops. It won't be my fault. It'll be yours. I'll tell them I can't work with you around. I can't concentrate. You're a nuisance. A distraction."

"You won't get away with it, kiddo. *Mein shiksa.*"

"I'm coming."

"No, you're not. I'll walk."

That's how their nightly conversation started the first two weeks she was in Waco.

Then he tried a new tack.

"You gotta see me. I gotta show you my new plane."

"You don't have a plane."

"Wait till you see it. I designed it myself."

"I don't believe you, in the first place. In the second place, I'm not interested."

"Baby, if you think you is gonna win this one, you doesn't know your competition."

Every one of those long, hot Texas nights she practically hung up on Marty North.

And couldn't get back to sleep.

The hotel was air-conditioned. But the ranch twenty miles out of Waco where they were shooting wasn't air-conditioned. The heat of the Texas summer was almost insufferable. She got back to the hotel drained, inert.

Then came that call.

It was like a narcotic. It would jab her from a deep funk into such an upper she'd be awake the rest of the night.

And dead on the set the next morning.

"Leave me alone!" she screamed at him one night. "You're ruining my health. I must get my sleep."

"So must I. We must get it together."

"That's not the answer."

"Cable me when you get a better one."

"Marty, for God's sake, get lost!"

"Kimmie, without you, I *am* lost."

He sent her bundles of flowers every day. Shipments of packaged dinners from the best restaurants in Los Angeles came every day by air, as if Texas was starvation country.

"You're stark raving mad," she told him.

"No," he said. "Maybe a little *meshugge*. But not mad."

Bits of romantic poetry he had written and dedicated to her arrived regularly in the mails.

Sometimes there was romantic music in the background when he called. "I'm dancing," he'd croon into the phone, "and dreaming that I'm holding you in my arms."

She wondered how she'd look dancing with a man inches shorter than she was. Then she realized she had almost forgotten he was short and had begun to think of him as tall. It must be because he talked so big and had all this wild energy and drive.

"You're going to get a boot out of being married to me," he declared in one of the last calls she got in Texas. "It'll be an education."

"The smart thing for you to do," said Kim, "is forget about me and find yourself a nice Jewish girl."

"No thank you. I had me one of those the first time around. Christ, she nearly drove me deaf with her yakittyyak-yak. She had a mouth as big as the Mississippi. No, I've found me the girl I want."

"If there were no other arguments against it," said Kim, "and I can think of a million, we're not of the same religion."

"What religion are you?"

"I really don't have any," she answered honestly.

"We have the same religion."

The day shooting was over, Marty North sent his plane for Kim to bring her back to the Coast. It was a Lear jet and not something Marty had designed himself.

Marty was waiting for her at the airport. At the sight of her he let out a whoop and a holler and threw his ten-gallon hat in the air. He made a lunge for her and grabbed her in his arms. The cigar came out of his mouth so he could kiss her.

It was their first kiss.

Her senses spinning, Kim knew she had lost the battle with Marty North.

And was ecstatic to have lost it.

Chapter 30

As he promised, Marty North *was* an education. He educated Kim about a lot of things. Too bad that education was cut so short.

Kim's marriage to Marty was the one I thought would really take. I know Kim thought so too. Marty was the husband of Kim's I really dug. He was a long way from being an angel. He had a violent temper and he never got tired of telling you he was the greatest. He drove a tough bargain and he wasn't above stretching the truth or conning people to gain his ends. But he was such a fascinating man. So creative and explosive. I don't know if he was a genius but he was the nearest thing to one I ever met in the flesh.

The first thing Marty taught Kim was to think big. Really big. He put a rock on her finger as big as an egg. Her wedding ring. That was just for openers.

"I credit Marty with whetting my appetite for jewelry," she said later. "Geordie Harmon gave me a few little trinkets. Grosvenor didn't have enough to buy me anything. Not that he would have anyway. Those New England Yankees are the cheapest breed going. No, it was Marty who taught me what a woman's best friend is."

When *Land of Kings* began shaping up as a big multimillion dollar grosser, Marty showed his muscle at the Studio. He went into the front office and yelled and argued Kim's case. Soon he was boasting—truthfully—that he was married to the highest paid woman under contract in Hollywood.

The house Marty moved Kim into was something else. Marty nicknamed it The Pearly Gates. You were up so high and the views were so spectacular, one step more and you'd be in heaven.

The house was a gigantic palazzo with huge wings on either side and a cobblestone courtyard in front. It went with the canyons of Southern California about like an adobe hut in Greenland. What made The Pearly Gates so fascinating were all the special effects. A band pavilion big enough to seat the whole Los Angeles Philharmonic. A canal that circled the property like a moat with honest to God gondolas floating around in it. A movie theater carved out of the side of the mountain like a cave. And a swimming pool, so help me, in the shape of two melony boobs.

"Fabulous!" everybody exclaimed seeing it for the first time.

"It should be," said Marty modestly. "I designed it myself."

Kim sold the Benedict Canyon place and moved her mother and Indiana to The Pearly Gates.

It took a staff of fourteen to keep The Pearly Gates going.

When they entertained, which wasn't often, whole catering crews were imported. On those special occasions, Marty always dreamed up a special motif. His parties always had to be bigger, costlier, and more artistically wrought than anybody else's.

Seeing Kim with Marty, I had no doubt that the scars had healed. I had no doubt that she was all wound up in him. It was more than love and desire. He electrified her. She found him continuously engrossing and entertaining and magnetic. And a little exotic, like someone from a mysterious land halfway around the world.

"Oh, God, Gina," she exclaimed. "He's a dynamo! The atom bomb fell on Hiroshima and rose in him."

As I say, I liked Marty. Liked him a lot. With all his bragging and bullying and yelling and bouncing around, there was an underlying sweetness and sensitivity. And that capacity for deep tenderness you find in so many Jewish men.

Whatever problems Kim might have with Marty, I couldn't think that infidelity would be one of them. He struck me as a one-woman guy who had found his woman. He looked at her with eyes that could have turned icebergs into warm Gulf Streams.

Marty could be kind and generous when he set out to be. I have him to thank for a couple of nice dubbing jobs I got at the Studio. In those musicals it's me you hear singing while the nonsinging heroine mouths the words on camera.

I also have Marty to thank for introducing me to my future husband, Matt Berliner, the ace lawyer at the Studio. Actually I remembered Matt from the days when I was a child at the Studio. Remembered him for all the girlish fantasies I had had about him and because I had never been able to get him out of my mind.

But it was Marty who introduced me to Matt. For that I have Marty to thank. Thanks but no thanks.

My invitations to The Pearly Gates were always for Sundays. Usually it was a swimming and brunch sort of thing. We'd sit around the vulgar-looking pool sipping whiskey sours or Bloody Marys (weak spritzers for me) and relax until mid-afternoon, when we'd go in to tackle the groaning board.

Marty was darting here, there, and everywhere. From the pool phone to the bank of phones in his office to the phone in the band pavilion. Marty's voice barking into the phone was always the backdrop for whatever conversation or activities might be going on.

The Sundays I was there the group was always small. Never more than six guests.

The only two guests I saw there regularly were Eileen Wyman and Bernie Miller. Eileen and Bernie had been man and wife for eight or nine years and had some kids. Eileen was America's Singing Sweetheart. She had starred in half a dozen or so Studio musicals that had done okay. Bernie was a nightclub comedian whose *shtik* was impressions. Now he was just starting to make it a bit in movies, where he was usually cast as the comic sidekick of the hero.

Both Eileen and Bernie had dimples. They looked cute and healthy and wholesome. The whole country had embraced them as their Favorite Young Couple. I personally found them boring. Don't look to comics to be funny offstage. Especially a Bernie Miller who bought all his material when he worked the clubs.

I think Kim felt the same way about them.

"Somebody should put them in a movie together," she said, "and call it *Apple Pie Meets Coca-Cola*."

It was Marty who wanted them there. But why?

Jealous Kim looked sharply for hints that he had designs

303

on Eileen. But she had a hard time finding them. So did I. Eileen would never in a million years be Marty's type. Even in a bathing suit she seemed to be wearing a long gingham dress with a Peter Pan collar. She was dull, dull, dull.

Marty apparently found her that way, too. Most of his attention focussed on Bernie. Between them there were all kinds of exchanges, mostly in Yiddish, which only they seemed to understand. Marty could never pass Bernie without tussling his thick wavy hair or giving him a little pat on the cheek.

"If I have to bust my balls doing it," he told Kim, "I'm going to produce something that'll put that kid up there where he should be. I'm not going to stand by and see him play second banana to that tight, squeaky cunt he's married to."

So a darker suspicion entered her mind. Was Marty's interest in Bernie maybe . . . well, homosexual? But she doubted that there was any of that in Marty. Not from the way he went at her as soon as they hit the sheets.

It must be some bond between them, that of their shared Jewishness. Both of them had grown up in ghettos (Bernie was from Newark). Marty was older and on top now and was just trying to pass along his good luck to someone who could still use a boost.

She got a clearer idea of what the relationship might mean by something Marty said to her one night in bed.

"If you'd take that damn thing out of your cunt," he said irritably, "we might have some kids of our own."

"No," she answered. "It stays in there. No kids." It was then it occurred to her that Marty treated Bernie like a son.

One Sunday the tension lurking beneath the calm exterior of Eileen and Bernie's marriage erupted.

When the houseboy came around to take refill orders on the drinks, Bernie ordered another Bloody Mary.

"Oh, Bernie," said Eileen, pursing her rosebud lips, "should you?"

"Should I what?"

"Have another drink? That'll be your third."

"Haven't you anything better to do," Bernie snapped, "than to count my drinks?"

Marty was darting from phone to phone in one of his familiar con acts: "No, Don, I don't see how I can cut you in on this one. Not unless somebody backs out . . ."

Yelling into another phone, so Don couldn't help overhearing: "Sam, everybody's dying to get aboard and we don't

304

need 'em. We were oversubscribed from the second the word got out what we were up to . . ."

No Sam on the other end of the line, and Don screaming to plunk down some big ones into Marty's new hot property, in which no one had as yet invested a dime. All the while Bernie and Eileen bickered. Kim was bored, and maybe peeved with them. If they couldn't be interesting, at least they could refrain from pouting.

Mostly to break away from them, I guessed, she slipped into the pool and stayed there. When the rest of us went in for lunch, she said she'd stay in the pool a while longer.

We had hardly sat down when we heard her blood-curdling scream.

Marty got to the scene before anybody else. By the time the rest of us got there he had already lifted her out of the pool and laid her gently on the ground, still screaming in pain.

She had slipped on the steps of the pool as she was coming out and had gone bump, bump down to the bottom of the pool on her fanny.

Marty summoned the ambulance, and then practically turned the hospital upside down to get the whole staff to drop everything and come dance attendance upon Kim.

The doctors took X-rays and stuck pins in her back. They tickled her feet and legs with feathers.

"See, Marty?" she said. "I can feel that. There's nothing wrong with me."

"You're staying right here. Flat on your back."

In a few days she couldn't feel the feathers. She couldn't feel anything in her right leg even when they stuck pins in it and drew blood. She couldn't stand on it. The leg was paralyzed.

Marty summoned a bone specialist from Boston. The bone specialist only confirmed the diagnosis that had already been given by the local staff.

Kim faced an operation and a long, slow recovery. Three discs were gone completely.

They cut away all the dead bone right down to the nerve center. Bone was taken from her hip, her pelvis, and from a bone bank. They made little matchsticks from these that formed into clusters and finally calcified and became an extended column, maybe six inches long.

Then came the real agony. To keep the bone from sagging in any one direction they had to rotate her body every three hours for almost three weeks. They had a sheet pulling one way and a sheet pulling the other to get her body rolled around.

The rotation process was almost unbearably agonizing.

"I don't care how much goddamn pain she's in," Marty screamed to everybody who was attending her. "I don't want you shooting her up with drugs. She has a low tolerance for drugs."

In a softer voice, I heard him say, "Of course I care about the pain she's in. I'd let you chop my right arm off if I could be in that bed instead of her. I just want to make sure she walks out of here alive."

I loved Marty for that. He was showing his true colors. And he kept showing his true colors.

Kim was in the hospital for six weeks. Marty was there almost every hour she was awake. He postponed all his plans and activities to stay at Kim's bedside. He never made or took calls there. He held her hand all day long and his warm eyes never strayed from her.

She had the best of rooms. But the best of rooms in the best of hospitals always seem to be painted snot-green. Marty brought his Wyeth and Monet and Degas from The Pearly Gates to cover up the vomity-looking walls. And he had a standing order with a florist so that fresh flowers arrived every day.

Plus all the expensive remembrances from the jewelers.

"Marty, you've got to stop this," Kim protested. The box she had just opened contained a pair of diamond teardrop earrings. "*Nobody* can afford all these presents."

"I'd rather die," said Marty, "than stop it."

One day Marty brought a guest with him. It was Bernie Miller.

"Here's Bernie to cheer you up," he explained.

"Say something funny, Bernie," said Kim.

"How are you feeling, Kim?"

"*That's* funny?"

Before she left the hospital, Kim had to learn how to walk all over again.

At home she had to spend weeks more recuperating before she could go back to work. Her next picture had to be postponed for nearly three months.

Marty's welcome home present to her was Boardman Robinson, the society portrait painter. Mr. Robinson, who didn't come cheap, had been commissioned by Marty to do her portrait.

"I want him to get you down the way you are at this moment," Marty said. "So you will be immortal. Immortal at your zenith. For the rest of recorded history. Robinson's hand will stop time. Long after you and I and ours are dust, generations to come will see you as alive and ravishing as you are today."

Kim found that posing for Boardman Robinson was marvelous therapy. The weeks in the hospital had made her svelter than at any time in her adult life. She was only months away from her thirtieth birthday, but her own mirror—and the likeness of her taking shape on Mr. Robinson's canvas—told her it was an inspired time to be sitting for her portrait.

While Boardman Robinson was painting her, Kim got some news that gave her morale a real hypo. For her work in *Land of Kings* she was nominated for an Oscar as Best Actress.

Marty's *Christopher Columbus Discovers America* was nominated for Best Picture.

"We'll show the rest of those fucking amateurs what it's all about," Marty boasted. "The Norths will both come away with an Oscar. Mark my words."

"Oh, Marty," said Kim, hoping with all her heart that he was right, "how can you predict such a thing?"

"*Predict?* I know. I know how those bastards in the Academy vote. They vote to save their own skins. A picture like mine that brings in umpteen million brings back hope to an industry that's been down so long it looks like up. Same with you. You star in a picture that cleans up. None of them dumb fuckers are sitting back and saying to themselves, 'Now I wonder who really gave the finest, most artistic performance? Not on your nellikins. They're looking at those *Variety* grosses. They're looking to vote for somebody who can bring 'em in. In some nutty way, deep back in their birdsize brains, they think that's the person who's going to save their asses. And another thing. The *schmucks* who run the industry like to peddle the myth that Hollywood is just a Happy Family, Main Street, U.S.A. So here comes us, Mr. and Mrs. Lovey Dovey—true blue and happily married—bounding right up that victory ramp together to claim our Price, Waterhouse prizes."

"Just this once, may my darling know-it-all husband Marty be right."

"Mark my words."

"Arky," Marty bellowed into the phone, "I don't give a fuck what you think I can spend or not spend. I don't need you to give me any of that bullshit. I'll take my business some place else."

"Who was that?" Kim asked.

"Just some half-assed accountant."

"Why were you so mad at him?"

"The fucking *schmuck* tried to tell me I was spending too much money. And I pay *him!* If he's worrying so much about the money I spend, I got a little economy to suggest to him. We can start cutting back on the larcenous fees he soaks me."

The day of the Academy Awards Kim woke up to find a large satin box on her breakfast tray. She opened it and lifted out a dazzling diamond tiara fit for a queen. It was every bit as spellbinding as any tiara she had ever seen on Queen Elizabeth.

She thought, I shouldn't be taking this out of the box. We can't keep it. We'll have to send it back. But not tonight. I can wear it tonight.

The accountant was probably right. Diamond tiaras and all the rest were maybe too much. Maybe more than they could swing, what with Marty's double alimony and all the big spending that kept The Pearly Gates going.

But like Scarlett O'Hara, she would worry about that tomorrow.

Marty took Kim to the Polo Lounge for lunch. There they held court almost the whole afternoon. Everybody who stopped by their table assured them they had it in the bag. Marty would win for Best Picture and Kim would take it for Best Actress. All the voting members of the Academy who spoke to them assured them they had voted for each of them.

Kim was in a jubilant mood as she dressed.

"Can a little girl from a played-out copper-mining town in Arizona find fame, fortune, and happiness in Hollywood?" she asked the mirror. "You bet your balls and boobs she can!"

A limousine provided by the Studio wasn't good enough for Marty. He had to get there in a Rolls Royce. He rented one of those knock-out Salamanca continental town jobs where the driver sits in the open. The passenger compartment was upholstered in red velvet.

I was glued to my television set.

When Kim alighted from the Rolls in front of Grauman's Chinese Theater, the fans went wild. Standing so straight, with head up, the tiara blazing away like headlights, she *was* the Queen!

She wore a white strapless chiffon gown that showed off as much of her boobs as the law would allow. A family of twenty-three could have lived the rest of their lives off the jewelry she was wearing. Excluding the diamond tiara. She had the fat rock wedding ring on her finger, of course, and the diamond teardrop earrings. New to my eyes were a diamond necklace and two bracelets encrusted with rubies and diamonds.

The camera swept over Kim and Marty repeatedly while the lesser prizes were being handed out. You saw them clapping heartily and flashing each other warm smiles. You saw them get tense during the last musical number before the big ones were to be announced. The camera picked up Marty reaching for Kim's hand, giving it a reassuring pat, and continuing to hold it.

Then it was over for Kim. She lost. The television camera panned in on her again to show her clapping, a brave smile on her lips. Marty was whispering something into her ear.

According to what she told me afterward, what Marty had whispered was, "Those fucking idiots."

His hand holding hers was hot and sweaty. It kept clenching and unclenching. She could hear his heartbeat and his teeth grinding. She knew he had already put her defeat out of mind. All he could concentrate on was the big moment coming up.

When it came, he was out of his seat like an uncaged tiger.

"I'll make it short and sweet," Marty barked into the microphone. "I won it. I deserved it. I would like to thank . . . myself."

He held the Oscar high. His mouth almost stretched to his ears in a captivating grin.

The audience roared with laughter. Then the clapping began. It reached thunder proportions.

It wasn't like Marty to be insensitive around people he cared about. But he made a giant blooper with Kim when he got back to his seat. You can only put it down to his feeling so happy and full of himself at that particular moment.

"Old lady of mine," he said, joining her again, "I guess you know who the genius of the family is."

His timing couldn't have been worse. Any other time she might have laughed it off. It was just Marty being Marty. But not tonight.

"If you'll just stand up," she said icily, "I'd like to get by."

"Get by? Where ya think you're going? We're going to the big celebration party at the Ambassador."

"*You* may be going. I'm not. I'm going home."

"Going home? Why? What the hell am I going to tell everybody at the party? They'll all be wondering what the fuck gives."

"Tell them any fucking thing you please. Tell them I'm expecting my menopause."

With great determination Kim smiled her way through the

throngs and into the waiting Rolls. At home she sat waiting for him in their pitch-dark front hall, still seething at her humiliation. To her amazement she didn't have long to wait. It couldn't have been more than an hour.

Marty stormed through the front door. Before he saw her sitting there, she said, "You can take your fucking tiara and shove it up your ass!" And taking it off her head, she aimed it straight for his crotch.

Marty yelped. "You little bitch!"

"Mr. Know-It-All. Had all the winners picked. Ha! Ha!"

He scooped her up off the settee and carried her to the living room. She was too surprised by his brute strength to put up resistance. Throwing her on a divan, Marty rolled her over on her stomach. Her chiffon dress was pulled up and her panties came down. His hand came cracking like thunder at her bare bottom.

". . . ungrateful, spoiled little bitch . . . bust my balls to try to please you and make you happy . . . can't even stand beside me in my one big moment . . . had to make up a fucking lie you were going to join some friends at a small private party . . . got no loyalty to me, pride in me . . . sorehead bitch . . . jealous of her own husband's success . . . making me look like a cuckold at my own party . . . selfish, mean, jealous, spiteful broad . . ."

The phrases kept spewing out like lava from an erupting volcano. Almost in rhythm with the hand that kept thrashing her backside.

Kim had no idea how long she lay there taking it . . . his verbal abuse and his spanking. She had thought if any man ever laid his hand on her she would claw his eyes out, but she just lay there, absorbing his punishment. The words hurt even more than his blows, and she was furious, hurting, weeping. And paralyzed, because beneath her tears and rage and pain she knew she was getting what she deserved, from somebody who could cut her down to size when she needed it.

Then the thrashing and the tirade stopped abruptly. Across her exposed rear end teardrops were falling. Marty opened his mouth and howled at the top of his lungs.

"Empty! Empty! Empty! It should be the happiest night of my life and you had to shit on it."

Kim sat up and flung her arms around Marty. She cradled and rocked him. They wept wordlessly together.

"Marty, Marty," Kim cooed into his ear finally. "You're wrong. I'm not . . . all those awful things you say I am. That's not why I left."

"Why, then?"

"Because I was so hurt and humiliated. Everybody was

staring. And those goddamn cameras kept focussing on me. Then you came back and instead of saying something soothing you had to come out with that horrible, cruel, cocky remark."

"What did I say?"

"You said, 'I guess you know now who the genius in the family is.'"

"Did I say that? That didn't mean anything. *Bubeleh*, that was just a joke. I was all whacked out once I had my hands wrapped around that little guy. I know you were disappointed. I also know you're the greatest. Whether you get a prize or not. I always talk up a great game about myself. But I needed this crappy little toy they gave me tonight. I needed it to believe I'm what I keep hollering I am . . ."

"Marty," purred Kim. "You are only the most wonderful man and marvelous producer on the face of the earth. And you don't need any 'crappy little toy' to prove it."

She was all over him with her kisses and endearments and assurances.

"*Bubeleh*," panted Marty. "How'd you like to come upstairs? And take pot luck . . . with a crappy little toy?"

Kim said she spent the night on the ceiling.

She referred to Marty as "master of the eternal erection."

Kim: I'm almost glad I didn't win.
Marty: In a pig's ass.
Kim: I mean it.
Marty: In a pig's ass you do.
Kim: Honest to God! What normal, red-blooded girl wouldn't rather have a hot Peter inside her than a cold Oscar in her hand?
Marty: You remind me of Catherine the Great.
Kim: Remember all those lovely people who stopped by our table and told me they had voted for me?
Marty: What about them?
Kim: Just that I never knew there were so many fucking liars in the Polo Lounge.

I wonder if Marty ever really caught on. I honestly doubt it. He was a genius in his field. He was shrewd about people and he knew how to manipulate them. Usually his antennae were sensitive enough to pick up any signals in the air. What was going on in other people's minds. But I don't think he saw through Kim's wiles.

Shortly after Marty won his Oscar stuff began arriving at The Pearly Gates with the initials IGMFY on them. Towels.

311

Napkins. Cocktail glasses. He even had the initials mono-grammed boldly on some silk shirts he ordered. And he had them painted on his plane.

Naturally they became a conversation piece. "What does IGMFY stand for?" was the first thing everybody asked him.

"Are you sure you really want to know?" Marty baited them. He'd keep on teasing them until they were about ready to pass out from curiosity.

"All right, you asked for it. I'll tell you. IGMFY stands for I Got Mine, Fuck You."

Kim thought it was funny but she put on a show of great indignation and ladylike disdain. "I think it's cheap and vul-gar," she told him. "And it's personally quite embarrassing to me."

"*You* think it's cheap and vulgar? And you're embar-rassed? Now look who's giving herself airs. A little cunt born in an outhouse . . ."

And they were off. It was a screaming and swearing and foul-mouthing match that sent the whole staff scurrying out of earshot. It ended with Kim throwing her arms around Marty's neck and apologizing profusely.

"I'm sorry, Marty," she purred. "As usual, you're right and I'm wrong. You always set me straight on everything. It *is* funny, and it makes people laugh. If you make people laugh without hurting anybody, it has to be a good thing."

It was a warm reconciliation that led straight to the bed-room.

Hours later, Kim sighed, "Marty, you're sensational. I have a movie idea for you. One you yourself should star in."

"Let's hear it."

"Well, the title would be *The Case of the Everlasting Hard-On* . . ."

In Mocambo one night she criticized his necktie and cuff links and told him he really didn't know how to dress. This started an argument. Their voices kept rising and rising until the whole place went dead silent to hear them out. Kim flung down her napkin and rushed out, with Marty in hot pursuit.

At home she threw herself upon him, begging his forgive-ness. She was in the wrong. She shouldn't have criticized him. She didn't even mean what she had said.

"What was eating you then?" Marty asked.

"I was jealous. I thought you were making eyes at the woman at the next table."

"What're you talking about? I never saw who was at the next table."

"I'm so jealous I guess I got to imagining things."

312

"*Bubeleh,* when you're in the picture I don't know anybody else is alive."

They were soon in the sack, where Marty "extended" himself again.

There were other loud-voiced arguments in public places followed by hasty exits. Soon they were the talk of the town. Sob sisters were predicting an early end to another of Hollywood's seemingly perfect marriages.

"The Marty Norths are raising eyebrows Up To Here," one columnist wrote, "with their public screaming matches."

"A spokesman for Marty North and Kimberley Hudson vehemently denies the rift rumors," someone else was reporting.

Kim went with Marty to London for the British premiere of *Christopher Columbus Discovers America.* Naturally they had to hole up at Claridge's. They were the talk of London. Not only because of the picture's enthusiastic reception and Marty's flamboyance and Kim's fame and beauty. But for a violent argument that started in Mirabelle's and raged through the lobby of Claridge's.

They sailed back on the *France.*

When they docked in New York, Ryder Downey persuaded Kim to meet the press aboard ship. They were all dying to see her and the easiest thing would be to hold a press conference and get done with it.

"Is your marriage with Marty North on the rocks?" was the first question. "You always seem to be fighting."

"I'm madly in love with Marty. He's the most exciting man I've met in my whole life."

"How come you're always fighting, then?"

"Well, there is a reason. I'm not sure you want to know."

About twenty voices yelled in a chorus, "Yes!"

"If I tell you, it'll have to be for the record."

"Yes!"

"And I want to be very sure that I'm quoted accurately."

"Promise!"

Kim looked very serious and lowered her voice confidentially. "The reason Marty and I scrap so much is that . . . it makes the fucking so great afterward."

Raucous laughter.

"Miss Hudson," said the reporter who had put the question to her, "we can't print *that.*"

"You promised to quote me accurately," said Kim in a mock-hurt tone.

"They were putty in your hands," Ryder assured her afterward. "They all adored you."

Marty was spinning new projects like tops. He was going to produce this and produce that. He was flying to Paris and Mexico City and Rome for the premieres of his picture. Kim accompanied him when she wasn't working.

"*Bubeleh*," he greeted her one evening, "I'm to get the DFF Award for Outstanding Citizenship. They want me—us—to come to Memphis—"

"What's DFF stand for?"

"Daughters of the Founding Fathers."

"Oh, those fat farts," said Kim. "I hope you told them where they can ram their award."

"Are you kidding? Of course I'm going. So are you. Fat farts they may be, but if this industry is going to save its ass, it'll have to start getting these fat farts and everybody connected to them back into the movie houses."

Of course she would go. Just to be with Marty and keep him company. The award was to be made at a Saturday luncheon during the annual convention of the Daughters of the Founding Fathers. They would fly out Friday night and take a suite at the Peabody. They would sleep Saturday morning until it was time to pick up the award. Then they would make a beeline for the airport.

But at the last moment Kim backed out.

All day Friday she had been feeling generally lousy on the set. In the afternoon she began to have stomach pains. She diagnosed it as the quickie virus that was going all around. She also felt strangely depressed and sad. Maybe that came out of feeling so lousy physically.

Nothing was helped by Marty's attitude. He didn't believe her for a minute. He blew his stack.

"If you're not the whole cheese," he stormed, "you don't want to play. If somebody else is going to grab the limelight for one second, count you out. Look what you're doing to me. Standing me up and making me look like a horse's ass. After I promised them you'd be there and they're all waiting to see you. The one time I need you beside me and want to show you off, you have to take a powder. You know what you are? You're just one spoiled, selfish little bitch. All take and no give."

Kim was in tears. "Oh, Marty, no more. Please. I would go if I could. But I'm feeling so terrible. Can't you see I am?

"It's an act. With you everything's an act. You're either blowing hot or you're blowing cold. Who the hell knows what gives. Or if you ever have one honest-to-God emotion you really feel."

On that note Marty walked out and slammed the door.

314

She shed a few more buckets of tears after he was gone. How could he be so cruel? Why couldn't he see that she wasn't faking . . . that she was really miserable? Had she pulled too many tricks and switches of mood to be taken seriously?

She cried and cried . . . and the pains grew sharper. And the depression became blacker.

Marty was halfway to the airport when he turned around and came back. "I believe you," he told Kim. "I was out of line. My goddamn ego keeps kicking up. I know you're not feeling well. You just go to bed and shake that damn virus and by the time I get back you'll be your real self again." He took her in his arms and kissed her tenderly, and started off again. But he was back ten minutes later, apologizing profusely for his hot-headedness and accusations against her.

They had another tender farewell scene.

She could hardly believe it when he came back a third time.

"*Bubeleh*, I'm so happy, happy, happy being married to you. I don't know if I could make it without you. I wake up having nightmares that something might happen to you."

"Marty, you're crazy," she protested weakly. "You'll be late."

"It's my plane," he said. "It goes when I say it goes." More kisses and professions of eternal love.

And then finally he was gone.

On the way to the hospital she thought, Whatever it is, I don't care. Now Marty will know for sure I wasn't faking.

Chapter 31

The Los Angeles night, she remembered, came right out of *Wuthering Heights*. Thunder. Cracks of lightning. A pea-soup fog. A fine drizzle. She remembered thinking of Marty with a ghastly, twisting knot in the pit of her stomach. Then the darkness enfolded her.

In some timeless future she awoke. There were people standing around her. A doctor, a nurse, and her mother.

"Where am I?" she asked.

"You're in the Queen of Angels Hospital, baby," her

mother replied. "You've had an operation and you're going to be just dandy."

"That's right," said the doctor. "We had to remove an ovarian cyst. It's all over now and you're doing just fine."

If she was doing just fine, why were the three of them looking at her so grimly?

"Where's Marty?" she asked.

Doctor, nurse, and mother darted anxious glances at one another.

"Ryder's waiting to see you, baby," her mother said.

The nurse scurried from the room and brought in Ryder Downey. Kim took one look at Ryder's face and screamed, "No!" Ryder simply shook his head up and down.

She was out of her bed and would have run into the street in her nightgown if she hadn't been held back.

"No!" she screamed.

"It was probably a bolt of lightning," Ryder explained. "His plane went down in the Ozarks."

Her screaming terrorized the whole hospital. Then she stopped abruptly and got a tight grip on herself.

"Where is Marty?" she asked Ryder.

"In New York. What's left of him. His brother wants him to be buried in the family plot in Woodlawn Cemetery."

"I must leave right now," she said. "I must get there in time for the funeral. Ryder, I want you to arrange this. Immediately."

The best of arrangements were made.

Against the advice of the whole hospital staff, she was released.

The Studio chartered an American Airlines commercial aircraft to fly her to New York and back. She wouldn't have to face up to a scheduled flight and the stares of a greedily curious public.

Bernie Miller asked if he and Eileen could go on the plane with her. If it had been anybody else but Bernie, she would have said no, but Bernie was the only other person who loved Marty anywhere near as much as she did. Bernie was the only other person Marty honestly loved.

She made the flight with Bernie and Eileen and her personal physician. Just before they landed, Dr. Christiansen gave her a sedative.

The whole funeral was a nightmare to her. It was a numbingly cold day in January. The cemetery was jammed. In the howling glacial winds, with four inches of snow on the ground, a crowd of fifteen thousand people (according to police estimates) swarmed all over the place. It was hideous, unbelievable. It could have been the circus coming to town. Kids sat on tombstones with blankets spread over their laps. Blankets were spread all over the grounds too. Family groups huddled together drinking hot coffee out of thermos jugs. Braziers were set up everywhere and hawkers were selling bagels and roasted chestnuts. Used napkins and empty soda bottles and wax paper wrappers swirled in the wind, blowing across the hilly spaces and drifting up against the tombstones.

As her car inched toward the gravesite, Kim saw them claw their way toward her. Swooping on the car like a gaggle of vultures, ugly, frightening, ravenous. Their faces were gruesomely distorted. They stretched their talons straight out like they waned to smash through the car windows and scratch her eyes out. They screeched and screamed.

Kim was wearing a charcoal gray hat with a semi-veil. It was all she could lay her hands on in the frantic rush to get away. Through the closed windows, half-drugged, she heard them:

"No widow's veil!"

"She looks terrible."

". . . like death warmed over."

"Older, too."

Through a police cordon she walked slowly to the grave. A tent over the grave shielded her from the voracious public.

"Come out, Kim!"

"Let's see you, Kim."

"Kim, we're here! Your fans!"

After the coffin was lowered, Kim said softly through the canvas, "Please, everybody. I beg of you. Please leave."

She knelt and said a prayer by Marty's grave. She came out of the tent by herself.

The crowd went wild. The police were no longer able to hold them back. They rushed for her. Bernie Miller got a grip on her and guided her to the car. But they were plucking at her, yanking at her dress, stroking her, pinching her.

Bernie shoved her in the car and slammed the door shut, and went in search of the missing driver.

They swarmed like maggots over the car. Their faces pressed against all the windows, like starving children. They pooled their brute energy to start rocking the limo.

Kim screamed. "Please! Please! Go away. Leave me alone. You *animals!*"

Kim remembered giving one order to the household staff: "Don't touch his clothes. Don't even change the sheets."

Back in the hospital she lapsed into a drugged sleep that lasted for two weeks. The first time she was distinctly aware of being awake was when she woke up in her own bed. In the bed she had shared with Marty. Sleeping on the same sheets they had slept on the night before Marty flew to his death. She could still pick up the scent of him on the sheets.

She dug her nose into the sheets and buried it there.

In Marty's closet was the laundry bag with his soiled shirts, socks, and underwear. She caressed each article and held it against her face. This was all of Marty she had left and she wouldn't let go of it. She stayed in bed for days.

I tried repeatedly to see her and comfort her. She put me off. She didn't want to see anybody.

"I appreciate it, Gina," she said. "But what's the point? It wouldn't cheer me up. How could it? My life's over."

I think the thing that kept her from going around the bend completely was having to go back to work. Production on *A Marriage in Heaven* had all but shut down. Each day the Studio called, nervously asking if she could possibly come back tomorrow. Each day she told them no. Then, finally, after four weeks, she told them, "I might as well get done with it. But I'm warning you not to expect much."

Kim was all right as long as she was playing Barbara, but the sound of "Cut" drew her back into herself. In her dressing-room she would turn on the television and see nothing. She would try to read but the lines of print in the book jumped and dipped and came together in dizzy waves before her eyes.

It was a cruel film for her to be making; it was a fantasy thing about a blissful marriage suddenly interrupted by death and resumed in the afterlife. As the bereaved widow Barbara, Kim had to say lines like, "Oh, Robert, I never thought you'd leave me. I had it all planned. We were going to live to be a hundred and ten. I was already drawing up the guest list for our diamond wedding anniversary."

At night she came home to a house full of servants running around. But the only presence she felt was the ghost of Marty. The food that was brought to her bedroom went mostly untouched. The television set droned on; she saw or heard nothing. Newspapers lay spread out and magazines open, unread. Night after night she quietly drank herself into oblivion, the drink slowly exorcising the devils of loneliness, grief—and guilt. Sick or not sick, she should have been on that plane with Marty, going down in flames with him.

One night she got a call from Marty's accountant. "I've been holding off till you got a little bit of a grip on yourself," he told her. "But I'm afraid I've got some bad news for you."

The bad news was that Marty had left this world in sad financial shape. A lot of money had come in but he had man-

318

aged to outspend it. He was in hock to everybody you could think of. The bills were mounting by the day. Unfortunately he had died without leaving a penny of insurance. He had some crazy belief in his own immortality that made insurance irrelevant. There would be more monies coming in from *Christopher Columbus*, which in time would help liquidate the debts, but certain decisions had to be made now. What to do about The Pearly Gates? It was mortgaged to the hilt and the cost of maintaining it was prohibitive. Would she want to assume that kind of burden?

Curiously the bad news gave her a kind of lift. It provided the escape she was looking for but couldn't galvanize her energies to initiate.

"Oh, Arky," she told the accountant, "I don't want to stay here. I just want to walk out of here next week when the picture is done and never see the place again. Get rid of everything—or get somebody to get rid of it. Use the money to pay off all you can and I'll try to make up the rest."

Besides her work, which was an obligation, this was the first concrete step she had taken back toward life. If she had tried to stay on in The Pearly Gates she would turn into a ghostly caretaker of a shrine.

When she walked out of The Pearly Gates, the only thing of Marty's she took with her was the pair of cuff links she had criticized that night in the Mocambo. Dear, dear Marty. The cuff links somehow symbolized the excitement, the white heat of their love. She would always keep them with her.

Kim couldn't face up to any homemaking plans. When the picture was finished, she decided, she would travel. She would take her mother and Indiana off to Europe. She had a month between pictures. They would go to London for the first week or so and move on to the Continent, maybe to Paris and Switzerland. . . .

But, as usual, Kim's plans went awry. She didn't make it to Europe.

She could have flown over the Pole to London directly. But Bernie Miller was in New York. Kim thought it would be nice to stop off and see him. He was opening up the current bill at the Copa.

She went to the midnight show and felt almost sick with the commotion she caused. She tried to close her eyes and ears to all of it. She tried to listen to Bernie's act and be supportive. But she hardly heard a thing he said. She laughed—mechanically—when the others laughed. Her thoughts were all back with Marty. Seeing Bernie brought Marty back to her so agonizingly and yet ecstatically again.

Bernie had provided his brother as an escort. After the

show they joined Bernie in his suite in the Hotel Fourteen above the Copa. Eileen was back on the Coast with the kids.

Kim and Bernie fell upon each other. As they embraced, they both began crying.

Bernie's brother quickly bade them good night and left.

To toast Kim's arrival, Bernie had a magnum of iced champagne waiting. The magnum was finished and another ordered. Until almost dawn they drank and talked and wept, recalling the man they had both loved so deeply.

"I never had an old man growing up," Bernie bawled. "Marty was everything I ever wanted in a father. I worshipped him. The things he did for me . . . was going to do for me!"

Kim was more miserable than she had been in weeks. The wound was open again. But at last, after such a long time, she was not alone any more. She was with the only other person who could feel any part of what she felt. Between them, with their memories and passion and tears, they could almost bring Marty back to life.

The lounge was long closed and the light was breaking when Bernie guided her drunkenly to the street to hail a cab to take her back to the Waldorf Towers.

She was hardly asleep when she woke up screaming. Her mother and Indiana were standing over her anxiously.

"It's nothing," she said. "It must've been a nightmare."

It was a nightmare, and she remembered it clearly. She was flying somewhere with Marty in his Lear jet. They were flying in a storm. Suddenly there was a bolt of lightning that cracked the plane wide open and set fire to it and they were plunging down in flames . . .

The departure for Europe was postponed. Tomorrow. And postponed again. Tomorrow. Tomorrow. Tomorrow.

Kim never went to see Bernie again in the Copa. But night after night she waited for him in his suite in the Hotel Fourteen. There they drank champagne and remembered Marty until in drunkenness and exhaustion they had to call it a night.

One night—it must have been three o'clock in the morning—Kim had hunger pangs, and she took this as a healthy sign. She could hardly remember how long it had been since she had felt an honest longing for food. Bernie took her to the Stage Delicatessen where they ate pastrami on rye washed down with Amstel beer. The Stage was hopping and they were the cynosure of all eyes.

The next day they were in Winchell's column: "Marty

North's beauteous widow being consoled by funnyman Bernie Miller."

Bernie was the only tie that bound her to New York, and the only tie that bound her to Bernie was Marty. Bernie was a derivative. He took his existence from Marty. When she looked at Bernie or listened to him, she was seeing, hearing Marty. But she needed Bernie to verify *Marty's* existence . . . to prove to her that Marty hadn't been just a dream that was lost forever.

After the Winchell item they stayed away from the Stage and other showbiz hangouts. It didn't matter. Wherever they went, the spies were waiting for them. Nowhere did they escape attention. And the attention became more barbed.

"Gotham is all agog," Dorothy Kilgallen wrote in her "Voice of Broadway" column, "at the touching tableau of the married young comic who's been cheering up filmdom's most beautiful widow in some of the smarter *boites* around town."

"A very much married comedian and a dazzling screen siren," warned another columnist, "are playing with fire."

"The Bernie Millers acting silly?" Ed Sullivan wondered in his column in the *Daily News*.

"They're all vicious," Bernie said to Kim. "Bastards."

But Kim was dismayed by the gossip. As far as the public was concerned, it was still a teasing guessing game. Except for that rather innocent mention in Winchell's column, their names hadn't really been spelled out. Nobody so far had been hurt. But it was ridiculous, unfair! Anybody listening to their conversation would know how innocent the whole thing was.

Bernie finished his gig at the Copa and left for the Coast.

Kim canceled her own plans to go on to Europe and flew back to California. She wasn't following Bernie. She just didn't have the energy to face Europe and all the crowds and gawking and mauling.

Back in California, alone again, she moved into the penthouse of the Holmsby Hills Towers.

It seemed the most natural thing in the world that Bernie would be coming over to see her. They had only each other to talk to about the vital force that had charged both their lives and was gone. Talking to each other was a way of keeping that force alive.

"Did Eileen love Marty too?" Kim suddenly asked Bernie one night at dinner. It was such a basic question she wondered why she hadn't asked it a lot earlier.

"No."

"Why not?

"She was jealous," said Bernie. "Eileen doesn't understand about a lot of things. The only thing that matters to her is her career and the image of the cozy little den mother all snug in her nest surrounded by her loved ones when she gets home from the studio. Marty had no place in that picture. She couldn't understand why I had to be so tight—close—with somebody out of the nest.—So she pulled the martyr act, pouting and pursing her lips."

Bernie spoke with bitterness. Kim realized, with some astonishment, it was the first time Eileen had got more than just a passing mention in their conversation. "Is it better now?" she asked him.

"No. Worse. Because of me, maybe. My moods. You see, aside from everything Marty meant to me, he had such plans for me. He had my whole future mapped out. I'd just sit back and listen and say, 'Uh-huh. Anything you say, Marty. I'll do it.' Now, without Marty, I'm scared for my skin. I'm not so sure I'm going to make it."

It seemed natural enough to Kim that two friends could have dinner together in a restaurant without putting the town in a spin. But apparently if the friends happened to be named Kimberley Hudson and Bernie Miller, that was something else. Kim pooh-poohed the "blind" items in columns that pointed to her and Bernie. All those know-nothing writers were putting one and one together and coming up with the wrong number. She defied all the well-meaning advice from people at the Studio who told her to take it easy, that she was flirting with danger.

"I'm not flirting at all," she shot back.

It seemed entirely natural and fitting (to her) that she should be sitting ringside the night her friend opened at the Coconut Grove. She even forgot to ask Bernie if Eileen would be there. Eileen wasn't.

By the time Kim got to his dressing room afterward Bernie was already besieged by reporters and columnists

"Where's Eileen tonight?" everybody was asking.

"She hates nightclubs," Bernie explained.

"That's something new, isn't it?"

"Well, you know," said Bernie, flustered, "with three little ones at home, it doesn't look too good for Mama to be out carousing at night."

Bernie and Kim handled the situation as best they could. But with Eileen at home and Kim in Bernie's dressing room, it was hard to convince a cynical press that this was just a jolly friendship.

When they were gone, Bernie said, "As a liar, I flunk out. They didn't go for that baloney about Eileen being home because she didn't want to be seen in a den of iniquity. Eileen's home because Eileen wants a divorce."

Kim gulped. "Oh, Bernie! How terrible!"

"Not terrible at all. It might be the best thing for both of us."

She could hardly bring herself to ask, "Is it . . . because of . . . the gossip?"

"No. The gossip isn't any more than the tip of the iceberg. It's been building up for a long time. I think it was a mistake from the very beginning. If we hadn't been in this crazy business and both so young, we probably wouldn't ever have gotten married. But when you hear a hundred people telling you how right you'd be for each other, well, you think they can't all be wrong."

But his face was sad. She couldn't remember ever having looked at him closely before. Bernie was thirty-two. But he had such a soft, boyish, apple-cheeked look that he could pass for twenty-two. Now in his sadness and vulnerability, he looked even younger.

Poor Bernie, she thought. Poor, poor Bernie.

Eileen made her low-keyed announcement that she would seek a divorce from Bernie Miller. It was the announcement heard around the world. What! The Perfect Couple coming asunder!

Eileen scooped up the kids and took off for Sun Valley to wait it out.

In the weeks since she had been back in California, I hadn't seen Kim once. None of her old friends had. Not even Lonnie Braintree.

When I called, she said, "Oh, Gina, I'm just not up to seeing you. It's not personal. I don't want to see anybody."

Except Bernie Miller, of course.

The morning after the big news broke, I called her again. Not to say let's-have-lunch or anything like that. Just to let her know I knew what she must be going through and I knew all the innuendos in the papers weren't true, and that I was still on her side. As always.

"Kim," I started out, "I've read the papers and I had to call you. I'm just sick for you."

"Gina, if there's one thing I don't need," she came back at me, "it's any of your pious Catholic moralizing."

And she hung up on me.

Kim was furious at the mounting gossip and accusations. In defiance of them she continued to be seen with Bernie in the most public places all the time Eileen was in Sun Valley. To stop seeing him or to start mucking around corners with

323

him in little hideaway cafés or lounges would be to acknowledge there was some truth to the rumors.

Bernie was badly shaken at Eileen's action. Kim thought it was her duty to keep him from sitting home alone brooding. Eileen hadn't threatened him at all or created any scenes. She just told him what she intended to do and then went ahead and did it. It put Bernie in a state of shock.

Luckily he was working. He was doing a couple of sketches in a "Big Broadcast" type of movie. He complained of the chill on the set. Apparently Eileen had a lot of sympathizers there who felt he had done her dirt.

In a different way Kim felt the chill too. She cut too much ice at the Studio to be mistreated, but there were all kinds of voices urging caution and discretion. On the set fellow actors seemed to be walking on eggshells in her presence. Some members of the crew politely—and distantly—addressed her as "Miss Hudson," when they usually called her Kim.

Eileen expected to occupy their house when she got back from Sun Valley. Bernie had to move out and the question was where.

"Bernie," said Kim on impulse. "Move in with us."

Bernie's left eyebrow lifted involuntarily. "Well, you are divorced. And God knows, there's enough room."

Bernie had hardly unpacked his bags before the news was racing to the far corners of the earth. Bernie Miller was house-guesting with Kimberley Hudson! Kim had hardly expected that Bernie's whereabouts would be a secret for very long. But this! There had to be spies hiding out in the potted plants in the lobby.

"God, if they only knew!" she said to Bernie. "All this *tsimmes* over nothing! And do you know what? They'd be disappointed as hell if they knew it was nothing."

Kim could pooh-pooh the gossip and its implications all she wanted to, she was still in trouble. For the first time in her life she was confronting an unfriendly press and public. The Studio insisted she get Bernie out.

"For Christ's sake," she yelled back at them, "I've got twelve goddamn rooms. Can't he sleep in one of them? There isn't a goddamn thing going on between us."

No one would believe that, they insisted, and suggested she read some of her recent fan mail.

"What's wrong with you?" one writer asked. "Are you some kind of nymphomaniac? Whatever you are, you are a disgrace to womanhood and common decency. Your husband hardly cold in his grave before you have to go and steal the affections of somebody else's husband! And to do a thing like that to one of the cutest, most darling girls who ever lived. And so devoted to her husband and children. We've always been fans of yours. But as far as this family is concerned, we've seen our last Kimberley Hudson picture. . . ."

Kim burst into tears crying, "Not true! Not fair!"

Bernie faced an uncertain future.

His manager had booked him into the Tropicana in Vegas, but after that, there were no firm commitments. He more than hinted that Bernie's divorce and "messy private life" weren't helping much.

Kim thought a lot about Bernie and his problem. And about herself and hers. An idea began to form in her mind. God knows, she had enough coming in to provide for Bernie as well as for herself. And it should shut up all the vicious tongue-wagging. Maybe she would be a little less unhappy if she tried to make someone else happy. And he so desperately needed her, someone . . .

"Bernie," she said, "I've been thinking. Maybe the best thing that could happen to both of us would be to get married. At least I can't think of any reason why we shouldn't get married."

Chapter 32

Nine fourteen.

At some point, with or without Kim, we're going to have to sit down and eat. Before we all fall down.

Weaving around the table again, I see there are no place cards for Grosvenor Forbes or Marty North or Bernie Miller.

Of course not.

It wasn't that whoever was in charge of the seating plan had a sudden attack of taste. Or was deferring to Kim . . . and her painful memories.

It's just that neither Grosvenor nor Marty nor Bernie had ever been a child star at the Studio.

"It's you, my dusky madonna!"

Arms encircled me. My cheeks were smooched and hot air was blown into each ear. "Your lover has come to spirit you away from this madness."

Lonnie Braintree. It didn't mean a thing. But next to Kim, I couldn't have been gladder to see anyone.

"This is Robert. Isn't he beautiful?"

I nodded. This was Lonnie's big new heartthrob. If this was what Lonnie loved these days, there was nothing but to go along with it. Because, like Kim, I've always loved Lonnie too.

But, Christ, what does Lonnie see in him? What's Robert got going for him except that he's young? Maybe twenty-two ... or half of Lonnie's age.

"So-o-o nice to see you again," Lonnie cooed. Squeezes. Nips on the ear lobes. Hot blasts into the ears. "You poor man's Sophia Loren, you!"

Dear Lonnie! Woo-cooing a woman up in public as foreplay to excite the lover beside him.

"Robert writes too, Gina. You should see some of the stuff he's turning out. Of course it's not quite in your genre. Not the sort of thing publishers think is commercial these days. But then publishers never thought Kafka or Proust or Joyce was commercial in *their* day ..."

Love is usually blind. In Lonnie's case it was chronically, hopelessly blind. Lonnie was always investing his lovers with qualities and talents they didn't vaguely possess. None of them ever began to have any of his quality or talent.

Of all of us kid performers, Lonnie was the only one besides Kim who still had a career in films. His physique and mannerisms are such he could never be a leading man type. But he is still a damn fine actor. He also has a brilliant mind, which is something you can't say about most actors.

Lonnie knows everybody in the world. From busboys to the Queen Mother. I think his most special gift is for friendship. He has the uncanny knack of knowing when things aren't going well ...

Kim has absolutely adored Lonnie since they were kids. In his own fashion he is crazy about her. They joked about their "middle-of-the-night passion." They are always calling each other from halfway around the world and at one end of the line it is usually the middle of the night. If Lonnie could have been really passionate about any woman, it would have been Kim. But Kim had never wanted that from him. She always thought of Lonnie as her dear buddy, a kind of sweet, close, combined brother and sister. If only she could have felt the same way about Randolph Jahr!

"What's keeping La Hudson?" Lonnie put to me.

"That's what I'd like to know. She's never been this late. I have a sneaking hunch she won't be here."

"Nonsense," Lonnie chirped. "I called her up in Lausanne

326

last week. She'll be here. She definitely said she was coming. You know Mama. When she makes up her mind to do something, she does it. I told her all about Robert and she's dying to meet him . . ."

Kim, Kim . . . qué pasa?

Chapter 33

"I knew it was a mistake almost before I said the vows," Kim said of her marriage to Bernie Miller. "It wasn't even a five-minute marriage. We should have stayed the way we were."

From this misguided union she came away with a moral: "Beware of pity. It can turn to loathing. Have pity, yes. Give money. Send a telegram. Offer help. But don't marry the pitiful."

"You don't have much luck with your marriages, do you?" someone said.

"No. I was lucky to have had Marty for the time we had together. Otherwise I guess I haven't been too happy in my choice of husbands. I don't seem to be alone in this, though. For a group of women who are supposed to be so beautiful and experienced and have the world to choose from, I'd say that Ava and Lana and Elizabeth and I are less than geniuses when it comes to picking men."

She never told anybody that the thing with Bernie was not meant to be a real marriage. She told Bernie but she needn't have bothered. He must have understood. He didn't ask any questions or raise an argument. They were going to be such good friends joined together mostly to perpetuate the memory of Marty North.

But it didn't succeed even at that level.

In order not to make a complete mockery of the sacrament of marriage, they had a wedding night of sorts. She closed her eyes and thought of Marty. The consummation of their union didn't light up the sky but that seemed to be okay by both of them.

I knew there was trouble in paradise two days after they were married. They had been secluded in her Holmsby Hills Tower penthouse, no doubt to give the impression of happy honeymooners who didn't want to be disturbed before going off to Vegas for Bernie's engagement at the Riviera.

327

"Congratulations!" I said on the phone.

"Congratulations? I hardly think that's the word."

Her bitterness came out of frustration. The marriage didn't accomplish any of its intended purposes. It didn't make anybody happy. It didn't advance Bernie's career. It didn't bring Marty back to life. And it didn't silence the criticism.

Kim had her first brush with a disenchanted public in Las Vegas.

She sat by herself down front at the midnight show on Bernie's opening night at the Riviera, dressed to the nines and wearing her best jewelry. She had slipped in during the opening production number so she wouldn't have to put up with all the staring and buzzing. But her presence was not about to go unremarked. Bernie hadn't warned her he was going to do it, and she could have killed him for it. But to be fair about it, if Bernie hadn't, the M.C. would have.

"And now, ladies and gentlemen," said Bernie, when he was taking his bows, "may I show off to you my beautiful bride? An obscure starlet by the name of Kimberley Hudson!"

The beam caught her and she stood up.

To a mixed reception.

Scattered applause. And the heckling and boos.

"Whore!"

It was a woman calling out from the upper tier.

"Tramp!" someone else called out.

"Home-breaker!"

The last came from a white-haired, grandmotherly type wearing rhinestone-rimmed glasses sitting just two tables away.

She could also have killed the son of a bitch working the lights. He kept the spot on her for what seemed like a dozen lifetimes. She had to endure it all with the smile frozen on her lips.

The second the light switched from her to the M.C., who was introducing the headliner, Kim picked up her drink and went over to the grandmotherly woman two tables away.

"Are you the lovely lady," she said sweetly, "who made the remark about my being a home-breaker?"

Behind the rhinestone-rimmed glasses a pair of eyes looked up at her in terror. Lips trembled but no reply came.

"Well, I'd like to take this occasion to thank you personally," she went on in syrupy tones.

Kim threw her highball in the woman's face. "Take that, you fat old sow!" she screamed. "I'm only sorry it isn't stale piss. Jack Daniels is too good for you."

The commotion was horrendous. First people stood up and

then whole masses of them were rushing toward the table. Several men in black were suddenly at her side joining hands in a protective phalanx around her.

"Please, Mrs. Miller," one of them said.

She allowed herself to be escorted out of the room and back to their suite.

"I'm sorry, honey," Bernie said shyly when he came in. "I didn't realize how many friends Eileen had in that house."

"Or how few you had," she shot back.

Bernie was too gentle to say anything about how many friends Kim had there.

"Why don't you sleep on the couch?" said Kim. "After what I've been through, I really need my sleep and I'd like to stretch out and not be bumping into anybody."

She went into the bedroom and banged the door shut.

She had planned to stay in Vegas with Bernie for ten days of his two-week gig. Then she was due to start work in *Sing Me a Merry Song*. Bernie woke up to find her with her bags packed. "I'm sure not going back into that nest of vipers," she told him. "I'd be eating the ceiling if I had to stay cooped up here. In which case, I might as well be back in Los Angeles."

One of the things Marty had done for her was to chop off two years from her contract with the Studio. For stars of her caliber, he had told her, the smart thing was to cut loose and be independent. She could choose her projects and name her fee. The old Hollywood order was passing. The long contracts with stablefuls of performers and the tyranny of the studios were on the way out. It spelled a bright new day for the real stars, while a lot of the lesser luminaries would blink out.

Kim had no understanding of business matters but Marty did, and she trusted his judgment unquestioningly. To get her free two years early, Marty said she would have to agree to do anything they gave her. But what the hell, he said, it was worth it to buy two years of freedom. The only other stipulation was that the Studio got first priority on her services for the first picture after her contract expired. But they had to meet or surpass the ante somebody else was offering. If they didn't, she was free of them forevermore.

The script for *Sing Me a Merry Song* was a disaster. She could either try to change it or sleepwalk her way through the picture.

"Look, Bernie," Kim greeted her new husband as he came through the door after his Vegas gig, "this is supposed to be a comedy and there isn't a laugh in the whole goddamn

329

thing." She held up the script. "I can't get away with going out and hiring new writers. But I can tell them I just can't say the lines they gave me so I wrote some new ones for myself. Now you're supposed to be the funny man. I'd appreciate it if you'd go to your room and write me some funny lines I can say."

The reference to "your room" was not lost on Bernie. Nor was there any protest.

In the morning Bernie offered her a few pages of jottings.

Kim glanced at them briefly. "Hmmm. I guess maybe I'll stick with the original script."

It was one thing to be having dinner with Bernie somewhere. It was something else to have him underfoot for keeps. This is what she came home to every night. Often he would have slept away the day and he would greet her unshaven in his pajamas and dressing robe.

"Say something funny," she'd goad him. "You're supposed to be the clown, so say something funny. God knows, there are no laughs in that turkey I'm making."

The sight of him at seven o'clock in the evening in pajamas sickened her.

"Bernie has such a lousy memory," she told me one day on the phone, with a harsh laugh. "He forgets the simplest things. Most days he even forgets to get out of bed."

She was enormously relieved to learn one night that Bernie's manager had lined up some work for him. He was going to have a week at the Concord, a weekend at the Latin Casino outside Philadelphia, and a couple of TV spots in New York. He would be gone almost three weeks. Kim felt as if she had been given a sudden vacation.

While he was gone, she thought about why her sympathetic comradely feeling for Bernie had so quickly turned to disgust. It had to be because of the marriage. By marrying her, Bernie had assumed the same position as Marty. And that was a ghastly joke. His career was on the skids without Marty to push him and make things happen. It was a new experience for her to be around somebody mediocre. All the men she had married or got involved with had been distinguished in one way or another. She had to admit to herself she didn't like the idea of being tied to anybody ordinary. It threatened her own sense of importance.

Over Bernie she was losing her good name. Marrying him had only added fuel to the bad-mouthing she was getting from the public. Now they were even writing editorials about her in newspapers and urging the readers to boycott her pictures. She was the villain, the destroyer, the husband-thief. It was preposterous. That marriage with little miss cutesy-poo was over long before she ever entered the picture.

Kim wept from self-pity. The unfairness of it all! Bernie had nothing to lose. She had everything to lose. She might not give a damn about what the public thought, but everybody who controlled her fate did. It would be one thing if she had wandered into the Garden of Delights and plucked a delicious plum. But what had she stolen? What did she have? Nothing!

Bernie came back from the East with his brother in tow. It was the same brother who had taken her to Bernie's opening night at the Copa. She thought he was sort of a *schnook* then and was displeased to see him showing up with Bernie. In their brief long-distance phone conversations Bernie had said nothing about bringing Phil out for a visit.

"Hi," Kim greeted them, as they came through the door, weighted down with luggage. "What's this all about?"

"You remember Phil," said Bernie. "He looked a little peaked and I thought he could do with a shot of California sunshine."

"Yeah," said Kim. "But not here. We don't have room."

"Don't have room!" Bernie cried. His arm swept around to remind her of the vastness of the place.

"That's right. We don't have room. All the rooms are occupied."

Bernie blushed to the roots of his hair. "In that case, Phil can bunk in with me."

"No." said Kim. "I'm afraid that won't be suitable."

"Suitable? He's my own brother. We slept in the same bed together until we left home. A few more nights won't hurt us, I guess."

"I think you'd better make some other arrangements, Phil," said Kim. "If I had been told anything about this plan I could have headed it off. We're just not equipped to put you up."

Bernie saw the futility of contending with her. He shrugged his shoulders, looking at Phil helplessly. He put his arm around Phil, grabbed Phil's valise, and led him out of the penthouse. There must have been a lengthy conference in the corridor. It was fully ten minutes before he let himself back in. Kim was waiting.

"Now don't you ever pull anything like that on me again," she said, "or I'll give you an even redder face. As long as I'm paying the rent, I call the shots. I don't like surprises and this most definitely is not a free boarding house."

Kim's last picture for the Studio was one of those epic things about several generations in a family. From loggers to lumber barons. It was called *North Star Country*. The setting was northern Minnesota. There were to be several weeks of shooting on location during the Minnesota winter. Location headquarters were set up in Duluth.

It was Kim's first real dip into winterland. At first sight, Duluth in mid-winter was magnificent to behold ... a stretched-out, hilly, lake-fronting city all a-dazzle in the snow ... a miniature San Francisco set in a northern latitude.

Kim (with Bernie) settled into maybe the grandest house in Duluth. At least it was the only house in Duluth with a ballroom. It also had an elevator. It had been built in the East End by a mining czar around the turn of the century. In recent years it had been occupied by a famous novelist who stayed long enough to get two best-selling novels out of Duluth that were turned into successful movies.

For Kim the overpowering factor of the Duluth winter was the cold. No matter how many layers of clothing she wore during the outdoor filming or how the thermostat was turned or how many fires blazed in the mansion at night she could never seem to get warm.

One evening she came from a long day of shooting in the hills back of Two Harbors. Most of the day she had been sitting in an open sleigh. The temperature hadn't gone above zero. Even foot warmers and hot water bottles, bundling up in furs and between-takes nips of brandy didn't help shake the chill. She came in to find Bernie stretched out in front of one of the fireplaces. He was still in his pajamas. It might be her imagination but she thought Bernie was starting to forget something else besides to get up in the morning and get dressed. He was forgetting to bathe. Every time she came within twenty feet of him she thought she could smell body odor. Then, again, it might be just her imagination.

"Get up," she ordered him. "Get dressed. I want you to go down to the Hotel Duluth and get me some of that glugg we had there the other night before dinner. I'm frozen to the clit."

"Joseph can go," said Bernie. Joseph was the driver who had been assigned to Kim on a round-the-clock basis.

"No," said Kim. "I want you to call up and tell them to start making it. By the time you get down there it'll be ready to pick up."

"I'll call up, honey. But why can't Joseph go down and pick it up?"

"Because I want you to go."

"But, honey—"

"Don't 'honey' me. When I say go, you go."

"It doesn't make sense," Bernie protested.

"Sense! You're looking for sense? I'll tell you what sense is. Listen, if I decide to go over to that coffee table and crap on it, I can tell you to clean it up. You'll clean it up. That's how much sense anything makes. And any time you don't like the terms of your employment, you can fuck off." She paused pregnantly. "May I add, it couldn't happen a second too soon?"

Bernie dressed and went for the glugg.

"Poor Bernie! I made his life complete hell. I started out wanting to make him happy and I only made him more miserable. I was dying from my own misery. If I had to die, I must've wanted to take somebody with me. He just happened to be there. It wasn't his fault at all. He was an innocent lamb led off to the slaughter. It was just his bad luck to connect with me during the only interval in my life when I've been an out-and-out bitch, when I probably couldn't have been decent to Cary Grant or Prince Philip, if either one had crossed my path. I've already hurt him enough. I don't want to go into any of the indignities I showered upon him. It's too painful for me to recollect, let alone want to talk about."

From *Kimberley*, by Ryder Downey.

Bernie brought Kim her glugg.

Two days later she was in the hospital, at death's door with double pneumonia.

The announcement that she was seriously ill was broadcast and trumpeted in headlines to the far corners of the earth. From all over the land—and Europe—the press converged on Duluth. They came by the hundreds, jamming the hotels and motels and rooming houses of the city.

Doctors from UCLA Medical Center and Peter Brigham were flown in to consult and observe. The daily bulletins issued to the press were maddeningly cautious and unrevealing: "There's very little change. Her condition remains grave." What the press wanted to know was, what were her chances, one way or the other.

But the doctors only replied, "We don't indulge in mathematical prophecies."

At some point Kim remembered that she woke up in a green room. The antiseptic smell telegraphed the message: "Hospital," and she could hear the squishy sound of nurses' shoes moving along a corridor. Frightening pipes were coming out of her chest, and she couldn't move her arms. They were strapped down. A man in white was sticking a big needle into a vein. She was suffocating, gasping wildly for breath. She must be drowning ... She must have drowned. She went out again.

When she woke up—a day, a week, a month later?—she couldn't talk. She tried, but only a whistle of breath came out. She was on a table. She saw a sea of green. Green walls, green caps, green masks, green gear. Gesturing for something to write on, she was given a pad and pencil. In a big childish scrawl she filled a page with the words: "Am I dead? Dying?"

Green eyes under a green visor looked down at her noncommittally.

She went under again.

"I nearly died in Duluth because I think I wanted to die. It taught me how potent the mind is in determining the state of our health. I just welcomed that disease into my system and gave it great hospitality. My life seemed to be at a hopeless dead end. Being married to Bernie was an impossible situation. But the thought of divorcing him was equally impossible. It would have washed me up with the public but good. Then what would happen to me? I had been making pictures since I was twelve years old. It was the only life I knew. By the old Studio contract standards I had made good money. But I had nothing to show for it. I hadn't had my first taste yet of the real pay dirt. I think, subconsciously, I felt why fight the disease? Dying was the only solution to my problems. I was a sick girl in more ways than one."

From *Kimberley*, by Ryder Downey.

Kim went in and out of comas for a couple more weeks while the world waited breathlessly for the latest bulletin from Duluth. When she came to, she saw that she was in an oxygen tent. A nurse was beaming broadly and flashing the victory sign.

The room was almost smothered in flowers. On the dresser were stacks of unopened telegrams and against one wall were piles of cartons jammed with letters.

"Read me some of them," Kim asked Bernie a couple days later.

He started reading and it was all music to her ears.

"Please get well immediately. You make the world a more beautiful place to live in ..."

"You are in our loving thoughts and prayers constantly ..."

"You are my very favorite actress in the whole world. I just adore you, as does everybody else I know. We would all send money or give blood or do anything to help you recover . . ."

She was alive! And to think her fans were so much more concerned about whether she lived than she herself had been! She started to cry. She almost cried herself into another coma. She wept for the sheer joy of being alive and loved.

There is no doubt that Kim's brush with death won her back all the sympathy she had lost over the break-up of Bernie's marriage to Eileen. As her life lay in jeopardy, the public that had been critical of her seemed to have an attack of conscience. Maybe they didn't know the whole story and they had judged her too harshly . . .

"I think one of my great assets," Kim joked some time back, "is being such a physical wreck. Whenever I get in a jam with public opinion, I can always be depended upon to come down with some horrible ailment that'll land me at death's door and get everybody back on my side."

The Duluth siege left her with a collapsed lung. Ever since then, she's had to spend at least one hour every day in a respirator sucking in oxygen. The respirator is so much a part of her life it's like a member of the household. She calls it Jimmy.

"Now every two-bit starlet in Hollywood'll want a respirator," one Hollywood wag predicted. "It'll be the hottest item since the invention of the vibrator."

She was convalescing in the East End mansion before resuming work on *North Star Country*, when she got a call from Harrison Winter, the distinguished producer. She asked Bernie to find out what he wanted.

"He's making *Helen of Troy*," Bernie reported back, "and he's still on the phone. He wants you for Helen and wants to know how much money you'd want to do it. He says it's going to be a real spectacular."

Helen of Troy! Oh, Jesus. Harrison Winter must be off his trolley. It sounded like one of those big bullshitty projects that puffed up a producer's ego to talk about but would never get off the ground.

"Oh, tell him a million dollars," she said. The figure was about as delirious as the idea.

"A *million*?" said Bernie.

"Yeah, a million."

A minute later Bernie was back, fit to be tied. "Harrison Winter says you've got it. Foremost Pictures has given him a budget of ten million. Production will start in London in the fall."

"Crazy," said Kim. "I don't believe a word of it. But call

335

Max Ackerman at the Studio. They still have first crack. Tell them Foremost is offering me a million to do *Helen of Troy*. You won't need to remind him that my contract with them expires after *North Star Country*. Just ask him if they'd like to match Harrison's offer."

A few minutes later Bernie was back in her room, shaking his head.

"What did Max say?" she asked.

"He said he thought you'd make a marvelous Helen of Troy."

Chapter 34

Helen of Troy was still making history thousands of years after the Trojan Wars.

Helen of Troy made movie history. And changed the lives of so many people connected with it. Including Kim's. And maybe not for the better.

There's the old saw about money being the root of all evil. From where I sit it's an observation that has stood the test of time. As the costs of *Helen of Troy* mounted from the estimated ten million to fifteen million and then to twenty million and finally to a staggering twenty-seven million, it was Harrison Walker who had to face the firing line of Foremost's irate stockholders.

"Where do you get off paying Hudson a million?" he was asked, almost in a chorus.

"Without her, there would be no movie," he answered them. "For Helen we needed the most beautiful woman in the world. Like Helen of Troy, Hudson's is the face that could launch a thousand ships."

When I talk about the evils of money, I sometimes wonder these days whether it's worse to be corrupted by money or to be going out of your mind wondering how you're going to lay hands on some. The latter happens to be my current status. I don't want to go into this too much. It's a digression. Besides, I've already told my story in a highly autobiographical novel. This is Kim's story. She's the star, front and center. I only bring myself into it because I see a parallel in our lives.

We were both embarking on the greatest adventure of our lives. She was going off to make the most publicized picture since *Gone with the Wind*. And I was getting married. To Matt Berliner, the Studio lawyer. As I said, as a child I had worshipped Matt's good looks and the smart, tough competent way he handled things. I had never stopped having fantasies about him. His name and picture were constantly in the papers. And he was considered one of *the* most eligible bachelors in Hollywood. So when I met him doing the dubbing job Marty North got for me, and when Cinderella started to snag her forty-three-year-old Prince Charming . . . Anyway, suffice it to say, the marriage was a disaster. It didn't take me long to discover I had made a mistake, but it took me eight years to finally break free.

Here again we come back to the insidious money thing! Why did I really marry Matt? Was it just because he was brilliant and charming and handsome? Or was I being just a little bit scheming? Was I thinking—and maybe not unconsciously either—that he was loaded and that would solve a lot of problems? Anyway, it's true that he bought Mama a house back in Brooklyn, where she wanted to be. And thanks to Matt, Mama spent the last two years of her life in that house without worrying about where her next meal was coming from or who was going to pay the gas and phone bills.

We married just a week before Kim was to leave for London. They were going to do the interior shots for *Helen* at the Pinewood Studios. I knew she didn't like Matt. But she graciously consented to be my matron of honor. She kept up a brave smile through the ceremony and the reception afterward at the Beverly Hills Hotel. But I couldn't help noticing how tense and drawn she looked. I presumed it was because she was so miserable being married to Bernie.

We had just a small second to talk together privately.

"I'm sure you'll be very happy," she said. It sounded like a robot talking.

"Are you all right, Kim?"

"Of course, I'm all right. Why do you ask?"

"You don't seem to be yourself. You seem a little . . . nervous."

"I probably am. I'm worried about the picture. With a million green ones on the line, they're going to expect an Academy Award performance out of me. I can't just wing it. They're bringing in the biggest guns money can buy. Jake Wilensky's writing a script and is going to direct. They've got Mark Willoughby for Menelaus and a whole slew of other English actors. And just today I learned they signed up David Glasgow to play Paris. They'll all make me look like a piker. I know I'll fall on my face."

I couldn't believe Kim was really worrying about the

money riding on her head. Or her reputation as an actress. Or her future. I think she was just plain miserable with the status quo ... and scared to death she could not get out of that misery enough to get through the important commitment she had made.

Helen of Troy was more than two years in the making.

By the time it was finished, it had taken its toll.

It nearly toppled Foremost Pictures. It rolled the heads of Foremost's top management team. It went through producers, directors, writers, and actors like Kleenex. It set off Byzantine intrigues and power struggles. It precipitated rages and enmities, broken friendships and marriages, bizarre new alliances and love affairs, illnesses, nervous breakdowns and suicides.

But the only *Helen of Troy* news the world hung on was the latest about Kim and David Glasgow. And how Bernie and Deirdre were taking it.

David Glasgow was not well known outside Great Britain when he went into *Helen of Troy,* but before the picture was completed, his name was a household word around the world. And his asking price had zoomed from peanuts to more than half a million a picture.

David Glasgow was a Scotsman, who had grown up in the roughest, toughest section of Glasgow, the Gorbals. His real name was David MacGillegowie. When he started to take himself seriously as an actor, people told him he should get a simple, easily pronounceable name. So he took the name of his home town for his stage name.

David had pulled himself out of the slums by the bootstraps. He had gone to Cambridge on a scholarship, where he cultivated a deep interest in literature. He also discovered he had a flair for acting, so he went to London and the Royal Academy of Dramatic Arts.

David Glasgow was maybe thirty-eight when he signed on to play Paris. Behind him lay a modestly successful career in films and on the stage, mostly in England. He had made three or four films in Hollywood. But they were of minor importance and nobody had been bowled over by his performance in them. He had scored his greatest successes in revivals of the classics, especially Shakespeare.

David Glasgow got the part in *Helen of Troy* only after Reginald Turner—who had originally been cast for it—had to bow out because of a severe attack of hepatitis. Many of Glasgow's fans were surprised and displeased to learn he had agreed to appear in the film. No matter who was making it, they wondered how it could be any better than any of the vulgar, overproduced De Mille-type spectacles that had poured out of the Hollywood dream factory. David Glasgow stooping to this! Among the head-shakers were some prominent critics who thought he held the promise of becoming the finest Shakespearean actor of his generation.

"What am I doing it for?" David Glasgow said in answer to a reporter. "Roughly sixty thousand pounds."

He had his responsibilities. He had two young sons, aged ten and twelve, and a wife of fifteen years, a lovely raven-haired Scotswoman who disliked London and the theater world. So their home was in Edinburgh. They went to London only when there was work there.

David Glasgow wasn't the handsomest man in the world, but he had an interesting, unforgettable face. It was lean and bony and angular and still had the traces of pockmarkings. His deep-set, rather melancholic blue eyes were topped by a high, intelligent brow and soft waves of blondish hair that fluttered rather poetically in the breeze. He was tall, lean, chesty, and still spoke with a slight Scottish burr.

For David Glasgow, as for everybody else associated with that ill-begotten picture, life would never be the same again.

I was completely out of touch with Kim all the months she was involved with *Helen of Troy*. During that time I was kidding myself I was happily married and that my only interest was my new husband.

In the Small World Department, one of Matt's buddies is a guy named Mike Mannings. Mike's a nice guy and we saw a lot of him when he came back to the Coast after *Helen* was in the can. Mike and I really dug each other and, who knows, if Matt hadn't been around . . .

Matt and Mike knew each other from the Studio. Mike was in the PR department then and had gone on to a better job at Foremost, where he eventually became publicity manager. Once Foremost got on the treadmill with *Helen*, the project took on such momentum that Mike personally set up shop in London. And then in Greece.

He could hardly believe his eyes or ears almost from the second he got on the scene. So this was Hollywood-on-the-Thames! So this was Hollywood-in-the-Aegean! For the sake of his own sanity, Mike began to keep a journal. Day by day he jotted it down like it was. If he hadn't kept faith with his journal, he said, he knew the time would come when he'd wonder if any of this had ever really happened.

Matt and I both told Mike he should publish his journal. It could make him a mint. It would tell readers more about the business of making movies than they'd learn in a dozen technical books on the subject. And it would give them a lot of inside dirt they'd never hear anywhere else.

Mike said that would be a great idea if he was retired. But not if he had hopes of staying on the payroll of Foremost.

Mike's no longer on the payroll of Foremost. He's gone on to become an independent producer. (*Summer Nights, Soft Murmurs* is his latest.) *Helen of Troy* is ancient history as ancient history goes these days—anything more than a month old. So Mike gave me permission to quote from his journal as I saw fit.

The entries from Mike's journal that I'm using here are just those that relate to Kim and that strange time in her life:

November 13. Hudson has been holed up in the Connaught for three weeks with a lingering virus. Who the hell—at least what red-blooded American—*wouldn't* catch something in a climate like this? Especially with no central heating.

The Script. Paris and Menelaus are in Sparta. Menelaus doesn't know he's about to be cuckolded. He doesn't know it's the destiny of Paris to love his wife and elope with her. He doesn't suspect a thing. And there's Paris writing "I love you" with spilled wine on top of the banquet table. And holding it up for Helen to see . . .

The Meeting. Hudson and Glasgow. They're scared to death of each other! Glasgow's introduced himself to everybody. But everybody. Down to the bottom grip and the thirteenth wardrobe mistress.

Hudson's frozen. Absolutely frozen. He's the great Shakespearean actor and he's going to look down his snooty nose at the Hollywood actress.

Finally Glasgow sort of dances around her, like a boxer. After a lot of hemming and hawing, he comes out with this: "Aye, you're a bonnie lass. All is dross that is not Kimberley."

"It seems to me I've heard that line before. Like from the script. Say something in Shakespeare."

She's bluffing. She's bluffed him down. Blushing, he backs away. He's supposed to be such a talker. But the cat seems to have caught his tongue.

November 14. Glasgow dug up some Shakespeare for Hudson. He approached her today, quoting:

"Shall I compare thee to a summer's day?
Thou are more lovely and more temperate:
Rough winds do shake the darling buds of May,
And Summer's lease hath all too short a date."

340

Hudson responded with that vulgar laugh of hers.

"Tell me more," quoth she.

November 20. Glasgow is coming on stronger. Today he serenaded Hudson with this verse:

> "He never saw, never before today,
> What was able to take his breath away,
> A face to lose youth for, to occupy age
> With the dream of, meet death with."

Glasgow gave her a courtly bow, offering apologies. "Sorry, luv. That's only Browning. I'm well aware of your devotion to the peerless Bard of Stratford."

"Balls," said Hudson.

That girl really has graphic powers of expression.

December 9. Glasgow is incredible. He comes on the set not only knowing his lines but everybody else's too. All the more incredible because the script is finalized about two minutes ahead of the shooting.

Oh, yes, Lonnie Braintree has arrived on the scene. He's Hudson's old buddy from their kiddie days at the Studio and she pushed her weight around to get him cast as Odysseus. Braintree, it turns out, is a pivotal figure in our cozy little circle of characters. He's not only Hudson's buddy but he's on friendly terms with Glasgow from the time they did *Julius Caesar* in London. On top of that, he's very thick with Glasgow's wife Deirdre.

The Hudsons (how could you call them the Millers?) are housed grandly in a rented house in Eaton Square. The Glasgows not so grandly in a flat in Chelsea. Lonnie Braintree's at the Savoy.

It's kaput with the Hudsons. A blind man could see that. But Bernie still looks at her with calflike eyes. She doesn't look at him at all. To her, he's just a go-for. "Bernie, see what they want and get rid of them." "Bernie, call the house and tell them we won't be eating until nine thirty." "Bernie, bring me a mirror."

Now Bernie's off to Switzerland for several days. Hudson's accountant has told her it would be smart tax-wise to establish residence in Switzerland, like a lot of the big ones in the mo'om-pitcher business are doing. Bernie's scouting properties in Klosters.

Glasgow has the reputation of being the biggest gash hound in the Western World. But he apparently has a good and lasting marriage and he loves his kids.

Too bad Glasgow and Hudson aren't free. Then if something got going between them it would be the publicity coup that could save this bomb-in-the-making.

December 11. She's outrageous! Audacious! Shameless!

When Menelaus brought Paris back to Sparta, he never dreamed there'd be any hanky-panky between him (Paris) and Helen. Under Aphrodite's spell, Helen loved Paris at first sight though he came on a bit much. Menelaus sees nothing because he is too grieved by the news of his father's death in Crete. After nine days of waiting, there's a favorable wind and he sets sail for Crete. That's when Helen and Paris get down to business.

Today they were doing the scene where Helen and Paris wave Menelaus off on his voyage. Afterward Glasgow was quoting something to Hudson in that bantering, insinuating way of his:

"I'll come no more behind your scenes, David. For the silk stockings and white bosoms of your actresses excite my amorous propensities."

He flashed her a meaningful wink. "Spoken by an extraordinary fellow Scotsman of mine. The inimitable Dr. Samuel Johnson, who was speaking to his friend Mr. David Garrick, the distinguished actor. I think the time might have been approximately Anno Domini 1749."

"Are you for real?" she put to him. "Or is it just bullshit?"

Well, there was a little bit more of backing and filling and feints and thrusts. By God, what did she do then but lead him right to her trailer! She has a trailer, incidentally, about the size of Madison Square Garden.

Doesn't she have to do her biggest scene on the trailer steps! Playing to a hundred crew members all standing around with their jaws gaping.

"Since I'm Helen of Troy," she said in a sweet but loud voice to Glasgow, "I hope you have a Trojan with you."

Loud guffaws from all hands aboard.

It was so brazen the way she did it we can only hope the help all wrote it off as grandstand clowning. That Glasgow was going in her trailer just for some drinks and gassing around.

I think Glasgow got more than drinks and conversation.

December 13. Hopes this might be a one-shot (no pun intended) ring-a-ding between Hudson and Glasgow have been blown (wow!) sky-high.

Hudson "entertained" him at another matinee today.

December 14. Bernie is back. Kim is depressed. David is being cool and proper.

Kim announces that she is buying a chalet in Klosters. But the announcement doesn't seem to make her happy.

December 17. Kim is suddenly beamish and vivacious. Could it be because Bernie's flying back to the States? Because he'll be doing a ten-day gig over the holidays at the Deauville in Miami Beach? On account of a last-minute cancellation?

December 19. Bernie's gone. Deirdre took the kids on the night train to Edinburgh and David's to join her there on the 22nd for the Christmas holiday.

That leaves Hudson and Glasgow.

Matinee-time. Yes.

If it were only the matinees!

Oh, no. Not for Mr. and Mrs. Excesses.

They had to go on and have dinner at Mirabelle's and . . .

December 21. The fat's in the fire.

The London papers yesterday all carried pictures of the couple as they emerged from Mirabelle's and stepped into their waiting limo. One enterprising wire services photographer tailed the car and caught Glasgow escorting Hudson into her Eaton Square digs.

Today's papers report Deirdre's reactions to the news.

What did she think of her husband's dining with Miss Hudson?

"I think it was a smashing idea," she said. "I'm sure they have a great deal to talk about. Since David couldn't have dinner with me and Miss Hudson couldn't have dinner with her husband, who's in the States, I think it's awfully nice they could have dinner together. It's dreary eating dinner by oneself. Especially for anyone as garrulous and gregarious as my husband."

What about Mr. Glasgow's seeing Miss Hudson into her home?

"Quite. My husband's always been the soul of gallantry. I expect him home later this evening and I look forward to hearing all about his night on the town with Miss Hudson."

A cable from Jake Wilkens, in Foremost's New York offices: "What the hell is going on?"

I wish I knew.

December 27. They not only celebrate Christmas here but something called Boxing Day the day afterward.

This is the first day in almost a week we've been in production. Glasgow's staying in Scotland until after New Year's. He doesn't have any scenes until then.

Hudson's on the set. She has a scene where she's gathering up all the palace jewels to stash away in the ship when she elopes with Paris. She seems pouty and edgy. I asked Lonnie Braintree what was eating her. He gave me a mysterious smile and said, "I think she misses a certain somebody."

Not Bernie, for damn sure.

January 4. Glasgow's back. So is Bernie. Which has Hudson smiling out of one side of the mouth and spitting out of the other side.

For the moment everybody is behaving. Whew!

January 9. Yesterday Hudson sent Bernie back to Switzerland. He's supposed to staff up for the chalet she bought. She gets a week off when we leave here and move operations to Greece. She'll stay there.

Coincidentally Glasgow has rented a house in Switzerland. In Davos. He'll put his boys in a Swiss school. Deirdre's an avid skiier and hates Greece to boot. The plan is David will fly to her on weekends.

When the cat's away, the mice will play.

Bernie was hardly on the plane for Zurich when Hudson and Glasgow staged another matinee.

January 11. If they'd only confine themselves to her trailer!

Last night they dined at the White Elephant and God knows what else. Attracting mobs and getting into the papers smiling romantically at each other across a battery of highball and wine glasses.

More static from stateside: "Whatever the hell's happening over there, stop it!"

January 13. Somebody *should* be speaking to Hudson. But for the moment nobody wants to burst her little bubble. Everything's going so peachy. She's effervescent as champagne, all jokes and smiles, and *giving a performance.*

My guess is she's taking this thing a lot more seriously than Glasgow is. He's an old seed-dropper from way back. But like a homing pigeon, he always circles back to Deirdre.

My hunches about him are supported by this bit of gallantry that was overheard and passed on to me. Glasgow, talking about Hudson, to an old crony: "She'll show up every fucking time I'm on the set. Her cunt is her Achilles heel."

January 14. Bernie's back. He's not very bright, God knows.

But he's heard the rumors and he's fuming. Hudson ignores his outburst. Admitting or denying nothing. She regards it as infra dig to even answer him.

January 18. Bernie is wanted for a TV show in Lisbon. *Lisbon?* He balked at going but Hudson told him to get his ass down there.

He'll be gone three days and that'll give her a little time to play.

January 20. Pictures of them gracing a table at Talk of the Town are everywhere.

Cable from New York: "Take immediate action!"

But nobody wants to approach her. Neither Harrison (the producer), nor Frank (the director) nor cowardly little me. Everything's going too swimmingly. Try criticizing her and she's sure to pull the sulks. Or some incapacitating illness.

Glasgow strikes us all as a cool cookie. Charming and amiable and all that. But opportunistic too, with his eye cocked on the main chance. It hasn't escaped his notice that he's suddenly a much hotter property playing opposite Hudson in a top-budgeted picture than he'd be in a lifetime of playing Shakespeare to rapturous notices.

I was designated to be the one to have a little chat with David. In the most delicate language I could summon to my lips, I pointed out how even the *appearance* of impropriety could have devastating consequences for the picture and all parties concerned. Especially in view of Miss Hudson's recent skirmishes with public opinion in America . . .

No dummy David, he said he'd have a word with Kim.

January 22. David's had his word with Kim. And she with him. Thank God for Lonnie Braintree! He's the go-between among all parties. He has everybody's best wishes at heart. He's also in the center of things—my primary source of information.

Glasgow told Hudson they should go on being the best of friends. But maybe no more. As for the rest, it had been just one of those things.

"Balls," said Hudson.

"I really think, luv, we must say fun was fun."

"Balls."

January 24. Glasgow must be trying to drive his point home. Today he had as his guest on the set a cheap, giggling little tootsie he must have found tending bar in some East End pub.

Afterwards he ostentatiously led her to his dressing room. Hudson was seething.

January 26. Hudson has checked into the London Clinic! Everything at Pinewood has ground to a virtual halt. We're putting out the story she has an abdominal virus. She's diagnosed her ailment as total fatigue and indicates it may be weeks before she feels well enough to resume working.

February 2. Hudson reigns! She's shown just who has clout around the joint. With all the daily visits and delegations to the London Clinic, the flowers and the telegrams and the frantic phone calls from New York and Hollywood, Hudson continued to languish. She just wasn't beginning to get her strength back. Maybe if she was going to be laid up too long they should begin to think about replacing her . . .

Harrison visited her today. With her characteristic slyness, when she's making a point, she allowed that a visit from her co-star might give her spirits a lift.

Her wishes will be done.

Glasgow came, saw, and brought a radiant Hudson out of the Clinic. Leaning on him, her arms entwined in his, she beamed her broadest smiles into the exploding flashbulbs.

February 5. Deirdre is in Switzerland putting the kids into school. Bernie is right here. *And they're carrying on right under his eyes!* He rages no more. He doesn't even whimper.

"Bernie," Her Highness told him, "if you don't like what you see, you know what you can do. And I wish you'd do it."

The London papers are having a field day. God, how the English dearly love a sex scandal!

It's on-again, off-again between both of them in twenty-four-hour cycles. One day they're remorseful, keeping their distance. The next day it's lovey-dovey and they're inside each other's armpits.

February 10. Deirdre, in Davos: "When you have a husband who is so talented and handsome and magnetic you know if you have any sense at all a great many other women are going to find him attractive too. And you must expect you are going to have to share him with some of them. For a moment."

March 7. Athens. The scene changes. And how!

To give Hudson and Glasgow more time at their respective domiciles in Switzerland, the big scene where the Greek fleet sets sail for Troy to rescue Helen was shot before the one where Paris and Helen actually elope.

The Stars have arrived. Everybody's holding their breath. Glasgow's holed up at the Athens Hilton, and Hudson & Entourage have taken over half a floor of the Grand Bretagne downtown on Constitution Square.

Ryder Downey persuaded Hudson to pose with Bernie for a big spread in *Vogue* to show off her chalet in Klosters. A masterful stroke. Implies the shaky truth that they're still very much married and their love nest is intact.

Today Hudson and Glasgow meet—presumably for the first time since London—to board the ship for Troy, which gets blown to Cyprus instead.

Hudson and Glasgow come together like strangers. Shy and proper and aloof. *Qué pasa?*

May it last!

March 9. The gods are against us! Hudson's housekeeper back in London has decided to spill the beans. For the pride of authorship—and a few hundred pounds—she's pouring out her guts for the *News of the World* in a series called "The Star and Her Gentleman Caller."

"Mr. Glasgow frequently accompanied Miss Hudson home after dinner or an evening in the theater," the good woman wrote. "If the hour was quite late, he would sometimes be an overnight guest. He was usually up quite early in the morning and he always enjoyed a proper English breakfast."

Hell is breaking loose on all fronts.

Hudson is furious. Glasgow is livid. The powers that be are apoplectic.

Methinks the housekeeper knows whereof she writes.

March 11. God bless the Greek press. They show a refreshing restraint in their coverage of the cavortings of movie folks. But the Italians and the English more than compensate for them. They're here in droves, the reporters and photographers, like packs of wild dogs.

The effect of all this notoriety—the housekeeper's memoirs, the converging of half the world's accredited members of the press on Athens, and the heat coming from New York and the Coast—has been the reverse of the desideratum. The ice is broken. That nice cool professional distance we hoped the Stars would sustain has vanished.

Today they were shooting the spear-throwing duel between Paris and Menelaus. Where was Hudson? Relaxing back at the Grand Bretagne? She was not. She was on the set beaming up at Glasgow the whole day, cheering wildly when Paris eludes Menelaus's spear, thanks to Aphrodite's intervention.

Lonnie Braintree let slip that the Stars were having dinner tonight at the Dionysos. "They'll be able to gaze up at the Acropolis," Lonnie cracked dryly, "and maybe derive some inspiration."

March 13. Their attitude seems to be, "If we have the name, we might as well have the game."

Last night (read, this morning) they ended up in a taverna in the Plaka, handkerchief-dancing and smashing dishes in the approved Greek fashion.

Today both are no-shows. Too much ouzo and retsina, no doubt. God knows what else.

The Ides of March approach. I shudder.

March 17. Hudson has moved out of the Grand Bretagne. No forwarding address. Ditto Glasgow. From the Hilton. Neither has offered any explanations to anybody. Including Lonnie.

March 19. The paparazzi are more resourceful than a big powerful movie studio in bringing to light classified information. They've traced her to a hideaway villa in the suburbs, which she's apparently rented. They also shot some dandy pictures of her sunbathing on the terrace with a familiar face that doesn't in the least resemble her husband's.

Bernie has been packed off to Paris to scout for paintings and objets d'art for the chalet.

March 20. Hudson's taking the offensive. Raving and ranting. She's the outraged citizen whose civil rights have been violated.

"Why the hell can't those vermin leave me alone? I'm not doing anything to attract attention. I'm going out of my way to avoid it. I just can't see why I'm all that fascinating."

Is she kidding?

March 26. The little idyll in the seaside villa has been interrupted. Maybe cancelled.

Deirdre is coming for the weekend and David's back in the Hilton.

Deirdre's a fascinating woman. Cool, sure of herself, seemingly simple, never leaves headquarters for the battlefield. From all the evidence, Glasgow is still very much in love with her. Nobody would give you any bets he's about to ditch her for Hudson. Hudson's just someone to get his rocks off with when Deirdre's not around. One of the hundreds he's poked his pecker into en route from the Gorbals to Greece.

April 2. Deirdre has prevailed. At least for the time being. She's come and gone and we're back to where we came in on Greece. The erstwhile lovers are apart. He's still in the Hilton and she's where she is.

They're back to their stiff formalities again on the set.

Underneath, Hudson must be seething. Who the hell does he think he is? *She's* the one who does the rejecting, not the guy!

April 4. Our spy overheard Hudson passing on this little tidbit to Lonnie Braintree. She was talking about Bernie.

"I'm going to keep him up there as long as I can. It's not only that I can't stand the sight of him, I can't stand the *smell* of him. I swear he never takes a bath. If he'd even change those filthy pajamas and bathrobe he never gets out of, that would be a help. In the pocket of the robe he carries a little toy pistol. He keeps pulling it out and aiming it at my heart and he goes, 'Ping, ping. You're dead.' I told him, 'Too bad you haven't got any balls, Bernie. If you had balls, you'd be waving a loaded pistol at me.' "

April 10. It's Operation Rhodes. The island of Rhodes becomes Troy. It's a big island with varied terrain, plenty of space for camps and battlefields and the waging of the ten-year Trojan War.

The plan is to finish all the scenes involving Paris and/or Helen first and then go on to the epic battle, the wooden horse, the sack of Troy, etc., afterward. In other words, to get done with Hudson and Glasgow before the powder keg blows up.

Hudson takes one look at Rhodes and decides she hates it.

April 24. Problems, problems, problems. Delays, delays, delays. Nothing's going according to SOP.

Hudson may be right. But for the wrong reasons. I hate this island too. But mostly because we seem to be accomplishing nothing fast.

Hudson isn't helping. She can be a mean, sulky bitch when she chooses to be. Maybe that's too hard on her. Fact is, she's a deeply unhappy woman. Plain to see, she's carrying a torch bigger than the Statue of Liberty.

Glasgow's in his own tent, being good as gold and true to his marriage vows. And lapping up the wine of the country. Yecch!

Hudson flies to Athens weekends. Alone. And comes back looking more dragged-out than when she left.

April 26. Hudson has everybody worried. She has that I-think-I'm-going-to-be-sick look. Like for about six months.

With the meter ticking away at about a thousand G's a second, it's a worrisome situation.

May 1. God bless American ingenuity! And ambivalence. Somebody—I refuse to speculate who (it would be too depressing!)—has put a bug in Glasgow's ear. The whole atmosphere is changed. It's all sunshine and smiles and warm Gulf Streams between them again.

Hudson and Glasgow have just set sail for a weekend of luxury cruising in the Greek Isles.

May 7. I feel sorry for Hudson. She can be a rough and tough customer, but there's a basic honesty to the broad. As she says, "I never pretended I was the girl next door or Mrs. America. I'm not like an ordinary housewife and I'm not trying to pass myself off as being like one."

There she is coming off the yacht in Mykonos to the screams of "Keem, Keem!" And she's smiling radiantly at a throng of maybe a thousand islanders who've never seen a big-time movie star before.

There she is caught in that pose, with her escort beside her, on front pages from Anchorage to Auckland.

I feel sorry for her looking so happy there, when there are sure as hell going to be repercussions.

May 9. Was I ever right about the repercussions!

First Deirdre was heard from through her conduit, Lonnie Braintree. Deirdre is not amused. Not that she's worried. She just doesn't like the publicity. Her concern is for the boys, who are getting all the wrong kind of attention from their classmates at school.

Bernie's got into the act too. He flew down here—to Hudson's surprise and displeasure—demanding an explanation. He got it.

"I'm in love with David and want to marry him," she reportedly told Bernie. "Now please go back to Switzerland like a good boy. Or allow me to finance you to a one-way ticket to America."

Hudson's had to take her lumps. They were delivered in person from New York. By no less than Barney McAllister, Foremost's president. He read the riot act to her. "If you break up another marriage," Himself told her in pulsating

350

fire-and-brimstone tones, "you'll not only be a woman without a career. You'll be a woman without a country. You won't be able to come home again. You'll be stoned in the streets."

Such piety! Such hypocrisy! Who the hell chartered the yacht and coaxed Glasgow into renewed intimacy with Hudson but men on McAllister's own staff? As a way of humoring her and cajoling her back into a working mood.

The moral of the situation: anything's cricket in movie-making—to advance the project and protect the investment—unless you get caught. But where is someone like Hudson going to hide?

May 11. Hudson's been confined to her trailer since McAllister dropped his bombshell. She'll see nobody but Ryder Downey and Lonnie Braintree. Ryder has discouraged her from making any statements to the press or offering any apologies. That would be an acknowledgment of wrong-doing. The best strategy, he told her, is to brazen it out.

Apparently she's remorseful one minute and raging the next. And crying right around the clock. Even if she wanted to work, it's doubtful if makeup could get her in shape to face the cameras. In his usual graphic way of talking, Ryder said her eyes "look like two angry ass-holes."

There is this fascinating sidelight to her character, though, signifying some underlying stability and vein of iron. Joe Brodkin, the ace hot-shot new movie producer, sent her a script that's a contemporary comedy and wanted to know what she thought of it as another vehicle for herself and Glasgow.

She pulled herself together long enough to scrawl Joe Brodkin a terse reply: "I'll tell you what I think of the script when you tell me what you think of $1,200,000 plus 8 percent of the gross for me and $600,000 plus 8 percent of the gross for Mr. Glasgow."

May 14. Will this picture ever be finished?

Hudson continues to languish in her quarters. Still to be shot, involving the Stars, are two vital love scenes between Paris and Helen. Then the death of Paris in the duel with King Philoctetes. And Helen's stabbing her hated new husband Prince Deiphobus to death.

McAllister had Harrison on the overseas tube today barking, "I want action!"

"Go to Hellas," replied the literate Harrison.

Hudson has summoned her doctor from London.

May 16. Hudson's checked into the American Hospital in Rome. Doctor's orders. He's diagnosed her as suffering from nervous exhaustion. No prognostications about how long she'll be hors de combat.

May 30. Here we go again, kiddies! The solution that was so simple a day-old idiot could have thought of it finally occurred to——? You guessed it. Barney McAllister. Wouldn't it be nice, he suggested, if David Glasgow paid his co-star a visit in the hospital?

A day-old idiot could also predict the results. A gloriously beautiful, healthy-looking, relaxed, and happy Helen emerges from the hospital arm-in-arm with Paris.

After a weekend in Corfu, the Stars will return to Rhodes for the filming of their final scenes.

June 16. It's over! *Mirabile dictu,* it's over! In more ways than one.

The Stars (lovers) came back from Corfu with the glow of happily married newlyweds. And with the hard grit of the professionals they both are when they want to be.

Down to business. (Yes, monkey-business too. On their own time.) And giving their very best. Those love scenes would melt the heart of a Gorgon! They're for real. Ditto Hudson's grief at the death of Paris. Those are honest tears she sheds.

Glasgow has to hang around for a scene they've added to the beginning, before he's met Helen. But they wanted to finish up with her first—those scenes after Menelaus has reclaimed her from Troy and they're being blown by perverse winds to Cyprus, Phoenicia, Ethiopia, and Libya as they try to make it back to Sparta.

Everyone was holding their breath, wondering: When she's done, will she hang around waiting for him?

But abruptly, with no good-byes, she fled! To Zurich. The only formal good-bye she said was to Glasgow, so formal it was written and hand-delivered by Lonnie Braintree. I don't think Hudson put him up to divulging the contents of the note but it's obvious she wouldn't be displeased since the note puts her in a favorable light. And nothing makes Lonnie happier than to put his treasured, controversial friend in a favorable light. Hence, his eagerness to quote Kim's message verbatim.

To David Glasgow, Kim wrote:

This seems to be the appropriate time and place to end

our friendship. There can be no question that it must end. To attempt to continue it would be too selfish on the part of either one of us. It could only bring about the unhappiness of other people who don't deserve to be hurt. Believe me, this is for the best—for all of us.

My best—as always,

Kim

Chapter 35

It must have been almost two years after she finished *Helen of Troy* before I had a tête-à-tête with Kim. God, how long it had been! How much had happened to both of us!

It was my first trip to Paris. Matt and I were there because he had business connected with a big Studio musical that was using the Left Bank for location shots. Kim and her by-now chronic co-star were going into the film version of one of those frothy boulevard comedies the French eat up.

Matt and I were at the Georges V.

Kim and David were ensconced in the Plaza-Athenée.

Holy Virgin Mary, how beautiful—how breathtakingly exquisite—she was! All cloudy and angel-like in a billowy jade-green teagown the exact match of her eyes. That face, that tall statuesque pose, the extraordinary burnished copper hair in a high pompadour. In the sheer ecstasy of seeing her again—seeing her like this—I reached for her. I was so hungry to hug her to me.

Glad as she was to see me, she backed away. The amazing thing about Kim is that she can fall into bed with men she hasn't been introduced to. But she doesn't like to be touched by other women. Even if she loves them and has known them a million years. Unless she's the one who initiates the touching. Like with Mama.

"It may not be the best hotel in Paris," she said. "But I wouldn't stay anywhere else. For the name alone. How can you get any closer to Athens than Athenée?"

Am I supposed to feel sorry for her? Because there might be a better hotel in Paris? The furniture may be ersatz Louis XV. But it looks pretty goddamn luxurious to a basically simple little girl from Albany, New York.

"Gina, I'm having something yummy," she said, pointing to

the bottle sticking out of a sterling silver ice bucket. "Dom Perignon '59. May I pour you a glass? Or would you like something else?"

"No, thanks," I said. Champagne has never sent me all that much. At three o'clock in the afternoon I've never had a taste for it.

"I guess you're dying to know what happened," she bubbled.

To paraphrase somebody or other, the more people change, the more they stay the same. How "in character" it was of Kim to greet an old friend she hadn't seen or talked to in years and ask them nothing about themselves! And launch right into a hunk of her own autobiography. But she was right. I was dying to know what had happened after *Helen of Troy*. In a sense I did know, of course. But I was dying to have all the blank spaces filled in.

"For once in my life," she said, "I acted unselfishly. I put the happiness of others before my own. I knew I must give David up. I was also determined to send Bernie packing. But that was no sacrifice. I came back to Klosters a shattered woman. It was summer and out of season and I don't believe I've ever felt so alone and deserted and absolutely up a blind alley. I didn't have a clue as to what the future might hold. And I didn't much give a damn."

Except for Indiana and her mother, she was totally alone in Klosters. She vegetated. She saw nobody. She tried to feign interest in her mother's hobby of needlepoint, but she was numb. Just going through the motions: eating and hiking and sleeping, leading the life of an automaton, day after day after day. For all practical purposes, she was dead. Where was it she had read that a rut and a grave differ only in their dimensions?

The last week in August—more than two months after she left Rhodes—she got a call from David Glasgow, who was calling from Davos. He invited her to have lunch with him.

It was a stupid idea, she thought. There was no reason to go. But in view of how empty all her days were, there was no reason *not* to go.

David suggested they should lunch at the Palace in St. Moritz.

Kim hired a young local named Gerhardt to drive her to St. Moritz. She arrived at the Palace and watched David get out of his car and walk slowly toward her. He looked gloriously tanned, and she wondered if this could have come from a Switzerland sun. He took her hand gently and lifted her out of the car.

"It's so nice to see you again," he said nervously.

And then the lunch passed in such a flurry—she was in a daze—that, later, she couldn't recall what they had eaten or a single word he had said.

Then he was helping her back into the car again. Like two very shy, awkward teen-agers on their first date, they parted.

That was that, she told herself, and she tried to put him out of her mind, but that was impossible.

About two weeks later, David called her again for lunch. This time they were not quite so shy with each other. They drank a lot of wine and relaxed and laughed away the afternoon. And when they parted, he touched her cheek with his hand.

It was another two weeks or so before she heard from him again. In terms of themselves, there was no talk of the past or the future.

"I couldn't see any harm in this," she said, "although Ryder and everybody else told me I was playing with fire. What could be the harm in having lunch with somebody? I was divorced from Bernie but David was still happily married to Deirdre. I really meant to put other people's happiness before mine. I didn't want to hurt David or Deirdre or their sons. I wanted to make myself available to David on his terms, whatever they might be. I wasn't going to try to catch him or trick him away from Deirdre. I wasn't going to try to make him jealous by pretending to have other romances. I'm really a one-man woman. As long as David was alive, it seemed inconceivable that I could ever become interested in another man. I thought I would go through the rest of my life alone living on whatever crumbs David might choose to throw my way."

Then Kim and David got called back to London to do additional scenes for *Helen of Troy*. She went to the Dorchester and the Glasgows went to the Savoy.

They thought it might take a week or ten days. But it was almost nine months before any of them got out of London.

While they were working at Pinewood, Kim got a call from Joe Brodkin and he said okay to her preposterous money demands to do his movie. He wanted both her and David—at their prices and percentages—to stay on and make the film in London. David had never dreamed he would command such money—in the movie business or any other kind of business.

"Crazy," said Kim.

So there they were, back where it all began. Kim in a rented house in St. John's Wood. The Glasgows in their Chelsea flat.

"I think men are maybe different from women in this re-

355

spect," said Kim. "I genuinely think a man can be in love with two women at the same time. I doubt whether it's possible for a woman—at least if she's anything like me. But I do think that was the impossible predicament poor David was in all those wretched months in London when nobody seemed to be happy. I was determined to stick by my vow of not doing one thing to entice him away from Deirdre. But I was also determined to do anything that would serve his happiness. His wishes would be my command. He could use me any way he wanted to. Whatever he wanted from me, I would try to give him. How could I feel debased if it was making him any happier?"

Nothing anybody did seemed to make anybody any happier. It was an impossible situation. On top of their tangled relationships, Kim and David had to contend with the abusiveness of worldwide public opinion. They were open and shameless in their indecency, their critics charged, cruelly oblivious to the suffering and humiliation of Deirdre.

"I'm going to have to piss or get off the pot, luv," David said to her one day. "The wicket's too sticky for rhyme or reason."

She waited ominously for him to go on.

"We are three miserable earthlings. Would that happiness, like Gaul, could be divided by three. It can't. Somebody must make way in the hope that two people can try to be happy together. In the hope that the third person can find happiness elsewhere."

He paused and she waited another eternity to hear him out.

"'In the dark night of the soul,' as Fitzgerald said, 'it's always three o'clock in the morning.' In the dark night of my soul I have decided that I want to marry you."

"It was, of course, what I wanted to hear with every atom of my being," she told me. "Even though I knew we'd both die a thousand deaths before we saw the sun again."

That old bromide, she said, about hell having no fury like a woman scorned should be changed to a woman *wronged*. Everybody in the world was on Deirdre's side.

"I don't think Adolf Hitler got more hate mail than I did. Some of the gentlest letters started out 'Dear Whore . . .' "

"How awful for you, Kim," I said. "It must have been pure hell."

"It was. In the eyes of God we may not be redeemed until we celebrate our golden wedding anniversary. In the eyes of the world our only hope seemed to be to show how much we really loved each other—and make the marriage last. But do you know what really saved our necks? The sweet smell of

356

success. It's remarkable how much you'll be forgiven if you're just successful. *Helen of Troy* could have been the greatest film of all time if they hadn't allowed the butchers to hack it up so it would fit into a nice 12-2-4-6-8-10 time slot in all the downtown theater houses. Even so, with all the down reviews, people were curious to see it and it's building into a solid box office hit. Who knows, in the twenty-first century, it might even break even. Anyway—" She stopped to refill her glass.

"Anyway," I picked up, "it's done okay."

"Which is more than can be said for *Day of the Butterflies*. But that's not the way the public gauges success and failure. They look at us and think, 'Jeez, they get paid all that loot to make a movie. They must be something special.' They've already forgotten what they were so mad about. They don't even care how lousy the picture might be or how lousy *we* might be. We're getting paid this stupendous amount of money, so we must be okay, all right joes, best people types. Wild!"

Deirdre consented to a divorce. Kim and David were married in Chicago, where they had gone for the premiere of *Day of the Butterflies*. While they were there, David got a call from Allan Mendelsohn, the producer, asking him if he'd be interested in doing *Macbeth* on Broadway. David replied he'd be very interested—with the proviso that his bride would be Lady Macbeth.

Kim let out a shriek when she heard David putting that little clause in the deal.

"I had never been near a stage in my life," she reminded me. "I was petrified. I might get creamed fifty ways to Sunday by the critics. But as David said, what did it matter? The public would still turn out in droves to see us."

The critics didn't exactly cream Kim's performance as Lady Macbeth, but they were ecstatic about David's Macbeth. David was prophetic about the public. They did turn out in droves.

"Well, you know how it was," said Kim. "You must've read about it. My God, it was wonderful and terrifying at the same time. If only Shakespeare had been alive to see the mobs he was drawing hundreds of years later! Only it wasn't Shakespeare, of course. It was the Glasgows. Gina, I've never seen anything like it. Every night it was worth our lives to get out of that stage door and into our car. If we hadn't had a whole battalion of muscular cops at our disposal, we'd have been dead ducks. They were all crying and clamoring just to touch us. We were staying in the Waldorf Towers and they had to put on extra guards to control the crazies who kept jamming all the doors around the time we would leave for the theater or be coming home. It was horrible, frightening!"

"And wonderful, as you said," I reminded her.

"It taught me what quick-change artists the great American public can be. Any public for that matter. You can be on everybody's 'Drop Dead' list one minute and the next minute you're being worshipped. I couldn't help wondering how many of those people screaming for tickets to see us and reaching out to touch us were the same ones who had been writing us the poison pen letters not so long ago. Nothing had changed, really. Except that we had 'got away with it,' so to speak. There were producers ready to pay us the craziest sums of money actors ever got paid. And that turned the tide."

If she was right—and she probably was—it was a sad reflection on John and Jane Q. Public.

"Where *is* David?" I asked. It had taken great restraint to keep from asking earlier. Never having met him before, I was dying of curiosity to see him in the flesh.

Kim kept me in suspense while she poured more champagne into her glass. "If he's where he should be," she replied, with a knowing smile, "he's in one of two places. He's either at the Buckminster Kennels in Neuilly. Or at Van Cleef and Arpels."

I didn't know what the knowing smile was supposed to mean. I asked what he'd be doing at a kennel or Van Cleef and Arpels.

"I got up feeling a little 'peckish,' to use David's word," she explained. "David's learned that when I'm feeling 'peckish' it's his cue to nip out somewhere and pick up a little comforter or two for me."

She left it to my imagination to guess what comforters David would be bringing back from the Buckminster Kennels and Van Cleef and Arpels.

I didn't have the time to wait and see. I had to get back and change. Matt and I were meeting some business contact of his for a drink in the Ritz Bar at five o'clock sharp.

"I'm sorry I didn't meet David," I said.

"I'm sorry I didn't see Matt again." On impulse, she added, "Tell you what, Gina. Can you have lunch with us tomorrow? Then you can meet David."

"I can. But I doubt that Matt can."

"Well, you come anyway. Meet us here at one o'clock. And while I think of it, I'll call for a reservation."

"Henri," she said. "This is Kimberley Hudson. We'll be four for lunch tomorrow. I'll want a table by the window."

"I know Matt can't come," I reminded her.

"I know," she said. "We'll still be four."

And she left me to wonder who the Mystery Guest would be.

Before I could be introduced to David the next day I had to meet Marmaduke. There was no avoiding Marmaduke. I heard him the moment I pressed the buzzer. Marmaduke obviously was what David had brought back from the Buckminster Kennels in Neuilly. He was a honey-haired Lhasa Apso with a great mop of hair falling all over his face. It was impossible to make eye contact. Who needed eye contact, with all the ear contact you were getting from his yah-yah yelping?

"Next to David, I've decided," said Kim, gathering the dog up in her arms and kissing him on the snout, "Marmaduke's the love of my life. David brought him home for me just yesterday and it was love at first sight."

There was David . . . tall, stony-faced handsome, sipping a drink, looking soberly into my eyes over the rim of the glass. He was wearing a blazer and a white silk shirt. He had a black and gold ascot tucked into his open collar.

"So," he said, "it's you."

"Yes."

"Whoever you are."

"David knows who you are," said Kim. "I told him about you."

She skipped into the bedroom and was back again in a second. "Look what David got me yesterday." She held up a chain of octagonal black onyx links studded with diamonds set in eighteen-karat gold. It must have cost ten grand if it cost a franc. David sure had made it to Van Cleef and Arpels.

"It's a knockout!" I gasped.

"Yes," Kim agreed. "It cheered me up considerably."

She put the chain away and we were off to lunch.

I don't think I've ever been through a lunch like that. Before or since. It was unforgettable in every way. Even getting there was part of the experience.

We rode to L———'s on the Champs Elysées in a chauffeured white Rolls Royce. Marmaduke sat in Kim's lap. I thought he would surely be deposited into the custody of the driver when we got to the restaurant. Not so. Kim had no notion of parting with Marmaduke for a second.

L———'s is one of the most beautiful and most expensive restaurants in the world. It's drenched in satin, chandeliers, and Dresden porcelain. I'm deliberately not mentioning the name because I don't think Monsieur L., who's still very much alive, would appreciate any publicity depicting the humiliation of his staff.

Henri's eyebrow did a small twitch at the sight of the dog. But he recovered quickly and led us to a window table that looked out upon a lush garden. Kim parked Marmaduke on the fourth chair.

"Will there be four, Monsieur?" Henri asked David.

Before David could answer, Kim cut in, "There *are* four, as it would seem to be quite apparent."

That cleared up the mystery about the Mystery Guest. It was Marmaduke.

David ordered two bottles of Bollinger '26. When he was told there was no Bollinger '26 in stock, he took it as a personal insult. The waiter suggested Dom Perignon '47. David glumly allowed the bottles to be brought.

David talked and talked and talked . . . a nonstop monologue pitched mostly to the rafters and the middle distance. Shakespeare, Strindberg, Chekhov, Olivier, Gielgud . . . the names rolled off his lips. He was on intimate terms with them all.

It turned out I was a much better audience than his wife, who was preoccupied with her new toy. Marmaduke.

We had to wait until both bottles of champagne were finished before lunch could be ordered. I had about a third of one glass. Kim almost kept up with David, refill for refill.

For appetizers four potted quail au foie gras were ordered.

It was a great disappointment to Kim that Marmaduke wouldn't touch the dollop of potted quail au foie gras she held out to him on her fingertip.

"Oh, Marmaduke, mother's so heartbroken you're missing one of the great delicacies of the world," she said.

"Perverse little beast," David commented.

"David!" said Kim, in mock horror. "Never, never call Marmaduke a beast. Let alone a perverse beast. He's our adorable child."

"Kimberley tells me you used to sing a little," said David.

It was the first personal remark he had directed to me. It came across as so insufferably condescending I couldn't let it pass. "I used to sing a lot," I said, "and I still do. Whether or not anybody is listening."

"Quite," he said. "I stand corrected."

On the basis of the waiter's enthusiasm, we all opted for the chicken Grand Palais.

"Three?"

"Four," corrected Kim. "We are four at this table."

It was the waiter's turn to twitch an eyebrow.

David ordered the first of two bottles of Château Latour

that he and Kim required to wash down their chicken Grand Palais.

How exquisitely everything is done at L———'s! The wine is decanted with reverence and poured into silver aiguières and the food is served in vermeil dishes.

David started working out on the Château Latour before we had our entrees.

The waiter served the chicken Grand Palais onto four plates and put them before us. I could almost hear him grinding his teeth when he set the plate in front of Marmaduke.

"Bon appétit," he said.

"Garçon," said Kim, "would you be good enough to give my friend a little help?"

"Help?"

"Yes. My friend isn't very handy with a knife and fork. Would you be good enough to cut up his chicken for him?"

For a millionth of a second the waiter's eyes flashed with pure loathing. He hesitated, as if he couldn't believe his ears. Kim sat back grandly, looking up at him, waiting for him to proceed. Even in plush, cosmopolitan L———'s, movie stars like the Glasgows are a magnetic attraction. I think every eye in the place was riveted on our table as our poor waiter was reduced to cutting up the chicken on the plate in front of the dog.

At that table, sad to say, I was the only one who had the grace to blush. It went beyond blushing. I thought I was about to go up in flames. I agonized with the waiter, knowing what he must be feeling.

Kim was spoon-feeding the diced chicken in its elegant sauce to Marmaduke, who was much more enthusiastic about this than he had been about the potted quail au foie gras. Kim didn't touch her food until Marmaduke had cleaned up everything on his plate. Including the wild rice and Belgian carrots.

"Oh, my little darling dumpling," Kim cooed, wiping his mouth with a serviette, "mother's so proud of you."

Kim was proud of Marmaduke again when he turned up his snout at the crêpes Grand Marnier.

"Oh, you're so smart, my darling. If your Mama had a brain in her head, she wouldn't be eating desserts either. Who's going to love her when she's fat and ugly? Only you, my darling."

The most I can say for that afternoon was that I enjoyed the restaurant and the food was great. But I didn't like either my old friend or her new husband very much. Kim's behavior was peculiar, to say the least.

An innocent observer might have wondered if she didn't

have her priorities bass ackwards when she said, "Next to David, I've decided, Marmaduke is the love of my life."

Chapter 36

I don't think I've seen Kim more than half a dozen times since that lunch in Paris. There have been several middle-of-the-night phone calls when she's half-crocked and wants to get something off that voluptuous chest of hers. To tell the truth, I've never gone out of my way to see Kim since she married David. I find David so off-putting. Maybe if I found him stone-sober just once I wouldn't feel that way.

You never know how to take him, what to expect. *In vino veritas*, the saying goes. Everything a man says or does in his cups reflects only what's really inside him waiting to surface. There are no secret demons in alcohol that take possession of a person's personality and distort it. What comes out, with drinking, is just what's always been there.

With most people you can predict what their behavior is going to be like when they're drinking. They get jolly or abusive or sad or talkative. Whatever. But there seems to be more or less one pattern of response. But with a mercurial temperament like David's, you never know what mood's going to come up. One time he's clammed up and casting hostile, glassy-eyed looks in your direction that say, "What the hell are you doing here?" The next time he's all over you like a puppy dog, practically licking your hands and face. He's in highest spirits or deepest depression. He's on a laughing jag or a crying jag, being charming or thoroughly disagreeable, spinning nonstop yards and anecdotes or snarling and grunting.

A strange, complicated man, David Glasgow, who manages consistently to make me feel uncomfortable. Even on the couple of occasions when he acted glad to see me and spread on the charm with a trowel. Those times I had the feeling that his mood could change in a minute and I didn't want to be around when it did.

So much of what I know or perceive of the Glasgow Years doesn't come from direct knowledge or observation. I've had to piece it together from such a variety of sources. Things I've been told by people who worked for them. Published interviews with them. Gossip. Talks with Kim's mother. My own intuitions.

Shortly after that bizarre luncheon at L————'s, Kim and David started filming the boulevard comedy they were in Paris to do. As comedies go, it was a lightweight. But it was a big success. Apparently millions and millions of people all over the world were willing to plunk out their hard-earned dollars or drachmas or pesos or whatever to see the Glasgows together in anything. Even just standing together reading from the telephone book.

"The success of the picture," Kim said, "is totally owing to David. David gave it that elegance and finesse that was needed for such a delicate little trifle. I couldn't have done it without him. He got me to, well, *float*."

In those days Kim couldn't give an interview without as much as saying that David had discovered *her!* For the record she was so sweet, demure, and submissive. What a target she would be for Women's Lib zealots if she were saying those things today!

Back in the States they moved in a perpetual fever, with everyone hot for their company, hot to sign them up. Hal Brooking was doing the movie version of *Who Needs Marriage?* It was a comedy-drama that had had a long run on Broadway and he wanted the Glasgows to play the leads. He discussed the project with them at the Regency Hotel in New York, where Kim had an additional suite just to house her wardrobe.

"We can be had," Kim told him. "You know our price."

"Please refresh my memory," said Hal cagily.

"One and a half million for me and seven hundred and fifty G's for David. Plus percentages."

"I thought it was one point two million and six G's."

"That was yesterday."

They got their price and gave their best to *Who Needs Marriage?* It made a beaut of a movie. A script like that would bring out the best in anybody. I think it was the last time they ever had a great script, either jointly or separately. Or were ever really first-rate, either jointly or separately.

After *Who Needs Marriage?* they did a dreary little melodrama that got panned by everybody. But the critics spared the Glasgows. The poor Glasgows, being wasted in a piece of junk not even their talents could rescue!

Then Kim was wanted—at the price she had become accustomed to—for a murder mystery. But David wasn't thought "right" for the male lead. He was too polished, too British. The male star had to be a rougher diamond, somebody audiences would accept as a hoodlum out of Hell's Kitchen.

"My husband's an actor," Kim argued. "A great actor. He
363

can be convincing in any role. As a matter of fact, he grew up in the section of a big city that would make Hell's Kitchen look like Fifth Avenue. He's just risen above it."

"And risen too high, I think, for our needs."

Kim read them loud and clear. They didn't want to carry the double load. They'd pay her price but they could get somebody for about a tenth of David's asking price. One Glasgow was better than two when it came to making your nut-plus in a picture like this.

"That settles it," Kim said to David. "I'll tell them to go shove it. Either they take both of us or they get the big finger."

"Don't be daft, darling. You take it. Always keep the old noggin mindful of that rainy day. Mindful of those biblical holocausts when it sometimes rained for forty days and forty nights. Take the loot and run."

"I won't," she said. "If they want me they'll have to——"

"Hold on, my lovely. It so happens the Old Vic would like me to have a fling at *Coriolanus*. With nary a nod to my wedded spouse."

"Oh, David! The Old Vic? In London?"

"The very same."

"You wouldn't consider it, would you?"

"I would indeed. I think *de temps en temps* we must part (such sweet sorrow!) to pursue our individual manifest destinies. You to the popular cinema. Me, perchance, to the classical theater."

"We'd be apart," she said, almost wailing, "a whole continent and ocean apart. You'd be thousands of miles away from me."

"True, my beloved. True and tragic. But as a celebrated apothegm composer once noted, 'Abstinence makes the heart grow fonder.'"

To ease Kim's pain, David nipped into Cartier's and presented her with a diamond and sapphire clip.

Taking their tearful farewells, swearing their deathless devotion to each other, both declaring that every moment they were separated would be sheer hell and tedium, the lovers parted at New York's John F. Kennedy Airport. David flew to London and Kim to Los Angeles.

David rehearsed five weeks and opened to glowing reviews in *Coriolanus*. And Kim, hard at work before the cameras in Southern California, read notice after favorable notice sent to her from far-off London. She glowed with pride and love until she began to hear the reports of David stepping out in London. First it was with actress Wendy Robbins.

"My darling," David reassured her on the transatlantic phone, "Wendy plays Virginilia, my wife, in the play. We had supper in the Savoy Grill one night and I dropped her off at her flat on Hertford Street and that was that. My darling, this apprehensiveness is unworthy of you. Surely you don't expect me to take all my meals in solitary, do you?"

"That seems to be how I'm taking mine," she replied tartly.

"I couldn't regret it more, if that's the truth. You have dear old friends all around you there. Can't you dine with Lonnie or Gina?"

Kim could, of course. But she couldn't help wondering if David's taking Wendy Robbins to supper was quite the equivalent of her having dinner with Lonnie Braintree or Gina Spinelli.

Then David was seen at Annabel's frugging with Jessamyn Aldrich.

"It couldn't be more innocent," David swore to Kim. "Jess is Valeria in *Coriolanus* and she lives in Berkeley Square. So we had ourselves a little jig and a glass to unwind after our Thursday night performance. What could be more natural?"

Kim bit her tongue to keep from saying, "I'll tell you what could be more natural. Your taking her home and fucking her. Which is what I suspect did happen."

There were other names linked with David's on the drinking-dining-dancing scene in London—names that had no connection whatsoever with the production of *Coriolanus*.

Kim fumed with jealousy all day. She called him every night just before she was going to bed. It would be about four o'clock in the morning London time. She took delight in waking him from a sound sleep and screaming at him. Nothing he said could dispel her doubts that he was screwing around and probably had some bird right in the sack beside him.

"Ducks, let me tell you something about a Scotsman," Lonnie Braintree said to Kim, trying to comfort her. "He'll fuck anything he can stick it into! But it doesn't mean anything. It's just getting his rocks off. Scotsmen are the horniest bastards on earth. But take it from me, David is smitten blind with you. Anybody else is just a socket to plug into for quick relief."

Kim didn't find Lonnie's analysis all that comforting.

In the interest of getting her own rocks off, Kim coldbloodedly seduced Turban Ankara. He was a romantic Turkish actor who had the second male lead in her movie.

Kim had room service bring dinner into the bungalow she was occupying at the Beverly Hills Hotel. (The house on

Mulholland Drive had been rented for a year to a writer from the East.)

As soon as they were through eating, Kim said, "Turban, you don't need to romance me in any way. No compliments or flattery or hand-kissing or any of that kind of shit. You don't even need to make conversation. We both know what we're here for. So let's skip the preliminaries . . ."

Before Turban's amazed eyes, Kim began disrobing.

"I'd appreciate it if you'd stay all night, Turban. I want you to fuck your brains out. I want you to keep hammering into me like a pile driver that just won't quit."

Kim had to tell somebody about it. Palsy-walsy as she was with Lonnie Braintree, it was not the sort of thing she could comfortably confide in him. So she called me.

"I'm telling you this in blood," she whispered on the phone. "If it ever gets back to David, I'll know where it came from. And if it's the last thing I ever do, I'll kill you. Before David kills me."

I swore eternal secrecy.

"Well, there isn't much to tell. Except these Turks are wild men. Never invite one to fuck you unless you really mean it. They don't do anything in a half-assed way. Turban tickled me silly with a French tickler and he fucked me all night long. What staying power! I never saw anything like it!"

Kim had never spoken to me so bluntly about sex. I tried to put myself into Kim's psyche. She had been humiliated by all the rumors of David's philandering and she had found her own secret way of saving face. On top of that, being the sexual creature she is, she had been satisfied . . . and there was the morning-after exhilaration.

"Gina," Kim rattled on, "looking back over my checkered career, I have decided I am a one-woman United Nations. Name a country and I've fucked at least one if its citizens. With the possible exception of Upper Volta and Chad. And I can't be sure about them either. And know something, Gina?"

"What?"

"All the time Turban was licking me and hoisting me to the moon, it didn't mean a goddamn thing. Except that I was getting my ashes hauled. And imagining that David was doing it."

Coriolanus was still running to packed houses when Kim finished her picture. She was on the first plane to London. Along with a couple hundred newsmen, David nervously awaited her arrival at Heathrow Airport.

For the benefit of the press, Kim staged a great reunion

366

scene, kissing and hugging David and nestling her face in his chest.

Inside David's suite at the Connaught Kim quickly drained a glass of champagne and threw the empty glass at David, splitting open his lip.

"What's that for?"

"That's just for openers!" she screamed. "You two-timing whoremonger! On the hunt for cunt the moment my back is turned. Making a laughing-stock out of me in front of the world. Mucking around like a common alley cat. Nobody pulls that on me. I'll soon show you who's running this show . . ."

David intercepted the Louis XIV chair she fired at his groin. He set the chair down. With one strong arm he grabbed her to him. He sat down on the chair and flung her over his lap, bottom side up, shoved up her dress and pulled down her panties. Then he began to spank her. Crack, crack, crack across her bare bottom.

"Silly, spoiled little bitch!" he said, timing each syllable to coincide with each crack. "You don't know what you're talking about. I love you to distraction. Awake or asleep, in darkness or light, I have your face before me. I never look at another woman but to try to find one feature that might remind me of you. But all is dross that is not Kimberley . . ."

The spanking kept pace with his outpouring of love and passion until Kim fell to the floor weeping.

She remembered that the only other time she had been spanked was by Marty the night of the Academy Awards.

"I love you to distraction too," she sobbed. "I've missed you so! I'm so insanely jealous. I can't help myself."

She positioned herself on her knees and wept onto his thigh.

When she stopped finally, she reached up and unzipped David's fly. She took his member out and began to fondle it. It was quickly erect. She ran her tongue lovingly around its head. Around and around she went until it was thoroughly lubricated. Then with the same loving, circular motions she lathed the shaft, tonguing her way lower and lower until she got to the base.

"Come, my love," he said quickly, breathlessly. And he scooped her up in his arms and carried her into the bedroom. "I think we have an urgent appointment."

He was still erect when he finally got his clothes off. It seemed like years before he stopped pleasuring Kim, again and again.

She didn't want to regain consciousness. As usual for her, after satisfying sex, she was famished.

"What will it be, luv? I'll give Room Service a bell."

"Enchiladas," said Kim. "I've got the maddest craving for enchiladas. I could eat a barrel of them. And I bet they don't have them here."

"You bet right. But maybe better luck somewhere else." David got dressed and put on his coat.

"Where are you going?" she asked him.

"To hunt down some enchiladas."

"Don't be gone long."

"Only as long as it takes to round up a barrel of enchiladas."

While David was gone, Kim called Harrod's and ordered a dozen wigs. She also called downstairs for a cab to go and pick them up immediately.

Whether or not she was around, she thought David would always be a man who liked a variety of sex partners. As long as she was around, he might not do anything about seeking out other sex partners. Even if he did, it might not mean a thing as far as his love for her was concerned. But his eye would always be roaming . . . and he'd always be fantasizing about this "bird" and that "bird."

Maybe, just maybe, there was something she could do to stop that roving eye and those fantasies.

David was gone long enough to put Kim in a panic and have her imagining the worst—that he was in the arms of another woman.

She waited for nearly seven hours only to see him come through the door empty-handed.

"Luv," he announced, "there's bad news and good news. There isn't an enchilada to be had in the whole vast, grand city of London. Bad news. But hang on. I've chartered a plane to go to Los Angeles and have called Gringo's in Los Angeles and instructed them to deliver two hundred enchiladas to that plane. The plane should be back early in the morning. That's the good news."

David delivered his message abjectly, hardly looking in Kim's direction. When he took a good look, he saw that he was looking at a platinum blond.

"Great heavens alive, Kimberley!" he exclaimed. "What the bloody hell have you done to your hair?"

"There ees some mistake," said Kim, faking a French accent. "My name ees Mimi."

Every night Kim wore a different-colored wig and had a different name. She was an ash-blond named Ingrid from Sweden. She was raven-haired Maria from Naples. She was red-headed Maeve from Belfast. She was even blue-haired Minnie from Miami Beach.

David threw himself into the game with the greatest of gusto.

"Oh, Ingrid, Ingrid, breathes there a man with soul so dead he doesn't dream of being the lover of a Swedish beauty!"

"Mia Maria, my little Neapolitan nougat! *Caressami!*"

"You see," said Kim, when she had exhausted her disguises, "I am your little harem. I can be all the different women you'll ever need."

"Of course, if you really loved me," said David, "you'd do what the women who love the sheiks of Araby do to prove their love."

"What's that?"

"They shave their heads. That's the true test of their love, if they're willing to part with their crowning glory."

David was speaking tongue-in-cheek. Of course he would never have asked Kim to part with a single strand of her glorious hair to prove anything.

But the next night when David came home from the theater Kim greeted him in their suite dressed in a nun's habit.

"Good God, luv!" he exclaimed. "I've done my share of wenching and I'm surely no angel. But one thing I've never got around to is banging Mother Superior. *Yet!*"

Kim knelt at his feet. As she did so, she threw off her cowl. Her head was as bald as an egg.

"No, no, Mother of God!" cried David. "I was only jesting. Oh, my darling Kimberley, look at what you've done to yourself."

He buried his face in his hands and wept.

"Look at me, David."

Reluctantly he raised his eyes to look at her.

"Now take me," she said.

It must have been like taking a nude, hatless department store mannikin to bed. Whatever he might have been thinking or feeling, David gave a masterful performance of desiring her.

"You tested me," said Kim afterward. "And I tested you. We both passed our tests. That proves we really do love each other and belong together. That settles it. We'll be together forever. No more working apart. 'Whither thou goest, I go too.'"

As an afterthought, she added, "And vice versa."

Chapter 37

Nine thirty-seven.

She's not coming. I know in my bones she's not coming.

Why?

What's happened?

No. Not that. We'd have heard that news. Missed the plane? A delayed takeoff? She'd have phoned.

Screwing her head off somewhere? Making it on every damn Alp with some new guy? Not likely. Getting laid—with any guy—was a movable feast that could easily be moved to Los Angeles.

Kim, where in the world are you?

I'm scared!

Chapter 38

Kim stuck to the vow she made that night in London's Connaught Hotel. They became like two peas in a pod, scarcely ever out of each other's sight.

Everybody who could type was sending them a script. They kept protesting they didn't want to be thought of as Rogers and Astaire or Abbott and Costello, but the fact was they did find a lot of things they'd be glad to work in together if somebody came up with the scratch. And they never parted to take separate assignments. If David was working, Kim was always on or near the set. When Kim worked, David was no farther away than the nearest saloon.

The point I'm making is they were together. Very together. With no vacations from each other. In the eyes of the world this adds up to intense romantic love. Kim and David's marriage has been called "The greatest love story of modern times." They themselves have been called the Lovers of the Century.

If you're married and spend a lot of time together, that's the kind of reputation you can get. Look at the Duke and Duchess of Windsor. Not long ago I was reading that the great love of the Duchess's life was not the Duke of Windsor at all, but some Argentinian diplomat who didn't want to marry her because she was a divorcée and that might put the kibosh on his political ambitions.

So you never know, as I always say, unless you're under the bed. And who the hell's ever under the bed?

Not so long ago a witty young actress was quoted in the *Hollywood Reporter* on what it was like to work with the Glasgows on location in Spain. The acidy tone of her remarks made it plain she didn't think too much of the Glasgows, or the chances of their marriage surviving into Kingdom Come. She said:

> The Glasgows have to be seen to be believed. Those two are really something. A typed time schedule is delivered to them each evening. The itemizations could not be more precise. The car arrives at the hotel at 10:02. It departs the hotel with the Glasgows at 10:04. The car arrives at the set at 10:23. The Glasgows disembark at 10:26. At 4:17 the Glasgows still have not deigned to bare their great thespian talents to the camera. Their Muse has simply eluded them today. And it's been so much more a-Muse-ing to recall their drinking excesses on three continents. Sipping brandy and sodas all day, they joust with each other and play guessing games intended to entrance all of us eavesdropping peons. Where was it they got so swacked from slivovitz? What was the name of the restaurant in the Haute Savoie where David sent the wine back five times? That coastal town in Denmark where they tried mixing aquavit and vodka, with Tuborg chasers on the side, and woke up in the local hospital? After a baker's dozen or so of brandy and sodas Glasgow is declaiming, "I am an ancient player in the autumn of my life. I am old and rich and wise and the triumph of my lapsing time on earth is to be married to the most incredibly beautiful woman who ever breathed." Mrs. Glasgow rose prettily to the compliment with her all-purpose word of approval, "Crazy!" Could they be mismatched in other ways as well as in their eloquence? A subversive thought, may the Lord and the President have mercy upon me.

After David's run in *Coriolanus* was over, the Glasgows went to Mexico, where they were both wanted—at their price—for *Three Tickets to Paradise*. Maura Anderson was also wanted for the picture. She would be "the other woman" in a troubled triangular situation played out against a lush tropical backdrop.

Kim had not seen Maura in years. Like most of the others in the old Studio stable of contract stars, Maura was on her own now. She never missed the opportunity to let the world know how much she prized her new independence.

Kim had mixed feelings about the reunion with Maura.

"I wonder if she's still so beautiful," she said to me during her Los Angeles stopover en route to Mexico.

"In all those pictures I've seen in the papers where she's with her bullfighter," I said, "she looks pretty darn beautiful."

"Yes, I've seen them too. I love Maura dearly. It will be wonderful seeing an old friend. But so help me, if she starts anything with David I'll scratch her eyes out. I'll cut her boobs off. When you get two people like Maura and David together who are both always leading with their groin, God knows anything could happen."

I had to smile to myself. If there was ever a case of the kettle calling the pot black, this was it. Kim was hardly one to talk about other people leading with their groin.

"I have a feeling you'll hold your own," I told her.

"I'd rather hold David's," she giggled.

Kim and David were quartered in a magnificent hacienda in the hills behind Mazatlan. It had glorious views of the Pacific and the breezes off the ocean made even the hottest days of summer delightful.

They were hardly off the plane when Kim decided she loved Mexico. And they were hardly inside the door when she declared that she and David must have a hacienda of their own someday. Preferably within sight of the Pacific and the feel of its exhilarating breezes.

Maura Anderson, for reasons of her own, was staying in a beach house south of Mazatlan. She arrived several days after the Glasgows, just thirty-six hours before filming was to begin. Kim invited her to the hacienda for lunch that last free day.

Kim had butterflies in her stomach as she saw her still-beautiful friend alight from her car, all bright and lemony-yellow from her slippers to the rims of her sun glasses and the wide floppy hat floating on top of her black mane.

"Honey, honey, honey," Maura purred, sweeping Kim in her arms. "I'm starved for the sight of you. Oh, my long lost girl buddy!"

Getting into the act and addressing himself to Maura, David said, "You are, you know, quite indecently, outrageously, and incredibly beautiful."

Maura laughed appreciatively. Kim's heart dropped like an express elevator.

"For real," Maura asked Kim, winking, "or standard bull-shit?"

"Let me qualify my encomium," said David. "You are the most indecently, outrageously, and incredibly beautiful woman in the world—next to my wife."

David gave Kim an affectionate pinch on her bottom.

"So this is the fabulous Mr. David Glasgow!" Maura marveled.

"The same, my dear Miss Anderson. At your disposal."

It was a boozy luncheon. Kim couldn't hang that on either David or Maura. It was she herself who kept postponing the serving of the chicken molé and avocado vinaigrette. It was a quick take between Maura and David. Panicking, Kim suggested another and another round of planter's punches. Nobody ever had to twist David's or Maura's arm to get them to accept another drink.

David quoted Baudelaire and Lord Byron through lunch and sang sea chanteys for Maura and regaled her with naughty backstage gossip about some of the greats of the English stage. Maura hung on every syllable. She laughed uproariously at his jests and off-color references.

When David excused himself to answer the call of nature, Maura exclaimed, "You got a prize, Kim. He's charming, brilliant, funny, sexy, beautiful—everything you'd want in a man."

"Yes," said Kim. Even numbed with alcohol, Kim had found none of David's talk and carrying-on either that funny or fascinating.

Maura looked at her closely. "Oh, my sweets. I know what you're thinking. But have no worry. He's all yours."

Kim felt relieved for a moment. Then a vague depression set in. "You mean you don't really find him attractive?"

"I find him *excruciatingly* attractive. But that's nothing you have to worry about. On the surface Mother Earth here might act like the Great Whore of the Western World. But underneath she does have a few scruples. She doesn't prey on the property of her favorite people in the world."

"The thought never crossed my mind," Kim lied. She felt that a ton of weight had just been lifted from her heart.

"Besides," said Maura, "at this time he's not my type. I'm in my Hispanic period."

Kim knew about Gilberto Cordoba, her bullfighter lover. But where was Gilberto now?

"In Sevilla," said Maura, "more's the pity." She pulled a sad face for half a second. Flashing a sudden smile full of April sunshine, she added, "But I have other fish to fry."

And she was mysteriously off to fry them, without waiting to say good-bye to David.

The whole world was waiting for fireworks to explode in Mazatlan. Kimberley Hudson plus David Glasgow plus Maura Anderson just had to equal fireworks. The flacks would have had a field day if it had happened. They did their best to suggest it was happening. Or about to happen.

Maura was an open scandal in Mazatlan, although she and David never sacked out together—to the best of anyone's knowledge. The behavior that shocked the Mexicans was not the kind of stuff the flacks were looking to publicize. It was their job to put a lid on that kind of stuff.

It started out such a lark. Kim was working with David and with one of the people she loved most in the world. Maura and David had eased into a buddy-buddy relationship, so they were like three old friends come together to have a ball. It was a better than average script, they had a good director and an easy-does-it mañana attitude pervaded the set.

The filming was done on a deserted island a few miles offshore, where the crew had constructed something that was supposed to resemble a dilapidated inn as background for most of the action. Cast and crew would go back and forth to the island every day by launches.

At noon they broke for a long lunch period that started with tequila cocktails and finished with a lengthy siesta. Filming might resume at four o'clock in the afternoon and stop at seven. Kim, David, and Maura would begin the cocktail hour in the launch going back to Mazatlan and continue it in the cafés or hotels in town. It was usually ten o'clock before they had dinner. But then that's the conventional hour for dining in Latin countries.

With coffee, Maura got her second wind and left them, saying, "And now I'm away into the night. I've got miles to go before I sleep." She blew them kisses and disappeared.

"I do wonder what that lass is up to," David commented the first time Maura left them abruptly.

"I've a damn good idea," said Kim.

It didn't take long for the mystery of Maura's excursions into the night to be resolved. The stories became the buzz of the town. Late at night Maura Anderson was bar-hopping the native cantinas, particularly those frequented by the beach boys. She was drinking tequilas with Bohemia chasers. Barefoot she jumped to the tables and danced orgiastically to the mariachi tunes on the jukebox. In the wee hours of morning, thoroughly drunk, she would stumble out toward her beach house, taking home with her a different beach boy every night.

"Is it true?" Kim asked her. "The stories I'm hearing?"

"Being an honest woman," said Maura, "I deny nothing."

For Kim and David the days went on in the glorious bliss of the Mexican idyll. They were never so together and noticeably in love. But suddenly a phone call from England shattered their peace.

The Nottingham Repertory wanted David to join them for a season. They wanted him to play Angelo in *Measure for Measure*. Then they would be doing *School for Scandal, Way of the World, Volpone,* and, possibly, *A Midsummer Night's Dream*. Like most serious British actors who have struck it rich in the fleshpots of Hollywood, David was elated at the opportunity to get back to "real acting."

"Nottingham!" cried Kim. "Where the hell's Nottingham?"

"You've not read your Robin Hood, luv," said David, "or you wouldn't be asking me the whereabouts of Nottingham."

"To hell with Robin Hood. Robin Hood or no Robin Hood, Nottingham is but Nowheresville."

"They have a fine acting company up there, luv. One gets a bit rusty in one's craft emoting on celluloid, y'know. Not many shillings involved, true, but a grand chance to brush up, shape up, and all that."

"How many shillings?"

"Who knows? Who cares? Not many. The game's the thing."

"I say no."

"What?"

"You heard me. No. N—O."

David went ashen. "May I ask why, sweet?"

"You may indeed. I'll tell you why. There are some things in life that just don't pay. Crime doesn't pay, and the classics sure as hell don't pay. So we won't be doing them. Unless some movie producer decides he wants to pay you a million to do *Hamlet* or *Henry V*. Without the old moola coming in, who do you think's going to pay the nut we got going for us? Me alone? Not on your balls, buster."

Saying nothing, David stormed out of the house.

It was late that night when Kim called me. David had not come home. Kim suspected he was out somewhere tying one on. From the croaky sound of her voice, I suspected she had been home tying one on.

As she relayed the scene to me, I couldn't help feeling she had made a terrible mistake. I think she realized this too.

"Oh, Gina, don't get on my back," she said. "I know I'm in

the wrong. Partly, anyway. But there is something to be said for my side."

"I won't get on your back," I said. "I know there's something to be said for your side."

"It wasn't just the money and all the creature comforts I was talking about," she confessed, "though they are important to me—us. I think there was some professional jealousy involved. I couldn't see myself sitting around drafty old Nottingham a whole winter doing nothing but watch David perform the classics. I didn't hear anybody inviting me to act in the repertory company."

I believed her. I think if she had been invited to act along with David she might have considered it. Maybe on a compromise basis. She might have agreed to their going for a month. Not a whole season.

"If you think you are in the wrong," I said, "you can always change your mind. That's a woman's prerogative."

"No," she said. "The decision has been made on that."

I felt sad hanging up the phone. There was no doubt in my mind she had made an important mistake. So important that it might alter the future course of their lives and their relationship to each other.

David came home roaring drunk that night after having closed the last cantina in Mazatlan. He woke Kim stumbling around and then being sick in the bathroom. In the morning—when Kim kicked him awake to start for the island—he had a ghastly hangover. He was in the doghouse with Kim more for disturbing her sleep than getting drunk and having a hangover.

The morning was agony for him to get through. When they broke for lunch, Kim was still not speaking to him.

"Maura, luv," said David, "when a chap goes out and makes a disgusting pig of himself with the drink and wakes up with the *cruda,* as our Mexican brethren say, what would you prescribe as an antidote?"

"You're asking *me* about hangovers?" Maura said incredulously. "Why, I'd be just about the last person on earth to ask. A tiny tippler like me." She winked broadly at both David and Kim. "What I do is I always go for the hair of the dog." Maura filled a water tumbler with tequila and handed it to him. "Hell, have a whole tuft of the dog."

Maura had other plans for the evening. So they didn't have their usual dinner *à trois.* Kim was relieved. She wanted to keep David in the doghouse a while longer. Afterward she admitted to herself that the punishment far exceeded the crime. Admitting this much, she also had to admit she might

376

be punishing herself too. Punishing herself for making a decision that could hurt her as much as David.

The following day was Saturday. Kim woke up to find David standing beside her sober, contrite, nattily dressed.

"Kimberley," he announced, "it must needs be that I make a hasty journey to the City of Angels. Matters that are urgent but not critical must be transacted. I shall return to your side before the sun sets."

He was gone before she grasped what he was saying.

Her first thought was that he was leaving her. But this was absurd. He might want to walk out on her. But he wouldn't walk now, in the middle of a picture.

Still, she spent a tense, unhappy day waiting for him to return. If he was going to return. David came back bearing a magic little box, which he presented to her with a solemn bow. The magic little box was from the Beverly Hills branch of Tiffany's. Inside it was a thirty-four-carat emerald ring.

Kim gasped and flung her arms around David.

"Not so astonishing as the color of your eyes, luv," said David, "but the nearest I could get."

"David, it's exquisite!"

"You know what they always say about diamonds?"

"Ask me something hard. If I don't know diamonds are forever and a girl's best friend, I don't know anything."

"Not so, my precious. According to what the chaps up there told me today, the colored stones are better investments. Emeralds. Rubies. Sapphires. Jade."

"Who's thinking about investments? I want that thing on my finger."

"And if I might be so bold, my Kimberley, before this night is out I'd like *my* finger in a certain favored place. My metaphorical finger, if you please."

Nothing ever stays the same for very long.

The Mexican summer wore on. The high spirits that launched the picture waned. The camaraderie of the three principals grew a little mannered and brittle. Maybe they had been together too much during the long hot summer. Maybe it was something else.

A new pattern developed.

After their dinners with Maura, David suggested they go on some place with her for a nightcap.

"You go, David," Kim said. "I'm totally zonked."

Hours later David would return to the hacienda, completely smashed and disrupting her sleep. She never suspected anything between him and Maura. They had their nightcap.

377

Maura went off to play her night games and David stayed behind—or went somewhere else—to get drunk.

Kim discovered it paid to put David in the doghouse. He must have been born with a sense of guilt. That Look and the Silent Treatment put him on several Saturday flights to Los Angeles. From Tiffany's he brought back such little peace offerings as an emerald brooch set in small diamonds, a diamond-and-sapphire clip with a forty-carat sapphire, and a truly fabulous Oriental pearl-diamond-and-ruby necklace.

The necklace must have cost a hundred grand. The sight of it nearly threw Kim into a faint.

"You're so extravagant, David!" she gushed.

"Nonsense, Kimberley. It's a trifling sum to have paid if it contributes to your happiness."

Much as she welcomed the offerings, Kim wished the occasions that prompted them wouldn't keep arising so regularly. She worried about David's drinking. She worried about it from the standpoint of his health. She worried about it because it meant he was less than happy, maybe deeply unhappy. And that had to reflect on her.

The picture was going along well enough. But so much of the early fun was gone. David's carousing and hangovers and morning-after remorses were one thing. But that wasn't all.

There was the problem of Maura. Mazatlan was too small a town to keep anything concealed. And too provincial a town not to be upset by unconventional conduct. Mazatlan was shocked by Maura's open flaunting of local mores. An unaccompanied woman who haunted low-class cantinas and made a drunken spectacle of herself was a lost creature. *Caramba!* Nor was the citizenry flattered that this famous gringo woman had taken such a shine to the young men of the community.

"I sometimes think," said Kim at dinner one night, "we'd all be better off if we didn't drink so much." Diplomatically, she included herself. "I think it might be interesting if we all decided to go on the wagon for the two weeks or so it'll take us to finish up here. Just to prove we could stop if we wanted to."

"A noble suggestion," said David, reaching for his wine glass.

"Are you kidding?" said Maura.

"How about you, David? Are you game?"

"Game as gamist. Starting tomorrow at dawn's earliest light."

"The time to start is tonight. Right now."

"Just a wee nip later, luv," said David. "Come. We'll all away and have a wee *après-diner* and then we'll start."

"I'm starting right now," said Kim righteously. "You and Maura 'away' and have your 'wee *après-diner*' and I'll be waiting for you, David."

Kim sat up waiting. If it took all night, she would wait him out. It was nearly two o'clock when he came home. He didn't stumble but from his bloodshot eyes she guessed he had a good load aboard.

" 'A wee *après-diner*,' my ass," she greeted him. "You're gassed."

"Scout's Honor, Bibles stacked up to heaven, I am not drunk, my Kimberley," David swore. He spoke coherently, without any slurring of his words. But Kim was still sure he was drunk. And she was furious with him.

"Tell you what, David. Let's put it to the proof. Let's have one round of miniature golf."

David had a miniature golf course built for them behind their hacienda. It was one of the first things he did after moving in. Experts from the States had worked round the clock so the Glasgows could indulge their new hobby. Since David had played golf before, and Kim hadn't, he always bested her by more than ten strokes, so now when she suggested they play a round under the night lights, he couldn't have been more pleased.

"An inspired idea, Kimberley! The mood could not be more upon me."

"If you win," she said, "I'll buy you a hacienda. This one if it's for sale. If it isn't, some other one. If I win—"

"If you win, dear Kimberley, I shall go in search of the most exquisite diamond on the market the moment our chores are terminated here."

Under the night lights illumining the little course, David and Kim played out their contest. Kim played as badly as usual. But David played even worse. He trailed her by a score of fourteen.

It was the first game she ever won from David. It had to prove he was drunk.

True to his word, the moment the picture was finished David set out in search of "the most exquisite diamond on the market."

He found it in New York, at an auction at the Parke Bernet. It was the famous fifty-seven-carat Kreuger Diamond, which all the experts had described as a near-perfect gem.

The only other contender for the Kreuger Diamond was Juan Bastinado, the Bolivian tin billionaire. He wanted it for his new American wife, the former Mercedes Cavanaugh. And Mercedes wanted it badly. Mercedes was the beautiful young widow of a rich governor from a western state, who had been slain by an assassin's bullet. For years she had turned up on the Ten Best-Dressed Women lists. As the bereaved widow carrying on bravely with three small children to raise, she had also turned up on the Ten Most Admired Women lists. In marrying the super-rich and elderly Juan Bastinado, she had won another listing from some: No. 1 Whore of the World.

Juan had cabled his bid of $750,000 for the diamond.

"I'll give you seven hundred and fifty thousand plus five thousand," said David.

The Kreuger Diamond was his.

While David was in New York, Kim decided that she hadn't really won, since David was incapacitated. Therefore they should both win. She bought him a hacienda.

Kim nearly expired at first sight of the Kreuger Diamond.

"If I live to be a million," she squealed, "I don't think I'll ever, ever behold anything so precious."

"Preciousness for the most precious," said David.

"Where in the world am I going to wear it?"

"Not here, certainly. We'll find some appropriate settings."

Kim gloated. "And to think you outbid Juan Bastinado and got it away from that gold-digging bitch Mercedes!"

David didn't drink a drop that night.

In appreciation . . . for his sobriety, for his spectacular generosity . . . Kim tried to give him a night he wouldn't soon forget. David gave as good as he got. And better. They couldn't stop pleasing each other that night.

Kim got into a giggling fit just before she dropped off to sleep. She jabbed David in the ribs, saying with each jab, "Now you bet-ter be good. Or else."

"Or else what?"

"It could be mighty costly for you."

"How so, luv?"

"Well, if you're not a good boy, it could cost you really a lot. Today I was reading somewhere about the Royal Blue Star of Venus sapphire. It has five hundred forty carats. They say it practically covers a girl's whole hand and once it comes on the market again it'll probably go for over three million."

David groaned.

Chapter 39

Kim didn't come into possession of the 540-carat Royal Blue Star of Venus sapphire. Neither has Mercedes Cavanaugh Bastinado. Yet. The Star of Venus came on the market in America not so long ago. I think the asking price was $3.5 million. I remember the owner saying it was a terrific bargain at that price.

I doubt it would have ever crossed David's mind to buy it for Kim, even if he had had the money—which he didn't. So Kim didn't get the Star of Venus on her finger. But sing no sad songs for Kim. Without the Star of Venus, her jewelry collection would make an auction by itself at Christie's or Sotheby Parke-Bernet.

If the Glasgows believed anything, they believed that money was a substance to be kept in circulation. Any place they ever visited they gave the local economy a real boost. They spent money as if the Supreme Court was about to hand down a decision declaring it obscene.

Let me give you a few vignettes from the Glasgow Years that reflect their life-style, to use the phrase of the day. They're culled from random and I quote without attribution:

Don't worry about the Glasgows ever not having a roof over their beautiful heads. They fell in love with Ireland during the filming of *Beyond Galway* and have just bought a castle in County Mayo. Never let it be said of them they're a one-home family. They still own the keys to the chalet in Klosters, the hacienda in Sinaloa, a flat in London's Belgravia, and the pied-a-terre in Beverly Hills.

Kimberley and David Glasgow sailed into Portofino to show off their new yacht to the Rex Harrisons. They've named their 116-foot boat *Pride's Crossing*. The boat's gold-painted, sixteen-ton Mercedes-Benz engines and twin stabilizers are valued at nearly $400,000.

In case you're thinking of offering Kimberley Hudson that movie script you've been cranking out on the old Remington portable, be advised of a few of her specifi-

381

cations: Basic fee, $500,000 with $100,000 for expenses; $1,000 per week for personal hairdresser; $1,000 per week for personal makeup man; $1,000 per week for personal photographer; $1,000 a week for her personal publicist; and from 10 to 15 percent of the profits. She will also name her own director and cameraman.

Say this for the Glasgows. They go first class. These days they fly hither and yon in a Boeing 720B, which has been tailored to their needs to the tune of $300,000 by the Los Angeles firm which rents the plane. *Starshine* (title courtesy of the Glasgows) has a bedroom with a marble fireplace and a double bed covered with a white fur bedspread, a bathroom with a shower, a mirrored salon and a club room with a player piano, stereo, two color TV sets, velvet couches and white leather.

Shhh! Nobody's supposed to know. But when Kimberley Hudson gets around to opening her Christmas presents, she'll find Santa's brought her a $125,000 blue mink coat. Every girl should be married to such a Santa!

I could go on. On and on and on. *Ad nauseam, ad infinitum.* But you get the picture.

With their work, with their restless natures, they were endlessly on the go. Roaming the face of the earth. By land, by sea, by sky. Like homing pigeons they always came back to the hacienda near Mazatlan. Again and again and again.

I think Kim knew what she was doing when she bought the hacienda. I don't think she did it on impulse or just because she loved Mexico. I think in some uneasy way she knew their time in Mexico was a kind of high noon. And I think she had a sneaky hunch nothing would ever be so good again. Either with their careers or between themselves.

Maybe if they staked out a claim here ... came back when they were free ... they could recover something they had had here for a little while. Call it what you will. Optimism. Confidence. Peace of mind. Joy in the promise of eternal sunshine and cloudless skies.

If she had that hunch, I think it was well taken.

I was too preoccupied with my own troubles in recent times to have much contact with Kim or anybody else. I am sure there are many occasions when she would have welcomed a supportive phone call from her old friend of a million years ago. I am sure she would have had many a woeful tale to pour out.

Many's the time, God knows, I would have appreciated a supportive call from her. But as Fitzgerald once said to Hemingway, "The rich are different from us." (Hemingway said, "Yes, they have more money.") To paraphrase Fitzgerald, "The big stars are different from me and thee." They're long on expecting thoughtfulness but short on extending it. In most cases. They're too full of themselves to be much tuned in to others. Self-involvement is so often the key to their survival. The unfortunate thing about self-involvement is that it breeds unhappiness. It's almost impossible, I've found, to be happy when all you're thinking about is your self.

On the plus side of the ledger of my marriage to Matt Berliner I would list the following items: plushy pads, a house for Mama in Brooklyn, unlimited credit in all the best places, an interesting and hectic social life, reasonably friendly relationship the first four years, and two beautiful children.

Our sex life started out so-so and progressed to blah-blah and finally to nada-nada.

The picture business was undergoing drastic changes. The Studio shifted so much of its top brass to the New York offices. Matt was part of that shift. We sold out in Beverly Hills and bought in on East 67th Street. A five-story townhouse with an elevator. I had four in help to insure my idleness. I also had the run of Bergdorf Goodman's, Henri Bendel, Saks Fifth Avenue, and charge accounts at the places the "ladies who lunch" frequent.

The thing that capsized my marital boat had probably been going on under my eyes on the Coast. But things seem to be a little bit easier to hide there. In one way Los Angeles is a small town. Or a series of small towns. But there's all that space to get lost in.

Manhattan is so compact. It's harder to keep a secret there.

In New York I discovered Matt's secret. He was so hung up on a kid named Sandy he couldn't be bothered to hide the clues. And Sandy's not a woman's name in this case. I let him know I knew the score. As far as our marriage was concerned, that was that.

Only it wasn't all that peaceful a parting of the ways.

It took another three years for us to see the last of each other.

At first Matt vehemently denied everything. When he saw I had his number down cold, he raved and ranted and screamed and turned on me with a deadly fury.

"You bloody bitch," he threatened me, "I'll never give you a divorce. I'll kill you first."

To drive his point home, he blackened my eyes and dislocated my jaw.

The next time I brought up the subject of divorce I got even more. I wound up with my arm in a cast.

During all my troubles with Matt I saw Kim just once. It was when she came to New York with David, who was getting a fat bundle for a week's work in a television spectacular. I met her for lunch one day at the Colony.

I told her how unhappy I was, how impossible my life with Matt had become since I had learned what Matt really was. I told her that all I wanted was out. Matt, for God knows what perverse reasons, was still refusing to give me a divorce. I asked her what she suggested.

"How terrible for you, Gina," Kim replied. "It's such a painful subject for me, too. You know how I went through this whole thing with Randy. Hearing you talk brings back so many painful memories of poor Randy. I do feel for you, Gina, but I wish we could change the subject."

See what I mean? If you've got a Superstar for a friend, all your problems are solved.

Well, I did get my divorce finally, but I never got a penny of alimony or child support.

When you're dealing with a sharp, devious legal mind like Matt's, what chance does a poor dumb ex-working girl have?

Kim's the actress. But her descent from the heights hasn't been anything so dramatic as mine. The general public may not have noticed a thing.

Oh, sure, you can't fool the public on the quality of the pictures. The pictures since *Three Tickets for Paradise* have been on a downhill toboggan. But the Glasgow years have gone on. The Glasgows still face life on the grand scale.

Still, I can't help thinking a significant corner was turned that time in Mexico when Kim said no, no David couldn't spend a season with the Nottingham Repertory.

After Mexico it was Jamaica and Denmark and Ireland and Morocco and Norway and New Zealand and Hong Kong and the Isle of Man ... and points east, west, north, and south. And a series of pictures ranging from not-so-hot to el bombos.

They keep working pretty steady. And spending just as steady. They must keep getting paid. And there must be an audience out there who will pay to see them in anything.

But something has happened.

What?

I have my theories. A couple of semidrunken phone calls from Kim gave me certain insights. Other sources have provided clues. As a life-long Kim-watcher, I could also make some speculations.

Human relationships are always complicated among the simplest of people. If there is such a thing as a simple person. When you get two enormously complex, volatile personalities like Kim and David bouncing their egos off each other—

Well!

From Alicante, Spain, came this monologue via the transatlantic phone:

"Oh, Gina, who am I? I feel like I'm dying and I don't know who I am. What will they put on my tombstone? 'Here lies ——' Here lies who or what? *Who am I?* Is there a real person here? Or am I just some animated object that's given a name, wound up, and told to move? 'Now you're Amanda Delderfield, a Texas pioneer woman.' 'Now you're Helen of Troy.' I feel like I'm just a scrapheap of the bones and rotting flesh of a hundred dead women I've pretended to be on the screen. But where's the real me? Is there one? I've spent my whole life impersonating other people. But what about me? Where am I? Do I ever really think or feel or say anything that wasn't fed to me somewhere along the way by a screenwriter? . . ."

I heard her out. Every time I thought she had run out of gas back would come that soul-rending wail, "Who am I? Who am I?"

"I don't think you need to worry about whether or not you really exist," I told her. "I can't pretend to understand you. But, then, I don't think anybody in this world ever really understands anybody else. I don't always like or admire you. But I've always loved you. I think you have to be basically lovable to be loved. I would write you up as 'My Most Unforgettable Character' for the *Reader's Digest* if I weren't saving you for my next book. I'm writing the story of your life, remember. I can't wait for you to die. Because in spite of your long and colorful medical history, I think you'll bury us all."

"Thanks, Gina." There was a lift in her voice but she didn't sound convinced.

"Where's David?" I asked.

"Well, it's only two o'clock in the morning here. I don't look for him until the last cantina is closed."

"Oh."

"He's going to come home carrying a beautiful basket of peaches. I must confess I probably drove him to it. We'd both probably be a lot happier if I didn't keep getting streaks of bossiness."

"What happened?" I asked.

"Oh, last night David was on one of his poetry-reading kicks. He can read poetry to Doomsday for all I care. But not *aloud*. He insisted on reading Rimbaud and Verlaine to me and I insisted I didn't want to hear any of it. I told him to knock it off. He was furious. He said, 'Who the hell's telling me to knock it off in my own castle?'

"I told him I was because I lived here too and I didn't want to listen to that junk. Well, he did shut up. But he pouted and glowered. I was a little p.o.'ed that he was acting like such an ass over nothing. So I decided I'd settle his hash for him.

"I got into my flimsiest, filmiest little shortie-nightie and doused myself with Joy. I slinked over to the chair where he was reading and went into a real seduction scene. I stroked his hair and laid my cheek against his. 'I'm sorry, dear,' I said. 'I was out of line. I didn't mean to be such an old cross-patch. Please forgive me. I'm off to beddy-bye now. Please don't be long. I'll be waiting.'

"I could tell from the look in David's eye he wouldn't be long. The second he hit the sack he was all for having his wicked way with me. 'Not tonight, darling,' I said.

" 'Not tonight!' he yelled. 'What the hell gives?' "

" 'Well, darling, you're just a little bit late. While I was waiting for you, someone else got there first.'

" 'What the bloody fuck are you talking about?'

" 'Just like I said. Somebody got there first. Another . . . er, friend . . . is occupying your normal berth. See for yourself.'

"I had my nightie hoisted way up to give David easy access. Well, Gina, he took one feel and roared like a shot beast. He was out of that bed faster than greased lightning. He got dressed and banged doors. And off he went to get polluted.

"I honestly thought he would be amused. You see what I had done. I had taken this giant dildo—and don't ask me how I happen to own a giant dildo—and eased it into my pussy. That's what David found when he reached out to touch his little pit of pleasure."

Kim started to giggle. Her giggling built up into a real hysteria and she hung up.

To use one of her favorite words, "Crazy."

Speaking of Kim's "long and troubled medical history," I must say she's had her troubles. You name it and she's had it.

386

Double pneumonia.
Ovarian cysts.
German measles.
Slipped sacroiliac.
Pleurisy.
Salmonella poisoning.
Bursitis.
Duodenal ulcers.
Broken vertebrae.
Inflammation of the hip.
Heart palpitations.
Viruses. From Asian to Zuzulandish.
Peritonitis.

The peritonitis turned out to be a real cliff-hanger. Again she had the whole world wondering if she'd make it. There were ghastly complications ... sensations of freezing to death ... a head swelling up to the size of a watermelon ... tremendous blotches over her face and body ... a heart stimulator pumping voltage into a failing heart.

It was a close one. When it was over, Kim's presiding physician had some stern advice for her:

"I can't tell whether you've always had this susceptibility. Or whether it's something that has built up through the ingestion of too many drugs. Including alcohol and pills. But you are a highly allergic person. You should at all times be wearing an identification tag that says you are allergic and lists all the known or suspected drugs you shouldn't be given in case of an accident or any kind of emergency. Starting with penicillin . . ."

"You should see the spiffy new dog tags I've got bouncing between my boobs," Kim teased Earl Wilson.

Earl Wilson was not averse to seeing anything that had to do with Kim's boobs. He asked her if she had joined the WACS. He thought only military personnel wore dog tags.

"David thought it would be too dreary," she said, "if I had to wear something around my neck that looked like a credit card or a driver's license. So he presented me with this cute little ensemble."

She took off a long thin gold necklace. The pendant was sterling silver embedded with diamonds. Engraved on the pendant:

ALLERGIC! PLEASE DON'T FEED ME

And underneath were listed all those known or suspect drugs. Starting with penicillin.

"It makes me feel like I'm an inmate in a zoo," said Kim. "You know those signs: 'Please Don't Feed the Animals.'"

Kim's "long and colorful medical history" had an important repercussion on her career. She became uninsurable. This isn't generally known outside the trade. But the fact is, the time came when no company would insure Kim. Not only for health reasons.

Besides real health threats, there were also all the feigned illnesses she could spring when things weren't going her way. And get some doctor to testify they were for real. And there were all the games and caprices Kim and David indulged themselves in. Sometimes to bug and/or punish each other. Sometimes to bug and/or punish the production.

Uninsurable, the Glasgows could be bad news. They had marquee value. But if you ran into any bad luck with them, they could end up bankrupting you. And breaking your balls for good measure.

Bye and bye only daredevils would deal with them. The amount of up-front money they got slipped, but there was always that percentage against the gross if something clicked. Still the pictures kept getting lousier and lousier.

Apparently no one connected with the making of them noticed. Or cared. Including David. Where was that old pride in craftsmanship?

It was a game both sides could play. The Stars could screw just as well as they got screwed. Throw them a lousy script, exploit them for their drawing power, and you knew what to expect. Not much.

The name of the game was: Take the money and run.

I wish I could have taken some money and run from Matt.

It was crack-up time with that jerk and I sure wasn't in the mood to be involving myself in anybody's troubles but my own. Had I bumped into Kim in the street then I'd have been tempted to say something like, "Nice to see you. I'll be seeing you in the papers."

After my break-up with Matt, come to think of it, that's the only place where I did see Kim. I wasn't even going to see her movies any more. Let alone anybody else's.

The face in the newspapers and magazines seemed to be changing. Not in just the way we all change with the passing of time, aging a little no matter how hard a fight we put up again the tick-tick-ticking of the clock. Kim was becoming *different-looking*. I would never have admitted it to anyone else but I thought she was getting to look downright sluttish.

She had put on weight. That accounted for some of the change. Her eating binges were famous. Before a new picture began, some of the excess lard was usually shed during a shaping-up session at Elizabeth Arden's Main Chance or the Golden Door.

I suspect this new slightly gone-to-seed look had to do more with drinking than eating. David had never made any secret of his drinking. How could he, with the public display he kept making of himself? From all reports his drinking was becoming worse. At some point, it's my guess, Kim must have said to herself, "What the hell. If you can't lick 'em, join 'em."

Nobody could ever match David drink for drink. But the way she started to look made you wonder if she wasn't trying to keep up.

It must have killed her—if she saw it—to read what one influential movie critic wrote about her after her last bomb:

Kimberley Hudson has changed before our very eyes from that fragile young angel with the woman's face to the stunning ingenue-goddess to the blowsy matron. Can this be the pattern of ex-child stars? The metamorphosis is not all that unlike the metamorphosis of Judy Garland.

Mike Mannings is my eyewitness to the Glasgows at Home. At least one recent day in their lives. And it sounded pretty depressing.

Mike, as I said, is now a producer. He was producing something in Rome. Kim and David were there making that god-awful *Savage Saturday*. Despite the fact they had given him giant headaches when they were making *Helen of Troy* and he was handling the publicity, Mike had always liked the Glasgows and kept in touch.

"I wouldn't put them in a picture," Mike told me, "if they offered to work for free—just too much aggravation, one way or another—but I've always found them fascinating. They're not like your next-door neighbors, the Smiths and the Browns, for damn sure. They can be charming and delightful company—David especially—if they're in the mood."

They weren't in the mood that particular Sunday. They had invited Mike to their big luxury apartment in Parioli for breakfast. They told him they might all spend the afternoon at the beach.

At eleven o'clock when Mike got there, David was moping around in his dressing gown, morosely pouring wine into a cup that had a couple of tablespoons of coffee in it. For the first time in Mike's memory David made no real effort to welcome him.

"How's the picture going, Mike?" he asked. His tone didn't indicate he was much interested in the answer.

Breakfast was served. David continued to slosh down cup after cup of red wine mixed with a little coffee, and that was all.

Mike ate alone. Madame had not put in an appearance yet.

It could be just a hangover, Mike thought. But probably not. David was an old hand at smiling and carrying on through hangovers.

"You're not your usual talkative self," he said to David.

"Sorry, old chap. I daresay you have caught me in a bit of a bummer."

What had got him down, he let drop, was a devastating review of his last movie. The review had come in yesterday's mail from the States.

The wine-in-coffee gave way to a glass of vodka laced with a splash of soda. After his third glass of vodka he produced the offending review.

. . . Perhaps the saddest spectacle of all is the bloated appearance—and performance—of David Glasgow. One can hardly glimpse the ghost of his former self. The deterioration of his acting powers has kept pace with his physical deterioration. Rarely has an actor promised so much and delivered so disappointingly little . . .

Mike tried to comfort him. But in his heart of hearts, he had to agree that the critic had called a spade a spade.

Kim did not appear on the scene until after two o'clock. She too was looking the worse for wear.

"Oh, hi, Mike," she said. "How's tricks?"

So much for catching up on what Mike had been up to since the last time they met.

She was in just as foul a humor as David. Her gripe, she let it be known, was that she had been slighted by the Vicontesse Alexandra de Sibes at a masked ball everybody but everybody in the international set had attended the night before.

The Viconte seemed inclined to want to chat with Kim. But the Vicontesse looked beyond Kim and said, "Come, Osmonde. We must not linger. We have so many *friends* to greet."

"That bitch," cried Kim, "I'll fix her trolley if it's the last thing I do."

"Come, luv," said David, "it wasn't personal. She didn't mean any harm."

"You bet your balls she did. And I'll find a way, believe me, of settling the score. Even if I have to fuck the Viconte and send her some memento of the occasion."

Kim started working out on a pitcher of Bloody Marys. With the afternoon half gone, the idea of an afternoon at the beach was never mentioned. Nor did lunch ever get served.

David and Kim settled into an alcohol-oiled, nonstop orgy of injustice-collecting. He with his near-straight tumblers of vodka and she with her Bloody Marys, then bourbon and sodas. He with his derogatory review and she with her social humiliation.

In subtle, devious little ways they were also sniping at each other.

"I've seen some drinking in my time," said Mike, "but nothing like this. His. I thought I'd never live to see the day it would happen. But they've turned into a pair of draggy bores. There's nothing worse than to be an artist and lose pride in your craft. That's what I think has happened to both of them."

Then I had another revealing phone call from Kim.

She was calling to congratulate me on the publication of my first novel. So she said. As usual, she was really calling to talk about herself and her troubles.

"David's drinking is truly getting me down," she said.

She sounded slightly three sheets in the wind herself. I couldn't help thinking how often we despise in others those very failings we ourselves have.

"You should be used to it by now," I said.

"I'm used to his drinking. I'm not used to it getting worse and worse all the time."

"Drinking is drinking. If you're already drinking a lot, what does a little more matter?"

"It matters."

"Are you worried about his health?"

"Oh, fuck his health."

"If you're not worried about his health—"

"Of course I'm worried about his health. But that isn't the point. I think he could drink two fifths of vodka a day and live to be a hundred and twenty."

"What is the point, then?" I asked.

"The point is drinking's become his mistress . . ."

She hesitated. I said nothing, waiting for her to go on.

"The point is," she said, "he can't get it up. And what the hell use is he to me if he can't get it up?"

The next I heard she was scheduled to do the Rob Haines Show. Alone.

Chapter 40

Rob Haines wanted the Glasgows for his talk show.

"Never in a million years," declared Kim.

"Hold on there a minute, sweetikins," said Ryder Downey. "Your old grandpappy here advises you to do it."

"He'd tear us to shreds."

"I think not," said Ryder.

"It is totally out of the question," said Kim.

Rob Haines would never make it as the best-rated late night talk show. But he was the most respected of the breed. He was the best and the brightest. He was the only one of the talk show hosts who aspired to quality. He could be tough and sarcastic. He gave fakery and pomposity short shrift. Usually he got a good interview out of his guests.

"He likes movies and movie stars," Ryder pointed out. "He'll be asking you about stuff you know cold. You'll both come off looking great. If Rob gets David going, David'll still be bending his ear five hours after the show is over. You can either sit back and relax. Or you can put your two cents' worth in when you feel like it. You're no slouch when it comes to talking. And you have a tremendous sense of humor. No, Rob Haines would dig you both the most. . . ."

In a delicate, tactful way Ryder suggested the exposure might do them a lot of good. Everybody in show business would be watching. As well as the rest of the world. It would be a great opportunity for them to be seen in top form. They would come off as the charming, congenial, talented people they were. Who knows, it might give somebody watching a big idea. A big million-dollar-plus idea for them . . .

"All right, I'll do it," said Kim. "I'm telling you this, though, Ryder. If I fall on my face, it'll be your ass."

"You'll both be sensational."

"There won't be any 'both.' I'll do it by myself."

"Without David?"

"Yes."

"Sweetikins, they asked for both—"

"They can take me alone or nothing.'"

Ryder used some more of his diplomacy to suggest that Kim spend a couple weeks at the Greenhouse before she was due for her guest appearance on the Rob Haines Show. Since she would be the only guest on the whole ninety-minute show, she should really come on looking her very best. At the Greenhouse she could trim down and tone up a teensy bit and emerge in really tippy-top shape.

I have all of this from Ryder, the details of that first meeting between Kim and Rob Haines.

Kim checked into the Penthouse at the Plaza. It had just been opened up for transient guests. It was some pad indeed. It should be. It cost $585 per day—before taxes. It was an eleven-room duplex with four master bedrooms, a living room, a dining room with parquet floors, a billiard room, a card parlor, a sauna, a whirlpool bath, a wine vault, and a large rotunda with a Tiffany skylight.

Kim called Rob Haines to let him know she was in town.

"Good," he said. "I'll have one of my writers come over to see you. He can go over with you the general line of questioning we'll pursue on the show."

"No," said Kim. "I don't want to meet your writers. You come here yourself."

Rob Haines heaved a sigh. "Oh, one of those."

"Yes, I'm one of those."

Rob Haines was a cool character. He came into Kim's luxurious digs wearing a corduroy jacket, a sport shirt open at the collar, chino pants, and sneakers. He was a tall beanpole of a man with abnormally long arms and legs. He was handsome in a Lincolnesque sort of way. High cheekbones, hollow cheeks, soft shocks of chocolate-brown hair falling over a high, creaseless brow, coal-black eyes mixing melancholy with mirth. He was young—thirty-two at the outside.

He didn't go into any genuflections or gee-whiz-it's-great-to-meet-you routine. "Am I to surmise," he asked her, with just a flicker of amusement in his eyes, "that the Glasgows are zigging when they should be zagging, as they say in the columns? The fact you insisted on this solo appearance?"

"You're free to surmise any damn thing you please."

"I see."

"There will be no questions on the air about my marital relationship with Mr. Glasgow."

"I see."

"Is that understood? I hope it is. Because, Mr. Haines, if you try pulling a cutie on me, I swear I'll leave you sitting there with egg on your face."

"Oh, one of those," he smiled.

"Yes, one of those."

"I should remind you, Miss Hudson, that this is being taped several hours before broadcast time. We would have plenty of time to edit out that egg on my face."

Kim might know volumes about the movie-making business but she was obviously naïve about television.

"Another thing I'm going to ask," said Kim, "is that those tapes be burned after the broadcast tomorrow night. I don't want any reruns of the show."

"Curious. May I ask why?"

"I'll tell you. What I say tomorrow night is true for tomorrow night. Time passes, life changes. Nothing ever stays the same. I don't want any playbacks six months from now of opinions and attitudes—or even a life pattern—that no longer represents me."

"Hmmmm. That's quite intelligent. You should be aware, however, there's nothing to prevent thousands of viewers from video-taping the whole performance and bootlegging it."

"I'll take my chances."

Kim insisted on taking him on a guided tour of the sumptuous premises before they settled down to cases. If she thought she was impressing him, she was in for a rude awakening. Either he had been in a lot of impressive settings or he didn't impress easy.

"Miss Hudson, why are you giving me the Baedeker treatment?" Rob Haines asked her, while she was pointing out the wine vault to him.

"I thought you might be interested in seeing how the other half lives."

"I've seen wine vaults before. But I don't see any living going on here. Do you?"

"What do you mean by that?"

"Just what I said. It's some setup. But I don't see any signs of life around the joint."

"I don't think you should be talking to me like this," said Kim. "It so happens I'm well acquainted with Mr. Thomas

Atkins, who just happens to be the president of your network, as you well know. One phone call and I could get you fired."

"I doubt that very much, Miss Hudson," Haines countered. "It would have happened long before you came along if it were going to happen. There have been many such phone calls. They're very respectfully received and I do get a memo from old T.A. 'I hear you've been a naughty boy again,' he'll write. 'Keep up the good work!' Of course a few phone calls from sponsors, cancelling, would be something else. Then I'd be in trouble. No, Miss Hudson, your case is dismissed."

"Oh, for Christ's sake, call me Kim."

"I think I'd like that very much."

His left eyebrow arched. She couldn't tell if he was putting her on.

"Since we're like best friends on a first-name basis," said Rob, "may I ask you something."

"Ask. That doesn't mean you'll get an answer."

Rob waved his arm to take in the whole penthouse. "Do you really need it? All this shit?"

"Yeah, I need all this shit. All this shit is what I've earned. Nobody gave it to me. It's what I deserve."

"Sad-making."

"I'd like to know what you mean by that remark."

"I wonder if you'd understand if I did explain it to you."

"Look, I think you're possibly the most insulting person I've ever met. If this is any indication of how—"

"Can I give it to you straight? The only reason I'd bother is that I sense that somewhere underneath all the camouflages and frou-frou there's a real person struggling to come out. A little girl lost who'd like to find the way."

"I don't know what you're talking about."

"I'm saying, 'Come home, Kimberley Hudson. You're out of style. The Super Jet Set and all its conspicuous consumption is out of style. The jewels and the yachts and the Rolls Royces and a house in every country and the endless roaming—even the heavy drinking—they all belong to the past. They don't cut much ice any more and anybody still hung up on them gets stamped as dated. That was yesterday. We're into a different time—a much more exciting time. And you're still hooked on passé values and status symbols. Come home, Kimberley Hudson. Get with it. Get yourself back. Discover your real self. You've sacrificed too much to Mammon. Including your own identity and professional pride. You've proved yourself more than once as a damn fine actress. Now you don't seem to give a fig about what you do or how you do it. Look at you. Pretty dishy-looking, don't get me wrong. But the two weeks at the Greenhouse can't erase the years of overindulgence. See those lines under the eyes? They don't belong to any thirty-eight-year-old woman who's been taking care of herself. You're still carrying around a good ten pounds of fatty tissue which doesn't serve any human need. Come home, Kimberley Hudson. You can sustain a bright, vivacious, chatty presence. But catch you off-guard and you catch the profile of a deeply demoralized, unhappy woman. . . .' "

Rob broke off suddenly. He had reduced her to tears. More than tears. She was bawling as if her heart would break.

"Oh, don't, don't, don't," Rob pleaded.

Then he was beside her on the settee, comforting her with his embrace. "There, there, there, I didn't mean to be an old bully," Rob told her. "I didn't mean to make you cry. You know something? Do you know why I shot off my mouth like that? Because I care about you. I've always cared about you."

"You have a funny way of showing it," Kim bawled.

"I have *cherished* you," Rob went on. "I've been high on you ever since *Wendy and the Golden Retriever,* when you and I were both kids. I've agonized with you through every illness and heartbreak. You are frozen in my vision as you were in things like *These Murdering Children* and *Land of Kings.* Not just because you were so young and pristinely beautiful. You projected something that grabbed me, held me spellbound. A radiance. An innocence. A basic honesty and authenticity. A vulnerability. A hunger—a reaching out to seize life's best possibilities. What I'm trying to tell you is I saw all these things in you and they fired my imagination and admiration. This was woman in all her magnificence. Time passes, as you say. Beauty erodes. But quality—or magnificence—endures. Or is recoverable if temporarily lost . . ."

After she had cried herself out, he dried her eyes and cheeks with his handkerchief.

"I care about you, old girl," said Rob. "Believe me."

"Yes."

Kim listened to him solemnly as he went down the list of things he'd be asking her. She had no objections.

"You'll be waiting in the green room," Rob said. "I do a little cutesy monologue at the beginning of the show and then I'll bring you out."

"I won't be able to make a sound. I'll be in a nervous collapse."

"You will not. You'll be riveting." Rob paused, wondering whether to say something else. "You can have whatever refreshments you want both in the green room and on camera. But may I tell you something? Cold sober, you'll be utterly fascinating."

He was nearly out the door when she called to him.

"Rob, there's something else you can ask me about if you want to."

"David Glasgow?"

"Yes."

"Gotcha." He poked his head in the door for a parting shot. "May I tell you one more thing? All my little carping and sniping aside, I sure as hell wouldn't pitch those slippers of yours out the door if I woke up some morning and found them under my bed."

He winked and was gone.

I guess all of America was watching the Rob Haines Show that night. He got ratings like he never got before.

Rob Haines was right. Cold sober, Kim was utterly fascinating. She was, to use another of his words, magnificent. Nothing short of magnificent. The very next day Rob was quoted in the television columns as saying it was the best interview he had ever done.

I thought she was incredibly marvelous. Quick, funny, ballsy, full of terrific anecdotes from the old Studio days. She was obviously having a great time and it was so good to hear that warm, earthy laugh of hers. I really feel sorry for all the people who missed that edition of the Rob Haines Show. It won't be aired again. The network gave in to Kim's demand that the tape be burned after the show.

There were so many good exchanges between Rob and Kim.

Rob asked her about the Boss.

"Well, of course, the Beast has been dead quite a few years now," Kim said softly. "Out of common decency and respect for the dead, I must tone down my remarks. Let me just say I never hope to meet such a consummate son of a bitch again as long as I live."

Finally there was the Question.

"Kim, it's fairly common knowledge that every talk show in the country has been hotly pursuing a guest appearance from the Glasgows. The invitation to appear on this show us repeatedly extended to both you and your husband. Yet here you are tonight by yourself. A great many viewers are apt to jump to certain conclusions from that. I don't need to spell out these conclusions. Do you want to comment on this?"

"Oh, I certainly do, Rob," said Kim thoughtfully. "Frankly, we're having our problems. Show me a married couple who doesn't have problems and I'll show you a pair of zombies. I think it's particularly difficult for two people who are both in show business. Especially people like David and myself, whose careers have been so intimately entwined. You have all the tensions and jealousies and competitiveness. Then, too, when you're thrown together all the time, you get the feeling you're living out of each other's pocket . . ."

After the show Rob Haines took Kim to Chinatown. The next day all the papers carried pictures with text. In the limo provided by the network Rob Haines took Kim to Wah Kee's on Doyer Street. Pursued by the press. In packs.

Wah Kee's does not have a liquor license. You're not even allowed to bring your own wine in.

I couldn't help thinking of all the pictures I've seen of Kim taken in some of the fanciest restaurants and nightclubs in the world. In front of her you always see the cocktail, highball, and wine glasses.

In the pictures with Rob Haines you see only a teacup in front of her plate. Rob Haines is trying to instruct her in the use of chopsticks. On Kim's face you see the happiest, giggliest, little-girl-in-toyland look.

It made me happy just seeing her look so happy.

Then she was off. Not back to London—and David. But to Switzerland. Mysteriously.

Chapter 41

The party was dying on the vine.

Everybody was milling around glassy-eyed. A few had already left. They had all come to see Kim more than anybody else. A few minutes of catching up had satisfied everybody's curiosity about everybody else. Then the talk went limp. Behind the empty words dropping around the sound stage, there was the oppressive waiting.

When would *she* come? *Was* she going to come?

At eight twenty I said to Lonnie Braintree, "I could kill her. Getting me all the way out here and not showing up."

"Were I you, I shouldn't throw in the towel just yet," said Lonnie.

"You don't think there's a prayer she'll show now, do you?"

"More than a prayer. A substantial hope."

"Based on what, I'd like to know?"

"Hmmm. Kimberley has business in America. I think this is where she wants to be."

"What kind of business?"

Lonnie gave me a quizzical smile. "That's a social secret."

Rob Haines?

Tinker Wells practically fell between us, dead drunk. "I knew that bitch wouldn't show her puss or pussy around here," he snarled.

Sober, Tinker is ugly enough. Drunk, he's grotesque.

"Miss Spinelli! Miss Spinelli! Any Spinelli here?"

The sound of my name made me jump.

"Over here."

A man who was definitely not a guest approached from the shadows at the back of the sound stage. "You Miss Spinelli? Yeah? Telephone."

Kim. It could only be Kim. At last. Later than usual. But better very very late than not-at-all.

I followed the man—who was probably a janitor, what else?—back in the darkness to a wall phone.

"Kim, where the hell—" I blurted into the phone.

I stopped short. At the other end there was the sound of hysterics. Hysterical weeping.

"Kim, Kim," I soothed.

She's been crying in my ears for twenty-five years. But I don't think the day will ever come that I won't be shattered by her weeping, by whatever current misery she might be suffering.

"Kim, tell me. It's me. I'm here. Your old friend from the roller derbies. Your old Italian mama's here. Gina the Wop."

When a woman is weeping, it can take a heap of patience to hear her out. When women weep, they can sound a lot alike. At least over the phone. That's the thing I learned that night and I don't think I'll ever forget it. Especially when you have the phone out at arm's length.

...back to my ear until the sobs start-
...knew it wasn't Kim.
...k her a few more choked sobs before she
...ue rest of my name.

..., Indiana. What's the matter, Indiana?"

I couldn't have asked a worse question. It set off a fresh
volley of convulsive sobs.

"Indiana—"

"Miss Spinelli—"

"Yes?"

"They called here."

"Who did?"

"They're here. They're pounding on the door. They're
beating on the windows . . ."

"Who, Indiana? *Who?*"

"The press, Miss Spinelli."

"The press? What are they doing there?"

More chokes and sobs. "Miss Spinelli, they called—"

"You already told me that, Indiana."

"They called. They said . . ."

"Who called, Indiana? Who's 'they'?"

"Mr. Glasgow."

"What did he say?"

"He said . . . she's dead!"

Chapter 42

Dead.

Kim *dead.*

Oh, God.

God, if she's dead, I shake my fist in Your face.

Can you believe it?

One of the most famous movie stars in the world dying in
one of the most expensive clinics in the world?

Here are the so-called facts.

Two days after the Rob Haines Show Kim entered the
Barbizon Clinic outside Lausanne to get "the works." A crash
diet that was about three calories away from total fasting. A

400

face lift. A body lift. Even her fanny got lifted. And she had the clinic's famous rejuvenation injections from sheep.

She died under anesthesia. The anesthetic was halothane. The time was early evening. She was anesthetized so they could take all the stitches out. The stitches weren't supposed to come out until the next morning. But no. Kim had to have them out that night because she was catching a morning flight to the States.

Under the anesthetic her heart simply conked out.

Do you think anybody has any satisfactory explanation of how it happened?

Get a load of Dr. Jean-Pierre Lazarre, who's the director of the clinic and who must be many times a millionaire from the gouging fees he charges.

"Miss Hudson has a formidable history of ailments and operations," Dr. Lazarre told the press. "Her body chemistry was certainly more delicate and complicated than you might guess with someone who always gave the appearance of good health. These things can have a cumulative effect. After so many encounters with illness and surgery, just one more encounter—however prosaic and controlled it might seem—can prove fatal. After the fact, too, we learned of Miss Hudson's extreme reaction to certain drugs."

"Where did you learn of that?" reporters asked him.

"From her husband. He was astounded that she had told us nothing of her pharmaceutical sensitivities. That she was not wearing the tag that identified her as an allergic."

"Did she have halothane before . . . when she was being stitched up?"

"Yes."

"Then halothane was not one of the drugs she was allergic to."

"Not necessarily. The second application of a drug . . ."

Another county heard from:

A group of Swiss doctors in no way related to the Barbizon Clinic.

If their theory is right, it's going to revolutionize the whole practice of medicine. Biorhythm is the catchword. We all have our own "body time" or biological clock, they claim, and there are certain times of the day when medicine or surgery works best—or can be fatal.

Kim may have been anesthetized at the "wrong" hour.

I bet she flaked out when they were halfway through the unstitching. I can see bits of the magnificent body strewn all over the gauze on the table ... snippets of breast and thigh and fanny.

I also bet, David, you're going to see that she really goes out in style. Alexandre flown in from Paris to do the hair. Sidney Gilleroff from the Coast to do the makeup. The best lighting guy in the business to put her in a soft light that won't show up the scars. Some blazing big rocks for her fingers and a ten-strand pearl necklace and an emerald brooch and a diamond tiara. And you'll be getting that guy on the Coast who does the floral arrangements for all the biggie wedding and parties out there. The one who lets all those white doves out of the bag.

Oh, David, I just know you'll be putting on the show of shows for the million jerk-offs who'll be streaming by the casket for one last peeky-boo.

"In her final appearance, the actress never looked lovelier . . ."

Poor Kim! She never had a real home. Her mother was just a dopey, dipso dame who would let anything happen to her if it would get her into the movies. She wanted a kid and he was born a freak. Twice she thought she had found true love. One guy was gay and the other was killed before she hardly got to know him . . .

And why was the curtain brought down on *us?* Me and Kim. Besides Mama and my kids, for better or for worse, through thick and thin, she was the person I loved most in all the world. But you can't call it circumstances, Kim. No, most of the time you were hardly your own best friend. You brought a lot of your troubles upon yourself. And you were a poor custodian of your health.

Every time I looked at your beauty, I'd think if I had just half your looks I could move mountains. I used to envy your riches ... But I'm here. And you're gone.

Where there's life, everything's possible. And suddenly wheeling a cart around the A&P and *schlepping* the kids to McDonald's for a "Big Mac" doesn't look too bad to me. May I be strung up and hung until I'm dead if I ever push my Julie or Timmy any nearer to the klieg lights than a school play!

You were only the most magical of all the make-believe children, Kim. Good night, sweet princess. Good night.

Ø

Big Bestsellers from SIGNET

☐ **PENTIMENTO by Lillian Hellman.** Hollywood in the days of Sam Goldwyn . . . New York in the glittering times of Dorothy Parker and Tallulah Bankhead . . . a 30-year love affair with Dashiel Hammett, and a distinguished career as a playwright. "Exquisite . . . brilliantly finished . . . it will be a long time before we have another book of personal reminiscence as engaging as this one."—**New York Times Book Review**

(#J6091—$1.95)

☐ **THE FRENCH LIEUTENANT'S WOMAN by John Fowles.** By the author of **The Collector** and **The Magus**, a haunting love story of the Victorian era. Over one year on the N.Y. Times Bestseller List and an international bestseller. "Filled with enchanting mysteries, charged with erotic possibilities . . ."—**Christopher Lehmann-Haupt, N.Y. Times** (#E6484—$1.75)

☐ **AMERICAN MISCHIEF by Alan Lelchuck.** He is a sexual dynamo whose sex life is what most men's dreams are made of. The sensational, X-rated novel about "the consequences of carnal passion . . . Brilliant!"—Philip Roth, **Esquire** (#E6185—$2.25)

☐ **FEAR OF FLYING by Erica Jong.** A dazzling uninhibited novel that exposes a woman's most intimate sexual feelings. . . . "A sexual frankness that belongs to and hilariously extends the tradition of **Catcher in the Rye** and **Portnoy's Complaint** . . . it has class and sass, brightness and bite."—John Updike, **New Yorker**

(#J6139—$1.95)

☐ **THE THREE OF US by Joyce Elbert.** When two beautiful sister rivals plunge into competition to prove which of them is the biggest swinger, the results are something that only the author of **The Crazy Ladies** would dare to put down between the covers of a book.

(#W5972—$1.50)

THE NEW AMERICAN LIBRARY, INC.,
P. O. Box 999, Bergenfield, New Jersey 07621

Please send me the SIGNET BOOKS I have checked above. I am enclosing $_____(check or money order—no currency or C.O.D.'s). Please include the list price plus 25¢ a copy to cover handling and mailing costs. (Prices and numbers are subject to change without notice.)

Name_____

Address_____

City_____State_____Zip Code_____
Allow at least 3 weeks for delivery

Have You Read these Bestsellers from SIGNET?

☐ **BRING ME A UNICORN: The Diaries and Letters of Anne Morrow Lindbergh (1922–1928) by Anne Morrow Lindbergh.** Imagine being loved by the most worshipped hero on Earth. This nationally acclaimed bestseller is the chronicle of just such a love. The hero was Charles Lindbergh; the woman he loved was Anne Morrow Lindbergh; and the story of their love was one of the greatest romances of any time. "Extraordinary . . . brings to intense life every moment as she lived it."—New York Times Book Review (#W5352—$1.50)

☐ **HOUR OF GOLD, HOUR OF LEAD by Anne Morrow Lindbergh.** The Lindberghs were the golden couple in a fairy-tale romance. And when their first child was born, the world rejoiced. Eighteen months later, tragedy struck. . . . "A totally expressive, often unbearable record of an extreme personal anguish that followed the greatest possible happiness. Mrs. Lindbergh has a great gift for communicating directly her joy and pain."—The New York Times Book Review
(#E5825—$1.25)

☐ **ELEANOR AND FRANKLIN by Joseph P. Lash. Foreword by Arthur M. Schlesinger, Jr.** A number 1 bestseller and winner of the Pulitzer Prize and the National Book Award, this is the intimate chronicle of Eleanor Roosevelt and her marriage to Franklin D. Roosevelt, with its painful secrets and public triumphs. "An exceptionally candid, exhaustive . . . heartrending book."—The New Yorker (#J5310—$1.95)

☐ **ELEANOR: THE YEARS ALONE by Joseph P. Lash; Foreword by Franklin D. Roosevelt, Jr.** Complete with 16 pages of photographs, this is the bestselling companion volume to the prize-winning Eleanor and Franklin. "Everyone who read Eleanor and Franklin will want to know the end of the story." —Life. "The story Eleanor thought was over when her husband died. . . . It is her capacity for love which shines through these pages."—Los Angeles Times
(#J5627—$1.95)

THE NEW AMERICAN LIBRARY, INC.,
P.O. Box 999, Bergenfield, New Jersey 07621

Please send me the SIGNET BOOKS I have checked above. I am enclosing $_____(check or money order—no currency or C.O.D.'s). Please include the list price plus 25¢ a copy to cover handling and mailing costs. (Prices and numbers are subject to change without notice.)

Name_____

Address_____

City_____State_____Zip Code_____
Allow at least 3 weeks for delivery